THE GATE TO REDEMPTION

RYAN KIRK

WATERSTONE
MEDIA

For Annie
Rest in Peace, Friend

PROLOGUE

The void of space trembled with its passing. It imagined the stars themselves would flee from it if they could.

It needed no food, no sustenance of any kind. It had left behind such physical concerns long ago. Dezigeth traversed the enormous distances with speed lesser beings couldn't even comprehend. But it still had some ways to go. The vastness of the universe impressed even it.

Stars passed by, pinpricks of light which grew into spheres of explosive energies as it neared. Sometimes the stars burned alone, defying the darkness of infinite emptiness. But others danced in pairs and triplets, finding some small solace in the company of others.

A newly awakened power called to it. At the moment, weak and fledgling, barely worthy of attention.

But in time, such power might grow. And in time, it might even challenge.

Experience had taught Dezigeth and its kind that even weak awakenings were best pruned early. Ancestors long past had argued about the justice of their actions, back when such quaint ideas had still held sway among the sentinels.

Its actions weren't about justice. They were about survival. About necessity. About the fate of all living creatures.

Because history taught one lesson to any who paid attention: power always sought more power.

Weak as this awakening was, it grew with surprising rapidity.

Such was a trend its brethren had noticed more often now. Some argued that another type of awakening occurred, one more subtle and more widespread than they suspected. The claims didn't strike Dezigeth as true, but as it slid through the void, it wondered. This awakening was greater in speed and depth than any it had felt before.

A portal had brought it to the edge of the sentinels' conquests. But the last leg of the journey had to be traveled alone, its destination beyond the outskirts of civilized space.

Dezigeth didn't concern itself with the outcome of its journey. When it arrived, a course of action would appear, and it would be followed. Excess thought was extraneous, a weakness expelled long ago. Regardless, it would establish a portal, so that the expansion of civilization would continue. It would shine light deeper into the darkness, and in time, the darkness would have no place left to hide.

That was the ultimate destiny of all living beings.

Dezigeth was a sentinel. An instrument of a pattern imprinted upon all things at the very moment of creation.

Those it approached considered themselves gods, another conceit its brethren had abandoned, along with justice, love, and compassion.

Soon, though, they would learn the harsh truths of the universe.

They weren't gods.

And their time of domination would come to a swift conclusion.

Dezigeth flew, and the space it soared through grew even colder as it passed.

1

L ight filled Brandt's soul.

It blinded him even as he squeezed his eyes against the onslaught.

The moment couldn't have lasted more than a heartbeat, but entire lifetimes passed within the distance of a single step. He was inside the gates, and he sensed the connections between all living creatures, tenuous filaments stretched across the planet like silk threads.

The light vanished, and he stumbled.

A perfect darkness overwhelmed his sight, so deep he couldn't see his hands in front of his face. He saw nothing at all.

His momentum sent him to his knees. The ground underfoot wasn't flat, and his day had been long. He'd witnessed the deaths of both his emperor and his prince.

Bile rose in his throat, and he vomited. The thin acid splashed against something solid, and a trickle of liquid ran along the edge of his palm as it supported his weary weight. The sickness came in diminishing waves, and after the third, mercifully ended.

He didn't dare stand. He breathed deeply through his nose and wiped his mouth dry with a dirty sleeve.

His senses returned, one at a time, like itinerant children wandering home as the sun fell at the end of a summer day. This space was dark, cold, and wet. It was familiar, somehow, though his fatigued mind struggled to recall where from.

A sharp, impatient voice interrupted his recovery. "Done?"

Brandt grimaced, the power behind the question sending a lancing shock through his skull. But the pain spurred his memory. When he'd last been here, it had been the queen's mental construct, and she had nearly killed him. "This is where you grew up."

A momentary silence greeted his observation. Then, "Clever, aren't you?"

Brandt thought of all that he'd left behind. "No, I don't believe I am."

A soft light flared to life before him, a dim flame that burned without fuel. It lit the cave, casting dancing shadows as the queen held it aloft. The space was exactly as Brandt remembered it, and it sent a chill down his spine. Besides the two of them, the cave was empty.

Brandt thought of the sword at his hip. The queen stood no more than five paces distant. Few opportunities would be as perfect.

But he saw the way her eyes rested on him. She expected an attack, and without surprise, he had no chance.

He set aside thoughts of murder and pushed himself to his feet, fighting his body's unsteadiness.

"A wise choice," the queen remarked.

Brandt gave as much of a nod as he could manage. Even that made the cave wobble in his vision.

Reflected light caught his attention. He focused on the source, then took a step back when he understood.

The cavern narrowed, forming a natural passage between what appeared to be two larger caves. Past that opening, Brandt thought he saw a gate. But it gave off no light.

The queen followed his gaze. "Care to inspect it?"

"May I?"

She nodded, and Brandt shuffled toward the gate, ducking his head to avoid the narrowing of the cave.

Illuminated by the fire that floated between them, Brandt saw that it was a gate, carved from the same diamond as the others he had seen. But the similarity ended there. He reached out, but was unwilling to touch the gate. Memories of previous experiences warned him.

"Why—" He couldn't find the words he wanted. His mind remained mired in the past, unable to understand what stood before him.

"—doesn't it overwhelm you with its power and glow?" the queen said, finishing his question. At Brandt's nod, she answered. "Because none in your lands know how to control a gate, not properly. Those experiences represent nothing more than wasted energy."

The implication was clear as day. Here, the queen wasted nothing.

Brandt pressed his palms to his eyes, trying to force life back into them. With every word and action, the queen reminded him of her superiority. Even the gentle flame still burning between them should have been impossible.

Ana.

The sudden thought of her last expression broke what little remained of his focus. The weight of his betrayal bent his back. It was all too much, far too much. He swallowed what remained of his pride and asked, "Would it be possible to rest, soon?"

"Of course," the queen replied. "I am due home, and you may rest there."

The queen meandered out of the caves, apparently showing deference to Brandt's weakened state. The show of kindness, small as it was, surprised him. In their previous encounters, she'd displayed nothing resembling warmth. He wondered how many of his previous impressions of her were accurate.

He supposed he would soon find out.

They passed through a small gap, barely large enough to walk through. Once beyond it, the queen gestured and a slab of rock descended, covering the opening. Brandt, exhausted from a day full of wonders, barely noticed. But he didn't think he could move the barrier, even with the gate-stone he possessed.

He studied the queen's back. Was it even possible to kill her?

The tunnels turned, and in places, he saw affinities had widened the stone to make an easier passage. Once, this cave might have been naturally difficult to access, but now the queen relied on the strength of her affinity to protect it.

They stepped into a blinding light, and the fire between them winked out, leaving no trace of its existence. Brandt squinted and covered his eyes from the glare of the sun.

A wave of heat greeted him as he emerged.

He was, it appeared, in the middle of a vast desert. He blinked again as his eyes adjusted, then turned his head as a sudden breeze blew sand into the air.

The change of scenery almost brought him again to his knees. Nothing like this existed in the empire.

Truly, he was alone and far from the empire.

A small caravan awaited them, which the queen gestured to. She smiled, though Brandt felt no warmth from it. "On behalf of all the Lolani, Brandt, welcome to your new home."

2

Shadows crawled across the land as the sun set over the jagged peaks and steep cliffs of Falar. Alena watched their progress from the corner of her eye, comforted by the solid presence of her brother beside her.

"It's too many," he said, his whisper barely reaching her ears.

She hoped Jace was wrong. All violence was pointless, but these continued attempts were pitiful. They had declared peace. These rebels struck out like a vengeful child, hoping to land one last blow against their sibling before a parent pulled them apart.

The rebel assault would fail. Ren and his war party had set up the tents for the night, but already they had crawled, out of sight of the advancing Falari below, to higher ground. Though Alena couldn't see them, she imagined them lying patiently in wait, bows eager for targets. If the advance came too close, Ren would give the order to fire.

She intended to avoid that outcome.

And now she had the power to make her wishes reality.

The abilities of two gates were hers to command, a power unimaginable to most. Surely by now the Falari advancing below them had heard stories, but few believed. Alena's affinities defied reason, and doubt was an unfortunately common reaction from their enemies.

"You don't have much time left," Jace remarked.

Well below the camp, Ren had erected a small marker of stone, visible both to Alena and the archers above. If the advance passed that marker, Ren would respond.

The rebels neared the edge of the trees. Once beyond cover, they would charge, their tactics as predictable as the last three groups who had tried the same.

Alena selected her boulder. She reassured herself her connection to the gates remained. Then she waited for the shadows to near. She sipped from her cup of cold water, her throat dry from another long day of hiking through the high elevations of Falar.

The attack came just as the sun dipped below the peaks of the mountains.

Jace's concern about numbers had been well founded. Nearly two dozen men and women broke from the trees at once, running silently up the slope toward the camp. Each carried their bow, eager to get in range.

Alena gestured, and the boulder beside her leaped into the air, breaking every natural law the Falari understood. Even Jace, familiar with her strength, widened his eyes as he watched. Alena flung the boulder a hundred paces into the air, then let it fall, nudging it in the direction of the advancing Falari.

The advance stopped the moment Alena gestured, and as they saw the boulder falling toward them, the small war party scattered, most running back to the safety of the trees.

The boulder struck the slope below with an ear-splitting crack, and Alena channeled a small amount of stone affinity to ensure no deadly fragments rolled down onto the fleeing war party.

Before the last of the Falari disappeared into the woods, they paused and turned toward Alena. They threw a rude hand gesture up in the air, a last act of defiance before they vanished from sight.

Jace laughed. "I'm not sure I'd have the courage to do even that much, were I in their position."

Alena wished she could find the humor in the situation. She was tired, an exhaustion far beyond what the long days on the trail justified.

Jace, ever attuned to his sister's moods, let his laughter die out. "You did well, Alena. The Falari will all come around in time."

Perhaps. Alena didn't know how long a people could hold on to the hurts of the past, but the cynical side of her suspected it was far longer than one would hope. Before the Battle of Faldun, the Falari had been nearly evenly split over the future of their people. Such divisions didn't heal just because one group won a single victory. The elders of Falar would need to rule wisely if they wished for the peace to last.

But the Falari weren't the cause of Alena's worry and exhaustion. That honor fell to the meetings still before them.

"What if he resorts to force?" The words broke from her like sheep eager to escape their pen.

Jace frowned, finally realizing her true preoccupation. He stirred the small fire in front of them with a stick, delaying his answer. "You don't think he would, do you?"

"I hope not—but I don't know."

Jace chuckled to himself, then silenced it when he saw her glare. But then he chuckled again, unable to contain it.

"What?"

"I was just thinking about how my sister is the most powerful person on the continent."

Alena shook her head. "I'm not, though."

Jace's grin didn't fade. "You possess the power of two gates and have the backing of both the Etari and the Falari. Personally, I think Olen has more to worry about than you do."

Alena supposed, but Jace's argument didn't sit well with her. This power wasn't hers. She had no right to it. She didn't understand why Hanns had bequeathed it to her.

"No matter how many times I see that, it never fails to amaze me."

The siblings turned to see Sheren. Alena moved over so the Falari soulwalker could join them. Though not officially a member of Ren's war party, she'd wanted to escort Alena and her other newfound friends to the border. More than anything, she wanted to join Alena in her daily soulwalking training with Toren.

Among the Falari, Sheren's soulwalking ability, and her willingness to use it, made her an outcast. But she was hungry for knowledge, and Alena had a feast to share.

Alena didn't mind. She enjoyed Sheren's company. Her mind was quick and she asked questions during their trainings that pushed Alena to understand her own abilities better.

Which she needed to do.

The world was a mess. Though the sun rose and fell as it always had, chaos had never been closer to seizing the empire and the surrounding lands. And now Hanns had given her this ability, leading her to believe that she was somehow responsible for solving it.

But she didn't have the slightest inkling. She had no solution to the threats hanging over the empire, no plan to bring peace to a world stumbling ever closer to war.

Every day as they walked she practiced with her gates. When she wasn't training others, she trained herself. And her abilities had improved. She could, for a while at least, soulwalk while walking, acting in both planes of existence at once. When they stopped, she explored her powers more deeply, and gradually, strengthened her connections with the gates. Hanns' had never been as strong as he believed, and she didn't want to make the same mistake. While the others rested at night, she wove more powerful bonds.

For all her work, though, she wasn't sure if it was enough.

Jace's hand on her shoulder slowed her racing thoughts. They'd spoken at length about her doubts, and no one knew her better. "Try not to worry. So long as you keep doing what you feel is right, I believe we'll be fine."

She smiled, though she didn't feel better. "Thanks."

The soft sound of rustling cloth announced Ren and his small war party. Toren and Ana were a part of it, their martial skills considered sufficient for the ambush. Alena tensed at the look of concern on Ren's face. Her first thought was that her tactic to scare off the attackers hadn't worked. Had the retreat just been a feint?

She caught ahold of herself. If that was true, Ren would still be up above, raining arrows down on the advance. "What is it?" she asked.

"While we were up high, we saw a scouting party two valleys over."

Alena frowned. That was a considerable distance, and

Falari scouting parties usually blended well into the terrain. No competent scout would be spotted so far away. Suspicion grew in her mind as she realized a likely explanation.

Ren confirmed it. "It's imperial, and they're heading this way. We watched them for a time."

The war leader paused.

"I believe they are looking for you."

3

Brandt stared at the lifeless desert as their carriage thundered along the narrow track. The dry air parched his throat. He constantly fought the urge to lick his lips. He'd been in inhospitable places, but none matched this. On foot, he wasn't sure he would have lasted a day.

Inside the black carriage, he should be roasting alive, an imperial dinner for the queen. Instead, he felt surprisingly cool. She was to thank. She channeled heat from the air inside the carriage through a small vent to the air outside. Brandt had never considered such a use of air and fire affinities, but the practice was so natural to the queen she seemed to do it without conscious thought.

He couldn't imagine her sweating.

Every moment within the carriage felt like an active betrayal. Not just of Ana. That was something else entirely, a decision he still couldn't bear to consider. If he did, he feared that he would shatter like glass.

This was a lesser betrayal, but the thought of it still twisted his insides with self-hatred. He should try to kill the queen. His sword should be out of its scabbard, seeking her life. For most of the day now, she had sat or stood no more than five paces from him, and he had yet to make a single attempt.

He told himself that his painful inaction was because of the certainty that he would be unsuccessful. He had seen the queen's abilities, and he had seen nothing that led him to believe that he stood a chance of assassinating her. For all her apparent ease, he was certain that if he made the smallest move toward his weapon, his life would be over.

No, he would wait. And in that time he would learn. The queen promised a power he had sought for nearly as long as he could remember. A wise man did not assassinate the bearer of gifts.

An excuse?

Perhaps.

But this continent was already a land of wonder, and he had seen nothing but the smallest fraction of what it offered. With every passing league, he learned something of the land the invaders came from.

To his knowledge, no desert of this magnitude existed on his home continent. He knew of one small area, less than a hundred leagues in diameter, which saw a little rain and was perhaps almost as arid, but the scale of this wasteland defied his understanding.

When Brandt finally tore himself away from the view, he saw that the queen was studying him with undisguised interest. She saw that she finally had his attention, and she spoke. "I am not used to people ignoring me for leagues on end." Her statement was devoid of malice, filled instead with curiosity.

Brandt saw no advantage in rudeness. "I apologize if I

have offended. But your land is unlike any I have seen before in my travels."

"My land is dying."

Brandt didn't understand, and his confusion must have been clear on his face.

"A land can only support so many," the queen said. "Under my leadership the population of my empire has exploded. But this land has little to offer, and we consume its resources faster than it can recover. Most settlements are along the coast, although you are unlikely to see them while you are here."

"Is that why you attack our land?"

The queen did not give an answer immediately, and Brandt felt as though he had just asked the wrong question to one of his military instructors.

She changed the subject. "Why have you not yet made an attempt on my life?"

The question threw him off balance, but the queen waited patiently for an answer. "I've been asking myself that question since we arrived."

"And?"

"Perhaps I am too scared. As tempting as these moments may be, I do not think I would succeed, and you have not yet shown me the power I seek."

The queen smiled. Although she appeared young, her eyes betrayed her true age. "I admire your honesty. In exchange, I will offer my own. I have not ruled for as long as I have without surviving countless assassination attempts. You are right to believe that you would fail. Perhaps, if you learn all that I teach, your attempt would stand a chance, but until then—" She shook her head. There was no need for her to finish that sentence.

They rode quietly for a time, but to Brandt it felt like an

anticipatory silence, as though the queen was gathering her thoughts.

"Throughout the course of your stay here, you will ask many times why I have taken a particular action. To save us both time, I can assure you that in almost every instance, the answer is the same." She paused. "It is because I am afraid."

Brandt's eyes narrowed. The queen seemed to be many things, but frightened was not one of them. Uttering the platitude felt hollow, though, so he said nothing.

The queen continued. "I am afraid because I have seen what is coming. For all the strength and skills that I possess, I am nothing compared to what now approaches. Every action I have taken, every decision I have made, is done with one end in mind: to fight the monster that even now approaches."

Brandt studied the queen with fresh eyes. He could detect no hint of a lie in her statement, but he wasn't sure that he would. This woman was unique in all the world. If she wanted to mislead him, he suspected she could

She waved one of her hands dismissively. "I can see you aren't sure if you believe me, and that is fine. But just know that this is my explanation, and in time you will see that it is the only one for what you observe."

With that, their discussion ended. The queen closed her eyes and appeared to relax, and Brandt resumed staring out the window at the endless expanse of desert. But the scenery no longer held the appeal it once had. Now, all he could think about was what kind of enemy was required to make the queen live so many lifetimes in fear.

4

Alena watched the scouting party approach, surprised by the amount of trepidation she felt. Questions without answers, paths with unknown destinations, and perils disguised as opportunities filled her thoughts. For a time, such thoughts had been weightless. But the approaching party meant that her thoughts would soon become decisions, and those decisions would carry a very real burden.

Alena had ordered their war party to a halt in an open clearing. She had no desire to shed more blood. They had already lost more than enough lives, but she feared it was little compared to what was yet to come.

Her eyes wondered briefly from the approaching imperial soldiers to Ana, sitting alone, a hundred paces distant from anyone else. Brandt's wife had been cordial enough throughout the trip, but Brandt's departure had started a war within that woman's soul. Three times Alena had worked up the courage to approach her, and three times Alena's offers of help had been politely but firmly rebuffed.

Her brother had better luck. Unlike Alena, he possessed

a gift, an ability to bond with nearly anyone. He informed Alena that Ana wished her no ill will. Alena hoped that her brother's information was accurate, but was hesitant to believe it. When Brandt had made his fateful decision, Alena was the only one strong enough to have forced a different outcome. But Alena hadn't acted.

For every moment of this trip she worried about the future, there were three where she cursed her past actions. She had done the best she could, but it hadn't been nearly enough.

And it had cost Ana her husband, the father of her unborn child. It was no wonder the woman didn't wish to speak much to her.

"Ready?" her brother asked.

His question brought her back to the challenge at hand. The imperial soldiers were now within bow range, and Alena could feel the tension building between the two forces. She took a slow, deep breath and centered herself.

The imperials stopped about two hundred paces from the war party. Mentally, Alena shook her head. She was still no warrior, but she now knew all too well the power and distance of the Falari bows. The imperials were too close for safety. Whoever commanded this scouting party wasn't familiar with these lands or the warriors who lived within.

A lone individual broke from the rest of the group, striding forward with confident steps.

One side of Alena's mouth turned up in a half smile. At that moment the soldier reminded her so much of Jace as a younger man, full of unearned pride and the certainty that the world would bend to his whims.

Before, Alena had found the attitude frustrating. Now she found it endearing, a trait she hoped the soldier would hold on to through the approaching storm. Ren met her eyes, and she gave a small nod as she rose smoothly to her feet. She checked to ensure that she still had access to the gates, then joined Ren in meeting the scouting party's commander.

Ren and Alena stopped about a dozen paces away from the soldier, far enough away to imply safety, but close enough to be heard without shouting.

Alena took the initiative. "Greetings," she said.

"Are you the one known as Alena?"

Alena frowned. She hadn't expected anyone to know her name, much less recognize her on sight. If Prince Olen had sent them, as she suspected he had, he was well-informed. "I am."

The commander appeared relieved. "My men and I are one of several scouting parties that have been sent to find you and the survivors of the Falari expedition." The soldier's eyes traveled beyond Alena to the motley collection of warriors behind her. Alena watched the young man as his concern mounted when he saw no familiar faces.

Alena sympathized. For her, news of the emperor's death was weeks old and countless leagues behind her. But for the rest of the empire this would be a fresh wound, an unexpected tragedy.

But she saw no reason not to let the commander before her know. She bowed her head in sympathy. "I'm sorry, but those of us you see are all that remain."

The commander's eyes widened as he understood all the implications of Alena's statement. Not just the emperor, but the prince as well. Alena didn't have the heart to inform the commander that it was the prince who had betrayed them all. That news would be Olen's to share or not.

To her surprise, the commander fell to his knees, tears freely falling down both sides of his face. Alena forgot that her views of the emperor were not shared by all. There were many, who, like this warrior, considered the emperor to be akin to a living god.

A god who was now dead, who had revealed, at the very end, that he was as fragile a mortal as any of them.

5

The sun rose and fell as the carriage made its way east. They made good time across the desert. Twice they stopped in small villages that had grown around tiny springs. At each stop, they exchanged horses with an efficiency that indicated long experience.

"We are far from your gate," Brandt remarked.

The queen waved her hand dismissively. "I seal it away where no one else may reach it without my awareness, and my connection to it exists regardless of my physical distance. Even now I can feel the power of the Falari gate coursing through my veins."

The mention of Falar sent a pang of longing through his heart. Ana and Alena would still be there, possibly still fighting through the aftermath of the civil war they'd been in the middle of.

Brandt nodded to the queen, his thoughts a continent away.

Until they crested a rise and a city came into view.

At first Brandt thought his mind had cracked, that the city was an illusion of both heat and exhaustion. But as they grew closer, the shifting spires solidified and Brandt realized he looked at a marvel. Beyond the city lay water, an endless expanse that could only be ocean. Brandt stared, not bothering to hide his amazement.

He noted the queen's pleased reaction out of the corner of his eye. Given their distance from the city, it was as large or larger than any city in the empire. It stood to reason, then, that he gazed on the largest city in the world. "Welcome to Valan, the heart of my lands."

Towering walls surrounded the city in a protective embrace. They stretched for well over a league. The amount of effort that must've gone into building such a wall was nearly beyond his imagination. And where had they quarried the rock from? The project must've taken decades to complete.

Though he burned to ask questions, he held his tongue. He refused to give the queen the satisfaction of his curiosity, at least for now.

She indulged him anyway. "The last time I had the wall rebuilt, it took nearly ten years, and the efforts of thousands of people. Should any invading army ever cross the desert, they will find that their efforts were for nothing."

"And if they attack by sea?" Brandt's strategic mind contemplated the possibilities.

The queen offered him a vicious grin. "Beyond the traditional defenses, I'm assisted by many with water affinities. No one unwelcome would ever near our shores."

Brandt chewed on his lower lip. He hadn't thought of that, which disturbed him. The gates in the empire were a closely held secret, for reasons Brandt understood and agreed with. But it meant that entire generations of generals and commanders had grown up not taking the exceptional power of affinities into account. Had he been in command of an invasion, they would've fallen prey to this misunderstanding.

Perhaps Alena had a point. The secrets that had built the empire might now be one of the greatest threats it faced.

The carriage rumbled on, and soon they were at the first of two thick gates, wrought with enormous quantities of steel. Brandt couldn't help but shake his head in wonder at the sight before him. He wasn't sure the empire possessed any siege weapons that could batter down such a defense. Not in any reasonable time, at least.

For all the wonders they had already seen, none prepared Brandt for the city itself. His first thought, which he was immediately shamed by, was that he had finally found a city he could live in. The streets didn't ring with the shout of merchants hawking their wares or people arguing with one another, as was often the case when too many people lived in too small a place.

The streets were largely empty, and those who were out walked with purpose, barely acknowledging anyone they crossed. Brandt imagined the homes they passed were full of people, but he saw little evidence of it in the streets.

Again he fought the urge to inquire.

The farther the carriage traveled into the city, the more uneasy Brandt felt. He appreciated the quiet, but there were too few people visible. Forces were at play he didn't understand, and again he felt the separation between himself and the empire he had left behind.

One final wonder awaited him. As the carriage followed a gentle bend, he could see out his side window a tower taller than any other they had passed. It looked to be made of obsidian, a black sword threatening to pierce the heavens. Another defensive wall circled it, higher even than the surrounding buildings. By itself, Brandt wasn't sure it could be taken by force, and it stood in the heart of this impenetrable city.

It was their destination. But at the gates, the carriage came to a stop that had a feeling of finality to it. He gave the queen a questioning look.

"I allow few within the palace grounds," she said.

They stepped out of the carriage together, and Brandt admired once again the strength of the wall. The Falari claimed that Faldun had never been taken by force, but Brandt suspected that even they would have no choice but to bow before this structure. The palace was enormous, and, if the queen spoke the truth, nearly abandoned. "How few?"

"Only one or two advisers are allowed within at a time. Anyone else who enters is under a strict compulsion."

Brandt's eyes narrowed, but he suspected that his judgment did not bother the queen in the slightest. "And me?"

"My first true guest in lifetimes."

The gates opened before her, revealing a vast and empty palace. "Welcome."

6

Alena, Jace, Toren, and Ana said a tearful farewell to Ren and the rest of their Falari escort. They exchanged pledges to visit and embraces. Relationships, it seemed to Alena, defied the expectations of time. Though she had only known the Falari for a couple of months, she found that she trusted them as much as those she had spent years of her life with. Leaving them proved more difficult than the span of their time together should have justified.

Leaving Sheren, in particular, proved difficult. Alena had a fondness for the soulwalker.

"You're sure?" she asked again.

Sheren nodded. "You have taught me enough for a lifetime, and now I must study on my own. But this is my land, and I miss my home."

Alena nodded, and they embraced again.

Again, as she had felt almost every day for the past three months, she was grateful for Toren. He stood beside her as solid as any mountain. Even if she spent the rest of her life expressing her gratitude, it wouldn't be enough. He didn't say much, but his presence grounded her.

Time and circumstances forced her forward. She had offered to tie a bond to both Weylen and Ren, but both had refused. Although the Falari were grateful for her efforts, their reticence over affinities could not be so easily overcome.

She mourned the loss of their company.

Her new imperial companions, at least, were far more pleasant than she expected. The commander, named Jon, might have lacked the competence necessary to survive hostile encounters in Falar, but he made up for it in curiosity. He hadn't expected to find Falari and imperial forces working together, so as they walked from the highlands of Falar to the plains of the empire, Alena found no shortage of conversation to distract her from the looming problems ahead.

Over the course of their travels, at night and around the campfires, Alena recounted the story of their adventures as best she could. Fortunately, as she had never come face-to-face with Regar, nor had she been present at his demise, she found it easy to remain circumspect about the details of his death. And because Hanns had kept the gates a secret, there was nothing for her to tell there, either. As far as the soldiers knew, she was nothing more than an emissary chosen by the emperor.

If they had any doubts as to that, they were polite enough not to speak of it.

She understood then some of the benefits to the secrecy Hanns maintained. She had little doubt the soldiers noticed the flaws in her story, but they made no comment of them, accustomed to not knowing everything.

Alena considered revealing more, but some doubt held

her back. Hanns had once implied that the secrets the first Anders had kept were responsible for the long peace the empire had created. Alena wasn't convinced, but she also wasn't so certain, or arrogant, to believe that her own viewpoint was correct. So she spoke of the emperor's and the prince's death obliquely and waited for the first meeting with Olen to decide more.

Her one regret from those days was not spending more time with Ana. With the arrival of the imperials, Brandt's wife had inserted herself with the scouts and spent the days roaming far and wide, and Alena suspected that the former wolfblade spent the days trying to outrun the feelings that threatened to crush her.

The days passed, and they continued to lose elevation. Their surroundings turned from glittering snowcapped peaks to foothills to plains, and one day, Jon announced that they were back in imperial lands.

Alena trusted Jon, but was disappointed that there was no change she could mark from one land to another. No unfathomable soulwork protected the empire, a reminder of how little the first Anders had actually known.

Jon led them straight to the outpost where Prince Olen waited. When they arrived, Alena was surprised to see that Olen had brought an army with him, orderly tents lined up in neat rows.

Some part of Alena had always realized how close their adventures had taken them to the brink of a war that would destroy the tenuous peace between the three peoples of this continent, but she hadn't truly understood until she saw the army. War had been only days away.

Though dusk was near, Jon brought Alena directly to the prince. For all the time she'd spent on the road, it hadn't been nearly enough to prepare. As when she had returned to Etar, she brought the news of the loss of a loved one. When, she wondered, would she ever bring words that people would welcome?

Olen quartered in the outpost itself, and within a single heartbeat of stepping into his chambers, Alena understood the mysterious prince. Everything in his quarters lined up perfectly, a collection of right angles. He sat straight as an arrow at a writing desk, and for a moment Alena wondered if his back even knew how to bend.

When he rose to greet her, Alena noted how stiff and jerky his motions were. Perhaps she had just spent too much time among warriors, but she found herself inexplicably disturbed by his lack of grace. It was no wonder the soldiers were rumored not to like him. "Alena, it is a pleasure to meet you."

His words were correct, but his tone and delivery were wrong. She kept her growing unease from her face as she bowed. "Prince Olen, the honor is mine."

"My father is dead, is he not?"

The question carried no emotion. But, Alena supposed, he made her task easy enough. "I'm sorry, sir, but he is."

The news appeared to hit him with all the same impact as if she had informed him it might rain a bit tomorrow.

"And my brother?"

"I'm sorry, sir, but he also died."

If it was possible, Olen's reaction to that news was even more muted. "Very well. I suppose you must tell me what happened. No embellishments, please. Just the details."

So, Alena told the story, for what she hoped would be the last time. This time, she told of Regar's betrayal, and the news didn't seem to surprise Olen. The only detail she left out was that of the gates, and the fact she now possessed them. She couldn't say why, exactly, but something about Olen made her uneasy.

When she finished, the prince dismissed her with a casual wave of his hand. "Thank you. As always, make sure no one knows. I must decide how best to break the news of the emperor's death."

She paused, wondering if she should mention that she had already informed the scouts. Small as her hesitation was, he caught it. His face darkened. "What?"

"The scouting party who escorted me is aware of your father's demise, sir."

Storm clouds built on Olen's brow, but he waved her away. "Tell no one else, then." She nodded and departed, uncertain what to make of her encounter with the prince. She had hoped that their meeting would resolve some of her worries, but it wasn't so. If anything, she was more confused now than before.

She hadn't made it more than a handful of paces beyond the outpost walls when a dozen heavily armored guards drew up to her with crossbows raised. It took her two full steps to realize they were here for her.

The one in the lead spoke with the voice of authority. "Alena, by the order of Prince Olen, you are under arrest."

7

Brandt ran through his forms in the empty palace grounds. He glided from one motion to the next, an uninterrupted flow of strikes, blocks, and movement. When he finished one form, he launched straight into another. He gave his mind no time to wander.

Sweat streamed freely down his face, but his breath harmonized with his movement.

When he finished his last form, he briefly considered starting the entire sequence again. He wiped the sweat from his brow. Other responsibilities weighed heavier, and he couldn't delay the inevitable much longer.

Brandt stared at the black palace looming above him, the rising sun hidden behind its enormity. It didn't seem real, and the grounds, immaculately maintained but abandoned, strengthened the feeling. He imagined the queen, high in her tower, looking down on everyone.

The sound of the main gate opening caused him to turn. A young woman entered and made a straight line for the palace. The gate slammed shut behind her. Brandt waved a hand in greeting, but her eyes never turned in his direction.

Brandt frowned, hand frozen in the air. The hairs on the back of his neck stood on end. His gesture should have drawn her gaze, at least for a moment.

He let his hand fall to his side, then shrugged. He returned to his own chambers, where he washed and changed into loose clothes provided by the queen. They fit well and he enjoyed the freedom of movement they provided.

A knock sounded at the door as he finished. He opened it to find the woman from earlier standing before him. Face to face, he quickly understood her earlier behavior. The girl's eyes were lifeless, reminding him of glassy pools.

Compulsion.

Brandt clenched his fist, nostrils flaring.

He closed his eyes and forced himself to breathe deeply. He'd known about the queen's compulsion before accepting her offer. She'd attempted the same on him once. Despite his own experiences with the condition, he could do nothing for the woman, and raging against the queen did him no good.

When he opened his eyes, he saw the woman hadn't reacted to his actions at all. She gave him a short bow, a poor imitation of imperial customs. "Greetings. My name is Sheela, and the queen has instructed me to follow all your commands."

Her words sent a shudder through him. He forced his fists open and gave his hands a small shake.

He returned the bow, determined to treat her no differently than he would any other person. "Thank you, Sheela. Did the queen have any requests?"

"She wishes to inform you that administrative matters require most of her attention today. While you are welcome to explore the palace, she suggested that I escort you around the city, so you may learn more of our society. She also wishes you to know you have complete freedom of movement, and I am to answer any questions you have."

The idea satisfied his curiosity, so he agreed. Sheela led him from the palace and through the main gates. Two palanquins waited for them.

"I'd rather walk," Brandt said. He wanted to feel the city, to smell its food and listen to the conversations within. He didn't want to observe it from within a box.

Sheela nodded and dismissed their transportation. As Brandt watched them vanish around a corner, she asked, "Is there anywhere in particular you'd like to visit?"

"Is there a market?"

Sheela looked uncertain. "I'm sorry, I don't understand this word."

Brandt blinked, realizing for the first time that speaking imperial hadn't been a problem since he'd arrived. But then, his only interactions had been with the queen, and now Sheela. Perhaps Sheela's imperial wasn't as complete as he'd assumed. He tried again. "Is there a place where people buy and sell goods?"

The lines of uncertainty deepened on her face.

Brandt tried one last approach. "Could you show me where people get their food?"

A smile lit Sheela's face, but combined with the emptiness behind her gaze, the effect was more disconcerting than comforting. "Of course! Follow me."

Brandt did, unease twisting his stomach into ever-tightening knots. He'd been a foreigner before, particularly in Falar. But the experiences didn't compare. Here, he didn't just feel out of place. This felt more like a wrongness, hidden under the veneer of a different civilization.

Just like yesterday, the streets were empty. Brandt asked Sheela why.

"Everyone has their duty to complete. Tonight, at first bell, if you are out, you will see citizens as they travel from their duties to their homes."

Brandt wasn't sure he understood, but he let the matter drop. Part of him doubted every answer Sheela gave him. Could he trust anything someone under compulsion said?

Which led to the next obvious question.

"Sheela, do you know you are under the queen's compulsion?"

"I live to serve the queen. It is an honored role."

Brandt rubbed at his chin, wondering if she understood. "Do you understand that not all your choices are your own?"

Sheela shook her head. "I have chosen to serve the queen."

Brandt let the question drop. Sheela didn't know. How much of her compulsion was voluntary was impossible to guess.

"Sheela, what is your life like when you aren't serving the queen?"

The glassiness of her eyes didn't fade completely, but the question surfaced something else in her. Her smile didn't seem so forced when she spoke about her family. "My husband helps maintain the palace grounds, and we have a young boy and girl who attend the local academy."

Brandt tried to imagine what life in Sheela's household was like, but couldn't. Her compulsion didn't seem to affect every corner of her life, though, so that was something. "What is academy like for your children?"

"It's different for everyone. Children are given an education according to their strengths. Our son has a head for numbers, and we believe he will someday become an adviser to the queen. Our daughter is much more physical, and I think she will join the army."

Brandt nodded along. He still didn't understand, but he heard the pride in Sheela's voice.

He hoped that someday, he would have the same pride in his voice as he spoke about his child.

Sheela stopped outside a building that looked much the same as any other. She gestured for him to lead the way.

Inside, the entire first floor of the building was one large room. The noise of dozens of people working filled the space. Sharp knives thunked against wooden cutting boards, and people shouted from one to another. Brandt breathed a sigh of relief.

At first, the space reminded him of markets he was familiar with. But the differences soon became all he saw. For all the food being prepared, nothing was being bought or sold. Instead, finished products followed a path he couldn't quite decipher, ending in piles near one corner of the room.

Sheela explained. "All day, the food is prepared and portioned for households. Tonight, after first bell, a representative from each household will come and pick up their food for the next five days." She pointed to the piles.

"And this happens throughout the city?"

"It happens in every village, town, and city throughout our land. Only rural families are exempt, but they have their own guides."

"People just accept whatever is given to them?"

Sheela nodded.

He watched for a while longer. Even food was strictly controlled in this land. But what else had he expected?

He asked Sheela if they could leave, which of course she

agreed to. The scene made him uncertain of his own feelings. In some ways, the system reminded him of the empire's own wage-earners, only with the money removed. But drawing comparisons between the systems did him no good. At a fundamental level, the assumptions he believed society operated on weren't true here.

Outside, Sheela asked him if there was anything else he wished to see. Brandt almost asked to visit the military, but he didn't feel well. Perhaps he suffered from some lingering exhaustion, but he asked to return to the palace.

They hadn't been walking long when Brandt caught movement out of the corner of his eye. He turned just as a slow-moving arrow streaked through his vision. The arrow struck Sheela in the head. Her head snapped around and she collapsed, but the arrow rebounded and fell to the street.

Brandt's sword leaped to his hand, but whoever had shot the arrow had scrambled out of sight. Brandt looked up, tracing the path of the arrow to a nearby rooftop. He became light, but before he could scale the building, a woman stepped into the street in front of him, hands held up. She said something, but Brandt didn't understand the Lolani language.

Brandt's gaze darted between the mysterious woman and Sheela. His guide still breathed, and he saw no blood. He looked more closely, confirming that Sheela hadn't suffered a visible injury. Then he looked at the arrow. Where the arrowhead should be, there was instead something small and round, wrapped in cloth. He'd never seen an arrow like it.

The woman took a step forward. She spoke again, in what sounded like a different tongue, but Brandt still didn't understand.

They appeared to be alone in the street. Brandt didn't sheathe his sword, but he relaxed a bit.

The woman frowned, brows furrowed in deep thought. Then she pulled a knife from a hidden pocket. Brandt tensed, but the weapon was still sheathed. The woman tossed it so it landed just in front of him. She gestured to the knife, then to him, then pantomimed carrying it.

Beneath him, Sheela stirred, drawing his attention. When Brandt looked back up, he saw a quick flash of clothing as the woman disappeared around a corner. Brandt refused to pursue. Not in a place where he knew so little, and not when Sheela still needed treatment. He picked up the knife and hid it, then helped Sheela as she regained consciousness. As she recovered, he grabbed the arrow and examined it. A rock rested where the arrowhead should have, and it was padded enough to still deliver a powerful blow, but was unlikely to kill.

Brandt looked up at the roof the arrow had come from. With an arrow weighted so unusually, he considered it an impressive shot.

He tossed the arrow away and helped Sheela to her feet.

Brandt followed her to the palace, the weight of the mysterious knife heavy at his hip.

8

Alena had never been imprisoned before, but she found the experience less frightening than she'd expected. As a young woman obsessed with theft, half the thrill had been avoiding capture. The reality of her cell was far less terrifying than the nightmares her imagination had conjured for her as an adolescent.

The guards had thrown her in a small cell that possessed only a single pot whose smell made its purpose immediately obvious. There were no beds, no thought at all given to comfort. But she wasn't tortured in any way, nor even treated roughly.

Alena sighed, then set to pacing the cell. Why had Olen arrested her?

Her first thought was the gates, but that made no sense. Olen couldn't know about her possession of them, and if he did, he wouldn't have bothered with this cell. As sturdy as her prison was, she could break the stone with a thought. Olen didn't strike her as being that foolish.

She didn't have long to wonder. A commotion erupted at the door as the guards brought in someone else, someone whose creative vocabulary made Alena's ears burn.

Ana.

Her hands were shackled behind her back, but she wasn't making the guards' task easy. Finally, about ten paces from Alena's cell, the commander of the unit had enough. He turned and slapped Ana hard across the face.

The blow only made the woman fight harder. Alena couldn't help but smile and shake her head. They must have caught her by surprise, or sleeping. She couldn't imagine Ana being captured by guards in any other way.

Her humor disappeared when the commander drew a sword.

In a moment, Alena was at the door to her cell, fully connected to the gates. If the guard tried anything, it would be his last mistake.

Ana noticed her, and at the sight, calmed.

The guard smiled smugly, believing that he had intimidated the former wolfblade.

Alena wanted to smack the smile off his face, but restrained herself.

The guards threw Ana in the same cell as Alena, still shackled. They slammed the door behind her, not even offering to remove the bindings.

The two women stared at each other for a few moments. Then Ana sighed and turned around. "Could you take care of these for me?"

Alena shook her head. "I'm sorry. I would, but I don't want them to know, not yet."

Ana sighed again, although she didn't seem surprised.

"What happened?" Alena asked. "Why are we here?"

Ana gave her an incredulous look. "You haven't figured it out?"

Alena's face must have been answer enough. Ana shook her head. "You told the scouting party about what happened to Hanns. Everyone is being arrested."

It took Alena a moment to understand. "All of this, because of that?"

Ana chuckled grimly. "You've been from the empire too long. We love our secrets." She sat down in a corner and rested her head against the stone wall. She closed her eyes and let out a slow exhale.

Alena paced the cell again, then stopped. It made her feel as though she towered over Ana. She sat across the cell from the former wolfblade, giving her space.

The sounds of adjacent cell blocks being filled reached their ears, confirming Ana's information. Alena listened for sounds of struggle, flexing her fist as she did. Confinement was one problem, but if any of the scouts suffered abuse tonight, Olen would rue his actions.

Alena remained alert to any fights, but it seemed that Ana was the only one who'd resisted arrest. Even Toren came quietly.

So they sat, and Alena snuck glances at Ana. She imagined and rejected dozens of attempts to bridge the gap between them, but Brandt's decision felt like a wall even two gates couldn't break down. Before long, guards brought an evening meal. Once Ana promised her best behavior, the guards entered and released her from the shackles.

They barely worried about Alena.

She delighted in their underestimation. It brought her back to the days of her youth, when no one suspected her of thievery. Sometimes, a meek demeanor was the most dangerous weapon in the world.

They ate their food, which was better than Alena had

expected. Most likely it was the same meal the soldiers had eaten tonight.

Content with a full stomach, Alena made her attempt. "The guards didn't hurt you, did they?"

Ana finished the last bites of her meal, then shook her head. She hesitated, then asked, "You would have attacked if I'd been in danger, wouldn't you?"

"Of course."

Ana took her bowl and slid it sideways through the cell door for the guards to pick up. She gestured, and Alena handed over her bowl so Ana could repeat the process.

"I'm sorry," Ana said. "I've—"

Alena held up a hand to stall the woman. She didn't need Ana's apology. She couldn't imagine what the warrior lived through. Whether or not Brandt's actions were justified, he'd ripped Ana's heart to shreds. Seeing this proud wolfblade with her head bowed was too painful for Alena to watch. "There's no need. He surprised us all."

"Is it strange that I don't hate him?"

Alena snorted. "Yes."

Ana smiled at that. "I understand why he did what he did. It doesn't make his leaving any easier to bear, but as much as I want to rage at him, I can't."

"I'm still going to drop a boulder on his foot when he returns," Alena said.

Ana laughed at that. "I won't stop you."

The weeks of silence and distance evaporated. One of Alena's burdens slipped away.

"Do you have a plan?" Ana asked.

Alena raised one skeptical eyebrow and looked around their cell. "Do I look like I have a plan?"

"Good point. Shall we work on one together?"

"Sure. I only have one requirement."

Ana listened.

"When it's done, Olen needs to regret he threw us in here together."

9

Sheela refused to enter the palace grounds, no matter how strongly Brandt insisted she needed care. Eventually, her stubbornness won out, and Brandt entered the palace alone.

The guards let him through the gate without question, and they made no search of his person. The palace grounds were as empty as ever, and he patted the pocket where the sheathed knife rested.

He entered the tower, surprised by the smell of cooking food drifting through the halls. His mouth watered, reminding him he hadn't eaten for most of the day. He'd asked, back in the building where food was being distributed, but they'd refused him. All the food was rationed, and no one received extra. Not even guests of the queen.

Brandt followed the smell. Even if it didn't lead to the queen, it would lead to a meal.

After several turns, his nose led him to a small kitchen. He stopped in his tracks when he saw who was there.

The queen stood over a stove, stirring vegetables into a

stew. She glanced up at his arrival. "I figured you would be hungry."

The sight of this ancient and powerful woman cooking her own meal froze Brandt's thoughts.

"I do most of my own cooking," she said. "It's one less path for assassination attempts, and I find it difficult to compel people to cook well."

Brandt couldn't help himself. After the events of the day, he laughed.

The queen looked up, anger flashing in her eyes before she brought it under control. "What?"

"You can direct a lightning bolt to strike countless leagues away, but you can't compel someone to cook for you?"

He saw another flash of anger in her eyes. "Power is never absolute."

"Despite your best efforts." Brandt didn't know why he pressed. Maybe because verbal weapons were the only ones he owned that had any effect on the queen.

He heard the songs of the elements intensify, and he suspected she'd connected to her gate. Perhaps he'd pushed too hard.

But then the songs faded. "If you wish to eat, you'll be wise to hold your tongue."

Brandt gave a small bow of acknowledgment, not wishing to die due to insulting his host. Then he remembered why he'd come here in the first place. "Sheela was injured during our outing."

"I know."

The answer stopped Brandt's next sentence in its tracks. "You do?"

"My compulsion, as you call it, allows me to have some awareness of what happens to her. She'll be fine, though.

They were wise not to kill her."

"Why?"

"Because training others in your language is a time-consuming task. I would have been frustrated, and taken that frustration out on them."

All Brandt could manage was a confused grunt.

The queen ladled the stew into two bowls, then took one. "Come, we can discuss it over supper."

The dining room was smaller and far more intimate than Brandt expected. It was nothing more than a small round table with two chairs sitting across from one another. All were of fine quality, but nothing as ornate as what they used in the imperial palace.

They sat down, and Brandt sampled the food. In yet another surprise in a day full of them, the stew tasted incredible. Some vegetables he didn't recognize, but the flavors complemented one another well, and Brandt ate with undisguised pleasure. He noticed, as he ate, the queen relax at his enjoyment.

That was when something that had been bothering him finally made itself understood. Why did the queen restrain her rage, or care what he thought about her cooking? He considered for a moment, but came up with no answer. He shoved another bite in his mouth, then leaned back.

"Why all this?" he gestured to the room, and the meal.

"What do you mean?"

"I'm here to learn from you, and if I succeed, perhaps kill you. There is no need to make me a guest in your palace, or feed me the same food you make for yourself. Why?"

She leaned back, matching his pose, studying him. "Because teaching you isn't enough."

"Why not?"

"Because I should have four gates under my control now,

with the fifth falling soon after. Instead, I have two. And even that was as much good fortune as strategy. The empire of Anders has resisted me at every turn, and I'm running out of time to conquer it."

"And you think I'll help?"

"I do."

The confidence in her voice unnerved him. It didn't carry the empty bravado of boasting, but a calm certainty. "Why not just compel me?"

"I've tried, as you recall."

Brandt did.

"In time, though, your defenses would crumble. Everyone's does, no matter their strength of will. But compelling someone takes something vital from them, a strength that warriors need. It is the same with cooking. I can compel someone to cook, but I cannot make them cook well. Compulsion is a tool, useful for some occasions, but not for others."

"Why not me? Why not now?" Brandt tired of vague answers.

"I've already told you I fear what comes. I am uncertain I am equal to the task, and you are the first warrior I've encountered in an age who possesses both the talent and the will to be useful in the war to come. Would you take your best sword and deliberately put notches in it?"

Brandt shook his head. "Having fought you, it is a difficult story to believe."

"You will, in time."

Not having an answer to that, Brandt turned back to his meal, finishing it in quick bites. When he leaned back again, it was with a contented smile on his face. Some habits of soldiering died hard. Nothing beat a full stomach and a warm bed. Give him those, and there was no limit to what else he could bear. "Thank you."

"You're welcome."

Brandt returned to the original subject. "You know Sheela was attacked, and yet you've asked no questions about the incident."

"There's no need."

Brandt frowned.

"I have little doubt you were contacted by one of the nascent groups of assassins that grow like weeds throughout my lands. I assume they rendered Sheela unconscious so they could speak to you without fear of me listening in through my connection to her. The details of what they said don't much matter. If they are as clever as they seem, I suspect they gave you some item, to see if it would pass the defenses I've put around the palace."

Even though the queen had been blinded, she'd deduced more about the group and their purposes than Brandt had. He supposed there was little point in hiding anything. He took the knife from his pocket and laid it on the table.

"Did they ask you to kill me?" she asked.

"No. They just threw this down before me and mimed that I should carry it. The language barrier was an issue, and there wasn't much time."

"They are clever, then." She explained before Brandt could ask her to. "Although they are invisible to your eyes, this palace is surrounded by wards. Anyone who tries to enter these grounds uninvited with a weapon is immediately compelled to kill themselves with that very weapon. I've found it a useful deterrent for would-be assassins."

"They wanted to see if I could bring a weapon across and still live." Brandt realized that if the group's experiment had failed, he would now be dead by his own hand, lying in a pool of blood at the gate of the palace. The thought made him shiver. They'd treated him as nothing more than a tool.

"They did. And by making it one of their own weapons, they ensured that you could bring any weapon in, not just your own sword."

Brandt followed her logic. "So, once they figure out the language, they can ask me to bring in all sorts of weapons, or ask me to act as their assassin." That thought led to another. "They immediately assumed that no matter who I was, I would want to kill you."

She nodded. "It is, unfortunately, a common reaction."

Brandt digested her words. He thought of the empty palace grounds and tower, and the layers of defenses the queen needed just to live through a day. Even Hanns, for all of his precautions, had never had to go so far.

"How long have you lived like this?"

She refused to meet his gaze. "Lifetimes."

Before he could answer, she continued. "But not for much longer. Soon it will all be decided."

"You fear this force that much?"

The queen studied him again. "I do." She played with her utensils, watching him. "I'd meant to wait to show you this, but perhaps it is best to do it sooner."

She stood up suddenly, her icy gaze focused on him.

"Would you like to meet this world's doom?"

10

The days rolled by, marked only by the passage of the shadows on the floor of their cell. Beyond the lack of comfort, Alena didn't mind the imprisonment. The guards were kind enough and provided them three meals a day.

The cells had never been designed for anyone to remain long. This was a military outpost, and Ana explained that the cells were most commonly used for soldiers who needed to sleep off a night of too much drink.

Alena used the time to consider her next actions, and to speak with Ana. Now that the wall between them had fallen, the conversations between them came easier.

While they waited, they listened. The guards, it seemed, weren't worried about what was said near the prisoners, so Alena and Ana overheard the important news of the day. They heard when Olen finally announced the death of his father and brother. Alena said nothing to the guards that day, but noted how many eyes were downcast.

A day later, Olen declared that he would assume the role of Anders VII. Alena watched the guards for their reaction to the news. She was underwhelmed. Though Olen's ascension to the throne was hardly a surprise, few seemed excited by the prospect.

The night before the ceremony, Alena decided it was time to act. She didn't know how long Olen intended to hold them here, or what he planned for them, but she'd waited long enough.

When she stood, Ana's eyes followed. The former wolfblade must have seen something in her posture, because she asked, "Is it time?"

"It is. You need not come with me, if you don't want treason added to your records."

Ana gave a small shrug as she stood up. "I'd rather follow you than Olen."

"That's what worries me."

Her imprisonment had given her plenty of time to consider different methods of breaking herself out. She could, if she wished, just destroy the cells, but she preferred not to make a scene. Alena opened her connection to the gates and picked up a pair of stones she'd slowly pried loose earlier. She'd smoothed the edges of each.

Alena floated the stones out through the bars of her cell, then took aim at the two guards.

The hardest part was deciding how hard to launch the stone. She only wanted the guards unconscious, not dead. And she'd never tried anything like this before. Toren would be better suited for the task, but they hadn't figured out a way to perform the action together. His cell with Jace was out of sight of the guards.

Alena flung the first stone forward.

Her aim was true, and the stone cracked into the side of a guard's head. The guard fell out of his chair, but he wasn't unconscious.

Alena threw the second stone at the other guard, this time a little harder. It, too, connected. The guard collapsed to the ground, and he wouldn't be getting up soon.

The first guard pushed himself to his feet. Alena didn't want to hit him again. Instead, she drove the stone into his stomach and pulled it toward their cell. The guard, still not sure what was happening, struggled, but soon found himself with his back pinned against their cell bars.

Ana wasted no time. She snaked her arm through the gap, wrapping it around the guard's neck. A few moments later she released the guard, and he collapsed to the ground.

Alena used the stones to pull the second guard, who had the keys attached to his belt, toward the cell. Once the guard was close, they grabbed the keys and let themselves out. After a moment of debate, they pulled the guards into the cell and locked them in.

Alena pushed down her pang of guilt. The guards weren't at fault. Later, she promised she would apologize.

Assuming her judgment of Olen's character was correct, and her plan worked.

The two women walked further down the row of cells. Commander Jon and the scouts filled the next three. Jon, having heard the commotion, came to his bars to speak to them. He eyed Alena warily. "I thought there was more to you than you let on."

Alena's estimation of the man improved. Others might have threatened or shouted. Jon trusted his instincts.

"I'm sorry I didn't say more," Alena said. "I wasn't sure what was appropriate."

Jon looked around his cell. "I'd say Prince Olen already thinks you said too much."

Alena conceded the point. "I intend to speak with him about that tonight."

"Do you mean him harm?"

Alena shook her head.

"Then we are with you, if you'll have us."

Ana laid a cautionary hand on Alena's arm, but the decision was an easy one. Besides, if Jon was trying to surprise her, it wouldn't work. She had two gates and two stones.

Yes, he could complicate matters, but she trusted him. And trust, she hoped, was better than secrecy. She opened his cell door and the others of the scouting party. "Remain here, for now. It will be easier for fewer of us to get through to Olen than for more. I don't want to fight if I can avoid it."

Jon nodded, and Alena proceeded to the last cell. Jace and Toren were inside, resting with their backs against the wall in nearly identical poses. When she got to the door, Jace greeted her with a mischievous smile. "Took you long enough."

"I don't have to let you out."

Jace chuckled as both men got to their feet. "That's okay. I think I've seen enough of the inside of this cell."

Before long, they were gathered together at the entrance to the cells. The group looked to Alena.

"I'll lead the way," she said. "Don't fight unless necessary."

They opened the door, revealing a long, narrow corridor. Alena led the way, opening another door at the other end and peering through. This door opened into a large storeroom, with plenty of places to hide. A pair of guards on patrol strolled by, but Alena and the others crouched behind stacks of barrels, avoiding them easily.

They exited the storage area once the guards were past.

The officers' quarters, where Olen was staying, were quiet. At this time of night, guard patrols were infrequent.

It was almost too easy.

Two guards stood alert outside Olen's door. Toren took one and Alena the other. They fell to stones easily enough. Toren and Jace pulled the guards aside, leaving Ana to guard the door.

Alena grimaced. It shouldn't be this easy. Toren could have completed this mission on his own if he'd been in Alena's shoes, and he was hardly unique among the Etari.

She went to the door and tried it. It was unlocked.

She hesitated for a moment. Perhaps it *was* too easy. Was it a trap?

She didn't think so. More than anything, it represented just how unprepared the empire was to fight against affinities.

Alena stepped inside.

Olen slept soundly in his bed.

Alena slammed the door behind her and used fire to light every lantern in the room at once. Olen practically leaped out of bed, his eyes wide with fear. They went even wider when they saw Alena.

She stepped forward and leaned toward him before he could shout. "Prince Olen, it's time you and I had a talk."

11

B randt followed the queen higher into the tower, eventually entering a room without windows. Several chairs sat in the middle of the space, and as Brandt approached, he saw they were an unusual design. Wide leather straps hung loose from both arms and the front legs of each chair. They looked like they were meant for restraint. His heart beat faster, thoughts of torture making him reach for his sword.

"It's not what you believe," the queen said.

Brandt paused, but his heart still raced.

The queen walked to the nearest chair and used her air affinity to brush a layer of dust off it. "This is where I come to share my memories and knowledge, and yes, to compel if necessary. But the restraints aren't to prevent you from escaping."

Brandt stepped away from the chairs, shaking his head. Death didn't frighten him, but he much preferred the clean, sudden end of a warrior in battle.

The queen shook her head. "Don't you think that if I

wanted information from you, or if I wanted you to suffer, that there would be simpler ways? Be rational, Brandt."

Brandt hovered between running from the room and stepping forward.

"The chairs have restraints because when I share my memories, people tend to panic. The straps prevent injuries."

"That's not reassuring."

The queen shrugged, then motioned to the chair she'd dusted.

Brandt sighed. At this point, what argument could he make? He sat in the chair and the queen fastened the restraints. She left them loose enough that he could extricate himself with a bit of time.

The queen approached another chair, her movements stiffer and more hesitant than usual, as though the seat was lined with needles. She paused for two long heartbeats before settling in.

The queen clenched her jaw and shot Brandt a questioning look. He nodded and a moment later his world vanished.

SOFRA WATCHED the adults hurrying through the streets. Her mother had ordered her to stay home, but Sofra wasn't sure if she should. Everyone else was running.

Her mother often said that Sofra was an old soul, sighing when she did. She wanted Sofra to remain a child, ignorant and naive to the ways of the world. But Sofra saw too much.

She saw the ways others treated her mother with respect when they spoke to her. But she also noticed that her home hosted far fewer visitors than most. Other children avoided Sofra, and their parents did nothing to discipline such behavior.

Sofra could only come to one conclusion.

Her mother was too strong, and they feared her for it.

Someday, Sofra would be as strong as her mother.

Her mother wouldn't stay home if she were in Sofra's place. Something had happened. It wasn't just the citizens running in the streets. Sofra could feel menace in the air.

Sofra ran through the house, planning out her actions. She grabbed a bag from a closet, then filled it with bread and other food, including a few treats her mother thought she had hidden well. She took their sharpest knife from the kitchen and the book that her mother spent so much time with.

If Sofra's mother returned home before Sofra and found such items missing, the gods alone knew what she would do. But that was a worry for later.

Sofra watched the streets. Everyone fled toward the sea. Why?

She climbed the stairs, up and up, ascending to their upper deck which looked over the city. Sofra and her mother spent many evenings up here, watching the sun set.

Today, no such pleasures awaited.

The woodland beyond the city walls burned, a plume of smoke rising to blot out the sun. But this was like no fire Sofra had ever seen. Her small heart beat even faster. This fire didn't burn. It destroyed. Trees exploded from the heat, and the fire advanced with unbelievable rapidity.

Sofra blinked. Why did the others even bother to run? There was no escaping this fire. It would burn the water from the bay.

She blinked again, and saw a lone figure standing on the wall. Even though the figure was little more than a speck in the distance, Sofra knew.

Her mother stood against the flame.

The wind picked up behind her, and a sudden storm appeared overhead, pouring rain down on both the city streets and the wood beyond.

The fire didn't relent.

Sofra jumped as lightning split the air. Once, twice, and then a flurry of strikes she couldn't count. Thunder rumbled, and the planks of the deck shook underneath Sofra's feet.

The lightning had all struck the same place.

Her mother's handiwork.

The flames separated, as though a curtain revealing an actor on stage. Sofra wished she had one of her mother's looking glasses, for she saw only shadow. But as she watched, it materialized into a figure.

More lightning flashed, a staccato series of bursts that ripped up the ground surrounding the mysterious figure. Sofra clapped her hands over her ears to protect them from the waves of thunder, though they did little good.

Her mother and the figure of shadows stared at one another. Then it raised a hand, and the fire vanished.

The world seemed to take an enormous breath.

Sofra squinted through the rain.

When everyone else ran, her mother stood.

When the world burned, her mother brought rain.

When Sofra was of age, she would follow in her mother's footsteps. She'd never been more certain of anything.

The air around her mother warped as though it were bread dough. Buildings disintegrated as though they were children's sand structures on the beaches. The wall itself collapsed, except for the section her mother stood on.

Her mother fell to one knee.

A pinprick of light grew, not more than a few hands above her mother's head. For several heartbeats, it was no more than that, a tiny, impossibly bright light that cast everything in stark whites and black shadows. Sofra almost turned away, but she refused.

Then the light expanded, swallowing her mother, what remained of the wall, and the city before them. Sofra squeezed her eyes shut and was still blinded by the intensity of the light.

A clap of thunder, far louder than anything Sofra had ever heard, shook her very bones. She felt not just the deck, but her entire house, sway from an impact, but before she could run, everything collapsed and her world went black.

BRANDT GASPED as the world returned to him. His heart thudded, and when he looked down he saw that his wrists were red from where he'd been fighting against the restraints.

Everything had been real. He'd been the queen, and he'd felt everything she'd felt, with the same intensity as she had in that moment. He thought he might be sick.

But his training took over, responding to his body's distress. He forced his mouth closed and breathed deeply through his nose. He focused on his breath, bringing his attention to the present moment.

Across from him, the queen looked almost as bad as he felt. He'd never seen her like this.

Vulnerable.

Human.

Their gazes met. "There's one more event I need to show you. Something it is better for you to see now, rather than later."

Brandt shook his head, but couldn't force words out.

"It must be done," the queen said.

"Please, not ag—"

Brandt's world slipped away.

.   .   .

SOFRA EMERGED FROM THE RUBBLE, *the skies dark overhead. For several moments she just stood, breathing in blissfully clean air.*

The shadow was gone. Sofra couldn't say how she was so certain, but she was.

Her mother was gone, too.

Sofra didn't have the time to grieve. That would come later. For now, survival was all that mattered.

She spun in a slow circle, numb to the disaster. The city she had grown up in was gone. Some buildings, like her home, had simply crumbled, but of others, she saw no sign, as though they'd somehow grown legs and ran off.

No fires burned and nothing moved. Sofra didn't expect she was the only one to survive, but she saw no evidence otherwise.

She wandered.

Everywhere, the scene repeated itself. If this city ever recovered, it would be a miracle. Whole neighborhoods had been leveled, wiped clean of any habitation.

The pattern became apparent in time. There were places where the destruction had centered. Those locations were barren. But as one walked from the center, buildings had collapsed instead. She imagined that if seen from above, the city appeared pockmarked.

At times she heard cries, but she didn't approach. Her mother had died for these people, and they'd never shown her respect. Mercy found barren soil in Sofra's heart.

She only stopped when she came to the edge of the city. The wall that was supposed to protect them was gone and she could look out on what had once been a forest.

Not even the roots remained.

At the sight of the absolute devastation, Sofra fell to her knees, and she finally cried.

It would be the last time she ever did.

. . .

ONCE AGAIN, Brandt returned to reality. He struggled for a few moments, then freed his right hand from the restraints. He wiped at the tears falling down his own cheeks.

The queen stood, her own face dry. But when she spoke, her voice carried the burdens of the memory.

"Now you know what we face."

Without another word, she exited the room, leaving Brandt to free himself from the last of the restraints.

The queen's memories were now his own. Whatever her technique, it destroyed the barriers between their consciousnesses. He had been her. Her fear was now his.

He tried to stand and failed.

He'd experienced the queen's power, and had thought that nearly impossible to attain. But if what he'd just seen was true, even that power paled in comparison to the looming threat.

Which left one inescapable conclusion: when the creature arrived again, their world would end.

12

T o Olen's credit, he didn't reach for the sword resting near his bed. After the moment of surprise passed, he rubbed his eyes and shook his head. "What's this about?"

The slight tremor in his voice gave away his fear. Beyond that, he gave no sign that a nighttime intruder in his private quarters was an unusual occurrence.

"The future of the empire," Alena replied.

Olen's sharp eyes settled on her, and she felt like a piece on the board of his grand game. "Do you bring guidance?"

Alena ignored the mockery in his voice. "And if I did, would you heed it?"

She found his gaze difficult to bear. Judgment, superiority, and confidence lurked in equal measure in his eyes, and she nearly wilted before it.

No wonder those under his command didn't care for him. She squared her shoulders and awaited his answer.

"Of course," Olen answered. "A wise ruler always listens to his subjects."

His movement was slight. Had she not been so focused

on him, she might have missed it. But his balance shifted forward.

She couldn't have that.

Olen believed he'd taken control of the situation.

She smiled, and Olen leaned farther forward, closer to his sword, probably thinking his answer had satisfied her.

Alena dropped into a soulwalk, found Olen, and forced him into her world.

She opted for a different environment from her usual choice. While she was most comfortable in her mother's kitchen, it wouldn't do for what she intended.

Alena chose the battlefield where she and Brandt had first faced the Lolani queen. Her memory had no problem recreating the lines of Lolani soldiers prepared for the invasion.

Olen's eyes went wide again as he understood what had happened. "You're a soulwalker?"

Alena snapped her fingers, not because she needed to, but because she wanted to disorient Olen. Shackles appeared around his wrists, and Alena forced him to his knees, chains pulling his arms to full extension. She pinned the chains in place with long stakes.

Olen fought, but his experience couldn't match Alena's. Here, she was stronger than anyone except the queen. Worry appeared on his face for the first time. "What do you want?"

"As I said before, to talk."

"Then talk."

"Not until you're ready to listen."

"I have been."

He still struggled, but his efforts did nothing to loosen the chains. Alena didn't need either her gatestone or the gates to keep him locked here. His lack of success surprised her.

Alena walked closer and kicked him hard in the stomach. She gave her blow a little extra strength, and Olen gasped and bent over, his forehead almost touching the floor.

She waited.

In a while, he raised himself back up, a snarl on his face.

"You're still not listening," she said. She stepped forward again.

Olen's fight was pathetic. But he still fought.

She kicked him again, grimacing as she did. The first kick had exhausted all her frustration at him. This made her feel uneasy, but she needed to break down his belief in his own superiority.

When he raised his head again, Alena saw that he was close to cracking.

But he hadn't yet.

Alena took a step forward, and then it happened. He shrank away from her, as much as it was possible, and tears started streaming down his face. "Stop! Please!"

Alena did. She waited a few moments as his body convulsed in sobs. When she was convinced it was real, she took a few steps back and made the chains vanish.

While he recovered, she looked over the horde of Lolani. Though she'd chosen this place for Olen, it served as a reminder for her as well. Every moment mattered.

Olen's snuffles ended, and he stood shakily on his feet.

"Are you ready to listen now?" Alena asked.

He nodded, eyes on the ground, and for the first time, she believed him.

"You've had several days to think about the events in

Falar and the impending invasion," Alena began. "How do you plan on responding?"

"Increase the size of our forces. Improved training, and station them at the border of Falar."

"You believe you can fight her?"

Olen's eyes rose in anger. "When I take the throne tomorrow, I will take an oath to protect the empire. So it doesn't matter what I believe. I will do all that I can."

His tone and posture were different than the other times she'd seen him. This wasn't the prince, or the emperor-to-be. She saw Olen, truly, for the first time. And this man she had a measure of respect for, a man who took his duties seriously.

"There's a larger problem."

"The force you claim you felt?" Olen's disbelief crept into his voice.

Alena exhaled a long breath. "You would be a fool to discount the possibility. I believe what I felt, and it is one of the few reasonable explanations for the queen's behavior."

Olen crossed his arms. "The queen's manipulations can be subtle."

The comment revealed much. Olen had firsthand experience of the queen's efforts, too. Unlike his brother, though, he hadn't turned. Alena took note.

She interrupted him before he could continue. "Stop. If you don't believe me, say so. I want to protect the empire, the same as you. But right now, I'm thinking perhaps the best way of doing that is turning over my two gates to the queen."

The verbal blow landed with every bit of the impact that she had hoped for. Olen's mouth dropped open, and for once, he had no retort ready.

Alena waited, but when no apology came, she waved her

hand dismissively, the same way he had to her during their first meeting. Even the air in this place now tasted bitter. She turned her back and prepared to drop out of the soulwalk.

"Wait!" he shouted.

She turned to face him.

Olen sank onto his knees, this time by choice. "You have the gates?" His body slumped, as though the ghost of his father had risen from the dead and snapped his spine.

"I do."

"Why didn't you say anything?"

"Because I wanted to get the measure of the ruler you will be."

Olen bowed his head to the floor. "I'm sorry."

Alena just shook her head. He was only sorry his plans hadn't worked. There was no remorse in him for imprisoning his own soldiers and citizens for days.

With a thought, she dropped them out of the soulwalk. Olen looked around, disoriented.

Alena hesitated. She had thought, when she'd first entered this camp several days ago, that she would turn the gates over to Olen despite her misgivings. But now it seemed their burden would be one she would continue to carry. She couldn't bring herself to trust the prince, and she wondered if she had discovered the reason why Hanns had given her the gates.

She left Olen's quarters, and the prince made no move to stop her.

Ana waited for her in the hall. She gave Alena a questioning glance.

Alena shook her head and Ana's face fell.

They gathered up Toren and Jace, and together made their way out of the camp.

13

Eventually Brandt stumbled out of the room. His legs wobbled, but he held out his hand, running it along the cold stone walls for support. When he reached the stairs he paused, gathering his strength to descend them.

He closed his eyes, taking deep breaths.

His first brush with death had been on patrol inside Falar, searching for a missing imperial scout.

They never saw the ambush. To his memory, it had been a quiet afternoon, with nothing but empty mountain terrain for leagues. Then the silence was shattered by the ear-piercing shrieks of the attacking Falari.

Arrows rained down on them as a war party emerged like ghosts from behind nearby rock outcroppings. Most of Brandt's training vanished beneath the angry glares of the enemy. He swung his sword wildly, any semblance of technique long forgotten.

Somehow, they'd survived. Brandt had killed for the first time. And today felt like the first moment of that first battle. Fear stole his strength.

His concern wasn't for himself. He'd always expected to die by the sword, and had made his peace with a violent end many years ago.

No, his thoughts were for Ana and the unnamed child in her womb. Brandt could fight and die without blinking. But to leave them undefended against *that*? He pressed his hand harder into the wall, drawing strength from it.

He made it to the ground floor and out the main doors of the palace. He needed air, a space to breathe. The deserted palace grounds weren't enough, but he didn't wish to enter the city. In his current state, who knew what schemes he would fall victim to?

His eyes traveled to the wall surrounding the palace, and his feet followed his gaze. He found a stair leading to the top and took it, climbing three stairs at a time in his haste.

From the top of the walls Valan stretched out before him, with the endless desert beyond. Brandt strolled along the wall, his thoughts and gaze as aimless as his path.

He caught new details of the city. To the north, there was farmland, no doubt intended to feed the growing population. To the east was the ocean, and the view from the wall made him pause. The gentle swell of the water soothed him, and when he finally looked away, he found his thoughts were more focused. He completed his circuit of the wall, once again looking out over the heart of the city.

The sound of the bells caught him by surprise, but as Sheela had promised, the city came alive underneath his gaze. People trickled out of buildings, and before long the streets were filled. He'd suspected the city held many people, but he was surprised by how many packed every passage.

Another set of bells seemed to serve as a warning, and

by the time the third set of bells rang, the streets were empty again, presenting their more familiar appearance to him.

Brandt heard the queen as she approached. She stood beside him and looked out over her city.

"This is all because of that creature?" he asked.

"It is," she acknowledged. "The bells help keep order, but they have a higher purpose, too. Should the worst befall us, everyone here will be conditioned to respond to the sound. They'll run to their houses as soon as the bells ring."

"It won't protect them."

"No, but it clears the streets for the warriors to fight."

Brandt turned the idea over in his head, like rotating a relic in his hands to examine it from all angles.

The queen had ruled for hundreds of years, at least.

Generations of citizens had lived and died under such control.

All for a momentary advantage in a fight the queen couldn't have been certain would even come to pass. "Is it worth the cost?" he asked.

"Isn't the survival of our species worth any price?"

Reluctantly, Brandt nodded. He wasn't sure how much of a decision it really was, but he'd made his. "I'm ready to train."

The queen stood taller. "Good. After today, I do not think we should wait. Get your rest tonight, and tomorrow, after my administrative tasks are complete, we'll begin."

The queen turned and walked back to the palace. Brandt watched her go. His nerves around the woman hadn't quite gone away, but with understanding came familiarity. She'd given him a year to learn. He hoped it would be enough time.

Night fell over the city, but few lanterns lit the scene

below. Why bother lighting the streets if no one walked them? Brandt watched, wondering if perhaps some young men and women, tired of living under the thumb of an oppressive queen, snuck out as children often did.

He saw nothing, though.

However the queen enforced her commands, it was enough to even convince the youth not to disobey. Remembering his own youth, Brandt was impressed.

Either that, he supposed, or they'd found ways to move about the city unseen.

As a military commander, he approved of the steps the queen had taken. Fighting in a city was always a miserable task, but having the citizens safely inside made it a little easier.

But who would want to live like this? If anyone here had ever known anything else, they wouldn't accept this style of rule. Even with the queen's incredible strength, it was remarkable that her reign had lasted as long as it had.

Alena had once told him that how he did things mattered. With every passing day, he saw more of the wisdom in her words. The queen prepared for an impossible war, and no doubt she saw her actions as justified now that the threat was returning.

But the cost—

Brandt shook his head. Such thoughts would only lead him deeper into despair. For all the queen's faults, she represented the best hope of saving humanity. So he would learn from her and use that learning to protect his wife and child.

Motion in the distance caught his eye.

A lone figure had climbed up to a rooftop several buildings away. Between the distance and the failing light, Brandt couldn't make out many details about the person.

But somehow, he knew it was the woman from the street.

The one who had given him the knife.

She stood there, perfectly still, and watched him until he turned his back to return to the palace.

14

No one stopped Alena and her friends as they made their way from Olen's encampment. None of the guards seemed particularly concerned about the motley group departing the area. Before the sun broke over the horizon they were already a league away, traveling deeper into the empire.

Alena's tired mind couldn't work through the encounter in Olen's quarters. Her decision to leave had been instinct, counter to every rational argument she made. Her stomach clenched just thinking of their exchange. But now, where did it leave her?

All the power in the world meant little without a title.

Jace laid a hand on her shoulder. "We need to rest."

He was kind enough to say "we," but he meant her. Alena fought the suggestion. She could walk for days, and still not be far enough away from the army. But Jace persisted, and Alena relented. Her feet were sore and keeping her eyes open took most of her attention. Jace found a comfortable depression, and Alena was asleep before Toren had time to prepare food.

She woke up sweating, the sun directly overhead. With a groan she sat up, blinking the cobwebs from her thoughts.

The others seemed at ease, but her waking drew their attention. She pressed her palms to her eyes, wanting one moment of peace before the questions fell like arrows around her.

Jace brought over a meal, which she devoured with speed that made the others flinch away. Though no one asked, she knew everyone had the same question. What next?

Alena had no answers, and she almost threw her empty bowl at them. She hadn't asked for the mantle of leadership. She possessed no more wisdom than anyone else here.

Her anger wasn't justified, though. She used the last bites of her food to calm herself.

When the last scrap of food was safely in her stomach, she answered their silent questions. "I'm not sure what to do next. I think I need to soulwalk first. With more information, we can make better choices together."

She expected disappointment. The others certainly desired more. But she saw only nods of approval. Alena stood and distanced herself from the group. Their proximity distracted her, and she would need all the focus she could muster if she was going to accomplish what she hoped to. She found a clump of bushes and sat on the far side of them. Just breaking line of sight made her feel more at ease. Why anyone sought positions of leadership was beyond her.

She settled herself into a comfortable position. The soulwalk didn't come as easy as it usually did, which she attributed to lingering exhaustion. As soon as she entered the soulwalk she saw several strands tying her to her friends, but she ignored those. Her attention was on a strand that took off in a different direction. Its presence reassured her. Brandt was still alive.

He better be.

Because she wanted to hit him with the power of two gates herself.

She followed the strand, curious to see if the distance was too great to follow. Distance had some meaning in the soulwalk, but not the same as in the physical world. She had some sense of the vast spaces that separated her from Brandt, but with the aid of the gates, she followed the thread as far as it would go.

It ended abruptly.

Or, at least, her pursuit of it ended. She came upon a weaving, reminiscent of the Etari boundary, but far more complicated. To her affinity, it appeared as a complex skein of threads, tied together in indecipherable ways. It had to be the queen's work.

Alena studied the weaving for some time. Parts she thought she recognized, but others were foreign to her. She didn't dare attempt to pass through. Brandt was still alive. Of that, she was fairly certain. It would have to be enough for now. She let go of the thread, returning back to her own body.

She remained in the soulwalk. One question remained, one she'd been putting off. She reached out to the stars, attempting to follow the trail she'd once accompanied the queen on. Despite the time that had passed, she found the process a simple one now that she had the aid of the gates.

She found it.

A spike, colder than ice, stabbed at her even as she observed it from a distance. Blacker than black, it passed through the void of space at unimaginable speed. She couldn't be sure, but it seemed to be moving faster. Their planet called to it.

Every fiber of her being demanded she run away. Against such an awesome power, what other action made sense? Through force of will alone she remained.

She sensed no malice from the creature. It didn't hate her. It simply sought the end of all humanity. And it had the strength to do so. Even with two gates, she was nothing more than a fly buzzing around its head.

But even a fly would get noticed if it buzzed close for too long.

Slowly, it turned its regard to her. Perhaps she sensed amusement, but in a flash, the creature swatted at Alena. It slammed her out of her soulwalk with physical force, and she doubled over in pain as every nerve in her body fired at once. She panted as she clutched at her stomach, the reaction instinctual but helpless. The pain lingered.

Eventually, she found the strength to sit up straight. She tested her connections to the gates, relieved to find they held strong.

Despair threatened to consume her. She could do nothing, nor could the queen. Even working together was pointless.

Alena gritted her teeth and shook her head.

There had to be a way. There was always a way. She didn't see it yet, but it existed.

She stood on shaky legs and returned to the group. With every step her stride grew more determined. Impossible or not, she refused to surrender.

That creature would rue the day it found them ready for its arrival.

Alena sat down in the loose circle her friends had made. She looked to Ana. "Brandt is alive, but I couldn't reach him.

The queen is protected in ways I don't understand, and I didn't dare approach too close."

Ana nodded.

"So why do you look like you've seen a ghost?" Jace asked.

"I searched for the force that the queen is so frightened of. It's close. Far closer than I thought. I can't tell how long it will take to reach us, but it's not long now."

Her response was greeted with sullen silence.

"So, what do we do?" Toren asked.

"The only plan I can think of is to return to Etar," Alena said. "If answers exist, they're in the gates, and the Etari one is the only one I can obtain access to."

It frustrated her. The imperial gates were closer, and she controlled them, but without Olen's support, they'd have to fight to reach them. Despite the need for haste, she couldn't bring herself to fight against imperial soldiers.

"Let's not be too quick to rule out the imperial gates," Jace said.

Alena looked up, confused, but then she saw what had prompted his comment. Banners flapped in the distance, slowly approaching.

Jace looked to his sister. "It looks like Olen wants another word with you."

15

The queen found Brandt as the sun reached its zenith. All morning he had watched a string of guests enter the palace grounds, each escorted by compelled servants and guards. From the quality of their clothing and their demeanor, he suspected most were advisers of one type or another. Even a tyrant like the queen couldn't run her empire on her own, and advisers wore the same smug expressions in every land.

Few remained within the palace long, and there were never more than two within at a time.

The queen's efficiency impressed him. His own empire could take lessons, although perhaps inefficiency was the price of greater freedom.

Watching the hurried comings and goings of so many others emphasized how much time she sacrificed on his behalf. Trust grew slowly between them, but he already possessed more of her attention than any of her subjects. That, more than any proclamations on her part, represented her own faith in him. Perhaps she deserved more of his own.

He followed her up the stairs of the palace to the windowless room. Brandt's throat dried when the queen gestured to the same chair as before.

"There's no need for the restraints today," the queen said. "While this technique poses unique challenges, self-harm is not one of them."

"What kind of training is this?"

The corner of her mouth turned up in the hint of a grin. "The best there is."

As Brandt sat down, she explained further. "We will dive into my memories once again, but this time, for learning. You will experience the same lessons I did, but without the associated struggle and the long periods of uncertainty. You'll be me, learning through a constant stream of little epiphanies."

Brandt couldn't hide his skepticism. "So I just sit down, close my eyes, and when we're done, I'm as strong as you?"

"Hardly. Do you teach dueling with live steel to a young warrior on their first day?"

Brandt shook his head.

"Consider this similar. For you to understand my strongest techniques, a foundation of knowledge is required. Today we begin that foundation."

Brandt caught a hint of hesitation in her voice. "What?"

"You are not the first candidate I have attempted to train," the queen admitted. "The others have died."

Brandt's eyes widened, and he took an involuntary step back from the chair.

The queen didn't seem to notice. "I have never been certain why. The foundational lessons have always gone well, and this is the same technique I used to imprint your imperial language on Sheela. But once I get to the more advanced lessons..." Her voice trailed off.

"Why?"

"I suspect it has something to do with strength of will. You've already experienced a variation of this technique when I revealed my memory to you. It isn't like reading a scroll or hearing me speak. In those moments, you are me, and I suspect your will must be equal to mine from that moment to survive. The powers we utilize are strong enough to rip a person to shreds. You've felt that yourself."

Brandt remembered the feeling of the first time he'd touched an active gate, the unimaginable powers flowing through him. Yes, he well understood. He'd never forget.

But the danger was acceptable. She'd told him the others had survived at first. And true learning carried a cost, just like affinities.

This was why he'd come. He'd risked everything when he'd stepped through that gate. It would be foolish to back out now. The stakes had always been life or death.

He sat down in one chair and the queen sat across from him. The world faded to black, and then he found himself in the ruins of an ancient city.

SOFRA HELD the book in her hands, reading and rereading the passages. It told of another world, a web of connection that spread among all living things. Those who traveled such paths were called dreamwalkers. Her mother had been one.

Several techniques were described. The simplest required the presence of another dreamwalker. Sofra had none available. Other methods involved domesticated animals.

Sofra looked up, taking in the destruction around her. She couldn't stay in the city for much longer. Others had survived. Far from banding together, though, hunger and despair transformed many into something less than human. She'd seen from afar what *the roving gangs did to the vulnerable they found, and she wanted no part of it.*

So, she needed an animal, then. That, she could find.

Three days and several attempts at a snare later, she had a rat tied to the ground before her. She'd had to hit it over the head so that its squeals wouldn't attract attention. Too many others had come too close to her hidden location for her to feel safe.

Sofra closed her eyes and fell into the meditative trance her mother had taught her.

It took four attempts and clubbing the rat one more time, but when it happened, the feeling was unmistakable. A web of interconnectedness appeared in the world around her. They appeared as thin chains, linking all living beings. Here, in this dead city, few chains remained. It had destroyed most of them. She followed a few, allowing her curiosity to guide her.

She discovered another person, closer than she expected.

She saw him watching her through his own eyes. Felt his hunger.

Sofra dropped out of the dreamwalk and ran, grabbing only her book and her knife..

BRANDT GASPED as the world returned to his senses.

He'd felt it.

He'd been Sofra as she soulwalked for the very first time.

"Soulwalking, as you call it, is the first skill you need to develop. Once, it was the first skill anyone with affinities developed. You've felt how it is done. Now, it will be your turn to perform it yourself."

Brandt worried that he might forget what he'd just experienced. If he was going to practice, he needed to do so soon. But he suspected the queen wouldn't allow him to practice on her. "Where?"

"There's a place in town where animals are kept before they are slaughtered. You may go there and practice. Sheela will guide you."

Brandt thought of the mysterious woman from the street. "And if I'm approached?"

The queen shrugged. "Keep Sheela safe. I don't believe they will harm her yet, but you can ensure they don't."

"That's it?" He'd halfway expected her to ask for more information on her foes, or kill them himself. But she didn't seem concerned.

"That's it. Good luck."

Brandt nodded, eager to attempt soulwalking for the first time. Then, maybe, he would finally possess the power to protect those he loved.

16

Olen surprised Alena twice.

First, his entire entourage numbered less than a dozen. Alena recognized the standards they carried and noted their comfortable posture in the saddle. Each one had the appearance of an elite warrior, with stares to match. If she gave them the slightest reason, they'd attack in defense of their new emperor.

She stood tall against their presence. If it came to violence, a whole army wouldn't be enough to protect him from her. She wouldn't be cowed by angry stares and sharp steel.

Second, he left even those guards behind to make the final approach to her. They fidgeted on their horses, but no one made a move to stop him. His step was hesitant, but his face betrayed nothing.

They met in the space between the campfire and the guards. Both groups were balanced on the edge of violence. She and Olen met as enemy generals on the eve of battle.

With luck, no steel would be drawn today. Their martial

skill needed to be held in reserve for the fight to come. There was no need to display it here.

Alena stepped to the side so that Olen could see her party. She introduced them all, then waited to see how he would respond.

She noted his reaction to Toren's presence. Like many imperials, it seemed he had no love for the Etari.

Olen looked torn between ordering his guard to attack and opening negotiations. Alena tried to make it easier for him. "Would you care to join us at our fire?"

He set his shoulders and nodded. A gesture kept his own guards back, and Alena had her friends open up a space for them both to sit.

The emperor picked up a long stick and poked at the fire. He kept glancing back at the guards he'd abandoned, as though he considered running away before completing the task that had brought him out this far.

Finally, he threw the stick in the fire. "I'm sorry," he said.

Ana and Jace both looked like they'd eaten something unpleasant, but Toren appeared confused. He didn't understand why they all reacted so strongly to this man's apology. The Etari had no equivalent for an emperor, so the import of what he observed was lost on him.

Alena studied Olen carefully. She still didn't believe him, but she couldn't say why. Nothing he said sounded genuine.

But he'd also come all the way out here with a small guard. He'd earned the right to be heard.

She still felt as though she was watching a play performed for her own benefit. Until she sensed a true intent behind his actions, she wasn't sure what to do.

Olen continued. "I am sorry that my reaction to your report was to imprison you. You had done no wrong, but I feared that news of my father's death would spread before I could secure the throne and ensure the stability of the empire."

Alena gave Olen her full attention. This, at least, seemed like a promising start. She got the sense that Olen was a supremely rational man, one who prided himself on logic and reason. Perhaps it didn't make him the most charismatic leader, but maybe what she considered insincerity was simply his manner of dealing with the challenge of leadership. "Why did you pursue us?"

Olen started to speak, then caught himself. He tried again. "I need the power of the gates if I'm going to protect the empire."

Alena glanced at the fire. She approved of his directness. "Let us talk about the gates, then. You say that you need them, but why? How would you use them?"

Olen glanced around the circle.

"You may speak as freely to them as you would to me. They were present for the Battle of Faldun, and know everything."

That proclamation made Olen shift uneasily in his seat.

"I need to protect us from the queen."

"But how?" Alena challenged him. "Your father made a lifelong study of the gates, and he could never stand up to her. Why would you succeed?"

Olen clenched his fists and almost stood. "I don't know!" He took a deep breath and relaxed his hands. "But the gates belong to the line of Anders. It is my responsibility and duty to use them in defense of the empire."

"Are you so wedded to tradition?" Alena asked. "The queen has given us less than a year, and our warriors are not prepared for the Lolani invasion. We share a common goal. The empire is my home, too. My family lives here." She swallowed the lump in her throat. She *had* been willing to give him the gates, hadn't she? Why didn't she just turn them over?

She considered it. She imagined doing it.

And it still felt wrong.

"I do not see why giving you the gates is a better option. Tradition alone is not a reason."

"Isn't it? Hasn't tradition kept the empire safe for two hundred years?"

"Tradition should be honored, but it should not be the sole guide to our future."

Olen surprised her again. He didn't become angry at her words, but considered them. When he looked to her, his eyes were sharp, and for the first time, she felt as though he was genuinely paying attention to her. "What would you suggest, then?"

"The queen is not the threat we should be focused on."

Olen tensed, but Alena raised her hand. "I know you do not believe, but if you wish, I can show you the true threat. A force approaches. The gates, I believe, were originally used to counter the threat, but they weren't enough. For all of the accomplishments of the first Anders, there is too much we don't know. I propose that we take a few weeks to explore the gates and find what they can tell us. Perhaps our answers are there."

Olen nodded. "The nearest gate is underneath the palace at Estern. We can be there in a week, if a relay is set for us."

Alena looked around the circle, but everyone deferred to her.

So be it.

She nodded, and with that gesture, they began preparations to travel to the capital, guests of their new emperor.

17

Sheela met Brandt on the palace grounds and led the way without so much as a greeting. The bruise on the side of her face hadn't completely faded, and he cast his eyes down when he saw it. Her injuries weren't his fault, at least not directly, but the lack of judgment in her blank eyes darkened his thoughts.

The first bell had already announced the end of the day, and more people walked the streets than Brandt's previous excursion into the city. Most kept their eyes on their feet. He slowed when a young man met his gaze.

"Hello," Brandt said.

The man's eyes widened, and his eyes darted back and forth, looking for an escape. Brandt looked to Sheela, who ignored the exchange.

Brandt introduced himself and asked basic questions, but the man never answered. He kept shaking his head and almost taking a step back. As frightened as he was, though, he didn't run.

Finally, Brandt turned away from the man, who scurried around a corner a moment later. He turned his frustration onto Sheela. "Why wasn't he willing to speak? And why didn't you translate?"

"You're a guest of the queen," she answered.

"So?"

"Laborers do not speak with queen, or to those who have contact with her."

She continued down the street. Others walking home gave them a wide berth, moving to the opposite side of the street, or in some cases, taking another street entirely.

Brandt considered Sheela's response. Not only did the queen not hear from her subjects, but even those who advised her remained separate from the laborers.

In the empire, most citizens didn't have access to the emperor. But almost everyone could arrange an audience with a local governor, provided they were patient enough. The governors served as extensions of the emperor's power. They were his eyes and ears, and his hands as well.

How could a ruler rule wisely when they didn't understand the lives of their citizens?

Brandt didn't know.

He understood the queen's fear. Thanks to her memories, he didn't doubt the object of her strategy. And yet the whole system felt broken.

Sheela's path led them to the outskirts of town, to a series of large buildings that smelled of animal. Behind them, cows grazed on irrigated grasslands. Sheela pointed to the cows. "The queen wishes for you to practice on them."

Brandt grimaced. Alena's first soulwalk had been through a wolf. Granted, he hadn't expected anything quite so predatory. But a cow?

He glanced at Sheela, wondering if she would allow him to attempt to soulwalk through her. Then he thought better of it. The queen had probably placed protections around the woman. Even if his intent was innocent enough, his attempts might run afoul of the queen's wards.

So, the cow it was, then.

Brandt set his lips in a tight line. He remembered the queen's first soulwalk. Her meditative technique hadn't been much different than those he'd learned to control his elemental affinities.

He imagined the look on Alena's face when he returned to the empire a powerful soulwalker.

It would almost make the suffering he'd caused worth it.

Almost.

Brandt stepped forward and placed his hand on the side of the cow. The cow didn't turn its head. Even the animals in this land ignored him.

He closed his eyes and focused on his breath, seeking the familiar meditative state.

When he reached it, nothing happened.

Brandt cracked open one eye, but the world remained unchanged. He wasn't soulwalking.

He tried again, attempting to duplicate the queen's mental state down to the smallest detail.

Every heartbeat passed slowly. The more he focused on recreating the queen's memory, the more difficult it became to achieve. His muscles tightened, and he took frequent breaks to shake out his limbs and try again.

Finally, he gave up.

The cow stepped away from him, as though trying to escape one ponderous step at a time.

Brandt paced under Sheela's watchful eye.

It should work. He knew now how soulwalking was supposed to feel, but despite his efforts, he couldn't bridge the gap between the queen's memories and his actions.

He rolled his head in a large circle and shook out his

arms. Being tense wouldn't help. The sun was almost down, but he wanted at least one more attempt. Soulwalking was the foundation upon which the queen's stronger techniques were based.

Brandt walked through the queen's memories one more time, looking for clues he had missed.

His attention landed on the chains.

Alena had described a similar web, but she saw them as threads, not chains.

Brandt's thoughts began to race. It had been there all along. The experience of soulwalking was different between the women.

Of course it would be. Affinities manifested differently in everyone. He heard the elements as songs. Others saw them as colors. It was common knowledge, but he hadn't applied it to soulwalking.

Maybe his mistake was in trying to duplicate the queen's experience too exactly.

Or maybe he'd just chosen the wrong cow.

Brandt smiled at his own jest, then approached a different cow and laid his hand on it. This one ignored him just as completely as the first. He repeated his meditative efforts, but this time, he listened.

For a long time, he heard nothing but the sounds of cattle feeding around him. He imagined pushing his awareness into the cow, of sensing the world through the cow's nose, eyes, and ears.

Then he heard it. A reverberating beat, deeper than even the largest drums he'd ever listened to. It vibrated his bones, but still he listened.

Stone had always been a low hum, wind a soft whisper. Life was percussion, the heartbeat of an entire world.

The rhythm surrounded him, a beat infinitely complex

and layered, and yet with an unmistakable pattern. It almost moved him to tears.

This was soulwalking.

Carefully, he connected to the gatestone he'd had since Faldun. The volume of the sound didn't change, but more layers of sound joined the first. It felt chaotic.

A few beats sounded more loudly than others, and he focused on those. One was completely even, a monotonous beat.

Sheela.

But there were others that demanded his attention. He explored.

Distracted, he almost didn't notice when Sheela's constant beat shifted higher. Then it faded, almost below the level he could hear.

The change broke him out of his trance, and he opened his eyes, just in time to see a giant of a man standing in front of him. Brandt just had time to see the fist before it landed on his face.

His world went dark and the beat faded away.

18

F or the next few days, it felt as though Alena had the whole of the empire serving her needs alone. It reminded her, in more ways than one, of when the Etari had decided that she and Toren would travel to Falar with all haste. When the carriages arrived for them, stocked with provisions and pillows, they seemed almost too good to be true.

As with the Etari, Alena only saw a fraction of the efforts made on her behalf. But having supported herself for most of her travels, she knew that dozens, if not hundreds, of people had labored to bring this transportation to her.

And when she stepped inside the carriage and relaxed within, she smiled and flopped onto the pillows, running her hands along the soft cushioning.

She understood then how insidious power and comfort were. Now that she'd tasted this mode of travel, would she ever want to walk again?

Once they were all situated, Olen gave the orders and then they were on their way to Estern, a city she had only ever dreamed of visiting.

For the first day, she enjoyed every amenity their travel had to offer. She ate until her stomach felt ready to burst and napped for long stretches, catching up on the sleep she'd missed since she left her home with Ligt. But by the second day she began to feel uneasy, and it took her some time to understand why. Part of it was the enormous efforts undertaken to transport her. In almost all her travels, she'd made her own way, usually on foot. To be ferried from one location to another felt too passive, as if she hadn't earned the right to reach her destination.

Alena noted that when she traveled with Ana, the warrior constantly stared out the windows at the riders. She wanted to be out there more than she wanted to be in the carriage.

The endless days of pampered travel also gave her too little to do. Her every need was taken care of, and with nothing to occupy her hands or mind, her worries increased. Problems both large and insignificant grew in her thoughts, until her head was filled with little besides concern.

In a way, it was a relief when Olen summoned her to his carriage during a stop to exchange horses. She climbed in as the carriage jerked into motion.

Olen stared out the window. "I never asked you to prove your possession of the gates."

Alena arched an eyebrow and gestured to the carriage. "This is more effort than trust alone would justify. I assumed you had some method of confirming the possession." She could have, if their roles were reversed.

And she suspected his affinities were more developed than he led her to believe. As the expected Anders VII, he would need to know at least some basic soulwalking to bond with the gate.

Olen shook his head. "I don't, actually. I needed to return to Estern anyway. In this way, I solved two problems with one decision."

Alena leaned back and made herself more comfortable. She studied him, deciding if she believed him or not. An emperor didn't just help transport citizens across a large part of the empire unless he had reason. So she pushed.

"So why believe me?"

He shrugged. "Truth is often far stranger than the stories we tell ourselves."

She waited for him to explain.

"Few people know about the gates, and even fewer know that my father possessed two. I knew you were with him at the end, and if my father understood the risks he assumed, he would have had a plan in case he failed. When your party was first found, I suspected one of you might be in possession of the gates, knowingly or not. Frankly, though, I expected it to be your brother. He is well-favored in Landow."

"Impressive reasoning."

Olen shook his head, refusing her compliment. "Nothing more than understanding my father and cause and effect." He took a long breath. "Only one question troubles me. Why you?"

From someone else, Alena might have taken offense. But Olen didn't seem to understand the effect his words and tone had on others. His was a world built on logic and reason, not emotion. Perhaps his judgments as emperor would be wise, but they would lack compassion.

"I don't know," she said. "I didn't realize what he'd done until after he'd died. Before his final fight with Regar, he and I had argued."

Olen's glittering eyes rested on her. "Over what?"

"The secrecy the empire is built on."

For a moment, it looked as though Olen might resume the argument, but with an effort, he cut off his initial response. "My father always possessed regrets about the nature of his position."

Alena leaned forward. Hanns had hinted of something of this when they'd spoken. "What regrets?"

"The role of an Anders is not what most believe. They call us emperors, but it is more accurate to call us stewards. We carry the original Anders' dream forward into future generations. Perhaps we make some small changes here and there, but there is one lesson we learn young: our duty is to uphold the practices of the original Anders."

Alena couldn't resist. "I've met him."

Olen's eyes widened, if only for a moment.

"I wasn't impressed," she said.

Olen's eyes expanded a bit more, the most emotion she'd ever seen from him. She pressed her momentary advantage. "Do you know why Anders structured the empire as he did?"

Olen shook his head. "No."

"Neither do I. He destroyed all the records of our past, erasing them so we would have no choice but to accept his word. Maybe his choices were the best, but maybe not. We have no way of knowing. So why abide by the edicts of a man who lived two hundred years ago?"

"And what would you do?" Olen challenged.

Alena shook her head. "I don't know. But I'm not going to rule the empire. You are. I do know your generals aren't prepared to fight the Lolani. They use affinities, and the queen's own acolytes are formidable warriors. Even the Etari suffered enormous casualties when they faced a small

Lolani raid. Anders' insistence on secrecy might have forged the empire, but it will also destroy it."

Olen didn't argue that point. "And yet, you still don't believe the queen is our greatest threat."

"I do not. I can show you, if you wish."

Olen shook his head. He resumed staring out the window, avoiding whatever subject really haunted him.

"What?" she prompted him.

He turned to her. "There is another explanation, one that makes far more sense, in my opinion."

"And that is?"

"That you are being manipulated by the queen."

Alena clenched her jaw. "I know what I've sensed."

"But our senses can be deceived. You're a soulwalker, and a skilled one. You know this better than anyone. This threat you speak of, you've never experienced directly, but only in the soulwalk. And as you've said, your first encounter only came with the queen as your guide."

Alena shook her head, not willing to believe. She'd felt the creature's cold regard. That was as real as her family, or the carriage they now rode in.

"There's no shame in it. The queen attempts to manipulate anyone in the empire connected to the gates. As soon as my brother and I received our gatestones, her influence became clear. As a younger man, my jealousy of my father and brother intensified by the day, even as my father warned of the queen's influence. Only through reason and logic did I escape the poisonous thoughts she inserted into my dreams."

"That's not what happened to me."

Olen held up his hands. "I only ask you to consider. Use your own reason. By creating a threat even greater than her, the queen makes you more amenable to her ideas. Even

Brandt, a man loyal to the empire, abandoned his wife and unborn child because he believed her so strongly. These are not the actions of rational people. What if you eventually come to believe the queen is the only one who can save us from this threat only you know of? As you implied in our earlier meeting, you might consider her the reasonable choice."

Olen's words hammered into Alena, and the carriage suddenly felt as though it was moments away from tipping over. She shook her head. "Stop."

Olen kept his hands held up, surrendering the conversation.

"No. Stop the carriage."

Olen signaled for a stop. The carriage slowed and Alena stumbled out, barely keeping her balance. The carriage with Toren stopped beside her and then the Etari was there, holding her up. Olen gave them one last indecipherable look. "Think on what I've said."

Then he slammed his carriage door and signaled for his driver to resume the journey, leaving Alena alone with her newfound doubts.

19

When Brandt opened his eyes, he found himself far from his new bovine friends. He stood in tall grass, prairie stretching on for leagues. It almost reminded him of the heart of the empire. But the air felt thicker, portending disaster.

Not even the slightest breeze brushed against his skin, and the silence was unnatural. Even the wide open spaces at the heart of the empire weren't silent. Wind blew through tall grass, small game rustled nearby, and birds chirped off in the distance.

He cursed.

He'd had just about enough of soulwalkers.

Brandt blinked and found himself in another place. Again surrounded by grassland, but this time a collection of huts stood nearby. The sound of children reached his ears, and the scent of roasting meat wafted past him.

Brandt steeled himself. It didn't take a gift of prophecy to guess the flavor of what came next.

Fire swept across the plains, racing to burn down the village. Families screamed and scattered, but nothing on two legs could outrun the inferno. Homes burned, some with the victims still inside. Ash filled the air, and the final desperate cries of burning children echoed in his ears.

Brandt's first affinity had been fire. He'd used it in war, turning it against enemies who had no recourse. He'd always watched, not because it gave him any pleasure, but because he felt he deserved to suffer as well. Monstrous deeds needed witness, else he feared he would turn into a monster as well.

The voice came from his left. "Do you shed no tears? Do you have no heart for the suffering these people have endured?"

Brandt turned from the horror in front of him to see the woman from the street standing beside him. She watched the same scene, tears trickling down her cheeks as she clenched some of the fabric from her clothes in her hands. "On the contrary. I know all too well this suffering."

"And you do not turn away?"

"There is no greater sin than to turn one's attention away from the horrors before them."

She blinked rapidly and looked away. She didn't speak for some time, and the scene in front of him faded to gray. Brandt ignored the ash settling on his shoulders. None of it was real, no matter what his senses proclaimed. "Your memory?" he asked.

She nodded.

"I'm sorry."

"The past is dead. My thoughts are only for the generations to come." Harsh as her claims were, her voice cracked as she spoke them, putting lie to her words. Her past was still very much alive within her.

"The queen, I assume?"

"She is no queen of mine. No one who brings such suffering to the people she rules is fit for a title."

"Why show me this?" Brandt suspected he knew the answer, but better to hear it firsthand.

"So you can see why you must kill her."

"I, too, am horrified by what she has done. But I cannot kill her."

"Cannot, or will not?"

"Both."

She studied him, circling him as though he were prey. He expected the behavior was designed to intimidate him, but with every moment in this soulwalk, he became more comfortable. He said a silent thanks to Alena for gradually familiarizing him with this affinity. Instead of trying to track her with his eyes, he closed them, listening.

Brandt heard her immediately. The beat of her soul was strong, and everything in this space echoed in time. She was the center of this realm, but he felt the pulse of his own affinity. If he wished, he could take over. For the first time, he could take control in a soulwalk.

So he did.

The woman gasped, and when Brandt opened his eyes they were outside the ruins of the monastery where he and Ana had lived for so long. Brandt's own breath caught as he saw once again the destruction the queen had wrought. Despite the devastation, he longed to return. Someday, he hoped that he would. "This is what she did to my home," he told the woman.

She shook her head. "Then why do you remain?"

"I must learn from her."

"So that you might become like her?"

"Not like her. As strong as her. Stronger, if possible."

The woman walked among the ruins of the monastery. "You do wish to kill her, don't you?"

"Once I was certain. Now, I am less so."

"Why?"

"I believe there is another threat, even greater. Perhaps a threat that even justifies her actions."

The woman's glare hardened. "Nothing justifies what she has done."

Brandt grimaced. Part of him longed to share the conviction this woman held. But another part of him was frightened by it. When belief became certainty, reason was the first casualty.

The woman looked up to the sky, as though seeking answers in the clouds. "I must think on this. She allows you weapons within her palace."

Brandt nodded. "But she was not surprised by the knife I carried. If anything, she expected it."

A bitter grin flashed across the woman's face. "I would expect no less. I may hate her, but I do not underestimate her. That is the mistake too many have made. Most who resist her only see her tyranny, but they do not see the genius behind it."

The woman took control of the landscape again, using a force that sounded like an enormous gong to Brandt's affinity.

She was stronger than she'd first let on.

"We do not have much time. Her search will find you soon." For the first time since this meeting began, the woman looked uncertain. "My name is Perl, and I would like to contact you again. Would you permit me to create a connection with you?"

Brandt's own curiosity needed to be satisfied. "I would."

Perl moved quickly. She wrapped a leather cord around

her wrist and his. Brandt listened. The tone of Perl's soul changed, the beat becoming lower. His own matched hers, and soon their beats formed a complex pattern.

Brandt suspected that if he listened for Alena, he would hear something similar.

Perl stepped back from him. "We will meet again."

With that, the vision faded into blackness.

The transition to the physical world wasn't as smooth as he was used to. His head ached, and when he brought his hand up, he felt the bump where he'd been hit. He made a note to be more mindful of his surroundings when he next dropped into a soulwalk.

Beside him, Sheela was tied up and gagged, her eyes wide with fear. Brandt moved to free her, but when he approached, she attempted to scramble away from him. He stopped, not wanting to frighten her worse.

The sounds of doors being slammed open distracted his attention. A low voice spoke in a foreign tongue, but Brandt recognized the sound of orders being given, no matter what language they were given in. Given Perl's fear, he suspected these were the queen's forces, here to search for him.

He looked back to Sheela. Her eyes were focused on him, but he saw only terror.

Then he noticed something else.

There was no hint of recognition in her eyes. Her compulsion had been stripped from her, and now she had no idea who he was.

Brandt didn't know what that meant for Sheela, but he knew one fact for certain.

The queen was going to be furious.

20

After all the wonders she had seen, Estern struck Alena as a living contradiction.

Once, she would have adored every nook and cranny of the city. Her eyes traveled to the rooftops above, unnoticed by most, packed tightly together. As a thief, she could have wandered from one end of the city to the other without ever touching a street. Down below, dark corners and narrow alleys provided routes of escape and evasion. And people walked shoulder to shoulder wherever she looked, a mass of humanity where one could blend in without notice.

She might have become wealthy, had her journey taken her here, before the fateful day she'd stolen the gatestone from the Arrowoods. The paths not taken seemed alive with possibility.

But such thinking did her little good. The past remained immutable, and although it reached out like a skeletal hand from the grave, eager to pull her thoughts backward, she needed to fix her gaze on the future.

Evidence of what might have been was all around her, though.

She was acutely aware of the fact she rode in an imperial carriage. As crowded as the streets might have been, the guards before them, riding on massive warhorses, cleared a path with practiced efficiency. The expressions on the faces of those they passed ranged from annoyance to anger. Little warmth was directed her way.

Did Olen see the same? His whole life had been lived within carriages and tall towers. When Alena saw a group of wage-earners clearing their horse manure from the street, she wondered if Olen even noticed.

Thanks to her father's skill at a forge, Alena had never known the life of a wage-earner. Nor did she want to. They'd always been a fixture of imperial life, but it wasn't until she'd returned from her time among the Etari and the Falari that she saw them in a new light.

When she was younger, she'd detested named families and the way they looked down on others. Now she watched the bustling city from the windows of a carriage, escorted by guards. Was she any better?

The carriage rumbled up to the walls of the palace. It was quieter here, and the houses larger. Named families lived here, and guards stood at attention near every corner.

Yes, Estern was impressive. It was considered the jewel of the empire, and for good reason. It was the height of architectural prowess, and buildings seemed to race one another to the clouds above.

And yet it lacked. Alena would have preferred either the vertical construction of Faldun or the constantly shifting arrangement of Cardon.

The carriage carried them through the main entrance of the palace, and the sound of the gate shutting behind them halted her thoughts. The neighborhood outside the gates had been quiet, but inside was an oasis of artificial peace. People strolled through gardens either alone or in pairs, and no one spoke much above a whisper. As Alena and the others alighted from the imperial carriages, all attention turned to them.

Olen gave no sign of noticing the gazes. He led them inside, and once there, gave orders as though he ran the place.

Which, Alena supposed, he did. It still didn't seem real. At any moment, she expected Hanns to come around the corner, a curmudgeonly look on his face. Olen gave instructions for servants to escort the others to rooms, then turned to Alena. "Do you need rest?"

Alena wasn't sure she would be able to, even if she wanted. Her mind raced too fast. She shook her head. "If you permit, I'd like to go to the gate. I mean to search for evidence of past events."

"You believe you'll be able to?"

She shrugged. "I hope so. It's the only way to find answers."

"Very well." Olen didn't hide his skepticism.

Toren signed to her, a discreet message where his hand never moved from his side. Did she want him to accompany her? He always had at the Etari gate.

She glanced at Olen and shook her head. As useful as Toren would be, she didn't believe her odds of introducing an Etari trader to the imperial gate were high. He signed his affirmation and wished her luck.

While the others followed the servants to their chambers to rest, Alena followed the young emperor. Soon, she was lost amid the twists and turns of the castle. Olen led them into a small study, piled high with books. A hidden door led them into the caverns behind and below the room. Alena noted how smooth the walls were.

This was the work of those who had come before.

Soon they stood before a gate.

Though she'd grown more used to them, the power emanating from the structure still astounded her. In a way, they felt alive.

Alena stepped forward, but Olen held out a hand. "You understand the trust I'm showing you, don't you?"

She did. Although she remained uncertain about Olen, there was no doubting this could have turned out many different ways. "I do."

"I'll remain here while you study the gate. When you return, I want to know what you've discovered."

Alena nodded and Olen let her pass. She approached the gate with a sense of trepidation. Would she ever be comfortable around such power? A part of her hoped the answer was no. Some fear was necessary. Comfort with power eventually became abuse of power.

Tentatively, she reached out and touched the uncut diamond. It felt warm under her palm. With a deep breath, she closed her eyes and fell into the soulwalk.

This close to the gate, she felt power fill every fiber of her being. But her breath never faltered, and she continued down through the levels of the gate with practiced ease. Part of her wished she'd tried to have Toren accompany her. He'd joined her on many of her journeys into the gates, and she would have felt more comfortable with his solid presence by her side.

With thoughts of Olen in her mind, she formed a barrier around both her and the gate. Maybe Olen deserved more trust from her, but she couldn't allow herself to be distracted by threats in the physical world.

She studied the gate from within the soulwalk. Its intricate structure filled her attention, and she felt the strength of the bond she had with it. She traveled along the bond, allowing her consciousness to merge with whatever the gate was.

A powerful force pulled at her, and she had little choice but to surrender. Her surroundings changed again, and she found herself in a study, not much unlike the one they'd just used to access the gate. Books lined the shelves.

She looked again and the room expanded before her eyes. This wasn't a study, but a library, filled with unmarked yet elegant books.

Alena picked up the first one that caught her attention and opened it. Again, there was a feeling of powerful transition.

HE STOOD BEFORE A TALL MOUNTAIN. *Though all he saw was stone, he imagined he could feel the gazes of the multitudes behind him. They had gathered for the occasion, immensely proud of their first son. The journey had taken them longer than expected, but all worthy journeys did. This would become a home to many, a place that honored the exploratory spirit of his entire people.*

And there was a nexus here, buried deep in the mountain. In time, they would uncover it.

He was nervous, yes, but also confident. He raised his hands, not because he needed to, but because the moment felt as though it required a gesture.

He channeled intense powers and the stone melted away before him. Before long, the first staircase had been formed.

Cheers erupted behind him, and he turned, a smile so wide on his face it almost hurt.

. . .

ALENA CLOSED the book and stepped back, holding it away from her.

It was a memory, but so much more.

She'd been there.

More than that, she recognized the place.

She'd fought the queen on that very mountain, when a city had been carved into its walls.

She looked around the room again, realizing now what this place was, the potential power held within. It took her breath away.

But there were so many books. So much to learn.

Her answers had to be somewhere within.

She put the book down and opened another.

21

The Lolani soldiers entered the room soon after Perl departed. If the rebel had waited much longer, her capture was all but certain. Had she known how much time she had, or had she gotten lucky?

Brandt guessed the former. There wasn't enough luck in the world to protect someone against the queen. If Perl still drew breath, it was due to her own abilities.

The soldiers cleared the room with violent efficiency, flooding the space with soldiers until it stank of sweat.

Brandt had only caught glimpses of soldiers thus far on his trip. The queen relied on none to protect her inside the palace, putting her trust instead in the complex web of wards she'd woven. No doubt it said something when she didn't trust her own warriors to protect her.

Nor were the soldiers often in the city. Now that he thought of it, he hadn't really seen any form of law. That would be a question for later.

Brandt had fought the Lolani once before, and as they now ensured his safety, their skills confirmed he didn't want to fight them again, even though these Lolani looked different than the ones he'd fought years ago. Strong and fast, these men and women weren't the desperate and hungry masses that made up the bulk of the imperial army. These were warriors, forged in the fire of combat. Their arms bore not just the strange tattoos he'd noticed in their first fights, but the scars of battle.

None attempted to speak to him, but through gestures indicated he was to come with them. Sheela tried to escape them, but bound as she was, had no chance. One soldier cut through the bonds around her ankles, but left the gag in and the bonds around her wrists in place.

Before Brandt could protest, they were led to separate carriages. The last glimpse he caught of Sheela was her kicking at a soldier as he threw her bodily into the second carriage. She might as well have been kicking a stone.

Then he was alone.

Although not quite. He felt the connection with Perl, a beat so soft it was easy to ignore.

He glanced out the window. They were in the city, but he couldn't see the palace, either because of the angle of the carriage or the dark of night. Without a reference, he had no idea where he was. The construction of the buildings was so uniform he was surprised anyone could find their way around.

He'd once thought the Falari architecture lacked heart. But compared to Valan, Falari constructions were ornate.

Brandt closed his eyes and rested his head on the back of his seat. He dreamed of home and all that he missed, wallowing in self-pity as the carriage, now guarded by almost two dozen warriors, carried him to the palace, safe into the protective embrace of the queen's wards.

He didn't open his eyes again until the carriage stopped. The door was opened for him and he stepped out, giving a small nod of thanks to the guards. The palace walls loomed above him, the open gates welcoming him home.

Sheela's carriage was nowhere to be found. Brandt almost asked the soldiers, but the language barrier was impossible to breach. Not only had Sheela helped translate for him, she had effectively kept him from having to learn any Lolani.

Brandt would have been surprised to find that hadn't been part of the queen's plan all along. Just like in the empire, knowledge was power, and language was the most dangerous weapon of all. It allowed ideas to spread faster than any ruler could stop.

As soon as he passed the threshold, he lost his sense of Perl. Whatever wards the queen had placed, they didn't permit a bond forged in the soulwalk.

Inside the palace, the succulent smell of roasting meat tempted him toward the kitchens and dining room. There he found the queen. She gave him one glance, then carved off some meat and put it on two plates. Brandt's stomach rumbled, reminding him he hadn't eaten in some time.

They sat down across from one another and Brandt attacked his food. The queen watched with an amused expression. When Brandt finally slowed down, she asked, "Were you able to soulwalk?"

Brandt finished chewing the last of his food. His initial protest died on his lips. Of course the queen wouldn't ask after his health, or about his abduction. She probably already guessed enough, and she had no interest in polite niceties. The longer he spent with her, the more he realized how much of her life had been shaped around a singular purpose.

The queen viewed herself as the savior of humanity.

And perhaps she was even right.

"I did."

The queen's smile was the most genuine he'd ever seen on her face. Her enthusiasm encouraged him, and he spoke of his experience, of the music of the soul. She listened with rapt attention, clearly fascinated.

When he finished, he couldn't help but ask, "And what about Sheela?"

The queen's contented expression soured. "Perl wiped her thoughts clean."

Brandt frowned, and the queen explained further. "Soul-walking, even compulsion, is a gentle art. That is one of the reasons why I insisted you begin by practicing on livestock. It goes without saying that a novice can easily damage another person beyond repair."

Brandt was reminded of his own experience with Kye. The former governor of Landow had compelled him, and the nightmare of that time forever lingered in his memory. Those weeks of wandering had been filled with confusion and physical pain. Sheela had exhibited neither in their time together. "You're saying Perl is a novice?"

The queen shook her head. "No. I don't know how she learned these skills, but for her to evade me for this long means she's learned them well. Her actions toward Sheela weren't an accident, but deliberate."

"What did she do?"

"Sheela doesn't exist anymore."

Brandt leaned back and shook his head. "What?" When the queen didn't respond, he pressed. "She's dead?"

"She will be soon," the queen said. "I've ordered my warriors to kill her."

Brandt stood up and slammed his hands against the table. "You can't! She's got a family!"

His outburst elicited nothing from the queen.

He almost went for his sword. Only the cold look in the queen's eyes prevented him. As always, she anticipated his reactions.

That took the fight out of him. Her behavior meant that not only would he not attack, he would eventually come to agree with her. He sagged into his chair.

"When I say that she is gone, I mean just that. Perl wiped everything from her. All her memories, all her knowledge. Sheela is now less than a child."

"Can't you fix her?"

The queen shook her head. "I could give her some of my memories, and if I wished, could provide an enormous amount of education in a short time. But then she would just be a shadow of me. Sheela's heart might still beat, and her body remain, but she *is* dead."

"Did her soul go to the gate?"

"I do not think so."

Brandt glared at the queen. "It is because of your rule that Perl believes her actions are justified."

"True."

The queen's acceptance of Brandt's accusation didn't placate him. It did the opposite. His spine stiffened and he leaned forward, hands ready to tear the table between them in two. "Then why do you persist?"

"You know why," the queen said. "That's not your real question. What you mean to ask is why don't I do better, right? You want my citizens to be happy and enjoy some of the same freedoms you do in your empire." Now the queen's aggressive posture matched Brandt's own. "The truth, Brandt, is this: what you see before you is the best there is."

The statement, uttered with such conviction, rocked Brandt back like a physical blow.

"When I first took power, I was a tyrant, much as you

probably imagine me now. But as the last flames of rebellion died, I tried other systems. I once had governors who were chosen by the people, then later a council of elders not unlike the Falari. Some systems worked better for a time, and yes, some increased the happiness of the people, at least for a decade or two. But I have reigned for more generations than you imagine, and all systems crumble, or they wander astray. Do you know why?"

He cracked before her vehement onslaught. He shook his head.

"Because humans will always want more. Even when my people were wealthy, they demanded more. They forgot the terrors of the past and focused only on the pleasures of the future. Nothing I gave was ever enough, and given enough time, corruption and greed always caused my dreams to fail."

Brandt stared at the table. He cursed her, but he believed her.

"So in the end, there was only one choice. Only I remember, and only I know what needs to be done. I know what my reign looks like, and yes, what it is. But there is little crime, and although my citizens lack the opportunities you had in the empire, my warriors are stronger and my lands prepared for the invasion to come. When disaster strikes, we will survive, and we will save the world. Your empire will burn."

The queen stood up. "You are right to grieve for Sheela, and Perl now has my attention, as she no doubt intended. You are even right to lay some of the blame at my feet. But you need to think bigger. Because as tragic as Sheela's fate is, what is coming is much worse."

With that, the queen walked from the room, leaving a cold wake behind her.

lena felt her exhaustion in her bones. Time passed differently in the soulwalk, so she knew she hadn't been in this construct for as long as she thought, but it still felt as though she'd been living entire lifetimes in the space of a single day. New memories filled her, lessons from generations of masters now a part of her.

The gates weren't just sources of power. They were a record, maintained for hundreds of years, documenting the rise and rule of a civilization beyond anything Alena had ever conceived possible.

Those that came before.

That was the term the Falari and Etari used to describe them. Accurate, perhaps, but lacking any of the wonder that Alena now associated with them. Any fool could tell that those who had come before were more advanced than any civilization that currently existed. Faldun and the gates were conclusive evidence of that.

But it hadn't just been the works of their hands that so endeared them to Alena. They'd been artists and explorers, dedicated to the pursuit of understanding. For a time, at least, they had conquered the planet, and when that was done, they sought to conquer themselves. Their civilization had stretched not just across this empire, but into Palagia as well.

They'd been scholars, and farmers, and philosophers.

And she'd been many of them.

For all that Alena had just experienced, though, it was but a fraction of what the gates held.

Unfortunately, she found nothing about the fall of the civilization.

But she'd only gone through far less than a tenth of the books, and she hadn't been able to discover any order to their arrangement, so it was certainly possible she just hadn't found the right book yet.

But she needed a break. This research was more than just reading. It was living, over and over again. Her stomach rumbled and her eyelids felt heavy. She extricated herself from the soulwalk slowly, ascending through the layers of the gate until she returned to her physical reality.

Alena broke her connection with the gate and looked around. Down in the caves, there was no way to judge the passage of time, but enough had passed that Olen had left. Perhaps due to boredom, or perhaps the duties of the young emperor pulled him away.

Exhausted as she was, she owed him an explanation of what she'd just done. He had, after all, trusted her to come this close to the gate. She trudged up the tunnel and found guards waiting for her outside the study. She asked to be escorted to Olen, and they led her though the castle.

They took her to a receiving room, where Olen was meeting with a group of men huddled close to him. He noticed her entrance and soon dismissed the others. They left, several of them openly staring at her as they passed. One sniffed in disdain.

Alena lifted an arm and realized how much she smelled. They'd been in the carriages for days without a break, and she had gone straight to the gate when they arrived. She was hardly fit to have a private audience with the emperor.

Olen looked exactly the opposite of her. His clothes were fresh and he appeared as though he'd enjoyed a long night of peaceful sleep. "You were there for some time. What did you find?"

Alena recounted, briefly, the outline of what she had discovered. For now, she kept most details to herself. Fascinating as they were, they didn't pertain directly to the task she'd been given. "Did you find what killed them?" he asked. "Did you find the evidence of the threat you so fear?"

Alena shook her head. "I did not. But—"

Olen cut off her rebuttal. "I know, there is more research to be done. I understand. But, do you see now why I have the right to be worried? For all the lives you've just lived, you found nothing. Not even a hint. Of course, there are other explanations. Maybe you just haven't found them yet, or something prevented those who came before from documenting their demise." He paused, staring coldly at her. "But there is another, simpler explanation, isn't there?"

Alena nodded. She knew what he wanted her to say. But she couldn't.

Olen's gaze missed nothing. "I will not give you any orders, yet. But you have your own evidence in front of you. Soon you must decide."

Then he dismissed her.

A kindly guard escorted her through the castle to her room, where she found Toren waiting for her.

She collapsed on the bed that had been provided for

them, and Toren made a hand sign, asking if she was fine. She nodded, then rubbed at her eyes. Her body demanded rest, but her mind refused her any measure of peace.

Toren moved so that he sat beside her. He said nothing, but held her hand in his own.

Alena sat up and squeezed his hand tightly. "I searched the gates for memories of what destroyed those that came before, but I found nothing." She spoke of what she had experienced, the wonders she'd witnessed. She spoke of the study filled with books and the magnitude of the task in front of her.

"But Olen believes your lack of evidence supports his claim," Toren guessed.

Alena nodded.

He let go of her hand and used that arm to wrap around her shoulders. He held her close, and she melted into his embrace. "Is he right?"

"I don't know," Toren said. "But I trust you to figure it out."

"I'm not sure I trust myself."

Toren gently pushed her away. "The Etari gave up soulwalking long ago. You know why?"

"Because Zolene destroyed your gate."

"Yes, but not just that. The elemental affinities are powerful enough on their own, but soulwalking opens up possibilities that are even more frightening. An elemental affinity might kill an enemy, but soulwalking can bring down an empire."

Alena stared at him. He was trying to say something, but her tired mind couldn't piece it together.

"We ran from soulwalking, Alena. And we've been running ever since. We saw the challenge it presented, and our elders wanted nothing to do with it. But that wisdom could never hold forever. These gates must be mastered, and soulwalking must be understood. I think, although they hated the idea, it is why the elders allowed me to accompany you. And I believe you, more than anyone else in the world, will be the one to unlock their secrets. It is why I follow you."

Alena arched an eyebrow. "Is that the only reason?"

Toren smiled as he ran his hand down her back. "Not anymore. But it is why I began." He began massaging the back of her neck. "I do not have answers to the questions that trouble you. It is possible the queen has misled you, but you have sought out the force on your own and found it. Though that, too, might be an illusion, I doubt it."

They lay down in the bed in unison, Alena's head resting on Toren's arm. Toren continued. "My people didn't trust themselves. Don't make the same mistake. Proceeding cautiously and asking questions is always ideal, but trust your own judgment. I do."

Alena's eyes drooped. Toren's words were kind, and wise, but it was his presence at her side that comforted her. She didn't seek answers alone, and if she couldn't trust herself, she could at least trust her friends to guide her when she misstepped.

Before she knew it, she was asleep.

23

Brandt gazed out over Valan from the walls of the queen's palace, seeking solace but finding none. If anything, the sight of the city streets only increased his disorientation. The army had appeared from the desert, as if they had materialized from the sand, and now filled the streets.

They went from door to door, never in a group smaller than four, searching for the woman who called herself Perl. Artists had made sketches based on Brandt's recollection, and the military spread out through the city with her likeness in hand.

Brandt didn't think any criminal had ever been pursued with such vigor in all the history of the empire. It made him uneasy, to see the force the queen brought to bear against her own subjects.

From his vantage point he watched the citizens opening the doors, faces white with fear. No one fought. No one even argued. For the number of people he could see, the city remained eerily quiet.

Should he do something?

He had more access to the queen than anyone in her own lands. Perhaps she would listen to him, make some change to ease the plight of her people.

He scoffed at the thought.

Even if he did argue, it would do nothing except earn her ire.

But in his silence, did he condone her methods?

He didn't think so, but what good would all his justifications do for those now having their lives invaded?

Brandt turned from the scene below. The queen waited for him inside. When he was ready, she had said, they would resume their training. She promised that this would be the time he learned how to become stronger.

THE DESERT STRETCHED AS FAR *as her eye could see, waves of heat bending the sight of the horizon even though the air itself didn't feel hot on her skin. This had once been a forest filled with more varieties of life than all the philosophers working together could count. Now, not even the most hardy creatures attempted to eke out a pitiful existence upon the barren soil.*

Describing the land as destroyed seemed too generous. Deep roots, old in the time of Sofra's ancestors, had been ripped from the ground, and burned as they were exposed to the unquenchable flames of the day of arrival. Glass shards poked through the last of the coverings protecting her feet, and water was a distant memory. These lands were empty.

Except for her and those who pursued her.

Much to her dismay, she hadn't been the only one to consider leaving their once-grand city. She had hoped, perhaps foolishly, that she would find a limit to the destruction, a place where life went on as if the arrival had never happened.

Hope had called her out into the desert, but hope didn't fill an empty stomach or quench a thirst.

A little food remained to her, and it was that food and the meat on her own bones that the others wanted. She knew because she had walked the dream and had found them. She had looked into their hearts and found their desperate desires. A group who, like her, had fled but who now sought to make the desert their home.

They had found a system of caves fed by a spring. They always had plenty to drink, but it was food that eluded them. They'd spotted her two days ago, and only by burying herself in sand, using a tube to breathe through, that she eluded their searches.

One way or another, this hunt had to end. Sofra only possessed enough food for another three or four days, but thirst would kill her sooner. She needed those caves, and they had no desire to feed another hungry mouth.

She studied the entrance, a fissure in the ground practically invisible unless one looked at it just right. If not for her journeys within the dream she would never have found it.

Sofra checked the grip on the kitchen knife. Out here, it had become her most valuable possession.

It was her turn to hunt. She would make them understand how it felt to be preyed upon.

She sensed only one young man at the entrance to the cave. He was barely a man—more a boy who had been thrust into the responsibilities of an adult.

Once, the thought of murder would have horrified her. But survival possessed its own cold and cruel logic. Killing equaled water, and she could feed on the flesh of her enemies.

Pacifism equaled death, and if she died she could never destroy the creature that had taken so much from so many.

The boy stood inside the cave, sheltering himself from the heat of the afternoon sun. In the darkness of the caves he would be as good as invisible to anyone standing outside.

Sofra couldn't see him, but she could sense him. She approached the entrance from an angle so that she wouldn't be seen. Then she fell into the dreamwalk, extending her soul out to him. He thought of one of the women deeper in the cave. Older than him, but not as old as his mother. The other men had agreed the boy was worthy enough to stand guard. It made him believe that the woman could be his, too.

Sofra recoiled from the boy's thoughts. Perhaps not uncommon, but impure all the same.

The boy should be plotting revenge, not worrying about satisfying his lusts.

His distraction made her own task simplicity itself. Her skills in the dream were hardly required, but she used them anyway. She saw little point in unnecessary risk.

Sofra wrapped the chains of her sense around him, cutting off sight and sound. Lost in his self-absorbed trance, he didn't even notice at first. But it couldn't last for long. She sprinted the last few paces into the entrance of the cave, her trusted kitchen knife stabbing into the boy's chest. Through their bond she felt his pain, a sharp agony that almost brought her to her knees.

She clamped her hand over the boy's mouth. She'd missed the heart.

Her stomach roiled, knowing what was still necessary. She repositioned the knife and tried again, knowing the fresh agony that would greet her.

This time, she did fall to her knees. But the agony lasted only a moment and then she was someplace else, a flat and featureless plain with a single arch. She recognized that arch. She'd seen it within the books that her mother possessed. It was a nexus, a gateway between worlds. And it was here. Some specter of the boy she had just killed walked toward the nexus, and she felt its *pull herself. But she wouldn't follow. Some instinct, buried deep within her, knew what that place was. It was the realm of death, and she still had much work left to do.*

BRANDT GASPED as he came back to the world.

That was how she'd done it.

The first soul she'd accompanied to the gate.

The first rush of power.

He'd once tried to coerce Alena into teaching him this skill. She had refused, but the queen shared it freely.

Soon, the strength he desired would be his.

24

A lena awoke to the sounds of Toren moving around their room. She yawned and stretched, rubbing the sleep from her eyes. She sat up. "Thank you for last night."

His hands flashed his acknowledgment. "Want company today?"

She heard the desire in his voice, the curiosity that was an echo of her own. Ever since they had first met, he'd been almost as interested about the gates as she was. "I do, but I fear Olen's trust won't extend to an Etari soulwalker at the heart of the empire's most closely guarded secret."

"Then it's another day with Jace."

"There are worse punishments, I'm sure. I can't think of any, but I'm sure one exists."

Toren laughed. The soulwalker and Jace got along well. If they hadn't, the two would have come to blows long ago. But as far as Alena knew, her brother hadn't ever confronted Toren over her relationship with him. Though they were both adults, and she was older, Jace remained protective of his sister.

"Would you check on Ana, too?"

Toren signed that he would.

After they broke their fast, the two parted ways, and Alena, with the help of the castle guards, found her way to the study. From there she was left alone to wander down to the gate. She connected to it, shielding herself again to prevent surprises.

In time, she found herself in the memories of the gate. With a sigh, she began opening the books, immersing herself in a past long forgotten by the empire.

She watched the growth of Faldun from a small enclave into a large city, carved into the side of a mountain by powers long forgotten. She lived through the eyes of a string of leaders who built a city on the edges of an ocean, a city that made Estern pale in comparison. It grew in a location Alena couldn't place, with an architecture unlike any she'd ever seen.

She saw so many wonders that they almost became routine.

The vast majority of the scenes she lived were peaceful, but not all. Those who came before were more advanced than any civilization she knew, but arguments arose that sometimes led to violence. In each case, though, the violence was quickly resolved, and the power of the gates was never used. Those who came before built a strong society, but it wasn't perfect.

Alena wondered if humanity would ever rid itself of violence completely.

One fact remained constant throughout her experiences. Those who could access the gates were a special class, a ruling elite that guided the course of history. There were far more of them then, with most of them connected to more than one gate.

But for all their ability, they rarely used it.

That was most impressive of all. Massive cities and continent-spanning civilizations were one thing. But withholding one's strength was far more so.

Alena closed one of the books hard, snapping her out of the memory she'd just been experiencing. One of the keepers of the gates had been involved in some argument about the continued exploration of the oceans. Rumors of a third continent had surfaced, and the keeper had been approached about allowing a new expedition.

In another age, Alena would have delighted in living that memory. There were so many lessons to be learned. Not just about the discoveries and advances those that had come before had made, but in leadership and wisdom. Lifetimes of direct experience were at her fingertips.

But she couldn't find joy in that knowledge. Not today.

She had only one question, still unanswered. What had happened to those who came before?

Alena looked around the library. If the memories here were ordered, it was with a system she didn't understand. She could continue pulling out books at random, but she couldn't begin to calculate her odds of success. She didn't know how many memories in here related to the fall of these people, or if they existed in here at all.

She thought.

In the past, the gate had always responded to her will. Perhaps this library was no different. She imagined herself holding the book which held all the answers she looked for.

Nothing in the library changed. She grabbed a book and opened it, testing her theory, but the memory wasn't helpful.

She swore softly to herself as she closed that book. If she had even a single clue, she would know better how to proceed. But as it was, she couldn't guess. Did she keep searching? Or try another approach? Perhaps there was another source of memories she hadn't even discovered yet.

She extricated herself from the gate, returning once again to the physical world. Her stomach growled, which served as the only true indicator of how much time had passed.

She supposed she should speak to Olen once again. She'd rather not, but she wanted to keep him as an ally. He could make her life unimaginably difficult as an enemy.

She made her requests to the guards, who brought her to what appeared to be a receiving room. There was a bit of confusion then, as she was made to wait. One of the guards came to her and apologized. "I'm sorry, ma'am. He's meeting with a group of wolfblades right now. His instructions were that he wasn't to be disturbed for any reason."

Alena nodded. She had no hurry, nor was there anyplace else she particularly needed to be. And the guard made her curious. Both Ana and Brandt had been wolfblades before they'd found their way to the monasteries. When she'd first met Brandt, it had been as a wolfblade in Landow. What would the new wolfblades be like?

Her answer wasn't long in coming. The doors opened and a group of lean warriors stepped out. Danger radiated off them, and Alena was transported to her first interactions with the elite soldiers in Landow. Alena looked up, and when she did, her breath caught.

One face was familiar. Aged by more than a decade now, but in a sea of strangers, it stood out. Alena turned her head, hoping that she'd gotten a glimpse of him but that he hadn't had the same of her.

Niles Arrowood.

He had been a classmate of hers, back when she'd attended the academy at Landow. When she'd last heard of him, he'd been hunting for her, blaming her for the death of his father. She felt sick and clenched her hands together to keep them from shaking.

She remembered now. Brandt had offered a recommendation to him as a wolfblade in training. Apparently he'd passed and become one of the empire's elite warriors.

Had he noticed her?

She hoped not. She'd left her past long behind her, but it seemed the mistakes of her youth might haunt her yet.

The wolfblades passed without a single stutter in their step. If he'd noticed her, he gave no sign of it. She turned as he passed, watching him for any indication. She almost soulwalked into him, but convinced herself against it.

He hadn't noticed, and that was for the best.

It took her too long to gather herself, but eventually she went in to visit Olen.

25

The queen didn't ask if her lesson succeeded. Her eyes bore into him, and there was no place for him to hide, even had he wanted to. Whether by intuition, or by observation, she knew. She stood and gestured for him to follow. He did, down the stairs and out to the palace courtyard. At the front gate, a large contingent of guards joined them, as though they'd been waiting.

Brandt knew Sofra used soulwalking to communicate with her staff. The exact method eluded him, but her needs were always met, and there was no other explanation. She'd spoken to no one, and yet their journey was expected and prepared for.

"Where are we going?" Brandt asked.

"To a prison. You've learned the skill. Now you must use it."

Brandt blanched. He'd only ever imagined using the skill in a fight. But perhaps he'd been a fool.

The streets of the city still crawled with groups of soldiers. If Perl remained within the city, Brandt hoped she had a hole deep enough to avoid being found.

Or perhaps she'd already been discovered, and her execution would serve as Brandt's first test.

He wanted to run, but there was nowhere to escape to. He'd chosen this path, and the only way out was forward.

Brandt looked down at his feet. Had he really once been so eager to learn this? He thought of his fights with Alena, and he knew he had. He'd have accepted any stain upon his own soul.

An old master of his, one of the first swordsmen he'd trained under, had once warned him of being careful what he wished for. Because the world might just give it to you.

Brandt grasped the sword at his hip with his left hand, hoping to draw some strength from the blade. As much as he wanted to claim ignorance, he'd always worried a day like this would confront him. And he'd already chosen. Now he needed to find the strength to follow through.

He could be as cold and decisive as his sword.

If saving Ana required such sacrifice, he would bear it willingly.

It wasn't combat, but practicing here would allow him to use it more effectively when it mattered, when his blood was boiling and the chaos of battle surrounded him.

Still.

He'd come to terms with killing in battle, and the toll that exacted. But this was something different, something darker. Even if the prisoner he executed deserved death, which was questionable in this land, could he bring himself to slay one who meant him no harm?

They reached a squat, sturdy structure. From the outside, Brandt saw nothing that indicated the dark purpose of the building.

The queen led him in, then paused in surprise as she

glimpsed her prison. She turned to the man standing guard near the entrance and spoke in Lolani.

The guard bowed and answered.

The queen nodded and led Brandt to the next door. "The cells are overfull. They haven't found Perl yet, but many others have been arrested."

A wave of sound greeted them when the door opened, almost knocking Brandt back. He'd gotten used to silence, and for a moment, he was almost offended by the sound. Some fought, shouting at whoever would listen. Others wept, and some cried for mercy. He didn't know their words, but he understood them well enough.

It was the most emotion Brandt had felt in ages. "Were you searching for all these people?"

The queen shook her head. "Why?"

"How did your search for Perl result in the arrest of so many others?"

"Justice here is simple. If anyone is accused, they are arrested. These were all citizens accused of crimes by neighbors, friends, family, or other acquaintance."

Brandt stared at the full cells. "What happens to them?"

"There is only one punishment here, Brandt."

"No matter the crime?"

"Any tolerance is weakness. There is only one punishment because I do not wish to spend the time of my warriors and servants overseeing long processes in the search for an elusive truth. They have better ways to spend their time."

"But what about false accusations?"

"Also a crime, and so punishable by death."

Brandt swallowed his retort.

The queen walked past the cells, ignoring the threats, pleas, and curses sent her way. Near each cell door was a slate on which was written a list Brandt couldn't begin to decipher. The queen glanced at the first slate. "Here we have a thief, who stole more than his allotment."

At the mention of "thief," Brandt thought of Alena. It had been her act of thievery that had, in many ways, started this journey. But he'd also seen glimpses of the woman she'd become, putting her past behind her.

He shook his head, and the queen continued going down the list. "And here a woman is accused of sleeping with a man who isn't her husband."

Seeing his refusal, the queen went down to the next cell. "Here we are. One even you can easily condemn. Here is a man accused of rape."

Brandt swallowed his objections. He stepped closer to the cell and looked in.

The man was huddled in the corner of the cell. He looked pathetic, but Brandt didn't know if he was a rapist or not.

With a gesture, the queen had the guard come and unlock the cell. "It is time, Brandt. Do this for Ana, and for your unborn child. Do it to save the world."

Brandt stepped into the cell. It was just him and the man, and the man offered no resistance.

If the accusation was true, then perhaps Brandt could bring himself to follow through. Such a crime deserved no leniency.

Indecision stayed his hand, though. How could he be certain? In the empire, crimes were decided by judges after evidence had been presented. Here, it was nothing but an accusation.

Then he realized he didn't need to worry. He knew a way of finding out.

Brandt found his meditative state and fell into the soulwalk. The cells surrounding him pulsed with life, but he was able to find the accused man's beat easily enough. He listened to that sound and fell into it, and then they were linked.

Brandt caught flashes of memory, and he saw the truth. He saw the cycle of abuses the man had suffered, and the crimes for which he was accused. He didn't experience the memories the same way he did the queen's, but it was as though he was an observer, forced to watch one horrendous deed after another.

The man was guilty. Of that, there was no doubt.

Brandt drew his sword.

The man deserved to die.

His sword hung in the air, like an axe ready to fall.

But something stayed his hand.

Brandt wanted to kill the criminal. He had no compassion, not after what he'd seen.

But his hand refused to move, even though the killing stroke would be a thing of simplicity.

For a long moment, he wavered between one action and the next, his body swaying slightly as he argued with himself.

And then, to his surprise, he had an answer.

He sheathed his sword, met the queen's furious gaze, and shook his head.

26

Another day of visiting the gate's memories led to little more than disappointment. Alena brought her hand away from the gate. Despite her physical proximity to so much knowledge, she'd never felt further from answers. Every failed attempt made her more certain that what she sought was not within the gate's memories. But what did that mean?

Her greatest fear was that Olen was right. She had, somehow, been deceived by the queen.

Alena took another step away from the gate and sat down on the stone floor.

She couldn't run from the possibility, so she considered Olen's theory.

If she'd been deceived, Brandt had been as well. He'd been lured into the queen's grasp by the same threat.

That fact pained her almost as much as her own failure to intervene in Faldun. But it also nagged at her. The queen already possessed two gates and an army without equal. Why would she agree to a year's truce in exchange for Brandt if she saw no need for a new ally?

Alena rubbed at her eyes, exhausted. She had no answers, and no new information to work with. All she gained through this was more doubt and a headache. Toren had the right of it. Though her evidence was slight, she still believed that a threat approached. That belief had to guide her actions until she found evidence to the contrary.

Alena stood up and stretched. She was too tired to continue the investigation today. She returned to her chambers, privately proud of now being able to find her way without the assistance of a guard. When she opened her door, she was surprised to see both Jace and Toren within, clearly in the middle of a heated conversation.

The two usually got along fine, so warnings went off in the back of her head as soon as she saw them in such a state. They also both looked like children who'd been caught stealing candies. Neither of them would make professional thieves. "What?" she asked.

"I received something today," Jace said. He handed her a letter, which she took and read. Then she read it again, a smile growing on her face. It was a letter from the governor of Landow informing Jace that the position of lieutenant governor was still open and that it was Jace's if he so desired. She beamed at her brother, excited despite her own problems. "That's great news!"

One of her greatest fears was that Jace's decision to follow her into both Etar and Falar would doom the bright future he'd created for himself. She understood he'd made his own choices, and was proud of them, but she hated thinking that anything he'd done on her behalf would bring more pain to his life. She'd already hurt him enough.

But perhaps she needn't have worried.

The look on his face killed her enthusiasm before it ran away with her.

Jace took the letter back from her. "I don't believe the governor of Landow knows I'm here. If Olen sent a bird home the moment we arrived, and the governor immediately replied, perhaps the timing works. Which," he added ruefully, "is more or less what Olen claims happened. But it can't be."

Alena looked at the letter in her brother's hands. Was he creating imaginary problems to avoid the role he'd been offered?

A moment of studying Jace dismissed that possibility. Her brother's courage was unquestioned. He wouldn't run from responsibility. Not ever.

His concerns were valid. It was too soon for them to be receiving letters from Landow. If both the governor and the emperor had made communication with one another their first priority, it could have happened, but her brother was right. The correspondence was too fast to be believable.

"It doesn't sound like the governor, either." Jace added, "And it arrived without a seal."

Alena frowned. The speed of the correspondence, the tone of the letter, and the seal. Taken one at a time, each could be explained. But all together, she understood her brother's concerns. The letter smelled rotten.

"Jace isn't the only one having odd experiences," Toren added. "I've been told, politely, but firmly, that I am no longer allowed to wander around the palace without an escort. One adviser went so far as to tell me I might be more comfortable staying among my own kind."

Toren's news made her want to punch the adviser. On one hand, imperial prejudice against an Etari was hardly news. The two cultures only tolerated one another on the best of days. But Toren was a guest of the emperor. For him to be encouraged to leave, however gently, was an offense to Olen.

Then Alena made the connection. "Both of you are being pushed out of the palace."

Jace nodded, and she saw the two men had already figured it out.

"Which means that Olen is either hoping to pressure me into a quick decision so that I might remain with you."

"Or he wants to separate us," Toren finished.

Alena paced the room. She didn't know Olen well, but she thought she had some sense of the man. It wasn't that she didn't believe that he was above such manipulations, but that she wouldn't expect him to stoop to them. There was no need.

Something had changed.

She swore, bringing both men's attention to her.

Alena focused on Jace. "I saw Niles Arrowood yesterday. He's become a wolfblade, and had an audience with Olen. I hoped he didn't see me, but if he did—"

"He would have gone to Olen and told him all about the events in Landow."

"Why would that be a problem?" Toren asked. "Didn't you stop the Lolani outside of Landow?"

"Before that," Jace said. He looked to Alena, questioning what Toren knew and didn't.

"I'll tell you the full story later," Alena told Toren, "but Niles would have given Olen another reason not to trust me."

"Which he was already looking for." Toren signed that he understood.

"And now he's trying to split us apart," Alena finished.

"He's getting more aggressive," Jace noted.

"Which means that if I'm going to find evidence to

support my belief, I'm going to need to find it soon," Alena said.

She swore again. After all this time, to be held back by the mistakes she'd made as a girl! She would hit Niles if she saw him again, but the greater share of her anger was directed inward. She'd been a fool back then.

But she wasn't a fool now. They didn't have much time. It didn't matter if she was tired or not.

She needed to return to the gate.

She needed answers, and soon.

27

The queen's fury burned like a fire lit in a forest of dead trees. Brandt's refusal was the spark that lit a conflagration that threatened all who neared. She stormed from the cells, her rage a palpable thing. She took the carriage and left him behind.

He found his own way back to the palace, guards leading the way.

Brandt didn't see her for the rest of that day or the next. He didn't press, knowing that any attempts at forging peace between them were useless. He spent his newfound time training the techniques he'd already learned from her, as well as maintaining his own martial training. Had he not feared approaching the queen, he would have asked for sparring partners from her own ranks. He rarely advanced as quickly as he did when sparring against unfamiliar styles.

Despite his efforts to occupy his time, he frequently felt as though he was treading water. No amount of practicing what he already knew would help him in the fight to come. He needed the queen's instruction.

After finishing a training session, Brandt climbed the

stairs to the wall. Looking over Valan had become a way to fill the time. The streets remained disturbed. Soldiers hovered at every corner, and groups went from door to door.

The search for Perl continued.

No wonder the queen remained in a foul mood.

He couldn't help but smile at that.

The more time passed, the more comfortable he was with the decision he'd made in the cells. It had been the right one.

Now, more than ever, he wanted to travel into his past and apologize to Alena. She'd always had the right of it. He'd been so angry when she'd withheld the technique. At the time, he'd feared that she would doom them all, and he'd thought he was willing to bear the burden of so many souls.

In many ways, Alena now served as the guide he hadn't known he needed. Her words, once lost on him, now directed his footsteps. He couldn't be like the queen. He couldn't carry those souls. For the first time since arriving here, he felt centered, balanced.

The queen had valuable lessons to teach. She was, without doubt, the most accomplished soulwalker in the world. But her ways were not the only ways. For all the people she had killed, for all the strength she had sucked from the world, she still wasn't strong enough to face the foe that now approached.

She wanted to make him like her.

But he dreamed of becoming something more.

Perhaps someday she would see the errors in her ways.

The thought gave him courage, and as he looked down at the sight below, he knew there was more left for him to do. Perl wanted him. He could sense her now, though the bond she'd shared with him. The beats of their lives overlapped. Because of Perl's plans, the citizens lived in even more fear than usual.

He could bring an end to that.

Brandt glanced back at the palace. Visitors had streamed through the grounds all day. He imagined the queen, filling her time with advisers in her attempts to push him out of her thoughts. He should inform her, but the rebel within him decided against it. If she shut him out of her training, then she could pay the price for her decisions.

He left the palace grounds. As he passed through the main gate he held his breath, wondering if the guards would stop him.

They did not, and for the first time, Brandt walked the city without an escort. He enjoyed the moments while they lasted. If his suspicions were correct, it wouldn't be long before he'd have company.

Brandt wandered with no particular destination in mind. All the buildings looked the same, and even if he did have a place he wanted to visit, he wasn't sure he was familiar enough with the city to find his way there.

But none of that mattered.

Today he sought Perl, and the easiest way to find her was to let her find him.

He only wondered if she was bold enough to approach him with so many soldiers searching for her.

His question was answered soon enough. A child, eyes blank, approached and gestured for him to follow. Brandt's stomach twisted at the thought of what had been done to the child, but he followed.

The boy led him to a building in which several families appeared to live. He brought Brandt up some stairs and to a nondescript door. The boy pointed, then ran off.

Brandt looked around. Although the place was somewhat hard to find, there was nothing special about it. If this had been Perl's hiding place for the last few days, he suspected she would have been discovered.

So either she'd been moving, or something else was at play.

Brandt opened the door and stepped in, finding Perl in an otherwise empty room. Brandt's hand almost went to his sword. He hadn't really been sure this would work, and he had no plan for ending this duel between the rebel and the queen.

Perl noticed his motion, her eyes tracking his hands, but made no move to defend herself. She sat down with her back to a wall and gestured for him to sit across from her.

He accepted the invitation, and this time, he heard the beat of her life as it tried to merge with his. He allowed it, and fell into a soulwalk. That realm was the only place they could speak.

The sensation was more disorienting than usual, as he found himself in the same room his physical body was in. But when she spoke, he understood her. "You seek me out. Why?"

"Because this needs to end. People are suffering because of you."

"People suffer every day under her rule, yet you take no action to save them."

"I am trying to save them!" Brandt stretched out his fingers and relaxed his hands. "Just not from the queen. Not yet."

Perl gazed at him. "You believe in this foe she speaks of?"

Brandt nodded. "Don't you?"

Perl looked to the window in the room, gazing out at the city. "She has told us to prepare for the enemy for as long as our records stretch. Untold generations have lived and died in preparation for a challenge that has never come. Why should we believe now?"

"I have felt its power myself."

"Have you? In the dream, it is hard, if not impossible, to know what is real and what is not. And she is the most accomplished walker of dreams the world has ever known. Can you trust your own senses, when she is the one who controls them?"

"If I don't, and I'm wrong, the world ends. It is too great a risk."

"For some of us," Perl said with a grim smile, "that wouldn't be the worst possible outcome."

"Will you end this?" Brandt asked. "I can advocate on your behalf. Together, we can find a way forward."

Perl shrugged. "It is in your hands to end it," she said. "It always has been. Kill the queen, and the suffering of the people will end. She allows you weapons, a gift she has given no one else in generations. I will make no peace with such a woman, and I have much more planned than even she can imagine."

Brandt shivered. He believed every word she spoke.

She gestured to him. "So what will it be, foreign warrior? Will you fight for us, or will you be part of our destruction? Because there is no middle ground."

And with that, Perl vanished from the soulwalk, leaving Brandt alone with his decision.

28

Alena closed her eyes and opened her connection to the gates. Using their strength, she soulwalked beyond the realm of her planet and into the stars beyond. Her target didn't take her long to find, a fact that surprised her.

The creature, if that was even an accurate description, was close. Far closer than she expected. Although distance was impossible to measure in the soulwalk, it couldn't be more than a few days away. It approached with such incredible speed.

Alena only remained a moment. She didn't care to attract its attention again. She had learned what she hoped to. In moments, she was back in her chambers, sweat beading down her forehead.

Toren sat in a chair in the corner, his weight shifted toward her. He came to her as she exited the soulwalk, wrapping her in his arms. She leaned her head against his shoulder. Without her having to say a word, he understood. "It's close, isn't it?"

She nodded, and her eyes began to water. She buried

her face in his chest, drawing strength from his stability. "There isn't enough time."

Toren didn't reply, but she didn't expect him to. He was the rare individual who didn't bother with empty words of comfort. He understood that his presence was enough.

Alena allowed herself a moment of sorrow. She'd come so far, but she hadn't discovered the secrets she needed.

Eventually her pity for herself ran out. It was necessary to indulge at times, but it did no good. Her choice was the same as it had always been. If she gave up, there would be no hope at all. She dried her eyes, allowed herself another moment of comfort in Toren's arms, then separated herself. "I need to return to the gate."

Toren signaled for her to wait. "Are you sure this is the best use of your time?"

He gave voice to one of her deepest fears. Perhaps those who came before had never had time to add the memories she sought to the gates. Or maybe there was some other explanation for their absence. No matter how hard she searched, she couldn't find something that didn't exist. But she couldn't surrender, and she didn't have a better idea. "I have to keep searching."

He signed for her to wait again as she made to leave. "You don't understand." Her nostrils flared, and he made a sign for peace. "I know you're scared and desperate. I am, too. But I wonder if your focus is too narrow."

She crossed her arms, waiting for him to explain.

He spoke carefully, knowing that choosing the right words mattered now. "You're looking to the past for answers, but why? If those that came before had an answer to the force that approaches, they wouldn't be those that came before."

Alena frowned, not quite following.

"Alena, *they lost*. For all their knowledge, they were destroyed. I don't think you'll find an answer from them because they didn't have one."

His argument slapped her in the face. For all her searching, she'd never made that simple connection. With so much new knowledge at her fingertips, it had never occurred to her.

Her legs suddenly felt weak, and she stumbled over to a chair and fell in. She looked up at Toren, desperation cracking her voice. "So what can I do?"

"Keep searching, but not for some answer those who came before found. One of your own creation."

"Just like that?"

Toren flashed a hand sign for uncertainty. "Maybe you find a way, maybe you don't. But don't limit yourself to searching for what has already been tried."

Some of his confidence must have trickled into her, because she felt a slight stirring of hope. She wanted to hurry to the gate and ask it new questions. "Thank you."

Toren acknowledged her thanks and shooed her out of their chambers. She walked with quick steps, the path now familiar to her. Guards seemed to watch her with more attention than before, and when she came to the study she found double the typical complement of guards. She frowned, but the guards didn't stop her. Nor did they give her any reason for their presence. Was Olen here?

She didn't find him in the study, and as she followed the secret passage and approached the gate, she saw no sign of him. As near as she could tell, she was alone, as she had been the last several days. Still, she bit her lower lip. Was she becoming paranoid, or was her welcome in the castle wearing thin? The guards worried her.

In more ways than one, her time was running out.

As before, Alena made sure she was protected as she touched the gate and dove into its memories. Once she was in the library, she paused and considered Toren's advice. If she'd been misguided this long, which line of inquiry should she now pursue?

She sat in a chair. If there was an answer to the force that now approached, it had to involve the gates. But at the same time, if the ones that came before had died, control of the gates wasn't enough. Was there more?

She didn't know. For all the memories arrayed before her, she still knew far too little about the gates.

That was where she must start, then: at the beginning. Alena fixed the question in her mind and picked a book at random. She opened it and fell into the memory.

SHE ADMIRED THE TAPESTRY, *a treasure passed down through the generations. The needlework was exquisite, the product of a lifetime of diligent study. For all her own talent with a needle and thread, she could never hope to match the skill displayed before her.*

It was a worthy addition to the project. She nodded, and the chief who had brought it to her smiled. His gift was accepted and would be honored, marking this momentous occasion.

She looked down at her hands, surprised by how wrinkled they were. It seemed like just last week she had found this nexus and realized what it meant. But a whole lifetime had passed since then.

Would her own work be honored? Would anyone ever gaze upon it with the same wonder she'd just experienced while looking at the tapestry? She didn't consider herself vain, but she hoped so.

The chief was the last of her visitors for the day. All that remained was the final weaving, the event so many had traveled so far for.

Tisha looked down at her hands again. Once, they had been steady and strong. Now they trembled no matter how hard she tried to force them to stillness. It was possible that this final weaving might be the end of her. But she had been to the last gate once before. She'd already solved half of death's puzzle. Something awaited her soul on the other side. Her end held little fear. Only curiosity.

Death fascinated her. Ever since her first hunt, she had wondered. And with what she had created, there were new opportunities. Prolonging life seemed easy enough. She'd already figured out the weaving for that. But what was the point in living forever? She'd had plenty of pleasure and seen plenty of sunrises.

No, what interested her was transcending death.

That was the puzzle she wanted to spend her remaining days on.

But first, today. Her dream of transcending the final gate might be the very quest that led her to it without a way back.

She'd prepared the chiefs for the possibility of her demise. It wouldn't do to start a panic, not now. And her apprentices were well capable of carrying on the work she'd begun. Though she wasn't sure, she believed other nexuses must exist. The world was too large for just one.

She stepped from the tent that had been her home for more years than she cared to count. A small crowd had gathered, chiefs from many different clans. The fact they weren't fighting was a wonder enough, but she hoped to give them an even greater one before the day was out.

Tisha fell into the dreamwalk. These days, it almost required more effort not to straddle the worlds. Lines of connection sprung into existence, filling her sight. The web between the chiefs was a knotted mess, but there was beauty in chaos. The nexus had taught her that. Order was useful, but it was not the goal.

Life would always be messy.

She bowed to the chiefs, and as one, they bowed to her. The mix of emotions she received from them brought a smile to her face. Some were skeptical, others eager, and others awed by her presence. She knew well the stories that had spread throughout the land about her.

The woman who spoke to animals.

The woman who fire could not touch.

The warrior who defeated an entire clan singlehandedly.

A demon from another world.

Some of the stories were more true than others, but she didn't trouble herself with any of them. If all went well, her work here would eclipse all the other stories combined.

No longer would they have to fight among themselves. Her nexus would bring them together. It would give them a purpose greater than mere survival.

Tisha saw the threads, stronger than others, that led to the nexus. They were the web of life she'd first discovered, all those years ago. Today she could sense the life flowing through those threads, like blood through the veins of a body.

The entrance to the nexus was simple but smooth stonework. She despised pretention in all its forms. Let her work speak for itself. She entered alone, nodding to the six apprentices who guarded the entrance. They bowed deeply.

The tunnel descended, a straight line until a door was reached. Tisha opened the door and beheld the work of her life, inert for the last time. She'd found the uncut diamond here, buried under the ground, at the very place where the threads converged. And on that day her wandering had come to an end.

The sight of it still made her shiver. As she had worked, it had taken the shape of the last gate. Tisha still didn't know if that was due to her own experiences, or if there was some deeper meaning, a pattern she didn't understand. Regardless, the nexus before her looked nearly the same as the gate she'd seen on the day she'd almost died.

She held up her hand to the diamond, sensing the patterns she'd woven within. A lifetime of study. Endless days of labor, knotting and untying the threads that ran through the heart of this world. Years had passed as if they were days, every small advance a leap in understanding.

Studying it now, she wondered if her feat would ever be duplicated. If another nexus was found, could it be so shaped? Her apprentices were talented, and they would have a model to follow, but she knew she would not live long enough to build another.

Tisha began the final weaving, the one that would tie this nexus to the heart of the planet, that would allow those who could walk the dream to control a power beyond imagining. And that was only the first step.

There were days where she worried what they would do with the power. Humans had an unfortunate tendency to turn their advances to destruction. But she had hope. In the long arc of history, humans tended to move forward. In fits and starts, and sometimes they retreated from progress, but they always found their way ahead. She didn't know how they would use this strength, but she hoped it was in ways she couldn't even imagine.

The final weaving didn't take long. Only a single act remained, and it was done.

Power filled the room, giving her a vitality she hadn't felt since she was a young girl.

It warmed her heart.

The gate began to glow, a blueish light that reminded her of the twinkling of some of the stars at night.

How did one measure the accomplishments of a life?

Tisha didn't know. But if she died now, she would do so with no regrets.

The very pulse of the planet beat in her ears, channeled by the nexus.

She held out a hand and fire appeared above it. She watched it for a moment. Expected as it was, it still surprised her.

Tisha walked out of the tunnel, her steps light.

The chiefs awaited expectantly. Tisha stood before them. Once outcast, now courted by every clan.

She raised her hands above her head, and a pillar of fire rose into the sky, burning through the clouds above.

As one, the chiefs fell to their knees, and a new age began.

ALENA EXITED THE MEMORY GENTLY, replacing the book as though it were a treasure.

The gates had never been meant as weapons. And they hadn't been built to fight the force that even now approached. She'd been wrong about that. And how much more?

The hope and wisdom of Tisha impressed her. Would she be pleased if she now saw what her gates were capable of? What they were used for?

The memory also confirmed a suspicion Alena had long had. The gates drew power from the planet itself. And that was the power that drew the creature.

That fact gave her an idea.

She dropped out of the soulwalk.

She needed to see Olen immediately.

29

Brandt sat in the same room, now alone, looking out at the queen's city, wondering if there were any answers to be found in the empty streets. Perl had left long ago, leaving only the bare walls to witness his continued indecision.

He understood both Perl and the queen. In some ways, the queen had an unfair advantage with him. He'd lived her memories, and they now felt as though they were his. It was hard to judge her, having shared her emotions. Even if she ruled poorly, the heart that made those terrible choices sought to save the world, and from where he stood, he couldn't say that her intent was wrong.

But the price of her rule wasn't paid by the queen. It was paid by those born in these lands. They had no choice, and they were suffering.

In one hand, he believed he held the fate of the entire world. In the other, the well-being and happiness of tens of thousands of people.

How did he choose between two noble causes?

And when would such decisions stop tearing him in two?

The bell rang, signaling the end of the day, and Brandt watched as citizens filed out of buildings and made their way home. Some greetings were exchanged, but mostly they ignored one another, each lost in their own personal misery.

A flash of darkness caught Brandt's eye. He looked up and saw a small dark bird flying overhead, cartwheeling freely on currents of air.

It shook something loose in his head.

This wasn't a choice between two set options.

Life was rarely so well defined.

Other approaches existed. Fate had put him in a place where he was closer to the queen than anyone else, possibly the first person to truly interact with her in years.

As much as he was at her whims, he wasn't powerless. She needed allies, and as time grew short, he was one of the only ones she could turn to. It was thin armor, but it was more than anyone else enjoyed.

Brandt straightened, and a hint of a smile played across his face.

It was time to do some good around here.

He waited for the streets to clear. His presence among the people caused more problems than it solved, and if he was being honest with himself, he didn't trust Perl to remain peaceful toward him. If the woman felt he wasn't on her side, she might turn against him, and find some other way to use him against the queen.

Just as she had with Sheela.

Perl's hands weren't as clean as she imagined, either.

Once the bell rang for the evening curfew, Brandt left the room. Now that only soldiers walked the street, he felt safer. The soldiers paid him no mind. As the only foreigner in this land, they knew who he was.

Brandt didn't know his path exactly, but the tall tower of the palace served as guidance enough. As usual, the guards at the gate let him in without question. Even if the queen was aware of his most recent actions, she didn't consider him enough of a threat to fear.

He found her easily enough by following the line of disgruntled advisers leaving her receiving room.

When he arrived, two last advisers stood in line outside the door for their meetings with the queen. Both looked nervous, and from the way the door opened and an adviser scurried out, like a frightened mouse, such fear appeared justified.

Although he was certain he could have stepped into the room before them, Brandt decided to wait. Despite the import of what he hoped to accomplish, he felt light, more confident than he had in a long time. Let the queen conclude her business with the others first.

The two men ahead of him cycled through quickly, and each time the door to the receiving room opened, Brandt was almost certain he could feel the queen's anger radiating from within. He couldn't say why it didn't frighten him, but his breath was even and the beat of his heart steady.

When at last it was his turn, he entered the chambers with a confident step. He'd wondered if his presence would surprise the queen, but from the expectant look on her face, she'd known he waited outside.

He stopped ten paces from the throne and made a short bow.

Her eyes narrowed. "What is this?"

"I've met with Perl."

"I know." Venom dripped from the queen's voice. "Did

she finally convince you to kill me? Did she show you enough tragedy to ignite your useless courage?"

Her barbs didn't bother him.

He saw the queen in a different light now, and he wasn't sure why he hadn't seen it before. For all her power and all her longevity, the queen was still human, and she hurt. She'd been alone for a long time.

"Quite the opposite, in fact," Brandt replied.

The queen sat up straighter, her look sharp. She waited for him to explain.

Brandt went down to one knee. It was the same posture used when an imperial soldier pledged his life to the empire. When he'd kneeled before, Brandt had held out his hands to receive the sword he still carried. But there would be no such gift from the queen.

Instead, he offered his own gift.

He took the knife from his pocket, the one Perl had given to him upon their first meeting. He held it up in both hands and offered it toward her, then laid it on the ground in front of him and backed away from it. He spoke slowly.

"You have shown me your memories, Sofra, and I believe them. The threat that approaches requires the will and effort you've shown thus far."

She heard the objection in his voice. "But?"

"But your choices, as much as you might believe in them, aren't right. As you've told me yourself, in all your long years, potential allies have been scarce within your lands. It is due to the methods of your rule. Fear can only control a person for so long." Brandt paused, wondering if the queen would tear him apart with a thought. He still drew breath, which was about as much as he could have asked for. "I will not use the technique you showed me."

The queen clenched her fist, and he rushed to continue

before she ended this audience violently. "It's not enough. I think some part of you knows this. How many have died for you over the long course of your life? If I intended to reach your strength through such a method, I would have to cut my way through every home in this city. We must find other ways, and we can do it together." He took another deep breath. "Just as we will rule your land together."

When he looked up he saw genuine surprise and amusement on her face. "You intend to rule by my side?"

"For a time, perhaps. Call me whatever you wish. I have no desire to usurp your power. But together, we will find a new way forward for your empire."

The entire audience had been a gamble, a bet that he understood her. She might be a tyrant, but even tyrants viewed themselves as the heroes of their own stories. He offered her more than service. He offered her company and understanding.

It occurred to him then that he'd already gotten far closer to her than even she expected. He'd been inside her memories. The experience had been almost painfully intimate. And now he asked her to trust him further.

He was surprised when she nodded. "It was a bold move, coming in here like that."

"Timidity solves nothing," he said.

Just then, there was a knock at the door. The queen frowned, and an adviser entered, head bowed all the way to the floor.

"My queen, there is trouble at the barracks."

"What kind of trouble?"

"It's the soldiers, my queen." The adviser shuddered, as though fearing for his life. "They have gone mad, and now they fight and kill one another as though they are at war with themselves."

The queen's eyes blazed with fury as she stood from her throne. She stared at Brandt, as though questioning whether he knew anything about this.

The timing was too perfect to be coincidence. It reeked of a plan, the aim of which Brandt couldn't begin to guess. But he shook his head. It surprised him as much as it did her.

For what it was worth, she took him at his word. "Come with me, then," she said.

Brandt followed, afraid of what fresh nightmare he was about to experience.

30

E ven after she'd been announced, Olen made her
wait.

Alena tried not to take the gesture personally.
Olen, after all, was an emperor. No doubt he had countless
pressing concerns, each vying for his attention.

But given her revelation, it still felt like a slight. Olen
needed to hear her thoughts, and although she supposed a
slight delay wasn't disastrous, it felt that way. This wasn't
just the fate of the empire, it was the fate of the entire world.
Other matters could wait.

It seemed to her as though he was reminding her of her
place. She might control the gates, but he controlled the
empire.

Finally, she was admitted, only after two other confer-
ences were ended.

Olen sat on the throne, looking more comfortable than
he had the day before. Alena bowed. "I've found important
memories," she began.

Before she could continue, he cut her off. "Did they deal
with the end of those that came before?"

Alena frowned and shook her head.

"Then it doesn't matter." Olen stood from the throne. Combined with the dais the throne sat on, he now stood considerably taller than her. As with so much that Olen did, it felt calculated and cold. But it was also silly. She had no time or patience for games of status.

Olen practically spit his next words. "I've given you as much time as I can to make your case, but you've given me nothing. Now it is time for you to relinquish control of the gates. Your emperor commands it."

Alena took a step back, surprised by the intensity of Olen's reaction. "But—"

A sharp gesture cut her off again. "No buts. No explanations. No excuses. I've begun to believe that you plan to use the gates against the empire. Do I fear correctly?"

Alena shook her head, unable to form a cogent response to the verbal assault. How could he even think such a thing of her?

"Will you then transfer control of the gates to me?"

Alena gritted her teeth and found her balance. Logic and reason she could accept. Olen's doubts fueled her own. But no one ordered her around. Had Jace been present, he would have counseled the emperor against it. Her father had once called her stubbornness legendary, and it was one trait of hers that hadn't changed much since she was young. "No."

Had Olen allowed anyone else to be in the chamber, she imagined they would have gasped and recoiled in horror. One didn't refuse a command from the emperor. Ever. No straighter path to the executioner existed.

They stared daggers into one another, and Alena wondered if Olen had been bluffing. The cost of taking the gates by force would be enormous, but he had to have guessed by now she had no desire to fight. Still, Hanns had given her the gates, and she thought she was beginning to see why. She didn't trust Olen, and wondered if his father hadn't, either.

She broke the silence. "I discovered the history of the gates and when they were founded. They pull power from the planet itself, but I believe it is the use of that power that drives this enemy toward us."

Olen's eyes narrowed. "What are you saying?"

"If we stop using the gates, perhaps the creature that is now so close won't visit us."

He didn't respond for several long heartbeats. Then a low laugh escaped his lips. "Now you want us to stop using the gates? Without them, we're defenseless against the queen." He shook his head slowly as his laughter faded, as though realizing a truth. "But that's what you want, isn't it? She has poisoned your mind with these thoughts."

Was he really that paranoid? Alena realized her mouth hung open and she closed it. Her jaw moved, but no words emerged. This wasn't some complex scheme. These were memories that she had unearthed. "I only want peace."

His voice was as cold as the dead of night in winter. "Then give me the gates."

She didn't answer. Was he right? Was she the one who was being played the fool?

No.

Her experiences were true. They had to be. "Emperor, if we use the gates, it might draw more attention to us. The consequences could be disastrous."

"And they will be for certain if we don't use the gates. And anyway, there is a flaw in your logic."

Her glare matched his own.

"Even if we stop using the gates, the queen possesses two, and I don't see her breaking away from them. No matter what, the gates will be used."

"Then we must go and speak to her. I can show her my memory, and we can reach an agreement."

Olen laughed again, the sound harsh against her ears, laced with bitterness. "Do you really take me for such a fool? Shall I send some armies with you as well, as a gift to bolster her own forces?" He stepped off the dais and toward her. "Alena, you are a traitor, beholden to a foreign queen, and you don't even realize it. Hand over the gates. It is the only logical course of action."

Alena retreated from the force of his request.

She knew she was right.

But what else could she do?

Olen's patience and forbearance, such as they were, had run out.

She needed time. She couldn't think her way out of this, not fast enough. She couldn't surrender the gates, but she could give him a temporary victory. She cast her eyes down, hoping that he would consider her defeated. "Maybe... maybe you are right. I still believe in what I saw, but perhaps there is more to it than I realize."

"That's right," Olen said. Condescension dripped from every word.

"Would you give me a night to speak with my brother, Toren, and Ana? I've traveled with them a long way, and perhaps they can offer me guidance. Then, if we agree that you are right, I will transfer the gates to you."

The thought of such an action brought tears to her eyes. She was better suited to the gates than him, a far stronger soulwalker, but what could she do? He stopped directly in front of her and grabbed her chin with his hand, forcing her gaze to him. He stared into her tearful eyes. Then he nodded. "Very well. One night. Tomorrow morning, you will turn the gates over to me, or there will be war."

Alena nodded.

"And Alena?"

She looked to him.

"I don't want to risk the soldiers I would need to take the gates from you by force. If you don't turn the gates over to me tomorrow, I'll send out birds and messengers. I won't fight you, but I know all about your family in Landow. Your father won't have to worry about ever forging another tool again if you seek to deceive me, and your mother will never bake another loaf of bread. Am I understood?"

Stomach sick, Alena turned away. She wouldn't even look at the emperor.

She found her own way to her chambers. Toren took one look at her face and rushed to her. She held up a hand to stop him. "Find Ana and Jace. We need to speak."

Toren didn't ask a single question. He just nodded and left. It didn't take long before they were all together again.

Alena told them of her discoveries, as well as her theory that the only way to prevent catastrophe was to not use the gates. Which led her to her conversation with Olen. When she reported Olen's threat against her family, she worried Jace might jump out of his seat to find the emperor that moment.

"He can't follow through on it. I've got too much leverage." A thought occurred to her then. "Of course, I only have the protection so long as I have the gates. But don't worry, I won't let anything happen to them, even if I have to compel him."

Jace's eyes met hers. They both knew how much she

would detest such an outcome, and the very fact that she would even consider it said enough about her determination.

"But I didn't ask you here because of the threat Olen made," Alena said. "His doubt is—justified—I suppose, and I want your opinions. Am I being influenced by the queen?"

Silence greeted her.

Jace looked at the others gathered, and when no one else volunteered to speak, he did. "Do you think she is manipulating you?"

Alena shook her head. "I cannot be sure. Her experience dwarfs my own. But if she is, it is too subtle for me to detect."

"So you believe the queen speaks true, and that the gates shouldn't be used?"

Alena nodded.

Jace shrugged. "Good enough for me."

Toren gave Alena a look as if to say, "I told you so." Alena looked to Ana. Of the group, she trusted the warrior to be the most critical. When she nodded her agreement with Jace's thoughts, it almost brought Alena to tears again.

"Thank you," she said.

They spoke for a while after, but there was little to decide. Alena would go to any lengths to protect her family, and she had the ability to do so, even now. The entire group convinced her that she was justified in meeting any threat that Olen issued.

By the time they finished it was nearly evening. They returned to their own chambers then, and Alena and Toren retired early. By the time she fell asleep, Alena almost felt confident about the upcoming day.

When she awoke, she knew she hadn't been asleep long.

But her heart pounded as she realized what was happening. She shook Toren, who came awake quickly.

"Get the others," Alena said, as she began throwing her clothes on. "Olen is attempting to steal the gates."

31

Horses were already saddled and waiting for both the queen and Brandt once they left the palace walls. The queen gave Brandt a long, strange look, as though deciding something. Then they were mounted and riding.

Sofra was a woman who kept most of her emotions hidden. She showed anger and rage, but anything more intimate remained behind a mask of steel. Tonight was different. This was a side of her he'd not yet seen. Her face was set in a stern line, and she didn't waste a single movement. He held his questions, the sounds of their mad gallop drowning out any attempt at conversation.

Thanks to the empty streets and the speed of their horses, it wasn't long before they reached the outskirts of the city. They rode north, leaving behind the city walls. Dust billowed behind them, obscuring Valan. The queen rode her horse without concern for the animal, leaving Brandt little choice but to follow suit.

Ahead, the orange light of fire flickering against the underside of clouds pointed their way.

When they crested a small rise and saw the barracks for the first time, Brandt almost brought his horse to a halt. Only the queen's continued dash forced him onward.

From the report, Brandt had expected a fight no larger than a couple of dozen soldiers. Tensions within an army often ran high, and fights inevitably broke out between warriors. It was frowned upon, but when one trained for war, sometimes one went looking for a fight. A wise commander found ways to channel that aggression. But poor ones often let it build until it found release in more destructive ways.

But this was no scuffle.

Several of the buildings in the barracks were consumed by flame, and the sound of steel against steel rang louder as they approached. Plenty of blood had already been shed, and there was more yet to come.

What had happened here?

Flames licked at the night sky as they rode closer. Ahead of them, chaos reigned, a sharp contrast to the empire Brandt had lived in for the past weeks.

The queen finally reined in, maybe a thousand paces from the open gates to the barracks. She growled. "A dreamwalker is among them."

Brandt glanced over. He could pick out nothing in the mess before them, but he trusted the queen's assessment.

In his years as a soldier, one truth had risen above all others:

There were no coincidences.

A soulwalker among the soldiers, spreading rebellion? There could be only one culprit. "Perl?" he asked.

"I suspect so. I underestimated her skill. This—this requires more than just planning. It requires a strength I didn't know any in this land possessed." She looked to him. "Can you guard yourself against her?"

Brandt swallowed the lump in his throat. He was anything but certain. But he nodded.

His lie didn't fool her, but she didn't stop him, either. "Be careful. I'm not sure I'll be able to protect you once we're inside."

Brandt almost bridled. He'd been a warrior his entire adult life. He didn't need her protection. But she spoke true.

They galloped together to the gates. Once inside the walls, Brandt leaped from his horse. He was a competent enough rider, but he fought better on foot than mounted.

The scene before them was worse than it looked from a distance. Bodies lay everywhere, and the fights that Brandt observed were fought with an aggression and lack of self-concern that he'd never seen in his long history of campaigning. He caught flashes of one duel after another, the combatants fighting with a complete lack of concern for their own lives. Few bothered with parrying or dodging. Most just hacked at each other until one or both fell, and even those on the ground who still possessed the strength cut at any who walked nearby.

It was a living nightmare.

These warriors didn't fight as humans, but as crazed animals, devoid of any sense of self. Brandt backed up a step. Whatever this was, he wanted no part of it.

Then a warrior found him, and the battle was joined. Brandt's cut wasn't blocked, and his own sidestep moved him well clear of the wild attack. The man fell and Brandt stepped aside as he drew his final breaths. Even in his death throes, the man tried to cut at Brandt's ankles.

Brandt noted that he needed to make his cuts as immediately fatal as he could.

Several more warriors charged, but it didn't feel like battle. They attacked him with wild and strong swings, but without any thought given to defending themselves, they had no chance. It was a slaughter.

When Brandt finally succeeded in clearing a small space around him, he looked for the queen. She stood two dozen paces in front of him, and no warrior dared approach her. But the fighting that surrounded her was frenzied.

When the queen dropped into a soulwalk, Brandt felt it. The drumbeat of her power was deep, reverberating in his bones. Those close to her stopped fighting, a small island of peace in the madness.

Brandt cut down one warrior who attacked him, then stepped aside as she died. His eyes barely wandered from the queen. Would she be able to calm this? The oasis only spread for a dozen paces, and the sounds of fighting carried from everywhere else.

He noticed a curious fact. When warriors wandered into her sphere of influence, they calmed, but if they stumbled out, they attacked once again. Whatever she did, it wasn't permanent.

"Brandt!" she called to him.

"Yes?"

"Scout the rest of the battlefield from on high. Let me know the details of what you see."

She pointed to the nearest building that wasn't on fire. He figured only a hundred or so angry warriors stood between him and the structure.

Of course.

Brandt made himself light, sliding between cuts and sprinting toward the building. But his movement attracted attention, and soon he was stopped by a wall of swords. He backed up, scrambling away from the cuts.

Then he realized what a fool he was being.

He still had his gatestone, and Hanns had shown him a far better way.

Brandt summoned stone, and one large rock a little larger than his head rose from the earth before him. He didn't have time to find balance, so he hovered the rock above him and leaped for it. Thanks to his lightness, he had little difficulty grabbing onto the rock and holding on as he lifted it with his affinity. With the power of the gatestone, the cost was no matter.

He carried himself above the battlefield toward the building. A few warriors flung their swords at him, but they did so without control, and he had little to fear. In only a few heartbeats he was on top of the roof.

He looked at his hands, almost disbelieving what he'd just been able to accomplish.

How much good could he have done if he'd been aware of these skills earlier in his life, when he was campaigning on behalf of the empire?

He shook his head and focused, turning his eye to the small-scale war being fought below him.

At first glance, it all looked the same. The barracks were large, probably capable of holding several hundred warriors. From the look of it, almost all of them were currently out of their beds fighting one another.

But as he watched, he noticed details. The fighting wasn't the same everywhere. Most of the barracks were consumed with individual fights, lacking any order. But in some places, soldiers had gathered and fought together as a group.

They fought like soldiers.

As he watched, one of those pockets collapsed. One moment the warriors had been protecting each other, but it broke suddenly, warriors turning on one another as though betrayed. Brandt studied the group, closing his eyes and extending his affinities.

He felt her.

Perl was down there, in that direction. Her beat was familiar, and stronger than the storm of uncoordinated drumming coming from below. When she moved to another group fighting together, they too broke up.

Brandt searched for her, but in the mess of bodies and the darkness, he couldn't find her. But she was here. And she, somehow, was seeding the chaos.

He almost leaped down the building after her. Whatever she was planning, this couldn't end well. The queen's anger had been ignited, and who knew what she was capable of in such a state?

He could find Perl if he went down there. But the danger was thick in the places she visited, and he would be fighting a battle on two fronts. No doubt, her actions were compulsion of a flavor he hadn't yet experienced.

He swore.

Brandt. The queen's voice echoed loudly in his head.

He walked from one side of the building to another. The queen and Perl were almost on opposite sides of the barracks, and the difference couldn't stand out more. The area around the queen remained calm, but it seemed pitifully small from up high.

What do you see? the queen asked.

Perl is here. Not everyone is fighting one another, but she finds those resisting and breaks them apart. There aren't many left.

He didn't know if she heard his thoughts. Silence greeted him. Her next orders almost caught him by surprise. *Leave here, Brandt.*

He looked down at the fight. He couldn't leave, not yet. *I can help.* He didn't know how, but there had to be something he could do.

The queen didn't respond. Brandt saw her moving from her position back toward the gate. She hadn't fought a single person.

Brandt watched, a sinking feeling twisting his guts. He looked around at the barracks, descending further into chaos with every passing moment. If they had any chance of turning the tide, they needed to do so soon.

With every step the queen took, though, his hope died.

Self-preservation eventually won out. He summoned the rock that had carried him this far, and once again held on to it. He made his body light and let it carry him far above the fight below. He let the stone slowly rotate, giving him a view of the whole mess.

He came down next to the queen, about two hundred paces outside the front gate of the barracks.

The building he'd been standing on caught fire. Brandt watched, despairing. "What are you going to do?"

"She killed them," the queen answered.

Brandt gave her a questioning glance.

"Her power is strong, but it is unrefined. And I don't think she cares. She wiped everything from them, much the way she did with Sheela. And then she instilled nothing but fear and anger."

Brandt stared at the building as it burned, the madness within the walls of the barracks taking on new meaning. "And she's spreading it as she wanders about."

The queen nodded.

"So what will you do?"

Her voice froze him. "End this."

Brandt felt the power of the gates. This close, every nerve in his body lit on fire as she drew on her connection.

He looked to her. "Don't do this." He studied her face, looking for some hint of remorse, some bit of sorrow that he could use as a bargaining tool.

But she gave him nothing.

A wall of fire erupted between them and the barracks. It reached high into the sky, and Brandt was reminded of the horror he'd seen in the queen's memories. He knew where she had learned this technique.

Did she even know that she now visited that same horror on her subjects?

He reached out to her, but the wall rolled forward, moving faster with every heartbeat. Though dozens of paces separated them, Brandt felt his skin burning from the intense heat.

The fire broke over the wall, Brandt's objections dying on his lips. It rolled through the barracks, slowing a bit, but giving no time for anything to escape.

Perl must have thought that the queen wouldn't dispose of her troops so easily.

After all, what human could?

But the troops weren't any protection for the rebellious soulwalker. Brandt felt his connection with her snap, and he knew well enough what that meant.

The fire passed through the barracks, ending a hundred paces on the other side. Then it winked out, as though it had never been more than a figment of his imagination.

He stared, horrified.

The sounds of battle had faded, replaced by the screams of those burning alive.

But even those didn't last long.

And then there was only silence.

32

"What would you have me do?" Toren asked.

Alena's mind raced as she threw on her clothes. "Get Jace and Ana. I need to soulwalk."

Toren went to the door, but Alena never made it to her soulwalk. Four guards stood outside their door and prevented Toren from leaving. Toren bowed in fine imitation of imperial fashion, then closed the door again. Their eyes met.

Olen had anticipated their moves.

"Get ready to leave soon, if we must. I'll try to reach my brother."

Alena fell into the soulwalk. Seeking out Jace was no challenge. The bond she'd tied between them was stronger than ever, and she followed it to him, surprised to find him still awake. When she connected with him, she had the distinct sense that she'd been expected. They both materialized in their mother's kitchen.

Jace wasted no time. "Olen has posted guards outside my room. They were loud enough to wake me."

"He's trying to steal the gates."

"Figured."

"Can you reach Ana?"

Jace thought for a moment, then nodded. "If I have to. Our rooms are adjacent. If the guards woke me up, they did her as well. But it will mean a fight."

Alena grimaced. If only she'd had another few days. "Wait, then, but be prepared for anything. We might need to leave quickly, or fight."

Jace agreed, and she dropped her connection with him.

She paused for a moment. Her next decision would have ramifications. She could reach Olen in the soulwalk, or she could go meet him personally at the gate.

One meant fighting the guards, and that was something she desperately hoped to avoid. Stopping Olen would be far easier closer to the gate, but she decided to take the risk of soulwalking first. That way, there was at least some opportunity for peace.

Alena soulwalked to the gate. Even from a distance she could see Olen lashing himself to the structure, his attempts as clumsy as the first Anders'. Compared to the fine weaving she'd spent so long on, his attempt felt oafish. But it was still enough to grant him power.

"Olen!"

He turned at her shout. "You should have turned over the gates, Alena." He created a bubble around him as he continued the process.

It was a pointless gesture. With a thought, she shattered his protection. He turned, the first surprise she'd seen evident on his face. She came closer. "Olen, let's talk."

He waved her away. "The time for talk has passed. I gave you time. I invited you into the heart of the empire. But now I see that my judgment was mistaken. You aren't some confused fool from the outskirts of the empire, though you play one well. You've always been after the gates. Perhaps you've always been a servant of the queen."

Alena forced herself to open her clenched fists, to meet his gaze. "None of that is true."

"You're subtle, Alena. Clever, even. Perhaps almost as much as I. My father couldn't see through you, but I can. And I will save my empire." With one last look, Olen dropped out of the soulwalk.

Alena swore. He'd be coming for her in the physical world. Perhaps there was even a prearranged signal among the guards.

She glanced at his connection with the gate. She should destroy it, but didn't have the time. He'd thrown enough lashings around it that it would even take her a while. Toren and the others needed her now.

Alena dropped out of the soulwalk. Her eyes searched for Toren and found him. "Olen has possession of the gate, and he's coming for me."

Toren stood up, as though he'd been expecting nothing less. "Our gear is packed."

"I'll take the guards," Alena said.

Toren offered her a couple of stones from the bag hanging at his hip. She took them and opened the door to her room. The guards turned toward her, but she didn't detect any distinct threat. They were there to keep her in, not to assassinate her.

She launched the stones, driving them into heads one after the other. She tried not to send them too fast. The guards had done her no wrong.

Toren followed her into the hallway, wrapping his arms around one guard's neck as she attempted to stand after Alena's first blow.

A moment later, they were free.

Alena dropped into the soulwalk and found her brother. He appeared in their mother's kitchen. "Leave now," Alena said. "I'll clear the way to the main gate."

As quickly as she'd fallen into the soulwalk, she removed herself. Then she stopped. The castle would soon be swarming with guards hunting them. If they were going to escape, they would need every advantage.

It was hardly an ideal environment, but there was no better time. She dropped again into the soulwalk, but split her awareness between the waking world and the soulwalk. Her connections to Toren, Jace, Brandt, and her parents shone brightest, but the web of life surrounded her. She took a few tentative steps and found it to be doable. It required a relaxed but constant focus.

Then they were on the way. Alena led them, dividing her attention between the constantly shifting web that the soulwalk revealed and their own path. Twice she noticed and avoided guard patrols before they could be heard or seen.

Sweat beaded down her brow. How had the queen soulwalked and fought at the same time? For all Alena's growth, this exercise was proving to her how far she had to go to catch the foreign tyrant. Just walking took all of Alena's focus.

They made it to the main entrance of the palace, and from here there was no choice but to fight. Eight guards stood stationed at the entrance. Alena and Toren rushed them together, stones circling all around. By the time they reached the doors, all eight were on the ground, either unconscious or dazed enough not to be an immediate threat.

The empire was in no way ready to fight a war against affinities.

Together, they pulled one of the heavy doors open, and then they were in the enormous gardens that surrounded the castle. Several hundred paces away, the walls of the castle grounds loomed large above them. Alena pointed to the west. "Stables are there. We're going to need horses."

Toren only gave her a quick, dubious glance. "You can take the gate on your own?"

"I think so."

Then he was off without argument. Though he'd helped at the doors to the palace, she had fought most of the guards. His skill and precision might surpass hers, but her gate-augmented strength couldn't be matched.

Alena glanced behind her. The castle stood quiet, as if the pounding of her heart was a lie. But it couldn't last. Soon, Olen would find them escaped, and the alarm would be raised.

She turned her attention to the main gates. Guards stood along the wall, but from their height wouldn't be able to make out any details of those coming and going.

And Olen had made a mistake. He hadn't closed the main gate. They didn't have to fight.

Jace and Ana found her about the same time Toren returned with horses. His right eye was developing a nice bruise.

"Problems?" Jace teased.

"One of the stablehands really didn't want to let the horses go without an order from the emperor. And he had fast hands."

They mounted the horses, and Alena wondered at the silence of the castle behind them. There was no way their absence hadn't been discovered by now. And still she heard no alarm. She paused. Olen was no fool. Them escaping had to have occurred to him as a possibility, but he'd barely taken steps to stop them. The guards he'd set might have stopped most warriors, but he knew the abilities of those he hoped to imprison.

If he had a plan, though, she couldn't fathom it. And she didn't want to fight Olen here. The power of the gates would rip through the city without mercy. Though it pained her, running was her best option.

They rode toward the open gate, and Alena motioned for the others to fall in behind her. Though it exhausted her, she remained in the soulwalk, and she saw the guards before her. She connected with each of them and rummaged through their hearts, finding memories of exhaustion and sleep. She strengthened those memories, drawing them to the forefront of the guards' thoughts.

The guards stumbled on their feet but remained upright.

Alena pushed harder.

And then they fell asleep.

She worried the clatter of their weapons would alert the other guards, but those on the wall didn't seem to notice.

They rode through the gates unchallenged. Because there had been no challenge, the guards on the walls didn't pay them any particular attention. Only when they were a hundred paces from the wall without pursuit in sight did Alena drop out of the soulwalk.

The group rode in silence through the streets of Estern. The city was large enough that it never truly slept, but few others wandered the streets at this time of night. Those who did explore the streets kept to themselves, each lost in their own private world. None paid them any special attention.

Their next challenge waited at the walls to the city. But the guards there, too, didn't seem concerned.

Perhaps, Alena thought, Olen's desire for secrecy actually restricted his choices. Maybe he wasn't able to act in the way he wanted due to his desire to keep their presence secret. The thought didn't sit right with her, but she decided to test her theory by simply riding through the gates.

No one stopped them, and then they were beyond Estern.

They rode through the buildings constructed outside the walls, many of them almost castles in their own right. Alena glanced back at the walls of Estern, shrinking behind them.

Jace finally gave voice to her thoughts. "Anyone else think that was too simple?"

Nods of agreement were all around. Alena kept looking behind her, but never saw anything worrying. It seemed they had made an escape.

Eventually the homes surrounding Estern also fell away and they came upon the first intersection in the road. The rest of the group looked to her.

"We need to travel west," Alena said. "Hopefully, I can continue to discuss the situation with Olen through the soulwalk, but we should head toward either the gate at Landow or the one in Etar. Both require us to travel in the same direction."

No one had any argument, so they took the road leading west. Alena took the lead, and the others, sensing her mood, gave her space.

While they rode, she tested her connection to the gates. They still felt strong. Olen's connection hadn't weakened hers. Which was another interesting fact she would have to think about when she had time.

The sun was just about to break over the horizon when Jace rode up to her. "We've traveled some ways. I don't think a town or village would be safe, but we should find a place off the road to rest. I think we've ridden far enough."

Alena kept riding. They'd maintained a consistent pace, but they hadn't exactly ridden hard.

He saw her doubt. "It's okay, Alena, we're safe."

They crested a small hill, and both stopped dead in their tracks.

Toren and Ana drew up alongside them.

"Oh," said Toren, his gift for understatement still strong.

Alena turned to Jace, unable to resist, despite the situation. "What were you saying?"

Olen hadn't just outsmarted them. He had been thinking several steps ahead of any of them. Before them was an army, several thousand strong. And at their head, the emperor. They'd been waiting.

Alena understood the moment she saw. Olen hadn't cared about secrecy. No—he'd had the same concerns as Alena about a battle in the city. He'd set the ambush perfectly, and they'd walked right into it.

A cry rose up from the assembled warriors, and the army broke into an orderly charge, led by hundreds of cavalry.

Ana's voice was cool and analytical behind them. "We can't outrun them, not after a night of riding."

Alena agreed. Whether she liked Olen or not, she couldn't find fault with his cleverness. Their only options were to fight or surrender.

"Alena?" Jace's voice held no doubt. If she told him to draw his sword, he would, no matter the odds.

She didn't deserve such faith.

Alena connected with her gates. There were still options. She could raise a wall of flame between them and make this a battle between her and Olen. If it came to that, she suspected she could beat him.

Then she thought of the force, somewhere out in the darkness of the sky, approaching closer every day. If she pulled from the gates, would she attract it?

She swore. Either way she lost. Either to Olen, or to the arriving creature.

Her mind raced, but there was no place for it to go.

She held to the power of the gates, ready to unleash it in a moment.

Then she shook her head.

The creature frightened her more.

So long as she lived, there were options. "Keep your weapons sheathed," she ordered. "We're surrendering."

33

Brandt jogged in a circle inside the wall that surrounded the palace.

When he'd been a young soldier in training, he well remembered the runs his commanders had sent him on. A true warrior, they shouted at him, had to be able to run a league to the battle and be immediately ready to draw their steel. When he'd first joined the army, he hadn't even been able to run a league. He'd never had to. But by the time he finished his training, his commanders ensured that he was able to run and fight.

The physical training had been useful, of course, but he'd been surprised to learn that the running calmed his mind, as well. Whenever he ran far, he slipped into a trance. If he ran even farther, he found peace, no matter what troubled him.

He wasn't sure how far he'd run, but he'd completed countless laps. At first, he'd tried keeping count, but his focus for that had faded. Now he just ran, hoping to keep his problems behind him, or at least put them in proper perspective.

No matter how far he ran, though, he couldn't put aside the memory of the queen burning her own soldiers.

The murder of so many haunted his dreams, but it wasn't what truly bothered Brandt. Horrible as it sounded, he expected such actions from the queen. She didn't value the lives of others. Her actions were terrible, but not surprising.

No, it wasn't the fire itself, but the betrayal that ate at his thoughts.

When he'd finished his army training, he'd made a pledge to the empire that he would protect it with his life. Though others might see his choices differently, he believed he'd kept that oath through all his days.

But there was an implicit reciprocity in his oath. He would fight and die for the empire, but he also expected the empire to fight and die for its citizens. And the whole nation owed a debt of gratitude to its warriors.

The queen's actions spit upon that agreement. Whether or not her warriors had ever given their oath freely was irrelevant. She expected them to fight and die for her. Which meant they deserved her loyalty as well. It was a code he considered inviolate.

For all the horrors he was certain the queen had visited on her people, her actions against Perl were a step too far. She hadn't even tried to save those of her soldiers she could.

And no matter how far he ran, his thoughts on the matter didn't change.

To his surprise, she was the one who exited the palace, seeking him. He finished the lap he was on and jogged to her. She gave him a disdainful look as she took in his disheveled appearance. But he couldn't care less.

"You didn't show up to training today."

"I would have been useless. Focus is impossible right now."

The queen continued to surprise him. Usually such disrespect merited a verbal lashing that made him wonder if he'd finally gone too far. Today, she took his claim in stride.

She seemed more reflective than she had in the past. "You disagree about how I handled the situation."

"To say the least."

"I do too."

The admission made Brandt pay attention. Had the queen ever admitted a mistake to him before? If she had, he couldn't remember it.

"Not for the reasons you imagine," she said. "But I never should have let it get that far. Perl beat me. The action I took was the only one left, and that was because I underestimated her, terribly."

The queen gestured that they should stroll the grounds, and Brandt walked by her side, grateful to stretch out his legs already growing sore.

"As near as I can tell, it began with the search for her. I thought groups of four would be enough to prevent any compulsion. But I was wrong. I can't be sure, but I believe that Perl allowed herself to be found many times. But every time she planted a seed of compulsion in the soldiers who found her."

"A seed?"

"It is the best word in your language I can think of. She prepared their minds for something larger, making compulsion at scale easier to achieve."

Brandt thought of the soldiers, searching for days. Because of his kidnapping.

He traced the path backwards, from effect to cause. Perl must have been planning something like this from the beginning, just waiting for an opportunity like the one he'd presented her.

"But you won. You killed her. And all the soldiers searching for her were from those barracks, so the compulsion hasn't spread. What else matters to you?"

The queen turned an icy glare on him, but today it had no effect.

"I had to turn on my own soldiers. Yes, I will try to hide the truth, but in time, word will escape. And what soldier will fight for me once it does? It will take years to rebuild what was lost, if not more. I might have killed Perl, but she has struck a blow to the heart of my reign. She's accomplished more than any rebellion has in generations."

Brandt wiped away the sweat on his brow.

Then he looked at the back of his hand. He'd stopped running long enough ago that he shouldn't be sweating anymore.

The queen, her confession complete, looked at him. "What?"

He didn't answer for a moment, making sure he wasn't imagining things.

But he wasn't.

It was warm. Too warm. The sun wasn't even to its midpoint yet.

"Is it hot?"

The queen frowned. "I usually keep a slight breeze blowing around me. I wouldn't notice."

Brandt kept forgetting how the queen utilized her affinities in ways he'd never thought of. A constant breeze was a brilliant idea and had never occurred to him.

Still, it was too hot. "Something's wrong," he said.

He ran up the nearest steps to the top of the wall. As soon as he did, the problem became apparent. "Sofra!"

The queen came to his summons. If she despised the use of her name, she didn't show it. When she saw what he saw, she swore. Then swore some more.

Her face, already pale compared to Brandt's, turned almost pure white.

Off in the distance, in the sky, a ball of fire fell toward the earth. It burned brighter than the sun, and it burned a trail through the sky. Even though it had to be dozens of leagues away, Brandt felt the heat of it as though he was standing a pace or two away from a roaring bonfire. He squinted against the pain of it.

After a few moments, he felt as though he could track it.

It fell toward the now devastated barracks.

There were no coincidences.

In that moment, he understood.

The enemy that the queen had so feared was here. He glanced at her face, and she knew it, too. He'd never seen her expression of terror, but he did now. And it turned his insides to water.

The air continued to heat. His own face felt like it was melting. He took a cue from the queen and used his fire affinity, taking heat from the air surrounding him and pushing it harmlessly behind him. It took more effort than he expected, but the feel of cool air on his skin was well worth it.

Then the ball of fire hit. The planet rumbled underneath his feet, as though the whole world had been rocked by a punch. A wave of sand blew out from the site of the impact, obscuring his vision.

A moment later flame and smoke erupted high into the air, the top of it billowing out, making Brandt think of a grotesque oak tree.

How could any creature survive such a fall?

Unfortunately, he knew the answer to that.

The cloud of destruction spread, and then the wave of pressure washed over him. At this distance, it blew him back a step in surprise. But they were leagues away from the barracks.

He'd seen two gate-wielders battle before and thought he'd never see a power like it again. In a sense, he was right. This was something beyond compare. Even the gates didn't matter.

Their doom had arrived.

INTERLUDE

Winds buffeted Dezigeth as this planet's atmosphere desperately attempted to funnel air into the vacuum its passage had created. It stood in a crater deep enough to find the bedrock underneath the shifting sands, sensing the currents and powers of this new world. Even in a moment, it noticed that the situation here was more complex than initially believed.

It had followed the clear call of power, so recently unleashed in this very spot. Buildings had stood here before its arrival, but there'd been no life. The air smelled of death and fire, of flesh cooked too long and left to decay in the unforgiving heat of the sun.

A city lay nearby, but Dezigeth remained still. Its mind ran along the lines of power, remnants both strange and familiar. Action without knowledge was wasted. The more it knew, the more efficient its cleaning of this scourge would be. And what was time to Dezigeth? It possessed vague memories of a beginning, but few of endings. Its work here would be accomplished in its own time.

Dezigeth gave itself physical shape, modeled after a male

*human. And wings, as it had no wish to walk upon these burning
sands.*

*Nothing could stop it. Yes, there was power here. More than it
expected. But not enough. It was good Dezigeth had arrived now.
Before long, this planet would develop into a threat to the stars.*

A danger to it and the others like it.

*The core of this planet shook in response to its arrival. If the
mountains could bow, they would have.*

*No one with ears to hear or eyes to see would be ignorant of
Dezigeth's arrival.*

*It waited as more information poured in. Thousands of lives
and the connections between them, all understood in moments.*

More surprises awaited.

*There were several on this planet with power, close to ascen-
sion, to evolution. The strongest of these was close, in the city
nearby. No doubt she was the one who had visited the destruction
upon this place. Her power echoed within the crater. Another in
the city held potential, still largely unrealized.*

*But the greater surprise was that one of its kind had visited
before. Rarely did a people survive a first intervention.*

But it had been ages past.

*Interventions had been cruder then. Nowhere near the sophis-
tication of the tools Dezigeth wielded.*

There would be order.

All in due time.

*Too many people lived on this planet for it to guarantee their
extinction alone.*

So it would need help.

Dezigeth began gathering its powers, and the work began.

34

Alena swam in a sea of stars, weightless within an infinite void. No troubles worried at the edges of her thoughts. Her heart beat with contentment. The stars didn't twinkle, and she stared at them, her mind blank.

She simply was.

Suddenly, a rip opened in the void, and a bluish light, alive with energy, bathed her. Something shimmered through the rip and Alena reached out her hand for it. She didn't know why, but she knew she couldn't let that light escape her grasp.

Heartbeats passed, and then the rip closed, leaving her floating once again.

But her peace had been disturbed.

Bubbles of color floated before her.

Memories.

An army before her. The advance of a single man under a flag of truce. Behind him, a small retinue of other men, faces hidden under hoods.

Anger pulsed through her veins at the sight, but she couldn't say why.

Words were exchanged, but in the silence of the void, they didn't reach her ears.

Then motion from the retinue behind the man, and a sudden stinging in her chest. The image shifted as she looked down, seeing needles emerging from her tunic.

Then darkness and peace.

The images faded, taking her anger with them. Before long, she was once again calm, floating.

Whispers reached her, the words too soft, too indistinct to make out. She listened and they grew louder. The voice was familiar. Although she couldn't put a name to the commanding voice, her heart beat faster and her throat dried. It wasn't the voice of a friend.

The void faded, replaced by a more mundane darkness. She opened her eyes. A stone wall was before her, and a face.

Olen.

The name tasted bitter on her tongue.

Olen stared at her, his face uncomfortably close. He turned away, spoke something, then shook his head when whoever he spoke to replied.

This was the waking world, and everything about it was the opposite of the star-filled void. She felt heavy, and waves of emotion washed over her. But she couldn't hold on to any of them. Thoughts were slippery, and she lacked the energy to grasp them.

Olen's gaze returned to her.

"Alena!"

Her eyes opened wide, the sound deafening. Her tongue and eyelids both felt heavy, and she felt her vision fading to black as she closed her eyes again.

"Alena!" Her vision shook back and forth. She saw another stone wall and a wall of bars. Then her vision steadied. Someone held her head in their hands.

Olen turned away again. "She's still not responsive."

"A moment, sir. The effects take some time to wear off."

"Alena, can you hear me?"

She managed to raise her head just a bit, then let it drop into his hand again.

"Good." Olen let her chin drop and stepped back. Chin against her chest, Alena saw that she was on a bed, although it barely deserved the name. She still wore the clothes from her last memory, when the needles had jutted from her chest.

"Alena, I need you to give me the gates."

She still couldn't hold on to thoughts. She reached for them, but they remained forever elusive.

Suddenly, her whole world shook, strongly enough that she fell to the side. After a moment, Olen lifted her up to sitting once again. She was grateful. Her body wasn't listening to most of her commands.

"Alena, give me the gates."

A powerful need washed over her. Of course she needed to give Olen the gates. Why hadn't she?

She couldn't remember, but slowly she was able to access her thoughts, to hold them for more than a heartbeat. Olen deserved the gate. He was the emperor, after all. Anders VII. They were his responsibility.

She blinked and frowned.

That wasn't right.

"Alena, give me the gates."

Olen was rational and cared for his people. Alena saw that now. Who was she, to think that she deserved the gates? Hanns had been a foolish old man, deluded at the end of his days. She would give the gates to Hanns' son, the way it should be.

Her head hurt, distracting her.

"No," she said.

Why had she said that? She'd meant to say "yes," hadn't she?

"Alena, I've tried, but I can't take the gates from you. I can't break your connection. You need to give me the gates."

Olen was wise and strong, the leader their empire needed.

But she couldn't.

She didn't know why. It didn't make any sense, but she continued to refuse.

For another moment the battle warred between her desires and her actions. Then Olen broke his gaze. He turned to the side, where another person waited. "Give her more. It didn't work this time." He walked to the iron bars and looked back in. "Let me know when she begins to come around again."

Olen left the cell and nodded to someone outside. Shadows moved, and then another figure emerged to enter the space the emperor had vacated. This name came to her quickly.

Niles Arrowood.

Cold hatred burned in his eyes. He stepped past the apothecary, busy mixing ingredients in a small bowl. He knelt before her. "Do you remember me?"

"Niles." Her voice sounded like a croak.

"Imagine my surprise when I saw you waiting for a private audience with the emperor. It didn't take me long, once I spoke with him, to figure out what you were up to."

She blinked, unable to follow the flow of his thoughts.

"You've always been so perfect, fooling everyone. The

teachers at the academy believed in you. Your family certainly believed in you. But you're a liar, a thief, and a murderer. My father was a great man, but here you sit, somehow in possession of something that shouldn't be yours. Olen won't tell me what, but he tells me you'll surrender it now."

He slapped her across the face. She didn't feel much, but it sent her tumbling back into the bed.

He put his face close to hers. "I want you to resist. I want you to make it hard. Because I've already gotten the emperor's word. When you finally break, he'll turn you and your fool of a brother over to me for your punishment. And I'm going to savor our time together."

He slapped her twice more, then stood up. He nodded to the apothecary, who came over and tipped a liquid into her mouth. It was bitter and foul, but he plugged her nose between two fingers. Niles held her jaw shut, so that she couldn't spit. She had no strength to fight, and eventually had no choice but to swallow the brew.

Then her world went black, and once again she was swimming in a sea of stars.

35

After the cacophony, there was one long moment of silence, as though the whole world held its breath. Brandt realized he was, in fact, holding his and let it out.

As if that was the signal, cries began to echo from the streets below. Brandt tore his eyes from the growing cloud of destruction near the edge of the horizon to the city below him. For the first time since he'd arrived in this strange land, people congregated in the streets. One person saw the cloud and pointed. Another tapped a friend or family member on the shoulder. Soon they were all turned as one to where the barracks used to be.

Fortunately, the destruction was distant enough that the city had escaped significant harm. Perhaps a few windows had been destroyed, but Brandt couldn't see any damage worth worrying about.

Beside him, the queen gasped, her senses more attuned to the power concealed by that cloud.

Five enormous boulders, all on fire, emerged from the cloud. They traveled impossibly high into the air, and for a moment, it looked as though the sky held half a dozen suns. Brandt watched for a few heartbeats before realizing they grew larger. His eyes went wide and his breath caught in his throat.

The queen connected to her gates. Waves of energy radiated from her, making Brandt feel as though he'd stepped too close to a fire. She groaned.

Then she swore at him. "Help!"

Her sharp command snapped him out of his stupor, but his own gatestone seemed meaningless when compared to the powers at play. He lent what help he could. He connected to his gatestone, hearing the low hum of the boulders through his stone affinity as they began to fall.

No other force acted on them. They had been thrown and forgotten. But they'd been thrown hard, and all at the same time. The queen focused her efforts on one, pushing at it as it reached the apex of its flight. Brandt joined his efforts to hers. He was like a child next to her, but bit by bit, the path of the falling boulder was altered. As it fell, the little difference they'd made became more meaningful. They'd gotten it at just the right time, and it now angled down away from the city.

"Enough," the queen said. "Now the one in the center."

Brandt knew the one she spoke of. One of the boulders fell directly at the palace.

He hesitated. "Wouldn't it be best to let that one land? The palace is unoccupied."

"Brandt!"

He had no choice. Only a few heartbeats remained. Once the boulders reached their highest point, they fell with surprising rapidity, and he couldn't stop them on his own. He added his strength to hers, hoping the areas near the wall were unoccupied.

For a moment, the falling boulder blocked out the sun.

Even working together, they barely succeeded.

The boulder crashed into the eastern wall, the crack of stone against stone so loud it felt like needles pierced deep in Brandt's ears. The wall crumbled in that section, one blow abruptly erasing the separation between the queen and her people.

Brandt swiveled his head from his position on the wall. Four boulders had landed among the city, destroying buildings as though they'd been made of sticks, and spreading fire wherever they touched. Black smoke already rose, and wind spread the fire from building to building.

For several long breaths, all Brandt could do was stare. From their vantage point on the wall it wasn't visceral, but he knew that hundreds of people had to have lived in and around the destroyed buildings. Even the boulder that collapsed the palace walls had been large enough to crush a few structures that had stood too close.

His gaze returned to the cloud. It grew larger, dwarfing any mountain Brandt had ever seen. No further attacks emerged from the darkness, but the queen's attention was completely focused in that direction. "What do you sense?" Brandt asked.

"It's—building."

"Building what?"

The queen shook her head. "Something that rivals the gates." She squinted. "But it doesn't draw upon the power of our world. The creature itself powers the construction." She shook her head again. Whatever happened out there consumed her attention.

Cries below reminded Brandt that the city suffered. He looked down. "We need to help your people."

The queen stared off into the distance.

"Sofra!"

His use of her name caught her attention. "We need to help your people," he repeated.

She just gave a small shake of her head and returned her focus to the distance.

Brandt swore. She could stand here, enraptured by whatever happened within that cloud, forgetting the suffering of her people, but he wouldn't. Remembering the technique Hanns had once shown him, he used his stone affinity to summon a stone. He grasped it in one hand and made himself light, then flew from the walls. He ignored the boulder that had shattered the palace walls. Plenty of guards surrounded the palace, and they would focus their attentions there first. Better to help someplace else.

Flying above the destruction, Brandt's heart broke.

War was one thing. Soldiers, at least in the empire, volunteered for their duty, knowing what they risked. Most of the engagements Brandt had fought had taken place in wild country, where the only ones who suffered were those who fought. He'd fought only twice in cities, and even then, noncombatants had been left alone.

The destruction below him wasn't war. It was murder on a scale he'd never imagined. From high above, he saw countless bodies in the street. Those that had survived fled the fires that spread out of control.

Presented with an abundance of places to begin, Brandt chose one at random and dropped down. He used his fire affinity to pull heat from nearby flames, extinguishing as many as he could. He funneled the heat through his body and out his outstretched hand. Flames reached into the sky but died quickly with nothing to burn.

Those who were dead he ignored. He could do nothing for them. He gave what aid he could to the injured, and carried out those who were trapped and in danger if the fires reignited.

At first, Brandt worked alone. But in time, when the others saw that the fires weren't going to reignite, he was joined by citizens. He received some strange looks. Even dirty and grimy, he was clearly foreign. But the looks faded as he continued to pull people from the wreckage. Thanks to his gatestone, he could lift the heavier debris that trapped victims.

He lost himself in the effort. Though he couldn't speak to anyone near, it no longer mattered. Gestures sufficed. If he needed someone to help grab the legs of a victim, someone would appear as if summoned. They were connected by their shared humanity, a bond deeper than language.

Eventually, he tried to pick up an injured woman but found he couldn't. He stumbled and tried again, but his muscles refused to respond. He connected to his gatestone, but no affinity could help.

A strong hand rested on his shoulder. It was an older man, his own face lined with soot and grime. He extended a cup of water to Brandt and gestured for Brandt to step away.

Brandt took the cup gratefully, stumbling as he backed up a step. The old man caught and supported him, guiding him to a stone to sit on. As Brandt watched, two others took his place and moved the woman.

He sipped at the water, fighting the desire to gulp it all down in one swallow. It tasted better than even the finest ales in Estern.

For the first time since he began, he took in his surroundings. The effort of rescuing the victims brought everyone together, but it appeared that the worst had passed, at least as far as he could see. Most of those that remained trapped were dead, and attention turned to those who survived.

When he looked to the sky, he saw that it was darkening. He'd been here for most of the day. It hadn't felt like that long, but it explained his utter exhaustion.

Brandt closed his eyes and fell into a soulwalk. He struggled to ignore the beats of those around him, listening for one in particular.

Sofra remained in the palace.

Bitter disgust rose in his throat. He would bet anything she had never left.

Her true colors were revealed today.

Not just a tyrant, but a coward as well.

He stood, wobbling as he did. Had he ever been this tired?

As he walked from the scene of the destruction, back toward the palace, the others stopped their work to watch him leave.

Brandt kept walking, but then the old man who had given him the water stood before him.

Had Brandt had any more energy, he might have worried after his safety, but right now, even death sounded like a welcome release.

Instead, though, the man mimicked the gesture Brandt had once seen among the Lolani soldiers, their equivalent of a salute. All around him, the others moved as one, mirroring the gesture.

Their kindness almost brought Brandt to his knees.

He met the old man's eyes, then bowed.

Perhaps they didn't know the imperial gesture, but the intent transcended the boundaries between them.

The old man stepped aside, a few tears running streaks in the grime in his face.

·   ·   ·

BRANDT FOUND THE QUEEN, alone and in the dark. She sat on her throne, tall and regal, but there was no one to impress. To Brandt, her posture was the ultimate in futile gestures. Better if the throne crumbled underneath her, as her lands did outside these walls.

Brandt lit some of the lanterns along the walls with his fire affinity. Their eyes met, but he saw nothing in hers to ease his judgment of her actions.

He mastered his anger, barely. "Your people need you."

She didn't respond, her eyes locked with his.

"Hundreds, if not thousands, are dead. With your strength, you could have saved many today."

"I did," she replied. "Only four of the five boulders landed in the city."

"And you could have allowed your palace to be destroyed."

The queen stood. "You still think too small." She advanced on him. "That attack was aimed at me. Had I let it land, I might have died." She held up a hand to stall his outburst. "And before you argue that my life isn't worth the dozens or hundreds that were lost, remember that I alone have a chance at fighting this creature."

Brandt growled. He was tired of being reminded by the queen how important she was.

"I know what you would have of me, Brandt. But my sights are set on the days yet to come. I spent all day summoning my forces, preparing our strategy. It has arrived earlier than I expected, but we can still fight. We can still win."

She punctuated every sentence with another step until they were face to face.

Brandt knew he should be afraid. But he didn't care anymore. "How you lead your people matters, Sofra. Especially in the fight to come. Against this, they won't fight for a tyrant they fear. But they will for someone they believe in."

The queen twitched, and for a moment, Brandt thought that he'd finally taken a step too far.

Then she retreated a pace. "Perhaps. What do you suggest?"

"Walk among your people tonight. Help how you can. It doesn't need to be much. Extinguish fires. Save any who are still trapped. Word will spread."

Then another idea occurred to him. He held onto it for a moment, wondering what ramifications it would have. Ultimately, though, he didn't feel as though he had a choice. "And we should summon Alena."

The queen's eyes narrowed. "She wants nothing to do with me."

"But this is larger than you. And you've recognized her strength yourself. She'd be a powerful ally."

The queen decided faster than Brandt expected. Perhaps her earlier confidence wasn't quite as firm as she wanted him to believe. "Very well. If you leave the palace grounds and aren't near me, you should be able to soulwalk to her. If she agrees, we can travel to the gate and meet her."

With that, the queen began walking away.

"Where are you going?" Brandt asked.

She didn't turn as she answered. "To help my people, as you suggested."

BRANDT FOUND a place where he felt safe, a rooftop several blocks away from the palace. It was hard to access and was one of the tallest places around, so he didn't have to worry about a rogue archer making an attempt on his life.

His body demanded sleep, but he couldn't succumb, not yet. This took importance.

He found the beat of Alena's soul easily enough. It was one of the strongest he felt, reflective of the bond she'd tied between them. But he hesitated.

He hadn't spoken to anyone from the empire since he'd left. No doubt, they felt betrayed and hurt.

He swallowed the lump in his throat. Facing Alena would be hard enough, but he wasn't sure enough courage existed in the world for him to face Ana.

But he would have to sooner or later.

Brandt followed the beat of Alena's soul. But when he reached her, she didn't respond. He tried again and again, but still there was no answer. Eventually, he broke off his attempts.

There was no doubt she was still alive. Otherwise the bond would have broken. He'd felt it clearly with Perl.

Was Alena so angry with him that she simply refused his summons?

Probably.

But the more he thought on it, the more he doubted his conclusion. It didn't feel like he was being ignored. It was more as though she just wasn't there.

Brandt closed his eyes, fighting sleep.

He'd keep trying.

The more he thought about it, the more he was convinced that his friend was in trouble, too.

The void remained, but she was no longer alone. Though she could not say how she knew, there was another here. Someone kind, exuding warmth and concern. Someone close.

The space around her body warped, distorting the light from the distant stars.

She watched, her cocoon of peace undisturbed.

The space continued to bend, twisting on itself until she feared it would rip.

Perhaps it would rip her, as well.

The thought didn't bother her at all.

She lacked even the memories of fear, pain, and worry. The void was everything, and the void was peace. A peace someone stripped away from her one layer at a time.

But even the loss of that peace didn't bother her.

The final transition was quick. One moment she was in the void, the next she was in a monastery, a scene that looked familiar though she was certain she'd never stood here in the physical world.

She turned and there was a man, on hands and knees,

breathing hard. His name was on the tip of her tongue. "Brandt?"

"What—" he huffed and looked as though he might vomit, "what was that?"

She couldn't decide what it was he referred to. "I don't know."

"When I first reached out to you, I couldn't. It was like you weren't there, but the connection still existed. Then I pushed for you, fought to bring us here. But it hurt. It felt as though I was pushing through an endless veil."

Her thoughts returned, slowly at first, but more with every moment. Like a boulder falling down a mountain, the revelations gathered speed, relentlessly battering her mind. One drew more attention than the others. "I've been drugged by Olen."

"What?"

The world around them wavered, and Brandt fell again to his knees. He looked exhausted, pushed far beyond his endurance. She stepped to him and put her hand on his shoulder, kneeling down next to him. "What's wrong?"

He grimaced. "Rough day. I don't think I'll be able to maintain this long."

Her stomach twisted at the thought of him leaving again, with so much still unsaid. Now, after weeks of waiting, Brandt was finally reaching out. The man who had abandoned them all. She wanted to berate him, but there would be no time. His hold on this soulwalk was slipping.

He could soulwalk.

The realization stopped her cold, but only for a bit. She needed to make the most of this time. "What do you need?"

"It's here," he said. "It landed outside the queen's capital. Earlier today. We need help."

She shook her head, still confused. "What do you mean?"

"The queen wants you to come here." He paused. "I want you to come here. This—thing—is beyond anything I could have imagined."

The monastery around them wavered as though it were a mirage. Brandt's control continued to slip. It wasn't fair. She had so much she wanted to say, so much that needed to be discussed.

She couldn't help but doubt. "Is this you, Brandt? Really? Do you trust the queen?"

Brandt didn't speak for a moment. "Not that long ago, you angered me. You told me that how I lived and how I fought mattered. I didn't believe you at the time. I wanted the ability to defend others, no matter the cost."

Somehow, he found the strength to stand on his feet again. Alena stood with him.

"I was wrong, and you were right. And I need you now. We all need you."

"I'm locked in a cell, drugged by Olen, on a different continent. Getting to Palagia won't be a simple matter."

He smiled at her as the world finally began to shatter around them.

"Then you better get started," he said, barely a heartbeat before he vanished, taking the world with him.

She acted on instinct, as so many of her actions in the soulwalk were. She needed to hold on to her thoughts. As Brandt's sending vanished, she threw up a wall, protecting herself from the void that threatened to swallow her once again.

Her actions saved her. Though the darkness squeezed in on all sides, her thoughts were uninterrupted. She sought her connection with the gates and found it.

Unfortunately, freedom within the soulwalk didn't equate to her freedom in the physical world. Whatever the apothecary had mixed for her left her unable to move her limbs. If previous experience served as any guide, the condition wasn't permanent, but it did limit her options.

She sought Jace, an easy enough task in the soulwalk. When they appeared in their mother's kitchen, he breathed a deep sigh of relief. "Olen had us worried. How are you?"

"I've been better. He's giving me something that keeps me hovering near the edge of unconsciousness. Not sure I would have gotten out of it on my own."

In answer to Jace's questioning look she said, "Brandt fought his way into my head. I still can't move my body, but I can soulwalk."

"Brandt?" The tone of his voice implied he had questions, but they could wait. "Where are you?"

"I'm guessing in cells underneath the palace."

"So are we."

"How are you?"

"Fine for now. Your old friend Niles Arrowood keeps walking by, but mostly they've left us alone. I think they're mostly interested in you."

"Brandt wants us to join him with the queen. He claims the threat I've been fearing has arrived."

"So soon?" Jace leaned back in his chair, reminding Alena of better days in their mother's kitchen, waiting for the meal to finish cooking. "Do you believe him?"

"He seemed earnest. He said the queen would welcome our help."

It occurred to her then that Brandt hadn't actually invited everybody. He'd only asked her. She ignored that detail for now.

"Is he telling the truth?" Jace asked.

"I—I don't know," Alena admitted. "I never thought to check. One moment."

She kept her connection with Jace, but allowed her attention to follow the thread that connected her and Brandt. If he spoke true, she'd find the enemy somewhere near him.

It didn't take her long. The power was unmistakable, and even from a different continent, easy to find. She returned her attention to Jace.

"I'm guessing he was telling the truth," Jace said before she could explain. "You were a much better liar when you were younger." He watched her for a moment. "You want to go, don't you?"

"I think we have to. This trouble with Olen barely matters compared to that creature. And we're clearly not doing too well here."

Jace smiled at that. "We can agree on that much, at least." He stood up and stretched. "Fine. I'll talk to the others. Reach out to me in a little while, and I'll have an answer for you."

"Thanks."

"And Alena?"

"What?"

"Be careful. You've really made Olen and Niles angry. We can hear the shouting from here."

Alena nodded and broke the connection.

Her first task was to check in with her own body. She could wiggle her fingers now, but little else. Still, it was progress.

It also meant that it probably wouldn't be long before her cell entertained more visitors.

Probably best not to imagine she could fight her way free anytime in the near future.

But Olen had asked to be summoned. Which meant the apothecary would visit first. It left her a brief window of opportunity. Anyone else she felt she could deal with. But Olen could pull on the power of a gate. A fight with him would be destructive, and in her current state, not in her favor.

Her cell suddenly shook, freeing dust from the ceiling that settled on her. She couldn't move her arm to wipe it off, so she settled for blowing what she could off her face. It had been an earthquake, and she realized that it wasn't the first that had happened. But in her earlier stupor, she'd thought it was her that had been shaking. Was it the whole world, responding to the threat of the creature that had come?

Before she could reach out to Jace, she heard the sound of shuffling footsteps nearby. They stopped outside her door.

Keys fumbled in the lock, and a few moments later she heard the sound of metal grating against metal as the hinges fought against their duty. The apothecary entered her field of vision, and he frowned when he looked at her. "You shouldn't be awake yet."

When she didn't respond, he nodded and began talking to himself. "Probably already too aware. I'll make it stronger this time. Maybe three parts in five?" He continued to mutter, but Alena couldn't make him out.

She couldn't fight, and she didn't dare call upon the power of the gates. If she did, she was certain Olen would notice. Which left the soulwalk. Thanks to their earlier escape from the castle, she had a technique in mind, too. She focused, and a few moments later she heard the apothecary lying down in the corner of the cell for a nap.

Even though it was a gentle compulsion, Alena hated it.

In a way, violence seemed much more straightforward, cleaner somehow.

Her head now moved, and she looked up and saw that the door to her cell had been left open. No doubt there were guards somewhere nearby, but it looked as though Olen had put most of his trust in the apothecary and his concoctions.

Perhaps the trust wasn't undeserved. Alena still couldn't move her limbs, although feeling gradually returned to them. The pace of her body's reawakening was quickening. But she kept glancing toward the empty and open door.

As soon as she could move her limbs, she struggled to her feet. Her balance was unsteady, but the walls provided the necessary support. She soulwalked briefly. One of the closest people nearby was Jace. Olen didn't have guards in the halls outside the cells.

She took the keys off the apothecary. Then Alena stumbled out into the hall and worked her way toward where she felt Jace. Although the door couldn't have been more than forty paces away, she felt as though she'd run for leagues by the time she made it to their door.

She tossed the keys between the bars and sat down. While Toren tried the various keys, Jace knelt down next to his sister on the other side of the bars. "Are you okay?"

"Whatever they gave me is still wearing off. Wasn't sure how much time I had."

Jace laughed at that. "Plenty. We think this is where the empire keeps prisoners they don't want anyone to know about. There are plenty of guards at the end of the hall, on the other side of the door, but very few people are allowed in here. Your greatest risk is going to be if Niles decides to stop by for another visit. That man makes my blood run cold."

"I don't think he likes me."

Jace laughed again. "You always did have a gift for understatement."

They soon had the door unlocked, and they brought Alena in. Ana, Toren, and Jace had all been thrown in the same room, and Alena appreciated being among friends.

"So, did you all have a chance to talk?" she asked.

They nodded.

"And?"

Jace spoke for the group. "It was a tough choice between a life imprisoned down here or fighting against a creature that will kill us all, but it turns out, most of us really like freedom." He glanced over at Ana. "And she wants to beat up her husband."

Alena smiled. "That's fair."

Jace looked down at her. "We don't really want to fight our way through the castle, though."

"I don't think we'll have to."

Jace looked skeptical.

"Remember," Alena said, "I've spent the last few weeks going through the memories of the gates. I might not have found exactly what I was looking for, but I did learn. We're underneath the palace, as is the gate. Seems convenient."

"You're going to tunnel straight through?" Toren asked.

Alena nodded.

They all looked to each other, doubt in every glance. Toren spoke gently. "Alena, you can barely stand."

"True, but I'm still connected to the gates. Physical strength has nothing to do with my abilities. I can get us there."

"What about our parents?" Jace asked.

"Olen won't touch them. He can't take the gates from me by force, and if he actually followed through on his threat, he knows I'd never surrender them willingly."

Jace didn't look quite convinced, but what choice did they have?

Alena closed her eyes and soulwalked. The gate didn't prove too difficult to find.

But she worried that getting to it would be another story entirely.

37

B randt found the queen at the palace. Her clothes were burned in places and her hair undone. He guessed that she had returned only shortly before him. She stood in the kitchen, uncut vegetables and meat piled in front of her, but her hands were still. She barely looked up when he entered.

The smell of the food, even uncooked, made his mouth water and his stomach growl. How long had it been since he'd eaten? He couldn't remember, so the answer was too long. The attack from the creature served as a dividing line in his memory. There was his life before and his life now. For all the challenges in his life before, he would have given anything at that moment to go back.

He came to stand next to the queen. "Go, sit." He gestured to the chair where he usually sat while she cooked.

Wordlessly, she walked over and sat, her weight falling onto the furniture.

Brandt chopped the vegetables and began cooking. His own skills didn't come close to the queen's. She had a sensitive palate and knew exactly how to alter a dish to bring out the best of its flavors. Brandt could usually manage not to burn the food. Today, that would be enough.

As he cooked, he snuck glances over at his host. She looked as exhausted as he felt, but he suspected neither of them would find sleep anytime soon. Even he could hear the sounds of his affinities responding to the events in the desert. An enormous power grew with every passing moment.

"What is it doing?" he asked.

"I'm not sure," the queen said softly. "But the complexity and scale of its working is far beyond my ability."

He had no response to that. Any sympathy seemed wasted, and the queen didn't ask for any. The truth stared them all in the face, as though daring them to contradict it. They had prepared, but their preparations, as near as they could tell, came to nothing.

He changed the topic. "How are your people?"

"Suffering."

Her response didn't invite further conversation, so he let her be. He turned his attention to not burning the food.

"It's easier not to care," she said. "Easier not to let anything in."

He finished the meal and plated it, then brought it over. "It is. But we lose something then, too."

They ate in silence. The food wasn't as flavorful as what he'd become used to, but he had no one to blame but himself.

"Alena has agreed to help."

"Then she volunteers for her own death."

Brandt looked up. The more he learned of the queen, the more he believed he had misjudged her. Faced with an enemy she couldn't fight on her own, a new person emerged, one long hidden under the mask of a tyrant. "We can't give up."

She looked up from her food. "Why not? We can't win."

"Because we're human. We fight. It's what we do. Maybe we don't have a chance. But we fight anyway, because it's better to fight and die than surrender and die. And who knows? Perhaps, if we fight, we find a way forward. But if we surrender, there's none."

It was hardly his most inspiring speech.

It appeared, though, as if it was enough. She nodded. "Very well. Then let's head to the gate."

They finished their food and left once again. In a world that wasn't burning down around them, they would have had time to rest. But they couldn't delay. Who knew how long they had before the creature attacked again?

Outside the walls of the palace horses awaited them.

Brandt wondered at her choice of transportation. Perhaps it was pragmatic. Carriages would be difficult to drive through some areas of the city. But with her power, that shouldn't matter. And a carriage would at least offer them the opportunity to rest.

But as they rode, Brandt understood.

For once, she wanted to be seen.

And she was.

Brandt didn't know all that she had done while he'd soulwalked to Alena. But he saw that the fires had gone out across the city, and although fear still dominated the expressions of the citizens, there was now more. He saw hints of respect, too.

It wasn't much, but it was a step in a better direction.

Perhaps it wasn't too late for the queen after all.

They left the boundaries of the city and increased their pace. He remembered that it had taken them most of a day in a carriage, traveling quickly, to reach the city from the gate. On horseback they were a bit faster, but the journey would not be a short one.

Their pace left them little time for conversation. Normally, Brandt would have let his thoughts wander, but when they did today they traveled in dark directions. Despite his efforts at encouragement, he understood the queen's despair. She had used all her strength to deflect just one of the boulders sent toward the city. The creature had flung five without a second thought, and that initial throw took far more strength than the queen's deflection.

He'd figured they would be outmatched. But the magnitude of difference between them surpassed his expectations. An uneven fight he could prepare for. He glanced in the direction of the barracks. The cloud had long since blown away, but the power emanating from that direction still lit up the sky, even as evening fell.

If he let his thoughts wander further, all he thought of was the loss of Ana and his child. And the thought alone was enough to stagger him.

So he pushed the thoughts aside, shoving them into the dark recesses of his mind. He focused on the road ahead, the sensation of the horse straining underneath him. It became meditative and he slipped into a trance-like state.

A sharp pull on his thoughts brought him back to awareness. He blinked and took stock of his surroundings. The queen was well ahead of him, his own horse's pace slowing. But the distance between them had allowed Alena to reach out to him.

He reined his horse to a halt. Falling off in the middle of

a soulwalk would be both foolish and completely preventable. "What is it?"

"Are you close to the gate?" Alena asked. "I don't think we have long before we need to make our move, and our window won't last long."

"I think we're about halfway there."

She bit her lower lip. "Can you hurry faster?"

Brandt thought of the queen's abilities. "I suspect we can."

"Then do. We're going to be in trouble, soon."

She ended the connection, and as Brandt's awareness returned to the waking world, he saw that the queen had stopped for him. He hurried to her. "Alena is ready to come through, but she won't have much time. She wants us to hurry."

The queen eyed him. "Half the night remains if we ride, even at our quickest pace."

"Can we get there faster?"

"We can't. I don't trust my focus enough for both of us."

Brandt's spirits fell.

"But I can."

"Then you should. I'll keep riding, and I'll meet with you when I can."

The queen nodded. "You should pass by a small village if you follow a straight line. There are carriages waiting there."

She thought for another moment, then reached into her saddlebags. She scribbled a quick message and handed it to him. "This will get you what you need. Bring them."

Then she pulled out two very flat stones from her saddlebags, each about a hand's width wide. She set them upon the ground and stepped on them.

Without a word she was in the air, flying fast toward the gate.

He stared for a moment.

Brandt looked down at the horses. They were majestic, of course. The queen rode nothing but the best.

But now he didn't want much to do with them.

Now he wanted to fly.

38

Jace stretched out, twisting back and forth to loosen up. "Did you reach him?"

Alena nodded. "I trust they'll hurry."

The cells remained quiet, but they wouldn't for much longer. The guards had just tried the door that led to the hallway and found it barred from the inside, a simple piece of work that had been Toren's idea. The sounds of the door being battered from the other side increased. Alena assumed that if Olen didn't know about her newfound awareness, he would guess it quickly enough.

Alena turned to the wall of the cell, made of solid stone. She remembered the soulwalker from ages past, carving the first steps of Faldun into the mountain. With a thought, she began her task. Most of the stone she simply pulled from the wall. While it floated behind her she shaped the stone beyond with her will, pressing it into a smooth tunnel with wide stairs.

She only took a moment to appreciate her work. Years ago, this would have been a feat of wonder. Then she waved the others in. Toren and Jace, armed with lanterns, took their first hesitant steps in.

Soon she had carved out enough space for them all. She dug a little deeper to give them plenty of room, but once they all stood in the tunnel she took the first stones she had moved and rebuilt the wall. Perhaps it would disguise their passage and confuse the guards. But she didn't put her hope in that. Even if the guards were confused, Olen wouldn't be. More than anything she just wanted a barrier between her and their pursuit.

Satisfied that the wall would hold, at least for long enough, she continued digging.

Pace by pace, she tunneled toward the chamber where the gate resided. Never having done this before, she had hoped that the process would be faster. Unfortunately, it wasn't. The gates provided more than enough raw power for the task, but shaping the tunnel took all her focus.

They advanced, the only real marker of their progress the increasingly long tunnel behind them.

It was taking too long. By now, word of the escape had to have reached Olen. He would know she only had one place to run to. They ran a race and she was hobbled.

Then the earth rumbled again. Not strong enough to throw any of them from their feet, but enough to make Alena's heart race. It made her think of the suffocating weight of rock above them. She swore. She didn't want to be here a moment longer than she had to.

They were getting close. She had tunneled about three quarters of the way to the gate, but it wasn't enough. She gritted her teeth and split the remaining rock straight through, widening it with a single effort. Blue light and fresh air spilled through the jagged crack.

"Run!" she cried.

The sharp stone cut at their feet and arms, but they shuffled their way through the crack, emerging near the gate covered in dust and small cuts.

Sounds of stone cracking down the tunnel warned her of Olen's approach. He wasn't going to take the established tunnels, but follow in their footsteps.

Alena swore again. This had been exactly what she had hoped to avoid. Against Olen, the others had little chance. She needed to find a way to both fight and use the gate.

Alena closed up the crack they'd come through. It wouldn't stop Olen, but hopefully it would delay him enough.

She stepped close to the gate and put her hand on it. "Come close to me," she told the others.

Jace looked to her. "I can fight. I'll give you the time that you need."

The gesture was noble, but foolish. "You won't slow him for more than a moment. Come here."

He grimaced but listened.

Alena formed a shield around them, the same way she'd seen the Lolani priestess do so many years ago. Then she soulwalked into the gate, searching for the queen.

In time, she found the queen's gate. It drew more power than any other. Alena called in the soulwalk, but no response came. She could trace the queen's connections to her gate, but the queen shielded herself too well to reach. Alena had no choice but to wait.

And they didn't have much time. She forced herself to maintain her awareness both in the soulwalk and the real world. Olen's pursuit was relentless, and the last stone they had passed through cracked open again as he approached.

He'd come alone, as Alena had expected he would. He'd lived his entire life in secrecy and wasn't about to abandon it now. Anyway, in a battle between gates, what good would extra soldiers do?

Olen took in the scene before him with a glance. "What do you think you're doing?"

"We're going to the queen," Alena replied. "The creature has arrived in her lands, and we're going to help."

Olen paled. "After everything, you still believe the lies that woman fills your head with?"

Alena glared. "You can feel the world shaking just the same as us. It was never a lie, no matter how you wish it to be."

"The empire needs the gates, Alena. You'll doom us all!"

There would be no reasoning with him. His eyes were wide, and he reached out to her, desperate to prevent her from leaving. He spoke with sincerity. He believed that if she left, the queen would take the gates from her.

Once, maybe, Alena might have shared his fear.

Now she turned her attention back to the gate and called for the queen again. It was time for them to go.

Olen's attack slammed against her shield. The force of it surprised her. In the short time she'd been unconscious, he'd been practicing. Her shield held, but her certainty in their safety vanished. Had he been her only focus she could have resisted him, but with her attention divided, she wasn't sure. She called to the queen, again with more desperation.

Another blast pounded on her shield, driving her to her knees. The others, unaware of the magnitude of the fight, surrounded her. But their attention only distracted her further. Olen gave her little time to recover. Blast after blast struck the shield, and she felt it cracking.

"Alena," a foreign voice intruded on her thoughts. "I'm here."

"How do we use the gate for transport?"

"I can open it from this end, but you need to allow a connection to form between us."

"You want my gate?" Alena recoiled, Olen's fears now mirroring her own.

There was a pause, but only for a moment. She could hear the grimace in the queen's voice. "I can work through you."

The space around Alena altered, and she knew the queen was working a weaving. Had she the attention to spare, Alena would have watched, but between maintaining her connection to the gate and fighting off Olen, her attention was already fully claimed.

Then she sensed the queen, reaching out to her through the gates. "You need to make the last connection," she said.

Alena only hesitated for a moment, then reached out and grasped the queen's hand in the soulwalk. In the physical world, a bright light flared inside the gate.

"No!" Olen howled. He prepared another attack, but Alena dropped the shield and attacked him herself, a powerful gust of wind throwing him across the chamber.

"Go!" Alena shouted to the others.

Ana led the way, running through almost before the words were out of Alena's mouth. Jace and Toren followed a moment later.

Olen arrested his movement before he hit the wall and flung his attack back at Alena. She barely managed to deflect it, but didn't respond with another attack. There was no point. All she needed was to get through.

"I'm sorry," she said as she met Olen's gaze.

Then she jumped through the gate as he reached for her.

She emerged someplace dark and damp, barely lit. The

scene struck her as familiar, but it took her a moment to place it.

The queen's caves.

She found it unsettling, to be someplace she'd only been before in the soulwalk.

Jace and Toren's lanterns dimly lit the space, and Alena saw the queen and Ana toe to toe. It appeared that Alena had already missed some of the discussion.

The reason was easy enough to determine. Brandt was nowhere to be seen. Everyone was on edge. Hands hovered near swords, as if the queen considered that a threat.

"What did you do with him?" Ana demanded.

"He'll be along shortly," the queen replied. "He told me to hurry ahead, and from your appearance, it's a good thing that I did."

"Ana, I believe she speaks true," Alena said.

"Come," said the queen. "He will meet us at the entrance of the caves, and I expect he'll be here shortly."

Based on the look on Ana's face, Alena wasn't sure if Brandt's wisest course of action was to hurry here, or run the other way as quickly as he could.

39

In his life, Brandt had faced Falari ambushes, Lolani elite warriors, the Battle of Faldun, and the queen's nightmarish mental assaults. The memories of those events still haunted him, casting dark shadows over his thoughts more often than he cared to admit.

None held quite the same terror as the slit in the ground that led to the queen's caves and the women within.

Gathering the carriages had been a simple task. He'd found the village without problem, and he showed his letter from the queen to the first person to greet him. The rest took care of itself. The letter unleashed a flurry of activity, and all Brandt had to do was sit back and watch.

As near as he could tell, the sole purpose of the village was to serve as a way station for the queen on her journeys to the gate. In the darkness of night he couldn't tell if any were compelled, but he wouldn't be surprised if they were.

The citizens had the carriages prepared faster than Brandt expected, and before long he was back on his horse, now following the carriages as they hurried to the gate. He wouldn't have minded some more time back in the village.

Any opportunity to delay the fight before him would be welcome.

When the crack in the ground that marked the entrance to the cave system came into view, Brandt reined his horse in. The carriages drew closer, ignoring his hesitation. His limbs felt suddenly weak and his mouth dry.

He set his shoulders and rode forward. Delay, as tempting as it was, solved nothing. When he reached the opening, the carriages were already waiting with their doors open. None of the villagers approached within a dozen paces of the entrance. Brandt dismounted and one of the villagers took the horse without even being asked.

Brandt took a lantern from one of the carriages and entered the cave, wondering if he would ever see the sky again.

The passage to the gate was open. The queen, apparently, had hurried quickly enough that she hadn't bothered to seal it behind her. Had she been fast enough?

The answer revealed itself a moment later. The area around the queen's gate was crowded with familiar faces. Alena, Jace, and Toren all faced the queen, their bodies tense, as though a fight might break out at any moment.

Then he saw the queen and Ana, standing toe to toe, and he understood.

His entrance broke the tension as all faces turned to him. He waved sheepishly. "Hello."

And then Ana was in his arms, and all he could think about was how much her belly had grown in the time he'd been gone. He wrapped her up, feeling a tension drain from him that had been building since he'd left the empire. "I'm sorry."

The words sounded hollow, barely worth the breath he wasted on them. But they were necessary, all the same.

Ana said nothing, but broke apart from the embrace. She turned to the queen. "Where to next?"

Several weeks ago, such a tone might have spelled the end of Ana's life. Now the queen just arched an eyebrow at the show of disrespect. The queen looked to Brandt. "There should be carriages waiting for us."

He gave a small nod. "They await outside."

The group trickled out of the caves and the queen sealed up the passage behind them. Brandt tried to watch the expressions on the faces of his friends, but his attention was fully held by Ana. She looked out at her first glimpse of the desert as though she'd expected nothing else. She stepped into the first available carriage and gestured for Brandt to join her. He gulped and did so.

The others, wisely, piled into the other carriages. Toren and Jace took one, Alena and the queen the other. Brandt would have liked to have been a part of whatever conversation happened between the queen and Alena, but that would have to wait.

He and Ana sat across from one another as the carriage lurched into motion.

Her stare was hard, and she said nothing, gave him no opening.

He had to say something, but nothing did justice to the decisions he'd made. He couldn't find the words to capture the depth of what he felt. "Ana, I'm sorry. When the queen made the offer—"

Ana held up her hand, the single gesture silencing his apology. She stretched out the silence, and he had the impression that she, too, was searching for the right words.

When she spoke, her voice was low, barely audible over the sounds of the carriage. He leaned forward to hear her better. "I know why you did what you did. As much as I hate it, I understand it."

She cut him off again before he could respond.

"There is no fault with your motives. I've had time to come to peace with that much, at least."

He waited, knowing there was more to come.

"But I don't know if I can forgive your actions," she said. "Not because you didn't have noble intentions, but because you refused to let me help."

Her breath was uneven. Brandt wanted to reach out to her, to comfort her, but he knew that the advance would be unwelcome.

"When you left, there was nothing for me to do," Ana said, the words beginning to tumble forth. "I couldn't follow you, I couldn't soulwalk to you, I couldn't *do* anything. You might have been in any kind of danger, and I was helpless. Even when we disagreed in Falar, I always knew that we would fight together, that one of us would always have the other's back. But you tore that certainty away from me. You left, on your own. Do you understand? You abandoned me."

She swallowed. Brandt reached out to her, but she slapped his hand away.

"What can I do?" Brandt asked. "Name it, and I'll do it."

"There's nothing to do," Ana said. "What's broken is broken. Perhaps in time, it can be reforged, but I can't offer anything more, not now."

Her words twisted like a dagger in his stomach. He'd known his actions would divide them, and that there would be a fight. Although it wasn't Ana's way, he'd hoped that she would yell at him, maybe even hit him. He wanted a confrontation that was violent and quick. Something that hit like a powerful storm but then blew through, leaving clear skies on the other side.

But he wouldn't be so fortunate. For as long as he'd feared this meeting, he'd never expected that his actions might be the end of them. What was left to him, if there was no forgiveness? "I want to fix this, however I can."

"I hope for the same," she admitted after a long pause. "But I'm not sure I can forgive. How can I know you won't leave me again?"

Brandt had no response to her question, but he swore silently to himself that he would spend the rest of his life fighting to answer it.

40

Alena couldn't help herself. She kept glancing out the window, angling her gaze to see if she could catch a glimpse of Brandt and Ana's carriage behind them. The queen, of course, noticed her curiosity. "What is it you seek?"

She gave a small shake of her head. "Just concerned for a friend."

"You fear something?"

"The end of Brandt's life," she replied.

"Surely you jest. The woman isn't strong enough to kill him."

Alena hadn't been entirely serious, but the queen didn't appear to possess any sense of humor. It killed the smile beginning to creep its way onto her face.

"It's not that I believe they will come to violence," Alena said. "Not really." She couldn't imagine Ana resorting to such crude revenge. "But she holds his heart in her hands, and I fear that she will crush it. Brandt's strength comes from his convictions, and she might shatter those."

The queen frowned, uncomprehending. Then, apparently convinced she had nothing to worry about, focused her attention on Alena. "Brandt implied you had difficulty with your new emperor."

Alena eyed the queen warily. A few weeks ago, she would have resisted the idea of willingly telling the queen anything. The creature changed everything, though. There was no doubting its strength. Even without seeking it, Alena felt it as a constant presence in her head. Whatever threat the queen had once posed to the empire, they had far greater concerns now.

"Olen believed that I was being misled by you. That the creature was of your own creation, an illusion of the soulwalk."

"If only that were true," the queen said. "Although I suppose his doubt of me is justified. I tried many ways of convincing the line of Anders to turn over their gates to me."

Alena turned her attention toward the glowing light off in the distance. "What is it doing?"

"What do you think?"

Alena closed her eyes. The sensations emanating from the area possessed a hint of familiarity. But if true, she didn't dare contemplate the consequences. "Like it is building a gate."

"That is my best guess, as well," the queen said, a hint of despondency in her voice.

"Why?"

The queen looked over at Alena, waiting for her to answer her own question. Alena thought of her own journey, just completed across much of the known world. The gates represented power, but they also served as transport. "It's bringing an army."

"I suspect so. Its kind has visited once before, but this time, it plans on being more thorough."

The statement was complete conjecture, of course, but the conclusion felt right. "What can we do?"

"I suppose asking you to turn over the gates to me is a waste of breath?"

Alena glanced out the window at the otherworldly light. Sofra's request was Olen's worst nightmare come true. Perhaps even more worrying, Alena didn't find the idea to be without merit. After all the scheming and efforts, would she give the gates over to the queen without so much as a fight?

"I won't dismiss the idea," Alena said, earning a surprised glance from the queen, "but I'm not prepared to do so yet. Besides," she added, "are you certain that the addition of two more gates will make a difference?"

"No," the queen said dryly, "but I'm a little low on options at the moment."

"Then let's find some together."

The queen shook her head. "You imperials are all the same. Seeking togetherness. At the end of all things, we are all alone."

"That doesn't mean we need to live that way."

The queen didn't respond.

Alena repeated her earlier question. "So, what can we do?"

"If it seeks to bring others to this world, we must attempt to resist it. My soldiers are ready, but I assume there will be no help from the empire?"

"I doubt it."

"Then my people fight alone."

"Not alone," Alena insisted. "We are with you."

"That means little, unfortunately. All of you working together couldn't even stop me from taking a single gate."

"Then teach me. I've learned much since we last met, but there is more left."

"And would you use such knowledge to wrest my lands and gates away from me? To take advantage of my moment of greatest weakness?"

"No, but does it matter? As you've said, you're running low on options."

A hint of a smile flashed across the queen's face. "Brandt holds great potential, but I am saddened that it was not us from the beginning."

Alena nodded, honored by the recognition of her once and maybe future enemy. Then they spoke, learning more of what each knew. The queen was surprised by the extent of Alena's understanding, but many gaps remained. The largest deficit by far was that for all of Alena's study, she had little practice. As they rode, the queen shaped Alena's knowledge into skill.

They went through several horse changes, and in time, wisps of smoke could be seen in the early morning sun. Alena looked out the window to behold the largest city she had ever seen. Amazed as she was, the sight saddened her. The city behind the walls was impressive, but it had also been broken by the attack.

The carriages passed through the walls and Alena was taken aback by the sheer magnitude of the damage. The glowing light had to be over a league distant. Even with the power of the gates, Alena couldn't imagine throwing boulders so far, and certainly not such large ones.

"You see, now, what we stand against."

Alena nodded.

"How do we fight this?" For the first time, Alena heard the hint of desperation in the queen's voice.

Alena had no answer. But they had to try.

Before long they were at the walls of the palace.

They emerged from their carriages and Alena dropped into a soulwalk. The weaving around the palace walls was even more magnificent than the building. "How long did it take you to create this?"

"Years," the queen answered. Alena felt the queen's weaving, a gentle touch around her wrist. Alena looked down and saw the string hanging from her arm. "This marks you as friendly. That is all."

Alena tested it by stepping through the gate in the wall. As near as she could tell, the queen had told the truth. She felt no strings of compulsion, nor even the slightest pressure of other forces at work.

The queen repeated the process with the others, and soon they were all within the walls of the palace, unharmed.

The small group of imperial friends, and Toren, gathered as the queen made her way into the palace. Alena looked between Brandt and Ana. "How are you two?"

Ana spoke for them. "For now, fine."

The tone of her voice left little doubt as to their true state. But some problems wouldn't be solved quickly.

"Come," Brandt said. "I'll get you settled. I imagine by the time you've all had some rest, we'll be ready to take the fight to the creature."

41

Brandt paced the room as Ana slept. As soon as they'd arrived, Ana had fallen into bed, barely bothering to undress. She took one half of the bed and him the other. When he had reached out to hold her hand, she turned over, her back to him.

He hadn't slept well, and was up well before her. On a normal morning he would have gone out to the courtyard and practiced his forms, but he wanted to be here when she awoke.

She made him wait for a long time, but finally stirred.

She sat up and rubbed the sleep from her eyes. "Morning."

"Morning."

She rolled out of bed, and for the first time, Brandt saw how her movement was affected by the child now growing within. The difference was subtle, but she lacked some of the customary grace born of her years of training. He thought of the creature that lurked beyond the walls of the city, and a crippling wave of guilt caused him to weave unsteadily.

He had brought his friends here, to where the danger was greatest.

Brandt watched as she changed. Though she wasn't quite as fast as she had been, it would be a mistake to underestimate her. He suspected she would still beat most warriors in a duel.

Once she was dressed, she turned her attention to him. "I'm surprised you're still here."

"I wanted to be here when you woke."

He thought she might poke fun at him. In the past she would have, reminding him that she hardly needed him around to get out of bed. But today she held her retort. Instead of being a kindness, it reminded him of what was missing between them. She turned to more pragmatic matters. "So, what happens next?"

"The queen meets with her commanders this morning. I believe that after she hopes to speak with us." Her eyes had never left him, and he'd forgotten how hard it was to hide from that piercing gaze.

"What's wrong?"

He shrugged. "It's nothing."

She clearly didn't believe him, and it barely took her any time at all to unravel the truth. "You want to be at the meeting with the commanders, don't you?"

Brandt nodded. He'd never had much success hiding the truth from her.

"Why?"

"I want to be involved. I might have something to add, or notice something they are missing."

Ana clenched and unclenched her fists. "You never change, do you?"

The barely restrained fury in her voice made him step

back a pace. He held up his hands, but wasn't sure exactly what he was defending himself against.

"What would you possibly hope to accomplish?" Ana began ticking points off on her fingers. "You don't speak the language. You don't know the size or structure of any of the military units here, nor their strengths and weaknesses. On top of all that, you've never had a gift for strategy. You're a warrior, Brandt. Probably the best I've ever known. But you're not a commander."

Each claim, stated calmly, punched his pride to the ground. But it refused to surrender. He began to argue, but Ana cut him off with a sharp gesture. "What? What will you contribute? Tell me the one thing that I'm missing."

He searched for an answer but found none, his retorts empty of truth. He stepped back again.

But her assault was far from over.

"So why do you want to be there, Brandt?"

Brandt growled and spun away from her. He feared that if she continued he might lose control of his anger and say something he regretted later. He looked out the window at the city, still recovering from wounds too fresh to heal. "Maybe you're right, but if I don't do everything I can, I'm not sure I could live with myself."

"If you keep thinking you have to do everything, you might not have to very long."

Brandt turned back to her. "Would you just have me surrender, then? Let the creature do as it will?"

His anger didn't ruffle her a bit. "I'm not telling you to stop fighting. But this isn't about you. It never has been."

She was right, of course. He knew it. He turned to the window again, taking deep breaths until he calmed down. It took some time, but eventually he reminded himself that they were together once again, and that was good.

He smiled, and although it was forced, it improved his mood. "You win this round."

She gave a small nod. She knew she hadn't swayed him completely, but she accepted his truce.

"Should we find the others for breakfast?"

"That's a much better idea," Ana said. "You can't believe how hungry I am these days."

"You are feeding two."

"Feels like I'm feeding more than that."

She chuckled as his eyes went wide. "No—there's only one. But he or she eats enough for several."

Brandt gathered the others who, like Ana, had slept in. He took them to the kitchen and started to prepare the meal. Toren watched him cut an onion, then shook his head, stood up, and gently pushed Brandt away from the stove.

For a time, Brandt could almost convince himself that all of this was normal. While the tension remained between him and Ana, rejoining the others felt a bit like slipping on a comfortable pair of shoes. The conversation was easy, and by unspoken agreement they avoided the subjects that threatened to tear them apart.

Brandt hadn't felt this at home among a group of people since he'd been in command of his small pack of wolfblades.

The queen entered as Jace, ever the bard, finished recounting one of his stories from his days in the city watch in Landow. The group's laughter faded when they saw her, and for a moment, Brandt felt as though they were two separate armies staring across at one another over a deep ravine.

Alena built the bridge before he could. "Come join us. Toren made extra food, and he's a far better cook than Brandt."

The queen hesitated, then tentatively pulled up a chair at the table.

Jace launched into another story as the queen nibbled at her food. Brandt watched her, trying not to be too obvious about it.

How long had it been since she had heard laughter inside her palace? Since she'd eaten in comfort among a group?

From the look on her face, he suspected lifetimes. And his heart broke for the woman he'd once considered his greatest enemy.

When Sofra finished her meal, the conversation turned to the threat at hand. The queen led the discussion, informing them of what steps her armies were taking.

She had summoned them from across her lands, and they would begin arriving in the next day or two. Her opinion, shared by her commanders, was that the gate being constructed was a natural choke point. Their best chance of stopping any advance would be there, the moment foreign armies set foot in the desert.

Alena asked the first question. "I'm no military strategist, but does your army even matter? Couldn't this creature destroy it with a thought?"

"The army isn't the first line of defense," the queen said quietly. "It's the last."

"You're planning on fighting it, aren't you?" Alena asked.

The queen nodded, and Brandt felt the weight of that simple gesture.

All the years.

All the sacrifices.

They had all been for this.

He didn't think it was enough.

Brandt hated himself for having the thought as soon as it came, but he couldn't help himself.

"I'll join you," Alena said.

Jace reached out his hand, as though to stop his sister, but he quickly returned it to his side. He looked away from her, though, to hide the pain that twisted his features.

Brandt understood. The two women, remarkable as they were, wouldn't survive. All they had done was volunteer to be the first to fall.

But they were also the best and only hope the world had.

42

Toren, Jace, and Alena all stood in Alena's bedroom, an awkward silence between them. The queen would soon be waiting for her, and this was her chance to say goodbye.

But she couldn't allow herself to think of this moment in that way. If she did, she wasn't sure that she would find the strength to walk through that door. She *would* see them again, and soon.

At the same time, she had to acknowledge the truth of what was about to happen.

She turned to Jace first and took a deep breath.

He shook his head, warning her off.

She ignored him. "Thank you, Jace, for forgiving me for all I put you through. You always impress me, but that—"

He turned his back on her and almost tore open the door. Though she couldn't see his face, his voice was gruff. "I'll see you when you return."

Then he closed the door and was gone.

Toren stepped toward the door, but Alena grabbed his

wrist and held him back. "It's fine. Look after him, though." The words caught in her throat. "Look after him if anything happens. At least for a while. It will be hard for him."

Toren's chuckle was low. "And it wouldn't be for me?"

She leaned into him. "You'd forget me as soon as you return to Etar."

He gently lifted her chin and their lips met. When they broke apart he had a smile. "I doubt that. But I will stand by his side, and your family's, if the need arises."

"Thank you."

She held on to him, willing herself to remember his scent and the feel of his arms around her. "I love you."

"And I you."

With an effort, she broke away from him. He gave her a small nod. "Come back to me."

She signed her affirmation to him. "I'll do everything I can."

Then she stepped out the door.

She wasn't surprised to find Jace outside in the hallway.

Without a word he came and embraced her. He held her, even tighter than Toren had, and when they finally broke apart, his eyes were rimmed with red. They locked gazes, but there was nothing to say. He nodded, and Alena left to find the queen, the two men she loved most behind her.

THE DESERT, which had first appeared so expansive, now felt suffocating in its closeness. Although the queen's affinities kept the carriage cool, Alena dripped sweat. She kept shifting her position, but no matter how she angled her legs or reclined, she couldn't get comfortable.

Doubt assailed her, and the queen provided no comfort.

From the way Sofra's eyes constantly darted back and forth, Alena guessed the queen's mental state mirrored her own. The only peace this desert offered was that of a final trip to the gate. And that was a journey neither was eager to make.

She and the queen rode alone, excepting the team of compelled servants who drove the carriage. Alena had objected to the use of the compelled, but was silenced when the queen pointed out that any other servants were likely to abandon their post once the battle began. Brandt, Toren, and Jace had all offered to fulfill the role, but Alena insisted they remain behind. Strong as they were, without a connection to the gates they would serve as nothing more than distractions.

Brandt and Ana followed in a separate carriage, but promised to remain well behind. They would be witnesses only.

This fight belonged to her and the queen.

At times, their approach to the site of the creature's arrival felt like a dream, as though Alena's mind hadn't caught up with reality. She only registered sights and sounds a moment after her senses gathered them, like a distant observer of her own body.

But this dream was true.

She'd defied the emperor and traveled across the world to reunite her friends, only to depart again soon after.

Alena squeezed her eyes shut. Such thoughts did her no good. The creature ahead demanded her full attention. She glanced out the window, although there was little need. She could feel it.

They were close.

"Any ideas?" she asked the queen.

The queen's glare was answer enough.

They had no plan. Not any worth the name, at least.

They would attack the creature. If possible, they would prevent it from completing its creation. There was no greater strategy, no secret attack.

Alena had always wondered at the heroes of her childhood stories, who rode so confidently into the face of certain death. As a child, the stories had both inspired her and frustrated her. Of course she respected the courage, but a part of her had always thought there should be a better way. No one *needed* to ride into battle.

The thought brought a hint of a smile to her lips. Unlike her childhood heroes, she was anything but confident, and sometimes there was no other way. As poor as their odds were, this fight was inevitable. Better to be done with it.

Perhaps her childhood self would be disappointed.

But stories revealed deeper truths.

She understood that now.

The queen ordered the carriage to a halt.

Sofra threw open the door and stepped down from the carriage as though simply arriving home. Alena watched with undisguised envy. Her own legs refused her first commands to move. When she did finally stand, they wobbled underneath her, unwilling to support her weight.

If it was possible, the creature's strength intimidated her even more without the thin walls of the carriage for protection. Now that nothing stood between her and that force, she had to admit that perhaps the queen's decision to use compelled servants had been wise.

No amount of courage could convince a reasonable person to remain here.

The light emanating from the site fell just short of blinding. If she squinted, she thought she could make out shadows moving within the light, tracing a pattern beyond her comprehension.

Her decision to quest toward the creature in the soulwalk wasn't even a conscious one. Her curiosity simply took over before her rational mind could shout its disapproval.

The varied and powerful sensations almost drove her to her knees. She already knew of the creature's strength and cold regard. Neither of those came as any surprise. But this close there was more.

How did one describe a soul?

Toren had asked her that once long ago and she had failed to give him a satisfactory answer. When she quested in the soulwalk she found it easy to identify those she was familiar with, but she couldn't describe how. It wasn't like in the physical world where the cut of a person's hair, their posture, or their shape identified them. Instead, it was like a feeling, like the slight sensation of warmth in her chest she felt when she woke up beside Toren in the morning, only magnified. Describing the combination of feelings that helped her mark each individual was almost impossible, but it didn't change the fact that she could identify the souls she encountered with ease.

One of the lessons she had learned was that all humans, regardless of their sex, their birthplace, or their behavior, possessed common traits. When she explored the landscape of the living world, humans were easy to pick out.

The creature that threatened them possessed no human quality. And yet, at the same time, there *was* a beauty to its soul. If anything, the complexity of its thought made it even greater than human. It drew her closer to the creature, like moth to a flame, its pull irresistible.

In a way, the creature reminded her of the gates with the

complex weavings she couldn't quite decipher. This was a soul she wasn't sure she could comprehend.

But it had an identity.

Dezigeth.

As if summoned by the thought of its name, Dezigeth turned its regard toward her. They had been in this position once before, and the memory of its rejection then was almost enough to convince her to drop out of the soulwalk.

But she didn't. Instead, she set her shoulders and met the creature's examination with one of her own. She invited it into her soulwalk and she appeared in her mother's kitchen.

Within moments an inky darkness spread throughout the kitchen. Although this environment should have been Alena's to control, her breath was visible in the cold air before her.

The black shadow took shape, coalescing into the form of a winged man. It was of average height and build, unremarkable except for the wings and the energy that flowed through it. It took in the sights and smells of the kitchen, but if it had any effect, it didn't show on its face. Though it took the form of a human, it most clearly was not. She shuddered as she met its gaze.

"Why are you here?"

To her inquiry it gave no answer. It went to one of the shelves and began picking up ingredients, studying each for only a moment before returning them. It adjusted each as it set them down so that the shelves remained exactly as she had formed them. It almost seemed to treat her soulwalk delicately.

"Why are you here?" she repeated.

It cocked its head to one side, as though noticing her for the first time. "To bring order," it said.

Its voice was nasally and high-pitched, scraping against her ears. Then it gestured and Alena was thrown from her own soulwalk like a trespasser.

She stumbled backward and fell into the sand. The queen glanced down at her but extended no hand. "That was foolish."

Alena found her way back to her feet. "I won't disagree."

"Did you at least discover anything useful?"

"I don't think it likes us very much."

"I wouldn't have guessed," the queen replied, her tone drier than the desert air.

Alena sensed the attack a moment before she saw it. It began as a pinprick of light, impossibly bright against the afternoon sky. It expanded into a wall of fire that filled her field of vision. Glancing left and right, she guessed that it was at least four hundred paces wide and taller than any building she'd ever seen.

Alena's eyes went wide and she took an involuntary step back. Beside her, the queen remained motionless. "How many hundreds of years?" the queen was mumbling to herself. "I would've expected something more."

The wall of fire began to move, rolling toward them. Alena retreated another step. She'd known this was a foolish endeavor, but it wasn't until now that she understood just how poorly misplaced her bravery had been. Her greatest strength was soulwalking, where her imagination and will could bend the world to her whims. But here, against the elements, she was outclassed.

She retreated a third step but stopped.

It didn't matter. Whether now or in the future, this was a battle she would have to fight. She had made that choice when she had refused to give Olen the gates.

The first step forward was the hardest. The second and

the third were easier and then she stood side-by-side with the queen. She prepared to absorb the energy of the fire and use it against Dezigeth.

The queen shook her head. "It will just add more power until you can't control it," she said. "We can't fight it on even terms or attempt to match its strength with our own. Use just enough to protect yourself and then attack."

The queen demonstrated by forming a shield around them. Alena lent some of her strength to the effort, and the wall of fire struck. Alena grimaced against the heat and the force, but then the wall was beyond them.

Horses screamed as the attack struck the carriage behind them. The compelled died without a sound.

She blinked. Despite the ferocity of the attack, defending against it hadn't been as difficult as she expected. Even Olen had struck her shield harder in the tunnels underneath the palace.

"My turn," the queen said.

Another light bloomed before Alena. This one was much closer to them, maybe a half-dozen paces away. Incredible heat radiated from it.

The queen never allowed her attack to expand. The power remained focused, a miniature sun smaller than her fist. It shot forward into the shadows dancing ahead of them.

Alena held her breath. For a heartbeat or two she dared to believe that they had been successful. That all their fears had been for naught.

But then she realized that the weaving before them had not so much as stuttered.

Shadows emerged from the light in the shape of a man and Alena recognized it. She reached for stone, ripping it from the ground not far below the shifting sands. She gathered all the force she could summon and whipped the small boulder at the shape.

Not long after she threw it, the boulder altered course, tumbling harmlessly into the distance, kicking up a long line of sand high into the air.

Undeterred, Alena tried again, this time pulling the stone into smaller pieces. The queen had been right. If strength alone was not enough, then perhaps more finesse was required. She separated the stones again until six hovered before her. The queen, understanding Alena's intent, mirrored the effort, and they sharpened each one to a point. Together they launched the stones at Dezigeth. Some of the queen's moved so fast Alena heard the crack as they split the air.

Their attack never came close. Every stone they launched froze in the air well before it hit, then dropped to the ground.

The air between them felt thick. The initial exchanges had been completed, and to no one's surprise, Alena and her ally had made no progress. But they were still standing, so that was something.

Moments after the thought had passed, perhaps thirty points of light appeared in the air before Dezigeth. The queen's breath caught, and she said something that Alena couldn't decipher, but sounded an awful lot like a curse.

The queen weaved a shield, but this one was smaller, only protecting herself. Alena took one look at the lights floating like deadly fireflies and shook her head. Even if she could create a shield as powerful as the queen's, it wouldn't do any good. The strength and focus those lights represented were so far beyond her skill she couldn't even imagine.

Alena ran as the lights came for them. She sensed them

as small weavings of incredible complexity. The queen and Dezigeth fought for control over each one, nearly three dozen battles happening simultaneously. The first hit perhaps a hundred paces in front of the queen's position. Alena watched as she ran, the sand billowing up for some tiny fraction of a heartbeat before flame flashed from the point of impact. The wave of concussive forces punched into her back, lifting her off her feet and sending her skidding across the rough sand.

Small rocks and grit abraded the surface of her skin. She tumbled twice, then rolled onto her hands and knees.

She sensed the attack a moment before it hit.

With no time to weave a shield, she pushed at it with all the strength the gates offered her. It rose and scorched the air above her, causing a burning sensation to spread across her back where it passed closest. Once past her, she let it go and it slammed into the ground, this eruption slamming her on her side going the opposite direction.

She groaned and pushed herself up to hands and knees again, then slowly to her feet. Dust hung in the air, until a cold wind pushed it away, clearing the battlefield.

The queen was on her knees, and now her left arm ended just below the elbow. Thanks to the wind, Alena smelled the terrible odor of burned flesh.

Dezigeth had focused on the queen. He'd only spared one attack for Alena, and when she looked down at her torn clothing and bloody cuts, she realized it had almost been enough.

More lights appeared in front of Dezigeth, and Alena sprinted for the queen before she had even made a conscious choice. Dezigeth turned his back on them as the lights sought the queen's heart. Sofra made it to her feet just as Alena tackled her back down. Alena bent the stone below them, the same technique she'd used to create the tunnel in Estern. As they and the sand around them fell, she reformed the rock above them, as much and as fast as she could.

Then the lights hit.

43

From a distance, the battle sounded like waves of rolling thunder. Though Brandt remained at least half a league from the fight, the impacts of the attacks rumbled through the soles of his feet. Dust obscured his view, but the clouds of flame and sand that rose into the air were evidence enough that Sofra and Alena fought on.

Ana stood by his side. Her presence held him in place stronger than any chain ever could.

He wondered at that.

Most reasonable people, he suspected, ran for safety when violence erupted before them. What made him different? Rationally, he knew that if he joined the battle he would be little more than a distraction. But if not for Ana, he would be light right now, sprinting across the sands.

He'd argued against her even coming this far. He told her she would be safer in the palace, and she had agreed. Then told him, in no uncertain terms, that she would remain by his side. She placed the burden of her safety squarely on his shoulders, leaving the choice to him.

Thus, they stood about halfway between Valan and the fight.

Brandt shifted his weight from one foot to the other, and whenever a particularly large eruption billowed before them, his hand went to his sword. Then he would notice Ana tense and he would remove his hand.

His friend was out there, fighting for all of them.

He stood here, doing nothing.

He growled.

Ana glanced at him, but said nothing.

The ground beneath them shook as a series of devastating attacks were exchanged. The songs of his affinities pounded in his ears. He pushed the noise aside, searching to see if he could still hear the beat of Alena's connection with him. It was there, but faint.

He took a step forward.

"Brandt?" Ana's voice brought him to a standstill.

"I have to help. They're losing. I can feel it."

Her silence spoke volumes. That he was a fool to think that charging forward would change anything. That the choice was his to make, and the consequences his to bear.

Brandt straightened and rolled his neck. He wanted to fight, but he had other means now, ones that were potentially safer. "I'll soulwalk. Perhaps I can't fight like them, but I can at least distract the creature."

"Soulwalking is no less dangerous."

"True," Brandt agreed. "But at least I have a chance of making a difference."

A heartbeat passed.

"Then what are you waiting for?"

Brandt reached for Ana's hand and squeezed it. She was a remarkable woman, and he was a fool for endangering their life together. But he also couldn't turn his back.

He continued holding her hand as he dropped into the soulwalk. Finding the creature posed no difficulty. Beyond the waves of energy emanating from it, there was something about it that was foreign, like a splash of misplaced paint on an otherwise beautiful canvas.

Brandt didn't hesitate, fearing that if he did, he would never approach. He connected with the creature, pulling it into a world of his own creation.

He appeared in Highkeep, where he and Ana had lived for so many years. The sight of it tugged at his heart, a reminder of what had been and could never be again. It was the closest place he had to a home.

The appearance of another being in the courtyard banished the longing. It took the shape of a man, and yet it wasn't. The face, body, and stature were completely unremarkable. It revealed nothing of the true nature of the creature. The appearance was like a mask, but worn over the entire body. Though Brandt couldn't picture its true form, it did have an identity.

"Why are you here, Dezigeth?"

Dezigeth looked around, taking in its new surroundings with a lingering gaze. It ignored Brandt for a few moments, then fixed him with a stare.

Dezigeth had no fear of this place.

It didn't surprise Brandt. Attacking the creature here had always been a slim hope. But Brandt wasn't seeking to defeat Dezigeth. Distracting it would be enough. He just needed to give Alena and the queen time to escape, or regather for another attack.

"Your kind has a remarkable lack of respect for this realm," it said. Brandt felt it folding away, breaking the connection between them.

He attacked, drawing his sword and cutting at Dezigeth.

His strike was true, the blade hitting Dezigeth's neck.

The edge stopped before it could do any damage. Brandt looked at his sword, not comprehending. He hadn't even broken the creature's skin.

Although the attack had failed to harm the invader, it had succeeded in getting Dezigeth's attention. The creature no longer prepared to leave. Brandt felt himself flung into the air by an invisible force, then held in place with his arms and legs spread wide, unable to move.

Brandt understood the power of will in this realm. He struggled, fighting to regain control of his limbs. He imagined himself falling, cutting at the creature once again. But his body remained pinned in place. Dezigeth approached at a leisurely pace, and Brandt began spinning slowly in the air. Dezigeth studied him from every angle, as though Brandt was a curiosity it had found on the ground.

Brandt's heart beat faster and shame flushed his cheeks. He'd entered this realm expecting a fight. This effortless control over his will reminded him too much of his first experience of soulwalking, falling steadily under the compulsion of the queen. But as Dezigeth continued its examination, the feeling grew even worse.

He connected to his gatestone, but even then, he could only move a hair. Dezigeth watched his struggles with interest. "You fight so hard, though the result is inevitable. Why?"

For a moment, Brandt had no answer. Why fight when there was no hope of victory?

He'd never questioned that belief.

It had just always been true.

Brandt didn't bother searching for the reason. He wrestled and struggled, but nothing happened. Even in this realm, Dezigeth could crush him with a thought.

Dezigeth took another step so they were face to face. It

looked into his eyes and slowly reached out, wrapping its hand around Brandt's neck and squeezing.

It hadn't been long, but hopefully he'd distracted the creature for long enough.

Because he had nothing left to offer.

44

A muffled *thump* was all the warning Alena had as she reinforced her stone bubble. The rock around them cracked and sand poured through, threatening to bury them alive. Alena sealed up the rock. Dezigeth's attacks hadn't killed them, but their safety was tenuous at best. She tunneled away from the battleground, pushing rock to each side as quickly as she could work her will.

Unlike her tunnel under Estern, she gave no thought to smooth walls. All she needed was a space wide enough for them to stumble away. Rock melted before her, re-forming in unnatural shapes as she released it.

Alena fought to keep her breath calm. There was no light here, and only a little air to breathe. Judging from the quick gasps of the queen, what air they had wouldn't last long. So she hauled the queen to her feet and shuffled forward.

The queen was light, made of little but skin and bones. Alena struggled no more than she would supporting a child. Sofra didn't argue, but her breathing grew more ragged and the stench of burning flesh worsened as the air stagnated.

Alena waited for the next attack, but none came. She continued to tunnel. The effort was futile. It didn't matter where she surfaced. Wherever they emerged, Dezigeth would kill them. What did a hundred paces, or two hundred, matter to a creature that had traveled between the stars?

Still, she pushed forward.

The creature's silence puzzled her. Was it toying with them, or were they not enough of a threat to deserve its continued attention?

No explanation made sense, but would she even recognize Dezigeth's thoughts if she saw them? It wasn't from this world, and perhaps the differences defied any attempt at understanding.

Her eyes began to droop, and she fought her body's sudden and powerful desire for sleep. If they didn't surface soon, it would be too late. Alena tunneled another five paces, then split the bedrock where the tunnel ended. She hoped it was enough ahead of them.

Light and sand filled the opening, and Alena shielded her face against both. The fresh air made her feel alive once again. The pile of sand grew until it was almost waist high, then stopped. A slim opening remained, with a cloudless blue sky inviting them forward.

A glance at the queen revealed the extent of the woman's injuries. Her face was pale and her body sagged. She needed rest and care. The wounds could very well be fatal.

Alena grunted as she crawled up the sloping sand, hands and feet slipping back with every movement. She pulled the queen behind her, the woman little more than dead weight. Near the top, her hands slid too far and she sprawled face first into the sand. She spit the sand out and immediately regretted the loss of water. Then she pushed herself up to hands and knees and pulled on the queen's good arm again.

Almost there.

She could almost reach the lip, but it looked like a journey of a thousand leagues. She lunged, her hand seeking a hold, but she found nothing and she slid back.

Alena resumed her painstaking crawl. She wouldn't look behind her, certain Dezigeth watched her pathetic struggles.

Then she was up, no longer in danger of sliding back. She hauled the queen the last two paces and risked her first glance back. She had tunneled farther than she thought, and now Dezigeth stood a fair ways behind them, well out of bow shot. Not enough distance to rest easy, perhaps, but better than standing next to it. It could see them, but it spared them no attention.

Alena didn't question why. She got to her feet and threw the queen's good arm over her shoulders.

Now that they were on the surface, she moved as fast as she could, a jog that sometimes almost became a run. She spared no thought towards attempting to fight again. They had lost the day. Their best hope—their only hope—was to retreat and regroup.

Brandt and Ana were close. Alena saw them and made for them. Even from a distance, she knew something was wrong. Brandt wobbled on his feet as though drunk.

With a flash of insight, she understood why Dezigeth was distracted.

Brandt was a fool.

Although he was likely a fool that had saved their lives.

She reached the pair.

Before Ana could say anything, Alena passed the semiconscious queen to her. "Take her to the carriage and back to her palace. She needs a healer."

Ana looked at Brandt, her concern written in every line on her face.

"I'll bring him back if I can," Alena said.

Ana took the queen, threw her over a shoulder as though she was a sack of grain, and ran. Alena watched for a moment, dumbfounded. The woman wasn't that far from giving birth and was completing physical tasks Alena could only dream of.

Then her focus returned to Brandt. The former wolf-blade didn't have much time. It was a surprise that he still lived. Dezigeth could kill just as easily in the soulwalk as it could in the physical world.

Alena dropped into the soulwalk, then found Brandt. The link between them remained strong, and she followed it until she found herself at an all too familiar monastery.

Dezigeth and Brandt occupied the courtyard, with the warrior spread wide and suspended in the air. Dezigeth held Brandt's neck in one hand, and Brandt's face turned red.

The creature barely used any power to hold Brandt, and Alena broke its grip with ease.

Brandt fell to the courtyard stones, and Alena imagined herself beside him. She blinked and she was. There was no point staying here even a moment longer than necessary. "Brandt. Get us out of here. Quick."

Her worry was that he would be too distracted by the suffering he'd just experienced.

But Brandt was a wolfblade, and a warrior of consider-able skill. As soon as Dezigeth's hold was broken, he started recovering.

At Alena's command, the monastery vanished around them, and Alena found herself in the desert once again.

Brandt moved slowly, stunned by the quick changes of scenery. But as before, he adjusted quickly.

Alena looked back, seeing Dezigeth in the distance. Her blood ran cold at the sight of it. "We need to go. The queen is injured. We're returning to the palace."

Alena couldn't help but keep looking back at the creature as they half-ran, half-stumbled away. She expected it to attack every time she turned, but it never did.

They reached the carriage and began the return journey to the palace.

Brandt asked no questions about the fight, nor did Alena volunteer any information. She wasn't sure when she would be ready to relive that fight, but she didn't think it would be soon. Her whole body felt as though it had been rubbed over a grater.

Unfortunately, there would be no rest for her. They had barely passed through the gates to the palace grounds when Jace ran up to them. "It's good you're here. The queen is dying, and we need someone to soulwalk to her."

45

The hallways of the queen's palace were cold and unwelcoming at the best of times. No paintings or art decorated the walls. Most remained dark, day and night. In his weeks with the queen, Brandt wasn't sure he'd ever felt truly at ease. The only rooms he associated any pleasure with were the kitchen and the dining room.

As Brandt followed Jace and Alena through the now-lit passages, he imagined the palace vomiting them out. The hallways seemed to contract before his eyes. They were foreigners here, a poison in the bloodstream.

Brandt paused, bending over and putting his hand against the wall for support. He didn't feel sick, not exactly. More as though he was violently disgusted, but without reason. He looked at his hands and his stomach roiled. He closed his eyes and counted his breaths until the sensation faded.

Brandt caught up with the others a few moments later. They had carried the queen to one of the first rooms within the palace. The lanterns had been lit, giving him a clear view of the queen laid out on a table.

The only optimistic claim he could make was that her breathing was even. Unconscious, she looked more human than ever, less of an untouchable legend. He focused on her left arm, which appeared to be the worst wound of the battle. He couldn't remember seeing any injury like it in the years he'd served. A little flesh remained below the elbow, but not much. What remained had been burned. The same attack that had taken the arm had also cauterized it.

But he didn't know if she would survive.

Toren was speaking to Alena, and Brandt listened in. "—don't know what else to do. None of us are healers. Nor do we speak the language here, or if anyone else can even pass the barrier around the palace to help her."

Alena was nodding along as Toren spoke, stroking her chin as she thought.

"We think our best chance is to have you soulwalk to her," Toren finished.

Ana spoke before Alena could answer. "Or we could just kill her."

"No," Brandt said.

"We should consider it," Ana pushed. "She's a threat to the empire, and at least indirectly responsible for Hanns' death. Her demise would open up the way for Alena to control all five gates."

Brandt looked from face to face, horrified they would contemplate killing an unconscious, injured victim. Only Alena looked doubtful. He seized on that. If he could convince Alena, the others would follow.

"We can't," he said. "Without her, we're stranded on Palagia. And she's a strong fighter, with more years of study than any of us. We would be killing our greatest weapon."

Alena wavered, but said nothing.

Brandt took a step toward her. "Alena, back in the

empire, you taught me that how we live matters. I thought you were an idealistic fool. But I believe you now. The queen isn't innocent, but we don't fight her like this."

Alena bit her lower lip and turned away, pacing the room while moving away from them. How strong was the temptation of two more gates? Strong enough to reverse the positions they'd once held?

"He's right," Alena finally declared. "If nothing else, she has more knowledge about the gates than anyone alive. She can't die before she shares everything she knows. I'll soul-walk to her."

Brandt stepped between Alena and the queen. "Let me."

She questioned him with a look.

"I've spent the most time with her, and I suspect I have the best chance of evading some of her defenses. I'm the most likely to survive soulwalking to her, and if not, I'm also less valuable than you," he said to Alena.

Alena almost argued the point, then pressed her lips together and nodded. "Be careful. I can't imagine she'll make it easy." She turned to the others. "I'm going up to the wall to see what I can, and to be ready if another attack comes this way."

Toren and Jace offered to join her, and soon the trio was out the door, leaving him alone with the queen and Ana. "You could leave, too, if you want," he said.

"I'll stay."

Brandt nodded and took a deep breath. He pulled up a chair and dropped into the soulwalk.

When he connected with the queen, his mind created a landscape before him. He stood on a featureless plain, barren except for a wall before him, one eerily similar to the wall that surrounded the queen's palace. From within the wall he heard a slow, deep, booming sound, repeated about every two heartbeats.

The queen was in there, and the wall protected her.

He studied the wall for a moment. It was several times his height and perfectly smooth. There were no handholds to climb. Although this was a soulwalk, and Brandt's abilities were limited only by his imagination, he didn't attempt to jump or fly over the wall.

This was the queen, after all. Anything that might occur to him would be defended against. The wall was impassable, no matter what openings he thought he saw.

So he went to the gate, raised his hand, and knocked, willing the sound to be loud enough to be heard for leagues.

Then he waited.

Time was strange in the soulwalk, but he waited for some time. No response came from within the walls. The low beat remained unchanged.

Brandt knocked again.

The queen heard him. He had no doubt of that. But she remained silent within her self-made prison.

When he felt he had waited an appropriate amount of time, Brandt knocked a third time. He wouldn't give up, and he wouldn't leave.

He returned to waiting, but this time the gate swung open. The queen stood on the other side, looking hollowed out, her soul peering out through her eyes from a distant place. Brandt didn't step through the gate, wary. "May I enter?"

She looked at him for ten beats of his heart in perfect silence. Whatever injuries Dezigeth had inflicted upon her in the physical world paled in comparison to the deeper wounds she now displayed. But she nodded and stepped aside.

Within the walls there was nothing but the queen. This wasn't a memory of home, but a construction.

He turned to her as she waited silently. She offered no opening. His first words might very well be the only ones she afforded him.

"We need you," he said.

"No. There is no need. It is inevitable. I should have seen that lifetimes ago."

"Your people need you. The world needs you."

She shook her head. "It never has. Leave now."

He felt her gathering some of her energy. A minuscule amount compared to what she was capable of, but still more than he could fight. She intended to throw him out of the soulwalk. "If you give up, everything you've done will be meaningless."

She withheld her blow. "It *is* meaningless."

"Not yet."

"You still hope?" Her disbelief here felt like a physical burden on his shoulders, threatening to bring him to his knees. "You've seen what it can do, and now you've watched it beat me with ease."

Her words came faster and faster, a torrent that pushed him back. "Can you imagine the years I've spent, first clawing my way to power, just another orphaned child after the first visitation? The years of study and training? To have a plan that took not months or years to bear fruit, but whole lifetimes? I've given, and I've sacrificed, all in preparation to be the one person standing between these creatures and this planet."

He couldn't imagine the suffering Sofra now endured. But he was pretty certain of the path forward.

"Fight with me. Hope lives as long as we draw breath."

"Why? There's no point in fighting a battle we can't win."

"Can you see the future?"

The question caught her attention. "Of course not. But I still recognize a hopeless battle when I see one."

"If we only fight the battles we know we can win, we lose everything that matters."

"What?"

"Life isn't a question of why. We could search for reasons for our whole lives and get no closer to understanding. Life is a question of how."

She blinked rapidly.

He continued before she could interrupt. "I don't know what your purpose is. I can't say why you're here. No one can. But I do know that you have more strength and knowledge than anyone else. Everything you've done, everything you've learned, can still be used. It wasn't for nothing." He paused. "But only if you fight."

She still hadn't thrown him out of her world, which he supposed was a small victory.

"It's still hopeless," she said.

"Just because you can't see the end doesn't mean there's no hope. Perhaps we fall here. It's certainly possible. But we can never predict the effect our actions will have in the future. Even you, with all your years, can't predict tomorrow any better than I can. Maybe even our deaths, in some way we can't understand, prepare the way for those who come after us."

She shook her head. "How? How do you keep going, even when some part of you has to know the truth?"

Brandt smiled. "I don't know if you've noticed, but my wife is pregnant. I'm not just fighting for myself. I'm fighting for those yet to come."

"You're a fool."

Brandt laughed, feeling suddenly lighter than he had

before. The sickness that had assailed him, the poison that lingered after his meeting with Dezigeth, was gone. "It's been said before. But will you fight with me?"

For a long moment he feared he had failed.

She nodded.

Brandt bowed, hiding his relief, then dropped out of the soulwalk gracefully.

"How is she?" Ana asked.

Brandt looked at the queen. "Strong, still. She's a fighter."

"Are you angry at me, for what I suggested?"

Brandt shook his head. "It's important to ask the question. I'm actually glad we considered it."

"Really?"

"Yes. Because it reaffirmed what it is we stand for."

Ana eyed him with an unreadable expression. "Your time with the queen has changed you more than I think you realize."

"Hopefully for the better."

She nodded. "I think so."

Just then, the whole palace thundered as the world shook. At first, Brandt worried that they were under attack again, but when no further impacts came, he doubted it.

"What was that?" Ana asked.

Brandt shook his head. He wished he knew.

A third voice answered weakly. "It was the creature," the queen said. "It just finished building its own gate."

46

The wall under Alena's feet shook as the ripple of force passed through the ground. Thankfully, the wall withstood the assault. Some buildings within the city weren't so lucky. Plumes of dust rose as structures collapsed. Homes and workplaces, all destroyed.

Alena gripped the stone wall more tightly. She should help in the city, but just climbing the stairs to reach the top had taken a tremendous effort. Lacerations ran up her arms and blood mixed with sand had caked into the cuts. Infection was a very real possibility, but she had no healing supplies on hand, nor any idea where to procure any. Toren had gone searching.

As much as she wanted to help the victims in the city below, she couldn't even help herself.

And off in the distance, Dezigeth had finished its working. The gate it built thrummed with power, something she sensed even a league away.

The sound of footsteps behind her caused her to turn around. Jace climbed the last of the steps and stood by her side. He looked off in the distance as the light faded. There was nothing to see, though. "What happened?"

"It finished."

"What is it for?"

Alena shook her head slowly. "It might strengthen Dezigeth. Or perhaps it serves as a gate for more of its kind to come through."

"So, not good, then."

Despite herself, she laughed. "No. Probably not good."

They watched the last of the light fade. Now it appeared as though nothing but desert waited beyond the walls of the city.

"We should do something to help the people down there," she said.

"No, you should find someone to take care of your wounds. Then it looks like you should eat a feast and lay down for a day or two."

"I'm fine."

"You're barely able to stand, and you look like you just emerged from a week in the wild. And the wild won."

"Thanks." She paused. "But we do need to help them."

"No, we don't. If you burn out trying to help everyone, you'll be too worn down to save anyone. We need you to fight for all of us. Cold as it sounds, that matters more than anything happening down there."

"That's exactly the kind of thinking that leads to the queen's actions."

Though she intended the words to cut at him, he shrugged. "Because she's followed that path too far. And you'll go too far the other way, if just to prove your point. But you can't. We need you to focus on what you do better than anyone else."

"What's that?"

"Find the answers. You've learned more about our gates than anyone in the empire. Now we know, without doubt, that brute force won't work against that creature. So we need to find another way, and I can't think of anyone better than you."

Alena turned from the wall. "Help me to my chambers?"

Jace extended his arm for her to take. Though she would never say so out loud, she wasn't sure how well she would have handled the stairs on her own.

Too often, she thought of him as a child. Part of it, she supposed, was their history. She'd spent almost two decades thinking of him only as her obnoxious and energetic younger brother. And then she had vanished from his life, forced away from their home by the consequences of her actions. When she'd returned, years later, he was a young man. She'd missed his transition from boyhood to manhood. There was just Jace the boy, then a blink of memory, and then Jace the soldier. And the memories of Jace the boy far outnumbered those of him grown up.

But he was grown up, in more ways than one. She still saw the youthful exuberance that had so annoyed her as a more self-possessed child. But now he had focused that energy, sharpened it like the edge of a blade. And it was tempered by experience, from Kye's compulsion to the battles he'd fought.

She couldn't ask for a better brother.

And in this case, he was right. She needed rest. She needed time.

They made it back to her chambers, where Toren was waiting along with a compelled servant. The servant carried towels and a case. Toren gestured to the servant. "Healer. Compliments of the queen."

Alena lay down on the bed and allowed the woman to

begin her duty. Some unspoken message passed between Toren and Jace, and Jace left the room.

Toren's presence reassured her. The woman who cleaned her wounds worked effectively enough, but there was a lack of gentleness to her movements. With Toren watching on, though, Alena slowly drifted off to sleep, despite the pain of her injuries.

When she woke, it was to a dark room.

She could hear Toren's breath, deep and even, but not asleep. The difference was subtle, but they had spent enough time together that she could tell. "Toren?"

No response.

She shifted in the bed and sat up. Her arms and legs had been wrapped in bandages. Her head pounded and her throat was parched. But she was alive, and that was something. "Toren?"

Again there was no response. His breathing didn't alter at all, as near as she could tell.

Her heart pounded a bit faster, but she reached out in the soulwalk. He was there, and she followed him.

She found him before the representation of Dezigeth's gate. He studied it from afar.

Her first instinct was to caution him, but tossed the idea away as useless. Toren well knew the risk he was taking, and was a skilled enough soulwalker to protect himself.

"What do you see?"

"It's breathtaking," he said.

Her gaze followed his, and she took in the structure before them. Though they didn't dare get close enough to attract Dezigeth's ire, she understood how he felt. Their gates were a masterpiece, but what Dezigeth had created surpassed them. Tisha had spent her whole life learning how to create a gate. How much more time had been needed to learn how to make this?

The speed with which it had been created likewise astounded her. A gate was a lifetime's worth of effort, but Dezigeth had built this in days. All of which pointed to the vast differences in ability between them.

As they watched, the gate began to shift. Alena figured it out quickly enough, the technique an echo of one she'd experienced only a few days ago.

Something was coming through the gate.

A lot of somethings.

47

B randt's mind frayed at its edges, the strings of his calm pulled by events far beyond his control. The night past had been a long and restless one. To see the queen shaken, hiding away in her mental fortress like that, made his knees quake.

He hadn't realized, until that moment, just how much faith he had put in Sofra. The queen, after all, had dedicated her entire life to this. But when he saw the queen, broken in her own mind, his own hope shattered.

Despair knocked, demanding admittance to his mind.

He'd gone to bed hoping to make things right with Ana. But she had been exhausted, and turned over and fell asleep before Brandt even found the words to say.

He spent the night worrying interchangeably about Dezigeth and Ana. In both cases, the sands of time slipped through his fingers, robbing him of options. The idea of dying with so much unresolved stole his sleep.

Then Alena reported that the gate had opened and *something* was coming through. An army, she suspected.

Alena had soulwalked toward the new visitors. Unfortunately, most of her efforts had been wasted. Either the creatures had some technique to hide their minds from her exploration, or their minds were so different she couldn't read them. Either way, she couldn't soulwalk to them the way she could humans.

Still, she had gathered at least some information. The new invaders weren't like Dezigeth. So that was something. The downside, though, was that the creatures that were coming through were numerous.

Very numerous.

Unfortunately, there was little for Brandt to do, no action that could ease his mind. The queen recovered in her own private chambers, refusing to show her face to the world. But she did send out a group of scouts to see what they could learn.

Brandt spent the morning training out in the yard, then searched for Ana, but she still slumbered. The morning crawled by, but the scouts never returned. At noon, the queen sent out more, twice the number she had sent the first time, but Brandt saw little point. The result would be the same.

He stomped around the yard of the palace as the second group of scouts left, his feet barely keeping pace with his thoughts.

The queen lacked the energy and the will to do much more. Gradually she slipped back into her role of leader, but her healing would take time. Before long, Brandt's restlessness grew to the point where he would wait no longer. They needed information, and they needed it now. He heard Ana scolding him in his imagination, but he could stay safe.

He left the palace and found a corner where no one could watch him. Never having tried this before, he wasn't eager for an audience. Thankfully, most of the citizens of

Valan had resumed their habit of remaining indoors. He used his gatestone to pull a section of stone from the street. He flattened it until it was a long and narrow oval, just barely wide enough for his feet. Then he made himself light, stepped onto the stone, and lifted it off the ground with the aid of his gatestone. In a moment, he was in the air.

The technique took a little time to master. He'd never developed his lightness as much as some others, and it was key to making the technique work well. But his balance was steady and the gatestone gave him more than enough strength. In time, he was floating on the flattened stone and flying with ease and control.

Brandt practiced a few maneuvers, getting better at moving both the stone and him through the air. If the invaders didn't want him near, he wanted to have some techniques on hand for escaping. Soon he felt comfortable enough to make his approach.

As he flew toward the foreign gate and the invading army, he couldn't help but imagine a future in which anyone could surpass the cost. Techniques and power like he was currently using could change the world, not just by revolutionizing transport, but warfare, trade, and more.

But unfortunately, it could never happen. The cost remained, a wall that limited most affinities to tricks and tools of small convenience. Brandt guessed that even the Etari with their small gatestones wouldn't be able to channel enough power to do this. This gift of flight would never be available to most people.

He didn't have much time to daydream. Ahead of him he saw numerous dots, black against the washed-out colors of the sand. He pushed the stone he stood on even higher, unwilling to risk whatever fate had befallen the scouts.

Before long he floated high above the invading army.

It took him some time to believe what he saw.

At first glance, he hovered over what appeared to be a camp, but it was like no camp he had ever seen. There was no discernible order, and thousands of the creatures seemed to ebb and flow to no discernible pattern. Unlike an imperial camp, set up in organized rows and sections, there was no order to this at all.

He floated too high to make out the details he desired, so he dropped lower, picking up speed.

His first clear view of the invaders almost caused him to lose his balance.

The creatures were not human. They walked on four legs, and although Brandt couldn't be sure from the air, they appeared slightly shorter than the average human. Their bodies were thin and elongated, and they possessed what appeared to be two long arms without an elbow joint. There were three appendages at the end of each arm, but each arm, the part that Brandt's mind labeled as a forearm, though the title wasn't correct, tapered on one side to a sharp edge. Their heads, if they could be called that, rested on squat necks and were roughly triangular.

They resembled nothing that Brandt had ever seen.

A few launched spears in his direction, and although their strength was sufficient for the task, their aim was not. Brandt had seen more than enough. He escaped high into the air and began his flight back to the palace.

He had to warn the others what was coming.

48

A lena knocked on the door to the queen's chambers, then bent her ear toward the heavy wooden door to listen for any response. The queen's voice, muffled but clear enough to make out, called for her to enter.

The interior of the queen's chambers was no more welcoming than any other room in the palace. The walls were as bare as the floor, and the furniture was minimal and functional. Alena didn't think she could fall asleep in one of the chairs if she tried. Though the room was plenty warm, a chill ran through her.

The queen sat at a small writing desk. "One moment," she said.

Alena waited. She noted the heavy stones placed near the top of the missive that weighted the paper down, allowing the queen to write without it sliding across the desk. Her handwriting flowed across the paper smoothly enough, but Alena caught the small motions in the amputated left arm.

Her body's memories of the manner the task had once been completed.

The queen rarely left her chambers since the fight with Dezigeth. At first, Alena believed it was due to the extent of her injuries and the need for recovery. Watching her now, she wasn't so sure. Despite the injuries, the queen largely looked well.

Sofra finished her letter, folded it awkwardly, and sealed it. Alena watched in silence. With two hands, the task would have been the work of a moment. With one, it was painful to watch. She didn't offer her help, though. She suspected it would be unwelcome.

The queen finally turned to her. "You've spoken with Brandt?"

Alena nodded.

"It means to wipe us out. Every single human on this world."

Alena had come to the same conclusion. It explained the gate and the forces that even now continued to pour through. "Do you have any ideas?"

"None I'm satisfied with. My first priority would be to destroy the gate, but Dezigeth sits beside it night and day. And so I'm forced to sit in my palace and watch as the invasion establishes their post without resistance."

Sofra's voice almost cracked.

It was the hardest steel that shattered the easiest. Alena's father had taught her that well.

She led the conversation to less fraught waters. "You have a plan, though."

"Not much of one. First, we need better knowledge. How do they fight? What strategies do they use? What are their strengths and weaknesses? How hard are they to kill? One of my armies arrived late yesterday evening. Later today I intend to send a small force forward to skirmish with the invaders. I want them to test the enemy and live to return with the lessons."

Alena followed the logic well enough. She was no military commander, but it sounded reasonable. "So, why am I here?"

The queen glanced away at the question, casting her eyes to the floor, and Alena understood. "You want me to join them in your place."

"I do. Someone needs to test Dezigeth as well, to see how it will respond to various challenges."

Alena's first thought was to tell the queen to do it herself. These were her lands and her soldiers. She was the stronger of the two of them. The loss of a hand didn't change that.

Perhaps it did, though.

The queen's eyes still wandered the floor. Physically, there was no reason her wounds should hamper her abilities with the gates. But maybe the wounds Alena saw weren't the ones tormenting the queen. If Sofra's confidence had been that badly shaken, Alena would be the more reasonable choice.

Of course, it could be a ploy. On the front lines, Dezigeth might kill her, opening the way for the queen's control of the other gates.

The request didn't feel that way, though.

Alena believed the queen, but it didn't ease all her doubts. Supporting troops was a role completely foreign to her. She imagined unleashing a wall of fire and the death that would follow. Her stomach sickened at the thought. "I'm not sure I can."

"It will be them or us," the queen said. "I'll admit, I never possessed your reluctance about killing, but if there was ever a time it was justified, that time is now."

In the end, it wasn't as though she had a choice. Alena nodded.

LATER THAT DAY she found herself mounted on a horse, not quite sure she had made the right choice. A group of a hundred Lolani warriors marched before them, armed with sword, shield, spear, and bow. When the queen said she intended to test the invaders, she'd spoken true.

Alena rode well behind the column. The queen's instructions to her had been clear. At some point she was to fight. They wanted some idea of when Dezigeth would stir to action.

Beside her, Jace, Toren, and Brandt all guarded her. She was still riding for battle, but she would be the best protected person on the field. Any general would be proud of such protection, but it did little more than make her uneasy.

When their journey was about halfway complete, Toren rode closer to her. He spoke low so the others wouldn't overhear. "You'll do well."

She managed half a smile. "Do I look that nervous?"

"And then some."

"If I do this, I'll be guilty of the same crimes I accuse the queen of." She held up a hand to stop his reply. "I know. I understand the reasons, and I know it needs to be done. At least, I can't think of a better alternative. But what makes me any different than her, once I do this?"

Toren didn't even have to think hard about the question. "None of this would bother her."

"That hardly matters."

Brandt spoke up. Alena hadn't even noticed him also edge

closer. "Nonsense. Toren's right. It makes all the difference in the world. Back when I was a wolfblade, I had a practice that I tried to honor." He paused. "Whenever I killed an enemy with my affinity, I didn't turn away, not if I had a choice. I saw it too often with other wolfblades. They refused to acknowledge what they had done. I knew that if I could ever kill an enemy with fire and not feel anything, I'd gone too far."

They let Alena ride in silence, digesting their wisdom. She looked to each of her companions in turn. "Will you stop me, if I go too far? Or even if I'm about to?"

"We will," Jace answered.

Their first contact with the invaders came sooner than Alena expected. A small group of the creatures, no more than fifteen, wandering beyond the main camp, came upon them. "Scouts, or perimeter guards," Brandt decided.

When the invaders spotted the Lolani advance, they turned and charged directly. Alena looked to Brandt, hoping for an explanation, but he was leaning forward in his saddle, his attention focused completely on the battle. Why would the invaders attack, though? They were outnumbered almost ten to one.

Arrows raced from the Lolani side into the sky, and when they hit, creatures fell and didn't rise again. The scouts now numbered less than ten, but still they advanced, their charge eerily silent. Alena shuddered as she watched the creatures move, the four legs lending them a gait that was distinctly not of this world.

Three of the creatures carried spears, and they threw these as they came in range. The Lolani in the front of the column carried large rectangular shields, though, and the spears were stopped before they reached the warriors.

Alena saw a rock spinning beside her which suddenly

disappeared. Another of the creatures fell. She glanced over at Toren, who had a satisfied look on his face.

The remaining creatures ran headfirst into the wall of shields. They swung their arms, the sharp edges that ran along the forearms cutting into the shields. Their efforts halted the Lolani advance, but not for long. Spears darted out of the shield wall, and the creatures dropped soon after.

Almost as soon as the battle began, it was over. The skirmish had been a decisive victory for the Lolani, but how could it have been anything else? The creatures had no protection, yet they charged without concern for their lives. And they had all died without a sound.

The Lolani paused to check their equipment. Their shields bore deep scars where the creatures' arms had struck, but they had held. Brandt and Toren dismounted and examined the creatures more closely. Alena rode her horse close, but felt no need to drop to the ground.

Everything about the creatures, from their triangular heads to their grotesquely sharpened arms, screamed a wrongness. They didn't belong on this world.

Brandt stood up from his examination. "They die easy. A lot of these wounds are in different places, yet they all seemed to be immediately fatal."

"Why did they charge?" Alena asked. It was the question she couldn't get out of her head.

"Couldn't say," Brandt said. "It doesn't make any sense, especially if they were scouts. The whole point of scouts is to warn the main party."

Toren tapped Brandt on the shoulder. "I think they did."

Alena followed Toren's outstretched finger.

Off in the distance, several hundred of the creatures charged toward them.

49

Brandt couldn't say for sure how many of the creatures advanced on their position. They maintained no order, no rows that aided in the estimation of their strength. They seethed forward like one giant organism made of hundreds of smaller parts. As near as he could tell, though, their little advance party was outnumbered at least five to one.

He cast a worried glance back at Alena. Although it seemed that the creatures died easily, the sheer numbers might be enough to overwhelm the queen's forces. In the first brief skirmish Alena's gifts hadn't been required, but if they wanted to guarantee their victory here, they would need her. Was she up to the task?

The color of her skin and the way she clutched her reins as though they were some sort of lifeline didn't fill him with hope.

But they needed her. And the Lolani needed him.

"They need help," he said, gesturing to the soldiers ahead of them. "And I want experience fighting them."

The comment earned him skeptical looks from his other companions, but Alena seemed to understand.

"Be safe," she said. "I don't think even two gates would protect my life if I came back without you."

Brandt offered a small bow of acknowledgment, then ran toward the Lolani soldiers as they prepared to fight.

He worried that the Lolani might not accept him. But his fears were unfounded. One of the warriors, a tall female whom he assumed was a unit commander, welcomed him into her own squad, all carrying the wicked swords of the Lolani.

As Brandt became one with the others, stepping deep into the mass of people, he took one last glance at the rapidly approaching horde. Alena had told him to be safe, but as he watched them approach, the truth was that his safety was in her hands. If she failed them, then every man and woman he stood with would fall.

He wished he didn't doubt her as he did. She could be roused to violence, if it was required. But she had a kind heart that didn't belong on these unforgiving sands.

Then he was swallowed up by the Lolani, a couple of ranks behind the shield line. He took a moment and readied himself, glancing at the warriors to his left and his right. They held themselves well, and he saw none of the worry that often accompanied an inexperienced warrior. They all looked forward only, ready to meet this new threat. He stood among veterans.

This battle opened in much the same way as the first. When the creatures were within range, the Lolani archers unleashed their arrows. Unlike the previous encounter, they didn't stop with a single volley. Instead, once the range was reached, archers fired as quickly as they could nock and aim another arrow.

Though his vision was obscured by the people and shields in front of him, Brandt could well imagine the waves of enemies being taken down by the archers. With no shields and plenty of vulnerable body parts, it couldn't be any other way.

For several heartbeats, that was all there was. Arrows hissed as they passed overhead.

Yet something about the charge and the defense struck Brandt as unnatural. It took him a few moments before he placed it.

It was the silence.

The Lolani let out no war cries as they attacked, and the invading creatures made no sound when they died. It left Brandt with an eerie feeling, as though he wasn't actually in the middle of a battle, but standing instead at some target range as the archers fired overhead.

The illusion was shattered moments later. A loud barking order was issued to the shield line and the bulky soldiers there planted themselves firmly, embedding the bottom of their long shields in the sand and bracing their bodies.

The commander's timing was perfect. Pointed spears punched through the shields, and one warrior groaned as the point cut through his arm.

Besides that single injury, they had weathered the volley unscathed. Their good fortune wouldn't hold much longer.

If it hadn't been so obvious, his thought almost would have been prophetic. Again, there was no final shout to intimidate the enemy, no screams that boiled the blood. There was another command issued in Lolani, spears were thrust out through the gaps in the shields, and the battle began in earnest.

It only took a handful of heartbeats for the tide of this

battle to turn against the Lolani. The creatures who first struck at the shield wall died quickly, but their companions simply swarmed around, forming a horseshoe around the small defending party. Those soldiers stationed on the edges were armed with spears and fought valiantly, but the numbers were overwhelming. The creatures packed themselves in tight, managing to squeeze two or three opponents against every Lolani warrior. No matter how talented a spear a warrior might be, there was no defense against so many attacks at once.

For the first time, Brandt saw firsthand the terrible damage those sharp arms caused. They cut through flesh like steel, and the creatures used them well. Without the equivalent of an elbow joint, the creatures essentially had swords for arms, controlled by strong and surprisingly flexible shoulder joints.

Those on the outer ranks soon fell, nasty cuts and gashes covering their bodies.

Where Brandt had once been safe, he now found the first creatures beginning to reach his position. They attacked with abandon, and Brandt brought his sword up to defend himself.

Two of the creatures reached him at once, and his sword flashed quickly to block the flurry of strikes. When sword met flesh, sword won. The creature's arms, sharp as they were, weren't a match for imperial steel. But their arms did block otherwise fatal cuts, and a blow to the arm seemed to be one of the few attacks that didn't kill the creatures.

Brandt turned aside another two attacks in short order, finding several openings to stab into. The creatures fell to his sword as soon as he struck.

Brandt stood over them, flush with victory.

In many ways, he didn't understand this new world he

had been thrust into. The soulwalk and the powers of the gates still left him reeling. But this—this he could do.

He glanced over to where Alena should be. He suspected she was safe. The creatures were much more focused on the Lolani forces than on the couple of horses standing well behind the battle.

Still, she should have acted by now. Alena had to see that they were beset on all sides and losing lives. They had gotten enough information about these creatures, who were terrifying in their simplicity. They attacked and attacked, and were more than willing to die without thought.

But then Brandt no longer had time to worry. The creatures broke through once again and he raised his sword to defend himself. He parried and thrust at the first creature to attack, bringing it down with one smooth cut.

Two took its place and Brandt was forced to step back just to maintain solid footing. So long as he stayed in front of his enemies he could handle their attacks. Two at once was difficult but manageable, but he feared the moment when three fought him. Strong as he was, no swordsman was fast enough to fight off so many attacks. Even now, a single mistake would be fatal.

The press got thicker, and the bodies of his allies began to fall faster beside him, the edges of the unit whittled away. Brandt's protection to either side faltered, and the dust in the air from hundreds of trampling feet began choking him.

He channeled his own gatestone, lashing out at those nearest him. They died quickly but were replaced even faster by others just as eager for blood.

Brandt summoned flame and cleared a bit of space in front of him, but a spear flashed through the fire and cut the air less than a hand's width from his head. Brandt lost his focus and the fire evaporated.

The creatures piled through into the newly open space.

They possessed no fear, no sense of self-preservation. They weren't terribly hard to kill, but their numbers and their sheer relentlessness intimidated him.

He took the single heartbeat of peace and savored it as the creatures rose their arms to attack again. He looked for Alena, but the dust obscured his view of anything farther than a dozen paces away.

He hoped she was safe, because they weren't going to last much longer.

50

Alena's eyes locked on the battle happening before her, unable to look away. Even as blowing dust rose to obscure her sight, her gaze remained fixed. The closest she had come to a fight of this scale had been many years ago, with a fight between a small Lolani invasion and the Etari. Memories of that fight rose unbidden. The cost for the Etari clans who fought on that bloody day had been high.

As horrible as that day had been, she had at least found refuge in understanding the event. The Lolani had been trying to escort an acolyte to the gate outside of Landow. They had given their lives in the attempt.

The war that these creatures fought defied explanations. They charged forward, heedless of the slaughter of their fellows. When one fell, Alena saw no outpourings of grief, nor any suddenly inspired fighting. The creatures just continued their advance, as though they didn't even notice the casualties they suffered.

They were inhuman in their indifference.

Alena couldn't bring herself to do anything but watch.

She felt the power of the gates at her fingertips. It longed for release and strained against her control. But she contained it.

Before long, the creatures would overwhelm the Lolani soldiers. Even before the dust stole her clear view of the field, Alena had seen a number of the queen's brave warriors fall, cut by those monstrous arms. One on one, Alena would bet that each Lolani was a stronger fighter than the creatures, but this was no series of duels. This fight was about numbers, not skill.

Alena finally tore her eyes from the battle to stare off into the distance. Somewhere out there, Dezigeth waited. In her nightmares, the moment she unleashed the power of her gates, it would rouse itself to action, destroying her for daring to fight for her warriors.

There was no way of knowing. Dezigeth's actions didn't mirror human behaviors. With such power, it could simply pass over the land, leaving only a scorched and inhospitable world.

But it didn't, leaving these creatures to perform the task of wiping out humanity. And they would. They were numerous enough to crash over the world like a wave, burying everything in their wake, leaving behind nothing but the memories of human civilization.

Alena squinted. At the edges of the cloud of dust, she thought she saw a terror that froze her heart. A moment later, she was sure.

Some of the creatures behind the front lines were stopping, the Lolani scouting party temporarily forgotten. They used their arms to chop up their fallen fellows, then began to eat. Alena's stomach did a somersault as she watched, threatening to eject the little food she'd eaten that day.

Jace's call grounded her. She ripped her gaze away from the nightmare and looked at him. He gestured to the battle. "They need you."

Alena nodded. This had gone on long enough. She feared Dezigeth's reaction, but that was no excuse. She began weaving the affinities at her command.

Then faltered before she could unleash them.

She knew these creatures were here to kill all that she loved. And they ate their own upon the battlefield, so death meant little to them.

She had no reason to show mercy.

And Brandt was in that storm of dust. She saw a burst of flame, short-lived, flash through the battle, and knew he was still alive.

But not for much longer.

She wove the attack again, and again failed to release it.

She didn't want to be the one who massacred a people, no matter how she justified it. Against the gates, those creatures had no chance.

In all her life, most of the enemies she'd fought against were stronger than her. She'd been fighting for her immediate survival. None of that was true here. Now that she had the power of the gates, she was on the other end. She had the ability to be the bully in a fight.

A glance at Jace brought back a memory long buried, of a fight between Niles Arrowood and some poor victim at their academy. Niles had been the aggressor then, and she'd stepped in to intervene without a second thought.

If she unleashed the gates, it would bring her one step closer to becoming a person like Niles.

And that terrified her more than losing the fight.

Flame flashed in front of her again. She saw Toren and Jace edging closer, worried both for her and for Brandt.

She wondered, if only for a moment, if Brandt had embedded with the Lolani for just this reason. That some part of him had known how deep her fear of her power ran. And he had risked his own life, betting she would overcome that fear.

"Alena," Jace said, "if those creatures destroy the Lolani, it's only going to take them a few moments to decide to attack us. And that would do some real harm to my sense of self-preservation."

His words wormed their way into her mind, settling like a weight on some invisible scale in her thoughts. She still feared her power, but if she didn't take action soon, it wouldn't just be Brandt in danger. It would be Jace and Toren, two of the greatest loves of her life.

The scale tipped.

Alena wove the power one more time and unleashed her abilities.

Unable to see the exact lines of the battle, she had to guess, and so she drew a line of fire out at a distance she was sure was safe.

She didn't need to end this battle alone. She just needed to give the Lolani a break from the constant stream of reinforcements. They could take care of the rest.

The wall of fire she created roared several times higher than the height of the tallest warriors, reminding her of the attack Dezigeth had used against her and the queen. It walked across the battlefield, killing the creatures near the front lines and those behind, eating their brethren. Not a single scream answered her actions. The creatures, as always, died silently, even under the prolonged agony of the flames.

Alena swept the battlefield as well as she could.

She called upon wind, blowing the hanging dust away.

It allowed her to see the fighting still happening.

Hundreds of the creatures lay dead where her flames had already passed, but if anything, she had been too safe in her estimations. The front lines of the battle were well inside where the fires had begun.

Still, her actions turned the tide of the battle in favor of the Lolani. The queen's warriors dispatched the creatures efficiently, and now, for the first time, there weren't more creatures filling the gaps. Slowly, the battle ended.

Now that she had taken the first step, Alena found it frighteningly easy to continue using her affinities. She used her gate-assisted strength to attack pockets of the creatures, preferring stone to fire in the more confined spaces. Toren helped as well.

Eventually the battlefield fell silent, the Lolani victorious. Alena looked off in the distance, alert for any signs of Dezigeth or another wave of the creatures. But none came. The vast majority of creatures remained near the gate, and Dezigeth didn't stir, even in response to her unveiling her power against its forces.

The damage had been done, though. Of the hundred soldiers that had departed the city, Alena didn't think that half remained. Those that stood continued their tasks, though. They examined the corpses of their enemies, looking for weaknesses and learning just how difficult the creatures were to kill.

A lone figure emerged from the group, walking toward them. He was covered in dust and splatters of blood, but walked well and seemed largely unharmed. Alena released a deep breath. She didn't want to imagine having to return to Ana and report the loss of her husband.

Brandt stopped maybe twenty paces from the three of

them and met Alena's eyes. "Come with me," he said, more than a note of command in his voice.

Alena didn't even think to argue. Whatever he wanted, the tone of his voice allowed for no argument. She dismounted and followed him.

When they were out of earshot, he spoke quietly. "You almost didn't, right?"

Alena nodded. She waited for his condemnation.

"I understand, you know."

She glanced at him, then returned her gaze forward. Yes, he had one of the largest gatestones in the world, but it couldn't compare to the power of a full gate. The only one who might understand was the queen, but they were entirely different people. He couldn't know.

It was as though he guessed her thoughts, and they didn't bother him at all. "When I was young and my affinity developed, I didn't like to use it, especially once I entered the army. I wanted to prove myself, so when I fought, I fought without my affinities. In fact, I was almost passed up as a wolfblade candidate because no one believed I could control fire."

The story caught Alena's attention. She knew little of Brandt before he became a wolfblade.

"It's apparently not all that uncommon," Brandt said. "Most people have a reluctance to turn their affinities against others. The army actually prefers that attitude to its opposite. Even limited by the cost, affinities can kill. Perhaps the most valuable lesson I learned as a young wolfblade was that an affinity was a tool, no different than a sword. I didn't need to fear my affinity, but I did need to learn how to control it and when to use it. I think the gates are the same, but on a different scale."

"They didn't have a chance," Alena said.

"No, they didn't. But they did have a choice. They chose to attack us."

It seemed slim comfort, but Alena noticed that they weren't heading toward the rest of the Lolani. They were making for the first areas she had cleared with her flame. Her step faltered.

Brandt extended his arm for her to take. "I know. But you need to see this."

Alena slowed to a stop, then took a step back, understanding now what Brandt wanted of her. She shook her head.

"You wanted us to make sure that you never became like the queen," Brandt said, his voice patient. "This is the best way that I know how. You can't turn away from what you've done. You need to look at it. You need to know what it costs. And then you'll know that you'll never abuse this gift."

"If I see it, I'm not sure I'll be able to bring myself to use the gates again."

His eyes bore into her. "Then you aren't strong enough to be using them in the first place."

She swallowed hard. Then she took a step forward and grabbed his arm. At the very least, she wouldn't have to take this journey alone.

They walked to where the creatures had fallen. Many were burned beyond recognition, but she saw enough. The smell burned her nostrils, and nothing moved before them.

Though her legs were unsteady, they carried her through the battlefield.

Brandt didn't make her stay long.

"Will you be able to use your power again?" Brandt asked.

"I think so."

"Good, because I fear you will need to before too long."

Alena glanced behind them, afraid that she might see another dust cloud. There was none. But Brandt's prediction would come true. Of that, she had no doubt.

And she suspected the battles to come would put this one to shame.

51

Brandt and Ana didn't fall asleep until well after the sun had gone down. He had insisted that they speak, refusing to delay their reconciliation any longer. The conversation alone hadn't solved everything, but it gave him the opportunity to share his feelings and his fears. He was sure it was nothing Ana hadn't guessed or figured out on her own, but the very act of talking began the mending of their relationship.

When they lay down that night, Ana rolled toward him, resting her arm and leg over him. He felt the child within her, kicking against his side as though fighting for more space. It made him smile. The child wasn't even born yet and was already making demands.

Fatherhood was a dream that became a little more real with every passing day. When Ana had first told him she was pregnant, he hadn't quite believed it was true, and had only slowly grown accustomed to the idea.

Then her stomach had begun to expand, bringing the dream that much closer to reality. And now he could feel his child kick. His new future was almost real, but still not quite.

He didn't think he would truly feel like a father until the moment the baby emerged from Ana's womb.

Brandt would do anything to make that moment come true. No fight, no challenge, would stop him from being present for his child's birth.

He fell asleep to thoughts of the future comforting him, and the sounds of his wife gently snoring beside him.

He woke to the sound of panicked bells ringing throughout the city.

His eyes snapped open and he sat up. He went to the window, glancing out. From their vantage point high in the palace they could see most of the city, but it didn't seem any different than it had the day before. No fresh plumes of smoke greeted the dawn, nor did any wall of fire advance upon the city from the desert beyond.

Still, the bells rang urgently, and although Brandt wasn't a citizen, he could well decipher what they meant. An attack was coming.

Had he been back in the empire, he would have known what to do. Here, though, he lacked certainty. He reached out through the soulwalk until he found the queen. She allowed the connection, but he could feel her distraction pulling her attention in different directions.

"What would you have of us?" he asked, making his question brief.

She considered for a moment. "For now, nothing. The Takaii are moving toward us."

"Takaii?"

"The creatures that Dezigeth brought with it through the gate. It translates roughly to 'devourer' in your language."

Brandt nodded. The name sounded appropriate.

The queen continued. "I expect that they'll reach the

walls of the city by noon, and if their previous actions are any indication, they'll commence their attack immediately. I've ordered all my units into the city, and we should be prepared for the siege."

Brandt could see the queen didn't want to waste any more time speaking with him, so he offered a short bow. "Let me know if you need us."

She broke their link without even acknowledging his offer.

When Brandt returned from the brief soulwalk, he found Ana standing next to him. She reached out and grabbed his hand, and together they looked off into the distance. Soon a horde of the Takaii would be gathered at the walls. Brandt could only imagine that it would be a slaughter. He'd seen nothing yet to indicate the Takaii could mount a successful siege.

But would it matter?

They numbered almost as many as grains of sand in the desert they fought over.

He clenched Ana's hand tighter. Then told her of the queen's plans. "I think I'll go to the wall, so I can at least see more of what's happening."

"Shall I join you?"

Brandt looked down at her growing stomach. "I would rather you not."

To his surprise, Ana didn't argue. "Are we trapped here?" she asked.

"No," Brandt answered, with a confidence that he wished he felt. "If there's anyone who can figure this out, it's the queen and Alena. They'll find a way."

She let go of his hand then, and Brandt left their chambers with a heavy heart.

As always, the palace was quiet. Brandt walked down

and out through the deserted halls and through the empty gardens outside. It felt so odd, being separated from the world beyond.

Then he stepped through the front gate of the palace wall and into a city he had never seen before. The siege had brought the city alive.

He'd never experienced a siege of an imperial city, but he couldn't help but think that if he did, it wouldn't look anything like this. The bells had stopped ringing, and the streets were filled with people. But there was no shouting, nor crying. The people moved with grim determination. And it wasn't just the men. He saw women stringing bows and younger children honing knives. Brandt suspected that if the Takaii broke through the walls, they would have to fight every single citizen living within.

For generations, the queen had prepared her people for exactly this event. The cost of that preparation could be measured in more lives than Brandt dared to count, but in this moment, that preparation began to show its benefits. Everyone bent their backs to an assigned task, as though every member was part of the army.

Brandt passed through the crowds like a ghost. A few people acknowledged him, perhaps hearing the stories of the aid he'd given during the first attack, but mostly he was ignored, which suited him fine.

He walked through the city, taking in the full extent of the preparations and being continually surprised. From cauldrons of pitch being prepared to food being stored, everyone was hard at work.

The continual scenes of labor gave Brandt plenty to consider as he reached the city walls. He passed the warriors guarding the stairs without problem and ascended to the city wall. Even from here, there wasn't much to see. Perhaps a cloud of dust rose in the distance, but he couldn't be sure it wasn't just his imagination finding what it sought in the shimmers of heat.

Brandt waited and watched, not having anything better to do. For the most part, he watched the desert, but at times he would walk to the other side of the wall and admire the preparations happening within the city. If he was an enemy commander, he decided that this city was one of the last places he would want to besiege.

As the sun continued to rise in the sky, Brandt finally saw the Takaii come into view. He gripped the edge of the wall tighter. When he'd flown over a couple of days ago, there had been many. But that number had grown by leaps and bounds. From this distance they appeared as black specks crawling over the land. As before, they marched in no appreciable order. They possessed no ranks, no greater strategy. They just swarmed, reminding him of ants.

Brandt checked the sky. The queen's guess of noon seemed accurate.

He turned at the sound of the queen landing beside him. With a thought, she took her stone plates and placed them in a bag at her side.

She looked stronger than she had before, but somehow still less than when he'd first met her. Her eyes were sunken in her head, and she looked out at the invading forces without hope.

"I've never seen citizens so well organized," he said, hoping to turn her mind in more productive directions.

She glanced at him out of the corner of her eye. Given the history of the arguments between them, he wasn't sure which approach she would take. But she said nothing.

"Dezigeth?" he asked.

She shook her head. "Remains guarding its gate, although I cannot fathom why."

That was something, at least. Not nearly enough, but something.

Then the Takaii came into arrow range of the wall for the first time, and the siege began in earnest.

52

Alena walked the streets of the city, lost in thought. After a long period of activity, the roads were now quiet. For the most part, she had the streets to herself, from narrow paths barely wide enough for her to squeeze through to wide thoroughfares where six or more could walk abreast. Here and there a person passed by, their eyes forward, their pace and focus indicating they had a specific and important destination to reach. No one acknowledged that she existed.

Alena had no purpose here. All the Lolani had been preparing for this very event their whole lives. Their parents, grandparents, and innumerable ancestors had done the same. She, on the other hand, had only learned of Dezigeth's kind in the past year. She had fallen, more or less, into this crisis.

If she kept her eyes on the ground, she could almost convince herself that none of this was real. This was her first time in a city being besieged, but she couldn't help but think this wasn't how a siege should be conducted. She'd expected chaos in the streets, the shouts and screams of the injured and wounded as siege engines launched stone and fire over the walls.

Humans, she thought with a bitter smile, were odd creatures. She almost would have welcomed such a siege, because then at least life would be unfolding according to her expectations.

But as always, her expectations turned out to be worthless, uncertainty gnawing away at her. The Takaii, as the Lolani called them, brought no siege engines. As near as Alena could tell, the most weaponry any of the creatures carried was a single spear, and even that weapon seemed limited to a select few.

Yet they flung themselves at the walls.

The first day of the siege was almost done, and Alena had yet to hear a single cry or sound from the Takaii. She wondered if they weren't capable of speech, and if they communicated through some means she didn't understand.

The Takaii were a challenge, but they weren't the true danger. As Brandt was fond of pointing out, they died easily, and if they could figure out a way to cut off the flow of reinforcements, the Takaii could be dealt with in time. But every plan for survival knotted into an unsolvable puzzle when Dezigeth was brought into the equation.

They had no answer to its strength.

They lacked any understanding of its behavior, and so they couldn't predict its responses to threats.

With such a lack of knowledge, they were finding it impossible to create plans.

How did one defeat an enemy they didn't understand?

Today's siege was a perfect example of their growing confusion. Alena didn't know how many Takaii had died in service of Dezigeth today, but she assumed the number had to be in its thousands. But Dezigeth didn't stir from the gate, which continued to belch out more Takaii as if feeding from an unending source.

The rushed nature of the siege didn't give Alena and the queen much time to strategize together, either, which was the reason for this particular outing. The queen remained on the walls, leading the defense. Alena had decided to find her and see if they could find time to speak.

Alena reached the wall and climbed one of the tall, narrow stairwells that led to the top. She paused, closed her eyes, and took a deep breath as she neared the end of her journey. This was her second visit to the walls today, and she feared the memories of her first would haunt her for the rest of her days. The carnage grew beyond reason.

She watched the warriors and citizens at the top of the wall, surprised by the quiet competence everyone displayed. The Takaii had no weapons that could reach the top yet, so people moved calmly from one station to the next.

Lines of citizens transported pitch up and down the wall, dumping it down on the Takaii gathered below. When the pitch landed, one of the queen's acolytes would spark it with their fire affinity, burning dozens to death at a time. Though archers stood evenly spaced along the wall, few released any shafts. Once loosed, they wouldn't be retrieved, and the queen's orders had been to hold them for a time of greater need.

Alena steeled her stomach and glanced over the wall. The piles of Takaii bodies had grown, and in some places were almost twice as high as a human. The piles didn't reach close enough to be a danger to those on the wall, but the stacks of dead presented the only path Alena saw to the Takaii ever breaching the queen's defenses. She could hardly imagine the cost the creatures would bear to make such a breach possible.

Off in the distance, a flare of bright fire indicated the queen's position. Alena watched in horror as a pile of Takaii, similar to the one below her, vanished in flame.

And then she knew they would never breach the walls. Wherever the bodies piled, the queen cleared with her all-consuming flames.

The thought of so many creatures, even enemies, wasting their lives made her sick. This lacked even the imagined dignity of war. It was organized slaughter and nothing more.

Which made Dezigeth's actions all the more troubling. It couldn't be a fool, so what did it hope to accomplish?

Alena joined the queen, surveying the field beyond the walls. Sofra offered a small nod of acknowledgment, which was more than Alena had received in the past. "How are you feeling?" Alena asked.

The queen waved away the question. She still didn't look healthy, exactly, but her pallor had improved considerably since the last time they'd spoken. No longer did Alena worry that a strong breeze would finish her. Alena tried another approach. "May we discuss Dezigeth?"

"Do you have some new ideas for fighting it?"

Alena stared at the ground. "I'd hoped you might."

The queen grimaced. "Then we have no hope."

Alena wasn't so quick to fall into despair. "Perhaps there is an answer within the gates. Before Olen sought to break my connection to them, I was exploring the memories contained within."

The queen's gaze hardened. "There are no answers in the gates. I've searched them all."

"Perhaps if we searched together, we could find something we missed."

The queen growled and dismissed her. "Return if you

find something to discuss. Otherwise, leave me to the defense of my people."

Then she walked away, ending their brief conversation.

Alena left, dejected.

There was no need for her on the wall. What skills were required were more than fulfilled by the queen's acolytes. So Alena returned to the palace where the rest of her friends waited.

She found them in the kitchen, where Toren cooked the evening meal. The smells and scents of the meal brought her a measure of comfort, but the incongruity between the quiet, peaceful scene in the kitchen and the fighting happening on the walls unbalanced her.

The ongoing conversation she interrupted by her entrance was subdued, and in response to their questioning glances, she shook her head.

While Toren's food was delicious, it didn't fill the hole in her heart. The darkness of the queen's castle crept into her thoughts, and she didn't think she was alone. They largely ate in silence, even Jace's usual exuberance dampened. When they finished the meal they walked to the palace walls together. From there they had a clear view of the city walls, well-lit by hundreds of small flames. The siege of the city and its accompanying defense continued without cease, the lack of daylight not hindering the assault.

Did Dezigeth simply hope to wear the defenders down?

If so, the plan would cost him untold thousands of warriors. The queen scheduled her defenders in shifts, so it would be days, at least, before exhaustion set in.

That night, as she lay next to Toren, sleep impossible to find, she began rambling to him. "It doesn't have any regard for the lives it throws away."

His response was immediate. Like her, Toren found sleep elusive. "What do you mean?"

"No human army would function in such a way. Eventually, they would turn on their generals."

"Except in this case the general is as good as invincible."

"I suppose. But it doesn't make any sense. Why do they obey?"

"Do you think it's important?"

Alena shrugged. "Maybe. If we could figure out a way to turn the Takaii against Dezigeth, it could open up some opportunities."

But nothing came to her except sleep, eventually.

In the morning, she was surprised to find the queen also wandering the halls of the palace. Before Alena could ask, the queen reported. "The attack broke off in the early hours of the morning. We don't know why."

They broke their fast together, but silence reigned over them.

As the meal ended, the queen looked up in that particular way that indicated she was in the soulwalk with one of her acolytes. "They are coming again."

The news made Alena want to scream. The questions of why tormented her. If this was a strategy, it was one none of them understood.

The queen looked to Alena. "I think you'll be required today."

Alena's stomach dropped. "Dezigeth?"

Sofra shook her head. "No. But I believe this is their main thrust. The numbers are incredible."

Alena shuddered. If there were enough Takaii attacking that the queen wanted both of them to unveil their gates, she couldn't imagine the number. And certainly, in the face of such slaughter, Dezigeth would approach. No commander could possibly stand for such destruction of their forces.

So Alena finished her meal quickly and they all filed out the doors of the palace. None of the others intended to allow Alena to fight alone.

They made good time to the walls, where a double shift of soldiers waited.

Alena stood, mute, when she came to the top of the wall.

The Takaii advanced, an enormous wave of dark creatures that covered the land as far as the eye could see. Alena couldn't even begin to guess the numbers.

The queen connected to her gate, and Alena was a moment behind her.

A wall of fire, now a familiar sight, sprang up no more than fifty paces from the edge of the city wall. It marched forward, the work of the queen.

The Takaii never faltered. They ran headfirst into the flames, as though they hoped that by speeding through they might somehow survive.

Hundreds died with every heartbeat, a massacre of a scale Alena couldn't comprehend. She stood, stunned, as the fire maintained an impassable barrier. She forced herself to watch.

Dezigeth finally stirred to action. Alena felt the creature gather its power, far in the distance. Alena glanced to the queen, but her attention was consumed entirely by the maintenance of the fire. Perhaps she didn't even notice.

Alena focused, waiting for Dezigeth to make its move. But it remained near its gate. She felt it weaving something familiar—one of the destructive balls of energy it had used to such great effect in their earlier battle. It launched the blast from over a league away.

The queen didn't react, and Alena was now certain she

had no idea the danger she was in. Alena jumped to protect the woman that had once been her enemy. She bent her will against Dezigeth's attack, straining against its momentum and power. The blast raced toward them, traveling hundreds of paces without deviating so much as a hair. But gradually, as the distance from Dezigeth increased, she managed to shift it ever so slightly, always higher.

Dezigeth fought her action, but as the ball raced toward them, Alena's strength prevailed.

The ball burst through the flame, and the wall sputtered for a moment as the queen realized her deadly predicament.

With a groan, Alena lifted the ball a little higher. It passed over their heads and out over the sea behind them. The queen glanced over at Alena, a knowing look in her eyes.

Dezigeth gathered another attack.

This time, the queen felt it. After a moment, she let her flames die away. As soon as she stopped, Dezigeth did as well.

The message was clear.

"No matter," the queen said, loud enough for all to hear. "I'm not needed today."

The Takaii, indifferent, continued to advance. The queen gestured to one of her commanders, and arrows clouded the sky as they fell toward the invaders. Hundreds fell silently, but the wave still crashed upon the solid walls of the city.

Alena watched for a time, unable to look away. Even with the additional numbers, the Takaii didn't possess the strength to break the walls. And yet they continued to fight. Soon, the scene became little more than a repeat of the day before. The queen's warriors were efficient, and the slaughter continued.

Eventually, Alena took her leave of the wall. She couldn't stand to watch, and there had to be better uses of her time.

Dezigeth had a plan, but its contours were beyond her. She only hoped she would understand before it was too late to counter.

That afternoon she poured over the memories given to her by the gate, but she found no answers there, either.

In the evening the queen appeared, announcing that the siege had been beaten back for a second day. Tired and exhausted as she looked, there was a hint of triumph in her voice. After all this time, they were holding. It wasn't much, but it was something.

And then, on the morning of the third day, Dezigeth attacked.

53

From a distance, Dezigeth hardly seemed frightening, Brandt thought. Unless one was gifted with an affinity, it appeared much the same as any man. A man that had dark wings and flew, but a man nonetheless. Still, Brandt's feet shuffled on their own accord, ready to run down the steep stairs to the imagined safety of the city behind him.

Brandt feared, as he heard the songs of Dezigeth's affinities gathering, that no place in the world would be safe anymore.

A powerful feeling of remembrance washed over him. This, in so many ways, was a reliving of the queen's childhood memory.

Indecision froze his limbs. Against any other enemy, he would have seized a stone with his affinity and thrown it across the gap at lethal speeds. But against Dezigeth, the action wasn't just foolish, it was pointless.

Could Dezigeth even be killed? It had spent years among the stars, if Alena and the queen were to be believed. They all assumed death was possible and natural, but what did they really know? Against this enemy he was a child just learning how to name what he saw.

His affinities listened to a new song. It was, to his surprise, one of the most mesmerizing sounds he'd ever heard. The low, deep hum of stone harmonized with the whistles of wind. Fire and water blended into the music, the final result a song of ethereal beauty. Dezigeth worked with its power, building to a devastating crescendo.

Brandt braced himself.

Unlike the queen's memories, Dezigeth sent no wall of fire toward Valan. Instead, the air between Dezigeth and the walls shimmered, as though the normal bending of the air due to heat had been increased until one could barely see through.

Perhaps a hundred paces down the wall, the queen and Alena, standing side by side, responded, a complex song of fire and air.

The forces met well outside the walls, and the whole world rumbled. The air appeared to melt, running like water away from the point of impact.

For a moment he dared to hope, dared to believe that the two women had found a way to fight Dezigeth.

For a moment, they held.

Then, directly ahead of the women, tiny points of light began to appear in the places where the air twisted and melted the most. Once formed, they hung in the air, a visible reminder of the destructive potentials unleashed.

More lights followed the first, each in a place where the two forces fought one another for dominance. Lights spread for hundreds of paces in every direction, and fear for what was to come stole his breath.

His only warning was that the first to burst were the first that had appeared, well away from his position.

Each point of light erupted, the space between the forces no longer enough to contain the dueling energies. The bursts were blinding, and for a moment, silent.

Then waves of pressure crashed into him, followed closely by many others. Brandt clapped his hands over his ears as they popped again and again.

The first eruptions ignited the others, and soon a wall of blinding flashes spread across his vision. He closed his eyes and crouched into a ball as the pressure grew, buffeting him from all sides. The wall shook underneath him, rocking back and forth as though it had been built on top of sticks.

Brandt tumbled onto his side, his fall arrested by the low ledge on the inside of the wall. Others weren't so fortunate. He saw at least three warriors thrown from the wall, their screams lost to the constant barrage of explosions splitting the air. The rocking slowly subsided, but it took Brandt several moments to find the courage to stand and assess the damage.

The wall still stood.

How it did, Brandt couldn't say. Enormous cracks ran through it, and a glance at the number of warriors still on the wall told of a tragedy all its own. No small number of the Lolani had been flung to their deaths below.

He turned to Alena and the queen, who alone stood on one of the undamaged sections of wall. They had both been driven to a knee, but Alena was helping the queen to her feet.

Dezigeth remained floating well away, to all appearances unaffected by the energies they'd unleashed.

Brandt heard that same deadly, beautiful song building once again, and knew he wouldn't survive the next clash. "Get off the wall!" he shouted, gesturing to the stairs as he did. They might not understand his language, but everyone who heard him comprehended the message well enough. He led the way, taking the stairs three at a time as he listened to the queen and Alena's response.

He felt the forces rushing toward one another as he reached the bottom of the stairs, and he kept running. His retreat wasn't cowardice. He felt no shame. Standing against such a duel wasn't bravery, but foolishness.

The forces collided, and Brandt made himself light, putting even more distance between him and the wall. Behind him, a thousand suns suddenly burned in the desert, and he darted into a small alley, taking cover behind its stone walls. He closed his eyes, covered his ears, and waited for the worst.

It came a moment later. Although the blasts lacked the power he'd experienced high on the wall, he still felt each one, like a wave passing through his stomach, turning his insides to water.

And then the wall collapsed.

The work of years, the queen had said. And it had only lasted two attacks, both of them defended by all the power the queen and Alena possessed between them.

Brandt didn't see the collapse, but he felt it. Enormous cracks split the air and the stone crumbled, crushing the buildings which had stood for generations under the shadow of the wall.

When the rumbling began to fade, Brandt dared to open his eyes. A cloud of dust floated in the air, but when a breeze came in from the ocean, it cleared the dust and revealed the desert beyond. Where the wall had once stood there was little left but a few large foundation stones.

Something in Brandt's mind shifted then. This wasn't a battle to save the planet, or even to save the city. He saw the future clearly enough. Dezigeth would remove the queen and Alena, then send the Takaii in to finish the task.

Brandt's thoughts ran only to Ana and his child.

This was a battle for survival.

Brandt broke from cover, only sparing a single glance back behind him. The section of wall that held the queen and Alena still stood, a lone pillar among the devastation.

Again, it reminded Brandt of Sofra's mother, standing alone against the force of Dezigeth's predecessor. Even after so many generations, history repeated itself.

Although he supposed that Sofra didn't stand alone. Alena stood beside her.

Brandt hoped they would find a way to fight.

Then he turned away, fixing his gaze on the palace.

The streets began to fill with people, the order imposed by the queen for so long finally beginning to crack. Some rushed to the collapsed wall while others ran across the city to the harbor. The attitude at the moment was unsettled, but it wouldn't take long for complete pandemonium to set in.

Brandt ran, weaving his way through the crowded streets. For most the shock hadn't yet worn off, but soon navigation would be next to impossible. He reached the palace, where he found Ana, Toren, and Jace standing in the gardens. Both Toren and Jace looked ready to run toward the wall, tossing aside all reason to fight beside Alena.

"She's still alive," Brandt said. "She and the queen continue to fight."

His breath came easier now that he once again had walls separating him from Dezigeth. He understood that the safety they provided was nothing but an illusion, but even illusions could bring comfort.

"So, what do we do?" Jace asked.

Brandt looked around. The city wouldn't last long.

Dezigeth's attacks spelled its doom. Of that, there was no doubt. They needed an escape, but their options were poor, to say the least. The queen's gate was the most certain mode of transport back home, but it required the queen to send them back. The odds of her both surviving and having the time and willingness to send them back were slim.

Which left the ships and the harbor. Brandt was reasonably sure he could get them a boat, but what then? He had only the most general sense of where Palagia was in relation to home, and the journey was hazardous. Strong storms wiped out most ships that tried to travel between the continents, although Brandt wondered if that remained true now that Hanns no longer maintained the defenses.

Though it was a poor option, the ships were really the only choice. "We need to go to the harbor. Perhaps we can find someone there willing to navigate back home."

"What about Alena?" Toren asked.

Brandt glanced in the direction where he could still feel the queen and Alena fighting. He didn't want to go back that way, and he wasn't sure Alena could survive Dezigeth's assault long enough for them to arrive.

But he didn't want to leave her behind, either. And the others wouldn't follow if he tried.

"We'll have to get her from that battle, somehow," he said.

As he spoke, another rumble rolled over them, reminding them of exactly what retrieving Alena would put them in the middle of.

54

The air before Alena twisted, not with heat, but with weavings of pure power. The fight between the queen and Dezigeth tore the world apart, a duel featuring both intense energies and incredible control over the elemental affinities. Sofra fought as though she had nothing left to lose, flinging one weaving after another toward Dezigeth.

In contrast, caution defined Dezigeth's advance. It protected itself from the queen's attempts, but had halted its advance. It remained uninjured, and to all appearances, unimpressed by the power the queen commanded.

The two fought like giants while Alena buzzed like a fly around their legs. Every exchange between the two taught Alena how much she had left to learn. This fight wasn't just about power. Both her and the queen could draw a roughly equal amount from the gates. But the queen's skill with affinities far surpassed Alena's. When Sofra dueled Dezigeth, it was a battle of mental focus and imagination. The queen used more combinations of affinities in the space of a few moments than Alena would have thought of in years of practice.

Whether they possessed the same power or not, lifetimes of experience separated them.

And it still wasn't enough. The queen could have leveled several cities by now, but Dezigeth didn't even have a scratch.

Another back-and-forth exchange split the air, the thunderous roar barely audible over the constant ringing in Alena's ears. As usual, the energies met between the combatants. To her senses, the weavings knotted together until they erupted in sound and fury.

She squinted. Was Dezigeth smiling?

It was.

It didn't fear them.

Not in the least.

The constant exchanges paused for a moment, allowing the queen to catch her breath. She stood strong, the last defender of this last section of wall. For all the help Alena was, the woman might as well have been standing alone, standing between her people and Dezigeth.

Standing between the world and Dezigeth.

Still, the hints of exhaustion were too obvious to be ignored. Sweat beaded down her face, the first time Alena had seen the sight. Her good right hand gripped the wall tightly, as though she might fall if she let go.

The wall beneath their feet began to shake, but it took her a few moments to understand why. Behind Dezigeth, sand poured off of four boulders as the creature ripped them from the bedrock underneath. Alena's eyes went wide, guessing what was coming next from the stories she had already heard.

Dezigeth launched the boulders. They raced high into the cloudless sky before beginning their long descent down.

The queen cursed as she worked her energies on the boulders. Alena joined in, focusing her efforts on a second boulder.

Dezigeth fought them, keeping the boulders on their initial tracks. But the queen managed to get hers to shift direction, and in time, so did Alena.

But their efforts took too long, and the other two hit, collapsing buildings and throwing up clouds of debris. Alena didn't want to imagine how many people had died under that attack.

Dezigeth gave them no rest, no time to contemplate the horror of what had happened. It just prepared another strike.

The queen gathered her power, layering weavings together into seemingly indestructible balls of pure energy.

The attack, when the queen released it, was one of the most beautiful and horrifying sights Alena had ever seen. Fire and air, woven together into visible braids of destruction, lashed out at Dezigeth, snapping at it like a whip of impossible length. Shards of ice and stone, honed until their edges were as sharp as swords, rushed at Dezigeth from all angles.

Alena joined in with her own attacks, her large balls of fire insignificant in comparison to the queen's focus.

But perhaps she distracted the creature. Alena formed and launched her weavings of fire as quickly as she could, hoping that maybe one would somehow make a difference. It wasn't always the strongest that won the fight, but the one who made no mistakes. She hoped Dezigeth's confidence would be its undoing.

The queen's barrage didn't stop. Sofra screamed, the sound an echo of pain long buried.

She saw now that there was no apparent limit to the quantity of energy they could draw. They weren't limited by the cost, as they weren't using the energy of their own bodies. Instead they borrowed it from the gates, from the source the gates were connected to.

As the queen pulled more, Alena wondered if there was any limit. Did the well of power ever run dry?

There had to be. She suspected it was why the Etari gate slowly failed.

Would the true cost of their fight today be the loss of one of the gates? Or worse, what hope would they have if they used the last of the gate's power? What if they went to pull and there was nothing left to command?

But if there was a bottom, they had yet to find it.

The queen's attacks built into a deadly cacophony of destruction. The air around Dezigeth warped, and then Alena saw another sight she never thought she would. She saw it only for a moment, a breath between rounds of the queen's attacks.

Dezigeth had a cut, running deep across its face. Inky darkness trickled out of it and floated in the air before Dezigeth, apparently as immune to the pull of gravity as the creature itself.

And just like that, Dezigeth vanished, dissolving into a thick shadow that quickly retreated back toward the gate it had built.

The world fell quiet, leaving Alena with nothing but the ringing in her ears. She glanced over at the queen, then behind her, struggling to believe they still drew breath.

That they were still alive.

That the city still stood behind them.

The queen collapsed to her knees, her eyes closed. Alena feared the worst until she saw the rise and fall of the queen's chest.

"It won't last long," the queen said. "It will return."

"We can't hold here," Alena replied. Now that she had some time, her mind began to work on the problem again, whittling it away from different directions. "We need to escape."

"Where?" the queen asked.

"Back to the empire," Alena said, only justifying the answer after she had given it. "It's not ideal, but it should take the Takaii some time to find their way to the empire."

The queen shook her head. "I won't retreat from Dezigeth. Most of my people are still out there."

"If you stay and fight, you lose everyone. If we leave, we save some. There's no cowardice in it."

But when the queen opened her eyes, Alena saw that it wasn't cowardice at all. It was the most emotion she had ever seen from the queen. "There's no future in the empire, either." Sofra's voice was low and bitter. "There's no future for any of us. Once it is done here, it will find its way across the ocean, dragging those demons behind it. Isn't a quick death better than months of prolonged worry?"

Sofra's words were dark, but they weren't born simply of despair. If they left, they abandoned the rest of the queen's lands. Alena didn't know how many people lived beyond the walls of the city, or even how big Palagia was. But if the queen spoke true, Valan was only a small portion of her empire.

But if they didn't escape now, Dezigeth would have complete control over the area, and there would be no chance of leaving.

Alena was glad she wasn't in Sofra's position. She

couldn't imagine the burden of so many lives on her shoulders. Terrible as the plan was, leaving was the only way to continue the fight. "If you really believe that defeat is inevitable, if you've already surrendered, then give me your gates. I'll continue the fight alone."

Sofra closed her eyes, and for a moment, Alena thought she might just accede to the request. Then a hint of a smile turned up the corners of her lips. "Clever girl."

Together, they turned their back to the desert and Dezigeth. The city had been mortally wounded, but much of it still stood. Perhaps the buildings were dull and without much personality, but to Alena's sight, the city appeared proud.

Alena felt the queen begin a soulwalk, her mind stretching out to many throughout the city. It was, as Alena had been learning, how she ran her lands. Then she nodded to Alena. "Those who are left will gather at the palace. We will make the journey to your lands and see how welcoming they really are."

55

Brandt stood in the stirrups, craning his neck for a better view of the long line of Lolani stretching out in both directions. The merciless sun beat down on their backs, but most barely noticed. Their gazes were locked on the ground before them, their focus on the simple but exhausting task of putting one foot in front of the other.

The queen had hoped to make the journey across the desert in two straight days of walking, but quickly adjusted her estimate once the trek began. People needed to rest, and their journey was not without its share of trouble.

At first, their exodus had been uncontested. They walked through the night, only to find themselves facing a small army of Takaii as the morning sun rose. The queen and Alena had decided not to join the battle, concerned about drawing Dezigeth's attention. Brandt had fought, though, his gatestone helping him destroy vast numbers of the invaders.

Dezigeth's tactics remained indecipherable. At times, the creature seemed incredibly cautious, fleeing when it was injured and using the Takaii to do most of the fighting. But if it was truly cautious, it would have simply dropped boulders on the city from a distance endlessly, or simply overwhelmed the queen and Alena. Both women believed it had the strength to do so.

The Takaii were little better. Scouts reported skirmishes with as few as five of the invaders, but then a whole army's worth of them would appear without warning or reason. Brandt's only consolation was that the queen's commanders had no better explanations than he did. They all struggled against these enemies that refused to obey the rules of warfare all humans seemed to instinctively follow.

The column was only a day's march away from the queen's gate. All things considered, the retreat had gone better than Brandt expected. The Takaii, at least when unsupported by Dezigeth, were relatively easy opponents to fight. Their only strategy was to charge forward until every last one was dead. He'd never seen a single one retreat. The queen's commanders had adapted well to the simple challenge. Formations of shield walls had been reinforced. Swords were replaced with bow and spear, any weapon that allowed the Lolani to keep their distance from those edged arms.

Brandt assisted where he could, riding up and down the line to lend his gatestone to any of the larger attacks. But he was rarely needed. The Lolani fought well, and their losses were far less than Brandt would have believed possible. The acolytes caused plenty of damage on their own.

Which led to another point of confusion. Dezigeth had to command the Takaii, and Brandt didn't believe for a moment that Dezigeth was a fool. But even simple changes to the Takaii's assaults, changes that would make them far more dangerous, never came. The creatures just kept charging, dying by scores.

All the same, the Lolani were wearing down. The Takaii attacked at random, and with random numbers, which made organizing a competent defense a nightmare. The soldiers had received the least sleep of any, and it was beginning to show.

Brandt doubted that attrition was the Takaii's actual strategy, but it was brilliant all the same. Dezigeth had to know their intended destination. If he placed a large force near the end of their journey, the results could be devastating.

When he wasn't aiding the Lolani, Brandt traveled with Jace, Toren, and Ana. Alena rode up front, side by side with the queen. She hadn't left them behind, exactly, but had claimed she didn't want to be too close to them if Dezigeth suddenly appeared. Jace and Toren, not having anyone else to protect, had latched onto Ana. They both worried over Alena incessantly, though, knowing she hadn't been sleeping well the past few opportunities.

No one was particularly pleased with the situation. Ana complained, reminding them she was quite capable of caring for herself, but Brandt was quietly grateful. His wife's stomach seemed to grow more every day, a constant reminder of all that he risked. He wouldn't deny any protection to her. Even if the protection wanted to be guarding someone else.

The attacks continued through the rest of the day and into the night. Brandt couldn't as easily sense the activity at Dezigeth's gate like Alena and the queen, but the Takaii must have been pouring through in an endless stream. He couldn't help but wonder what life was like on the other side of that gate. He imagined countless rows of the mindless soldiers, collected in a disorganized mass, waiting their turn to pass through the gate to another world, most likely never to return.

Brandt slept little that night, the same as the two nights before. Whenever the sounds of battle drifted his way, he couldn't help but sit up and listen.

He was awake when the sun rose, and when the sun warmed his face, he felt the first glimmer of hope in a long time. Today they would make it to the gate and return to the empire.

The column came to its feet slowly. Up and down the line, people stretched, their eyes sunken against the horrors they'd seen. Did they have any hope left? They had lost their homes, and their lives hadn't been much even before. They trudged on, another example of life refusing to give up, no matter the cost.

The march continued, each step bringing them closer to the gate. Brandt rode up and down the line, but the morning seemed quieter than usual. He couldn't hear or see any attacks from the Takaii. Against a normal enemy, such a lack would have frightened him, but against the otherworldly beings, he could do little but shrug.

When the column slowed to a stop, his heart sank.

Brandt rode to the front. He feared what he would find, and as he crested a small rise, he saw that his worst fears were true. For the first time in this campaign, the Takaii had shown strategic genius.

He didn't think there were as many of them as had attacked the city a few days prior, but that didn't make their numbers any less intimidating. Thousands stood between the refugees and the gate.

Perhaps more worrying than the presence of the Takaii was the certainty that Dezigeth knew their intent and sought to block their escape.

There was reason to the creature's actions, even if Brandt didn't comprehend it.

He had little time to curse their fortunes.

Once spotted, the Takaii defaulted to their typical strategies. They charged silently, kicking up a cloud of dust that even those at the rear of the column couldn't miss. From the north, a constant stream of reinforcements approached.

The Lolani response was calm, displaying none of the worry Brandt was certain they felt. Shield walls formed and the warriors prepared to meet the charge.

Brandt joined a contingent of warriors, most of them now used to his presence. He remained mounted and summoned his affinity. He studied the developing battlefield.

Even if all Lolani citizens fought this wave, they would still be outnumbered. But that no longer bothered Brandt. They were now used to fighting under such conditions, and numbers alone no longer made him fear.

The one who did, fortunately, was nowhere to be seen.

More Lolani warriors rushed in from farther down the line, lengthening the shield wall to meet the Takaii advance. Brandt joined his efforts with some of the queen's acolytes, unleashing waves of fire at the approaching enemies.

As was now common, Brandt and the acolytes slaughtered untold numbers of Takaii, and as always, they continued their relentless assault, ignoring the losses they absorbed.

The Takaii finally hit the shield line, and soon Brandt's ears were filled with the sounds of flesh striking shield. The Lolani on the front line groaned with effort but held. Brandt and the other acolytes cleared as much space as possible, and spears darted out between the shields, bringing down those Takaii unfortunate enough to be squeezed between the shields and their charging allies behind them.

Alena and the queen did not join the fight. But they were far from passive. Accompanied by a group of elite soldiers and a full dozen of the queen's acolytes, the two women led the way through the Takaii toward the slit in the ground where the queen's cave waited for them.

The battle continued, and with every passing moment, Brandt believed that they were gaining the upper hand. The Takaii were unable to break around the shield wall in any large numbers, and the queen and Alena made steady progress.

All they had to do was hold.

Brandt thought they could.

Until he felt Dezigeth stirring to action off in the distance.

56

Alena felt Dezigeth's presence shift at the same time as the queen. Up until a few moments ago it had been content to let them fight their way through its endless supply of Takaii.

No longer.

Alena turned to the queen. She feared what had to be done, but could think of no alternatives. "You must lead your people. Open the gate closest to Landow and send them through."

The queen shook her head. "I can only travel between gates that I control," she said, a hint of an accusation in her voice.

"I'll give you that gate." Alena didn't want to, but she had no better ideas, and she was becoming increasingly convinced that the number of gates one controlled didn't matter as much as the queen and the line of Anders believed.

"As much as I would like to, I don't think Dezigeth has any intention of allowing us enough time to complete the exchange."

"So, it's Faldun, then? There's no other choice?"

The queen nodded. Alena chuckled grimly to herself, glancing back at the thousands of Lolani behind them. "This will be a disaster."

They were driven by necessity, though. There was no choice.

Regardless of their destination, their next actions were clear as day. In a different world, the queen might have offered to be the sacrifice instead of Alena, but not here. Only the queen knew how to use the gates to travel from one destination to the other.

Which left Alena alone to hold Dezigeth at bay.

A lump formed in Alena's throat as she considered the likely consequences. Then she looked at the line of people, stretching back toward the city, each of them looking for a new home, a new beginning.

And it was really no decision at all.

The queen gave her one last look, then nodded. "Thank you."

"You better get going," Alena said.

The queen did, following the path her acolytes had cleared and her elite warriors now held against the press of Takaii.

Alena looked out on the desert, watching not just the refugees but the creatures who attacked them. She knew she was delaying what she needed to do, but she couldn't help but take a moment and wonder about the point of it all. So many lives lost, and for what reason?

This close to her final journey to the gate, it all seemed so meaningless.

She took a step forward, only to be stopped by a hand on her shoulder. She smiled, and tried not to cry as she turned around to face Jace.

"It's coming, isn't it?" he asked.

Alena nodded.

"And you're going to hold off, aren't you?" He spoke softly, barely loud enough for her to hear over the din of the battle.

There was no point in her responding. They both knew this ended in only one way.

She embraced him. "I want you to go," she said.

Jace shuffled his feet for a moment, but then his back straightened, his decision made. "You know I would have stayed."

She didn't doubt for a moment. "I know."

They embraced once more, Jace's arms tight around her. "I love you," he said.

"I love you, too."

When Jace turned aside, he was replaced by Toren. "I'm staying," he said.

She shook her head. "No."

"I'm not going to leave you."

"I can't protect you, too," Alena said. "It will be easier if you aren't around." She swallowed. "And if it kills me, it would mean everything to know that you had lived."

Toren couldn't be budged. "No one should die alone."

She leaned in and kissed him. "We all die alone. I'm grateful I got to live among people I love." She paused, enjoying their closeness one last time. "Now go, before I compel you."

Maybe he realized that he had no chance of winning the argument, or perhaps he finally accepted her wishes. Regardless of the reason, he left, hugging her tightly one last time before rejoining the column.

Alena didn't see Ana, but she imagined that the wolfblade would be somewhere close to Brandt. In this battle, she wouldn't be anywhere else.

There was no more time for delay. Dezigeth approached rapidly. Alena gathered her affinities and wove them together using all the patterns she had learned over the past few days. Walls of fire killed hundreds of Takaii at a time, freeing up the queen's soldiers to reinforce weak positions and begin their own escape.

She fought the growing revulsion in her stomach, hating what she did, but doing it all the same.

She wondered if Brandt had felt the same back in Faldun when he had accepted the queen's offer.

Before her, the Takaii posed no threat. She didn't allow any to advance close enough to even throw their spears at her.

She wove more focused attacks, drawing more power as she grew more comfortable with the techniques that had once been the queen's alone. Her purpose was simple. She needed to kill enough of the Takaii, and summon enough power from the gates, that she would draw Dezigeth's attention.

Then she only needed to hold long enough for the rest to flee.

In the final few moments before Dezigeth arrived, she swept the desert clean with her powers, giving the last of the soldiers time to escape. The queen was within the cave, and Brandt was as well. She felt the Lolani pouring through the gate as fast as the space would allow them.

They would make it.

She would ensure it.

She turned her full attention to Dezigeth, and as the shadows in the distance formed into the shape of a man, Alena let her attacks fade, curious how it would respond.

Though her hope was that of a fool, part of her still wondered if they could somehow find peace.

Dezigeth had no interest in conversation. It lashed out with its powers, but compared to some of the attacks Alena had felt earlier, the blows seemed weak, as though it was holding back.

In response, Alena flung everything she could at the creature. Her techniques lacked the queen's refinement, but at the moment, she didn't care. As far as she was concerned, there was nothing for her beyond this moment.

As before, though, the creature batted aside her attacks as though they were the playthings of children.

Still, it didn't advance, and for every moment she delayed it, at least a few unexpected visitors were arriving in Faldun.

Her focus on her attacks was so complete she almost didn't notice when Dezigeth finally responded. She sensed the ball of flame when it was no more than ten paces away from her, and she barely wove a shield of air in front of her before it exploded.

The force of the blast knocked her back, giving her abrasions on her back to match those still healing on her arms.

Dezigeth gave her no chance to recover. Another blast followed the first before she could stand.

Again she managed to protect herself from the worst of the blast, but again the effort leeched away her focus as pain blossomed across her back.

A third assault, also barely defended, drove her even deeper into the sand. If not for the shield woven around her, she feared that she would be buried alive.

Then thankfully, mercifully, it was over. Dezigeth floated past her as a horde of Takaii ran toward her position, those sharp arms upraised and ready to cut her to pieces.

Alena fought her way to hands and knees, but could make no further progress. Her body simply refused to respond.

She rested her forehead against the shifting sands. Nothing she did made a difference. Dezigeth casually dismissed her even as a threat. The Takaii, it thought, were enough to finish her off.

She couldn't let it end, not when so many more still needed to escape this land. Grunting, she struggled to her feet, swaying in the wind with the effort. Then she dropped into the soulwalk and reached out for Dezigeth.

She knew it was the action of a desperate fool, but right now that defined her perfectly.

They appeared on the rooftops of Landow. Dezigeth turned and gave her its full attention. In that gaze she thought she saw something more than its usual cold dismissal. Perhaps annoyance?

She braced herself for the assault she was certain would come.

Dezigeth did not disappoint.

A wave of pure energy rippled the air and smashed into her, but for the moment her shields held, her will to survive equal to Dezigeth's desire to kill her.

In this world she found attack and defense a simpler matter, her imagination more powerful than her affinities in the physical world. Spears appeared out of nowhere and dashed toward Dezigeth. Like her, it had formed a sphere of protection, and each battered at the other while still protecting themselves.

When Alena became dismayed at her lack of progress, she reminded herself that she didn't have to win. All she had to do was distract it. Every moment she could drag out this fight was another life saved.

Despite her greater comfort in this realm, the result was still inevitable. The difference in powers was too great, and the longer she resisted, the more powerful Dezigeth's attacks grew. Soon she had no choice but to stop her own attacks, forced out of necessity to protect herself to the exclusion of all else.

Dezigeth's attacks battered against her shield. Landow faded as Dezigeth's will in the soulwalk became dominant, and the very fabric of the world seemed to fight against her. She fell to one knee, then curled into a ball, each an attempt to shrink her shield and keep it intact for one more moment.

Her shield began to crack, spiderwebs fracturing the sphere.

She could count the heartbeats of her life remaining on one hand.

Alena broke before her shield did.

She tried to escape. To her shame, she tried to flee back to the physical world, to breathe fresh air deeply once again. But Dezigeth wouldn't let her. Its own will locked her in place as its power battered at the very last of her defenses.

She imagined Jace, Toren, and her family calling for her to return, to not leave them quite yet, and a wave of anger began in her chest and rushed to the tips of her fingers and toes, making her feel as though she was filled with light bursting from within her. She focused that feeling and sent it toward Dezigeth, one final attack on behalf of the empire.

Her blow struck true, and the attacks against her abruptly ceased. She battled disorientation for a moment as the soulwalk solidified around her, Landow returning to focus. She didn't bother to search for Dezigeth. She could feel it like a disease within the soulwalk and knew that it still lived.

She fled the soulwalk, finding herself once again in the physical world, the Takaii now within a hundred paces of her body and closing the remaining distance in long, loping strides. While in the soulwalk she had fallen once again on her side.

She pushed herself to hands and knees, but she was done. Her body had no more left to give.

Then a shadow blocked out the sun, and she was certain that Dezigeth had come for her, one final act of vengeance.

Instead, she found herself in strong arms that held her tightly. She looked up, the simple effort of moving her eyes exhausting.

Brandt.

She frowned. She felt the wind blowing quickly against her face, but that made no sense. Not even Brandt could run that fast. And then the wind stopped, and it was dark. Then there were another pair of arms, even more familiar, around her, carrying her.

The darkness deepened, then suddenly became light. Alena caught a glance of a hard, angular face, and she finally surrendered to the exhaustion of her mind.

INTERLUDE

It did not howl, although some primal urge, buried under count-less years of perfection, suggested that such a reaction would be appropriate.

How long since it had eradicated a vermin so dangerous? How long since they had discovered an outpost of humans that so willfully upset the balance?

Its memory was longer than these short-lived humans could believe, but even it had to stretch to recall.

Their behavior exemplified chaos. Their actions remained beyond understanding or prediction. They drew upon the power of the heart without regard, and frolicked recklessly like willful children in the realm of souls.

Discipline alone, it feared, would not be enough. Such, perhaps, had been the intent of its predecessor, but the message had not been heeded. No, only extermination remained, a righting of cosmic scales.

If they possessed any decency, they would bow their heads and thank him for their just punishment.

Instead, they hurt it, using their recklessness to continually surprise it. It came and offered mercy, and they responded by attacking, pulling so hard from the heart it could hear the world scream in agony.

The situation sickened it. Humans sickened it. Such behaviors could not be tolerated, not if this universe was to survive.

It passed along its orders to those who had accompanied it here. Someday, the creatures would outlive their usefulness and they would meet the same fate as so many of the species they had destroyed. But they were wise. They would welcome its final judgment.

For now, they were an expedience, the right tool for the job at hand.

Not a single human could be left alive. Not this time.

It sent out a command to the hive mind of the creatures, ordering them to scour the land.

When this land had been cleaned, it would travel to the other continent and finish its work.

Then it could leave, and in time, if it wasn't too late, the heart could recover on a world devoid of humans.

The thought brought so much pleasure it broke its composure.

Dezigeth smiled and waited.

57

Once Brandt stepped through the gate, it was as though he had transitioned from a world of light into a realm of darkness and shadow. Just before he'd walked through the queen's gate, he had stared directly at the glowing arch, and the image of it hovered like a ghost in his vision. This journey had been no more pleasant than the last. He took another step and immediately ran into the back of another person, who grunted his displeasure.

Then there was movement behind him and the familiar blue light flared to life once again. The energies swirling around the gate subsided, and Brandt stood motionless, still dazed from the transition from one world to the next. The shifting of weight in his arms brought him back to the present. Alena needed his help.

Together with Toren they laid the young woman down, gently resting her head against the stone floor. The soft rise and fall of her chest let Brandt know she still lived. He looked up at the queen, hoping she would know more. "How is she?"

The queen's demeanor changed as she looked at Alena.

Where Brandt had expected a dismissive gesture, the queen instead knelt down next to the girl, gazing at her not unlike a parent. Gently, she laid her hand on Alena's shoulder and focused her attention. After a moment she nodded. "She'll live. Her last stand with Dezigeth must have taken everything out of her." The queen's gaze traveled up to Brandt. "What happened?"

Brandt shook his head. "I only saw Dezigeth from a distance, but it appeared stunned."

"Appeared?"

Brandt wasn't sure a human could fit any more disbelief into one word. He shrugged. "I felt its affinities falter, and I knew Alena was still alive. That was enough for me to attempt the rescue."

The queen looked from Brandt down to Alena and back again. "You are greater fool than I imagined."

The anger in her voice that was so often present wasn't now. Perhaps she hated to admit it, but she respected Brandt's courage. Brandt flashed her a smile. "It's a complaint that has been made before, I'm afraid. Probably will be again."

The queen stood, and Brandt could tell from her change of posture that she was beginning to consider her next steps. "What next?" he asked.

"I must treat with the Falari," she said, using the same voice Brandt imagined a child used when forced to eat something they didn't want.

He couldn't help it. He smiled again. His heart was finally settling, and he felt more at ease than he had in weeks. He wasn't home, but he was closer. Now, at last, he felt safe. Which made him feel like jesting. "Would it be safe to say that it's been a while since you've attempted diplomacy?"

The queen's answering stare could have frozen the forest.

Brandt glanced down at Toren, who nodded his permission. Alena couldn't be in any better hands than his.

"Then I'll come with you. I am still a Senki, or at least, I think I am. But I've been part of a diplomatic mission to these lands before."

The queen arched an eyebrow at that. "And didn't that diplomacy result in a civil war?"

The return barb had been perfectly placed. Brandt grimaced. "I suppose I can only do better."

The two of them made their way forward. The sacred tunnels of the Falari were now filled with refugees, citizens and soldiers milling about, equally uncertain of what would happen next.

The queen spoke in her native tongue, her commands not loud, but easily carrying to everyone in the room. Although Brandt couldn't understand the words said, the gentleness and concern in the queen's voice surprised him. When she finished, the Lolani began speaking among themselves, and Brandt had the sense that they were passing the queen's commands to one another.

He and the queen shuffled forward, and Brandt saw little hurry in the queen's actions. She spoke to a few soldiers who were injured, listening to them as they gave their report.

Brandt's perpetual smile faded when he thought of the queen's people. For as many as had been saved, he couldn't imagine how many more had been lost, both to the Takaii and to Dezigeth. He imagined that without the queen and Alena occupying their attention, the Takaii would begin spreading across Palagia. And as much as he wanted to help, there was little he could do.

And those that survived were not in a much better situation. While Brandt rejoiced at his return to the continent he had grown up on, almost everyone else in this cave was a foreigner, and no one had invited them.

He couldn't fight for those left behind, but he hoped he could help those that still lived.

Although the queen did not hurry, they did continue working their way forward. Outside the room where the gate stood, the ruins of a maze remained.

The sight humbled him. In his time visiting Palagia, he had forgotten that the queen's last visit had been an invasion. Now, he couldn't help but associate that word with Dezigeth and the Takaii. She controlled the gate, but it wasn't because of any permission the Falari had given her. And now she had brought thousands of her people through. Although they didn't come as conquerors, it was still another invasion of sacred Falari spaces.

Brandt hoped they could find a way to forge a peace together.

He supposed they were somewhat fortunate to have been forced to make Faldun their destination. Here, the gates were unattended. A longstanding cultural tradition meant the tunnels were almost always empty, and it appeared that tradition still held despite recent events. It gave them a chance, at least, to speak before a fight began.

The two of them continued to push forward, past the maze and higher up the long tunnels. As they progressed, Brandt realized they couldn't wait long. The Lolani were packed in the tunnels shoulder to shoulder, and although there was some airflow, it wasn't enough. They needed more air to breathe. Brandt thought of Alena all the way back where the gate was and hastened his pace.

Eventually they reached Ana. Despite her arguments back in Palagia, she had been the first through the gate once the queen opened it. She had been the logical choice. The queen had to keep the gates open, meaning she would come through last, and Brandt had been using his gatestone to protect the retreat. Ana was the only one left who could speak even a word of Falari.

And her departure meant she was far from Dezigeth, a situation that pleased Brandt.

He dreaded her reaction when she found out he'd run into the heart of the battle after she'd left. Even though he'd successfully saved Alena, he would receive an earful, at the least.

It appeared that after passing through the gate, Ana had been the one who kept them organized in the tunnels. The queen reported that Ana had made them stay back, had prevented the flood of refugees from washing over Faldun in a disorganized mess.

If they had any hope for peace, it was due to the quick thinking of his wife. But Brandt saw that even though she had packed the tunnels tightly, there were just too many Lolani. He hoped she'd kept them far enough away from the entrance.

It was close. When they reached her, Brandt estimated they were only a hundred paces and two turns away from the entrance to Faldun proper.

His relief at seeing her safe was mirrored on her own face. After a quick embrace she pushed him away. She gestured ahead. "Our arrival did not go unnoticed."

Brandt's heart sank. He stepped forward, and the queen joined him. He stopped her. "I'm sure my presence will be difficult enough for them to accept. But this might be easier if you remain behind for the moment."

She shrugged, and Brandt saw the return of the same queen that he knew so well. In her eyes, it didn't matter whether the Falari wanted her there or not. Her people needed shelter, and she intended to find it for them.

Brandt took a deep breath and started forward. It would be up to him to negotiate something that involved far less violence than the queen imagined.

He took the last few steps before the corner, forming air into a shield before him. It couldn't be seen, but it should protect him should some young warrior decide their best course of action was to shoot first and figure everything out later.

He saw daylight ahead and turned the final corner. He raised his hands away from his sword to indicate his peaceful intention. Thankfully, no one shot at him.

It was a good start, he supposed.

Although they certainly looked like they wanted to. Ahead of him stood a whole unit of Falari archers, all with bowstrings tightly drawn. Brandt figured that if he made one wrong move, over a dozen arrows would be searching for his heart.

He looked at the faces for any sign of welcome, but saw nothing. "Well," he said to himself, disappointed no one else could enjoy his sarcasm, "this should be easy."

58

Alena woke, surprised to find herself in a bed. Her last coherent memory was of endless sand and the Takaii rushing her position. Everything after felt unreal, like a hopeful dream before traveling to the final gate. Her head ached, and she groaned. The surprised shuffling of feet in response let her know that she wasn't alone. At least two others were with her.

She cracked an eye open to see both Jace and Toren hovering over her, undisguised relief on both their faces.

"Where are we?" she croaked.

Together, the two of them helped her sit up, two strong hands supporting her back. She groaned again as her body complained. Bandages were wrapped tightly around most of her, and served as her only real covering. She pulled the blanket of the bed over her, grateful for the warmth.

Jace offered her a mug of water, which she gratefully accepted. She had the presence of mind to sip it slowly. As the cold, clean water eased her parched throat, she swore it was as sweet as any honey she'd ever tasted.

"Faldun," Toren said, answering her question.

"We all made it?" She closed her eyes against memories of the Takaii and Dezigeth.

Toren nodded. "Brandt was protecting the last of the refugees, and then he refused to leave without you."

She almost called Brandt a fool out loud, but realized the observation might not land well with the two men. Instead, she said, "I'm grateful."

And she was. To still draw breath, to be here among Toren and Jace, after her pathetic attempts to stop Dezigeth, was a gift she wouldn't reject. She felt as though she had returned from the dead and been given another chance at life.

She wouldn't squander it.

Jace chuckled softly at her comment. "Don't be too grateful just yet."

Toren shot her brother a warning look, but Jace ignored it. She frowned at the two of them. "What?"

Toren grimaced, but Jace didn't bother shielding his sister from the realities of the world beyond this room. "Well, you've somehow managed to land in the middle of a mighty conflict even while you were sleeping."

"Dezigeth approaches?" If true, Alena wasn't sure she would be able to summon the will to fight.

Jace shook his head. "It's remaining stationary, as near as we can tell. No, your new problem is far more diplomatic." He paused, as though not quite sure how to proceed. "Everyone is waiting for you to wake up to prevent a war between the Lolani refugees and the Falari."

Alena's head felt as though it might explode. She squeezed her eyes shut, willing out the pain. "What?"

She thought about Jace's words another moment, leaving her even more confused. "Wait, what?" Questions tumbled around her thoughts, but she couldn't even order them.

Toren spoke softly. "Right now, the Lolani are being forced to remain in the tunnels behind Faldun. They've been given food and water but little else. The queen is furious and ready to destroy the whole mountain, I think, but Brandt has managed to calm her so far."

He paused. "It's been a tense day around here."

"What he means," Jace said, "is that the two civilizations are on the brink of war, and they need you."

"Why me? Couldn't the queen or Brandt mediate an agreement?"

Jace chuckled grimly at that. "He tried, but the Falari won't listen to him. They said that he lied to their council of elders, that he abandoned his friends and family in their battle against the queen, and that it is likely the queen compels his every action. He's being held in the tunnels now with the rest of the Lolani. They won't even let him visit Ana."

Alena grimaced on behalf of her friend. "Ouch."

She supposed, though, that two out of the three of the accusations were true. Brandt hadn't done himself any favors leaving the way he had.

"He was upset, too," Jace said.

"For a moment, I thought *he* might try to tear down the mountain," Toren added.

Alena almost asked why the Falari didn't deal with the queen, but that one was easily answered. She had, after all, invaded their lands and stolen their gate right out from under them. It wasn't exactly the strongest foundation for productive peace negotiations.

"And what, exactly, am I supposed to do?" Alena asked.

Jace gave one of his mischievous grins. "Don't know. That's why we've been waiting for you to wake up."

Alena tried to stand and found that it was difficult. Both men offered her their arms, but she shooed them away.

"Take your time," Toren cautioned. "Once you emerge from this room, you'll have no time to rest for a while."

Alena acknowledged his point, but said, "Every moment the Lolani remained trapped in those tunnels is another that the queen could lose what little patience she has. It's worth hurrying for."

Jace smiled, as though he had a secret he'd been holding onto. "Then you'll be pleased to see who's outside."

He went to the front door and opened it, ushering in a familiar face.

"Sheren!" Alena cried, followed quickly by, "What are you doing in Faldun?"

The Falari soulwalker ignored the question. "It's good to see you awake," she said. "When you first emerged from the tunnels, we weren't sure of your health."

Alena glanced to both Jace and Toren, and thought of Brandt. "I have quite a few people to thank for me being here."

"Did you tell her?" Sheren asked the men. In response to their nods, she turned to Alena. "You're wanted down in the council chambers, immediately."

Alena was grateful for the time Jace and Toren had given her. How hard had they had to fight to keep her to themselves? Given the imperative tone of Sheren's voice, had anyone else been here, they'd already be dragging her down to the chambers.

She had heard of them before, in the stories Brandt had told of his first visit. "The room with the truth-telling circles?"

"The same."

"How far is it?" Right now, Alena wasn't sure she could walk more than a few dozen paces.

"We're not far from the entrance to the tunnels," Sheren answered.

"I'll assist her," Jace said.

Sheren shook her head. "It would be wiser if Toren did."

At Jace's hurt look, she explained. "If all goes as well as we hope, today will be the day that all the people of this world begin to unite. If Toren escorts her in, then we have an imperial, an Etari, and me. The symbolism will not be lost on the elders."

"Except that I'm a wanted criminal in the empire," Alena said, "and you and Toren hardly have the right to speak for your people."

Sheren waved away the comments. "The three of us walking in as one will be a symbol regardless."

"Will she be in any danger?" Jace asked.

"No," Sheren said. "It's only been a few months since you were here, but stories of your deeds have spread. No harm will come to any of you."

Jace stepped aside then, satisfied.

Toren extended his arm and helped support Alena. Her eyelids drooped, and all she wanted was to sleep for a day or maybe three. She knew this encounter with the elders couldn't wait, but she wished it could.

Sheren led them, slowly, toward the tunnel. Alena could tell the Falari soulwalker was impatient, but she contained it well.

Alena had only entered the tunnels once before, but had approached the entrance from much higher up on her previous visit. Now her chambers appeared to be on the same level of the entrance. Sheren led them through the streets of Faldun, confident of every turn.

Alena wondered at the change in her friend. The woman had always been a perfectly competent navigator, but this confidence was something new. She hoped they would have the time to speak later on.

Assuming she didn't inadvertently start a war.

Despite the enormity of the task before her, Alena couldn't help but find herself distracted by the sights of Faldun, the most impressive artifact from the days of those who had come before.

Built into the side of a mountain, Alena could see for leagues whenever a view opened up between buildings. She couldn't begin to guess how high they were, but it was dizzying. The Falari, used to the high places of their rugged land, moved with ease, but Alena well remembered the vertigo she'd experienced when she approached the drops at the edge of the city.

There were also warriors everywhere. The only privacy in the city was found indoors. Outside, Alena found they were always in view of at least one set of warriors, if not more. They stood silent watch, and Alena thought she detected nervous anticipation in their stance. Many expected to fight soon, she suspected.

More surprising than the number of warriors, though, was the deference they paid to Sheren. Alena eyed her onetime traveling companion thoughtfully. "What happened to you in the past few months?"

"I didn't make it home," Sheren explained. "Weylen himself sought me out and found me not long after I departed your company. He has become a powerful voice after the Battle of Faldun, and he is a deeply pragmatic man. As the only Falari soulwalker he knew, he wanted me by his side. Through him, I've been granted more authority than I thought I'd ever have."

"Congratulations. You're moving up in the world."

"Despite my wishes, yes. Though I find life was much simpler back in my village."

It was the first hint of the woman she'd traveled with. The comment made her smile as she thought of her own life since leaving Landow. "Don't we all," she said.

They entered the tunnel, leaving the concerns of Faldun behind them. Before long they came upon the Lolani refugees. Here, there was enough space for them to walk single file, but little else. Most looked up at her, listless in the dark shadows. A strong breeze carried through the tunnel, and Alena wondered if it was Brandt or the queen providing the fresh air.

She was grateful when they took a different branch of the passage and she could lean on Toren once again.

The sight of the refugees strengthened her conviction. They were, when all was said and done, little different than her. She could well relate to the pain of leaving one life behind and starting another. If she could help them, she would.

They followed the turns that led to the chamber where the elders waited for them. They paused in a small antechamber, and Sheren prepared them. "Speak when spoken to. Not otherwise. Toren, when we enter, you must let Alena stand alone. You may escort her to a circle, but then you must stand apart from her and find your own. I will do the same."

When she was convinced that they understood, she nodded to the guards, who opened the doors.

Brandt had described the room to her, but seeing it with her own eyes put his description to shame. The walls formed a circle, at least a hundred paces in diameter. Around the circle stood the elders, the symbols beneath their feet flickering in a pattern Alena couldn't understand.

Her curiosity getting the best of her, Alena dropped into the soulwalk, traversing both planes of existence at once. The weavings around this room were nearly as remarkable as those of a gate. The walls of stone had been reinforced, and thin holes in the stone leading upward seemed to be inscribed with an air affinity to keep the space ventilated. She'd never seen their like. The circles that were found everywhere on the floor contained a weaving of a type that was also completely foreign to her. The whole room was a masterpiece, showing off the best of what those who came before had been capable of. She wondered just how cognizant of the wonder of this room the Falari elders were.

Usually, the work of those that came before inspired her. Today, it made her heart break. If a people so advanced, so knowledgeable in the ways of manipulating affinities, couldn't stand against one such as Dezigeth, what hope had she?

Toren escorted her to the middle of the room, where he left her within a circle, waiting nearby for a moment to ensure that she stood tall. Then he took his own circle next to hers.

"Thank you for coming," a voice said. It was soft, but she heard it clearly, as though the speaker was standing face to face with her.

"Yes. We have some understanding of the trials you've faced, and your willingness to stand before us after such a fight is noted by us all." Another voice, but this one also sounding as though it came from before her. Brandt had told her of the phenomenon, but it still awed her.

"You honor me, elders." She would have bowed, had she felt certain the motion wouldn't pitch her forward.

"We shall keep this brief, child. The arrival of the Lolani scourge was unexpected and unwelcome. The queen's power is feared, and rightfully so, but we also understand the consequences of Dezigeth's arrival. Tell us, if you were in our position, how would you act to protect your people?"

Alena noted the phrasing of the question. She knew of the abilities of the circles. In only a few words, they had trapped her into telling them what, specifically, she thought was their best course of action. Fortunately, she had no need to lie, to persuade them of something she didn't believe.

"I would seek an alliance with the Lolani," she answered.

She'd expected an outburst, but there was none.

"Explain," requested another voice.

"As we speak, Palagia is being overrun by an invader that even the queen and I, wielding the power of four gates between us, could not stop. The Lolani have been a threat, and may someday be one again. But in the war that will be coming to this land, we need every ally we can find. Imperial, Falari, and Etari must band together to fight Dezigeth if we are to have any hope at all."

She paused, then continued. "But even if that were not true, I would counsel the same. The Lolani have lost their homes, and their numbers are greatly reduced. By the end of the month, the Lolani in your tunnels may be the last left. I was raised to believe that a defeated enemy deserves the mercy of the victor."

She saw, out of the corner of her eye, the light flashing from the inscription of the symbol beneath her feet, but she paid it little mind. She knew she spoke the truth.

Another new voice asked the next question. "We would

know your thoughts on Brandt. He was once honored as Senki, but his actions cast doubt upon his worth as a warrior."

The question permitted her any number of answers, but she chose to answer directly. "Brandt is a man who will always do what he believes is right. He wishes to protect the empire and those he loves, and will go to any lengths to do so. It means that sometimes he will make questionable decisions, but his mind is his own. The queen has no more influence over him than anyone else."

"Thank you," the first voice spoke, bringing the interview to a close. "We will allow you to rest now."

Alena was grateful. She gave a small nod of her head, but when she stepped out of her circle, the edges of her vision darkened. In less than a heartbeat, Toren was there, catching her as she fell.

She felt him catch her, and it was her last memory before darkness swallowed her waking thoughts.

59

Brandt stopped, his hand caught in midair just short of the thick wooden door. For the past few days, events had crashed over him in waves, throwing him forward and barely giving him time to surface for air. It left him feeling disoriented and unsure of himself.

It wasn't as though he hadn't seen his friends recently. They'd all been together in Palagia, but there had been a distance there. They had been together yet still separate. The arrival of Dezigeth had hung over every interaction like a damp shroud.

The creature was no less a threat now, but the physical space between them created mental space as well. He felt like he had taken one deep breath over the last few days. His thoughts cleared, no longer shadowed by Dezigeth's actions.

So now he knew just how much space separated him from Alena.

Which prevented him from knocking on the door.

He'd heard of Alena's defense of the Lolani and her subsequent collapse. How could he not? Her tale was on every tongue, endlessly retold and speculated over. Gifts of food and clothing were piled outside her door, given freely from the little the Lolani had carried with them through the desert.

Though the queen was also in Faldun, it was Alena who now drew all the attention.

Her kindness overshadowed the queen's strength.

He hadn't seen her since they'd first taken her away in the tunnels several days ago. At first, his confinement kept him away from his friends. But then he was freed along with the rest of the Lolani, and it was his own fears that kept him away. She was the hero everyone spoke of. The woman who had held off the demon singlehandedly, then freed the Lolani into this new land.

He was the man who had left his wife and unborn child.

He knew they were stories, hardly reflective of the complex truth of their lives, but they still cut like knives. They fed his voice of doubt, telling him that he had no reason to be a part of her life anymore. That she would be happier if he were to fade away.

He'd invented plenty of justifications for his absence the past several days. There was far too much to do, and she needed rest more than she needed his company.

Then she'd sent a message to him, requesting that he come.

He couldn't refuse.

Brandt shook himself out and squared his shoulders. He'd fought far more terrifying enemies throughout his life. Alena was a friend and he had nothing to fear. He was acting no better than a fool. He knocked on the door before his momentary courage failed him.

Toren opened the door. When he saw Brandt, a smile lit his face and he reached out, wrapping Brandt in a tight embrace. "It's been too long," he said, pulling Brandt into the room.

The warm welcome immediately put Brandt at ease. "Only a few days," he replied, suddenly all too aware of how rude he had been not to visit.

"It feels longer," Alena said from the bed.

Brandt turned to her, then stopped when he took in her appearance. Recovering, he stepped toward the bed, but from the smile on her face, she'd noticed his moment of surprise.

"I know," she said. "I'm not really looking my best these days."

"You look like you've been run over by a regiment of cavalry," Brandt said before he could catch himself.

She laughed at that, easing his worry that he'd over-stepped his welcome. "It's good to see you, too. Everybody else coddles me as if I might break into pieces at an unkind word." She aimed a pointed glance at Toren, who ignored the look with an ease that indicated significant practice.

"It's good to see you, too. I'm sorry that I didn't come earlier." Brandt almost made an excuse, then stopped. This was Alena. Even before she'd been a soulwalker, she'd had an uncanny ability to separate truth from lies. Chances were, she already understood why he'd not visited. He let his apology stand alone. "How are you?"

"I've been better," Alena said.

"Do you know what's happening?"

"It's—been quite the couple of months," she said, "and I think my body is demanding some rest."

He looked her over again, more carefully this time. She'd lost weight, even from the last time he'd seen her. And she hadn't had much to spare to begin with. Her years among the Etari had shaped her into a lean and strong woman, capable of leagues of walking without tiring. She'd never looked so frail.

But her answer made her wishes clear. She had some idea what afflicted her, and she didn't want to discuss it. Brandt respected her choice and moved the conversation forward. "Why did you wish to see me?"

"Olen," she replied.

Brandt's stomach fell at that. He hadn't thought much of the empire since his return to Faldun. "You want me to travel to Estern?"

Alena shook her head. "I'm not sure that's wise. Of the lands we need to unite, it will be the empire that I suspect will be most difficult to convince."

"They're also the strongest force by far. If they decide to stand alone..." He trailed off, not needing to speak the rest.

"We need them," Alena agreed, "but considering the circumstances surrounding our departure, I don't think Olen will be interested in hearing from me. But I could find him in the soulwalk and connect the two of you. Perhaps you can convince him where I would fail."

"I'm not sure I'm any better a choice," Brandt said.

When Alena didn't immediately reassure him, he knew she worried the same. "I still think you'll have a better chance than me," she eventually said. "You were a wolfblade once, and perhaps that will count for something."

"When?"

"There's no reason to delay."

Brandt looked down at his hands, noticing the slight tremble in them. "I don't suppose you've got a strong mug of ale sitting somewhere nearby? I might need one for this."

She smiled, but left him no opportunity to escape. "Ready?"

"No, but go ahead." As Alena closed her eyes, he closed his.

He heard the sounds of her soulwalk, that steady beat of her heart, now closer and stronger. He felt a beautiful simplicity in that rhythm and allowed himself to become lost within it.

Her voice spoke to him, echoing in his thoughts. "Where would you like to meet?" Alena asked.

Brandt considered for a moment. "The monastery."

He felt her acceptance. "Form it in your mind. Hopefully Olen will join you soon."

Brandt did, appearing in his recreation of the place where he'd lived longest as an adult. As he looked around, he realized that while he still felt nostalgia for his time here, he didn't feel that same sense of being home as he had in previous visits.

While he waited for Olen, he wandered the courtyard, allowing memories of long days of training to distract him. He'd been so earnest back then, so convinced there was some way to reach the levels of strength he desired. Knowing now that the only way to surpass the cost was the use of the gates, it all seemed somewhat foolish.

But it was over the course of those days that he had fallen in love with Ana. Much of what was good in his life was due to this monastery.

He sensed the presence of another and turned around to find Olen standing in the courtyard.

Brandt had seen the prince from a distance a few times, but this was the first time they had stood face to face, even if it was in the soulwalk. Brandt bowed, realizing he now stood before his new emperor. "Sir."

The emperor gave him a quick glance, then resumed his

study of his surroundings. "I have been here before. High-keep, isn't it?"

"It is, sir."

"I understood it was destroyed by the queen."

"It was, sir."

"An interesting choice as a place to meet, then."

"I spent over ten years training here, sir. It is the place I know best, and the easiest for me to soulwalk within."

Olen gave no indication he'd heard Brandt.

Something in the young emperor's bearing troubled Brandt. It took him a moment to see it. It lacked humility. Hanns, for all his faults, had some knowledge of his limits. Olen, too young and too sheltered to have experienced anything of true failure, didn't possess any of the same knowledge. Though Brandt had the advantages of additional years and a wide variety of experiences to share, Olen's attitude towards him was dismissive.

Finally, he turned to Brandt. "I can sense Alena's influence in this meeting, but I see she hasn't shown herself. Why did you summon me here?"

"The creature has arrived and is in the process of destroying Palagia."

Olen didn't react for a long moment. Then he nodded. "If true, that's wonderful news for the empire. One less enemy for us to fight."

"It will attack our lands next, sir. The queen and her armies were powerless against it, and it has brought a force to bear we failed at containing."

"And what would you have of me?"

"We need to join forces. All the people of this world, fighting as one. With you, the Etari, and the Falari working together, perhaps there is a way to stop this threat."

"A noble sentiment, but there is one problem," Olen said. "I don't believe you."

Brandt worked to contain his frustration. "Why not?"

"Because I've learned of Alena's past. I know that she was a thief who has been interested in the gates since she was young. She might have manipulated my father into earning his trust, but I am not so easily fooled. This is yet another ploy."

The emperor's assessment of Alena jarred him after so many days among the Lolani and their respect for her. "It's true she made mistakes when she was young, sir, but she's more than made up for that now."

"You might believe so, but I do not. She won't settle until she has the power of all the gates at her command, and she's created an elaborate scheme to ensure her success."

Brandt shook his head. "Sir! She's telling the truth. Countless lives have already been lost. At the very least, prepare the empire for what is to come. Preparation costs you nothing, but could save thousands of lives."

Olen began fading from view. "Count yourself lucky that you've given so many years of service to the empire, Brandt. If you ever try to reach out to me on behalf of that thief again, I will destroy you."

And with that, Olen was gone. Brandt watched the space where he'd been, unable to believe what he'd just experienced.

Then he, too, dropped out of the soulwalk, worried that he'd just failed at their last chance to fight against Dezigeth.

60

Alena stared at the ceiling of her chambers, as she often had for the past several days. Dramatic events shaped the course of history beyond the walls of her room. Dezigeth and the Takaii flooded over Palagia, killing thousands of Lolani the queen had been forced to leave behind. At times, Alena could feel the gruesome work of the invaders, the web of life around the world vibrating at the sudden departure of so many human lives.

Steps were being made to formalize alliances between three of the four peoples on the continent. Alena had provided the spark, but the torch was now carried by the Falari elders. They were the ones that had sent representatives to both the Etari and to the empire. Toren had included his own report to travel with the delegation to the Etari, and Alena firmly believed that the nomadic warriors would join the cause.

She felt far less confident about the empire. Olen's thoughts were twisted in ways she couldn't unravel, and she went so far as to fear for the lives of the Falari who traveled under the banner of truce.

Here in Faldun, the Falari gathered for war. The Lolani refugees had been given shelter on the lower levels of the city, and the queen discussed what they had learned from their battles with the Takaii with the warleaders. Faldun, at least, would not be caught off guard.

In the midst of all of this, all Alena could do was stare up at her ceiling, or sometimes speak with Toren or Jace.

In all her life, she'd never felt so lifeless, so completely drained of energy.

She didn't want to sleep. Her mind raced in circles from morning to night, preventing her from finding peace. Even when exhaustion finally claimed her, sometime late in the night long after the others had fallen asleep, her sleep didn't refresh her. She saw memories of the pain and suffering the Takaii and Dezigeth had inflicted, the smells and sights as vivid as though she were there all over again. She would wake up in a cold sweat, with only a little time having passed in the waking world. So she stayed up late, fighting her body's demands that she rest, collapsing only when she needed to.

Food held little meaning. She knew she needed to eat, but nothing sounded appetizing. She forced herself to consume enough food to live, but there were times when even a single bite would make her feel sick. At those times she considered throwing up intentionally to purge the illness from her. But she needed the nutrients, so she refused to do that.

Her friends worried for her. She worried for herself, but couldn't find the path to wholeness. It was as if everything she'd been through had finally hit her at once.

Of particular concern, Alena also held onto a secret, too shameful to even admit to her friends.

She had become terrified of the gates.

She could still connect with them, but she wasn't sure she could command their power dependably. Whenever the thought of using the gates occurred to her, she then thought only of the Takaii rushing mindlessly into the walls of flame. She had probably killed more of the creatures than anyone except the queen, and the thought sickened her even further.

The logic of her actions in those moments had been clear. She had found herself in a situation where it was either kill or be killed. The reasoning was true, but she rejected it. The more she relived her memories at night, the more certain she was there had been another way, a way that she had missed.

Manipulating the gates, or any affinity, was an exercise in focus and an expression of will. These days, she could summon neither.

Her friends deserved the truth, but she couldn't admit it, even within the privacy of her chambers. Perhaps, she thought to herself, in a day or two she would be past this affliction. The evidence of such recovery was sorely lacking, but it was the only hope she had.

Despite her lack of physical ambition, Alena had never been one to do nothing, even on her worst days. She might lack the will to leave her bed, but her soul could still wander. She fell into the soulwalk and quested for the gate hidden underneath Faldun. An idea had occurred to her, but she wasn't sure it was even possible.

She'd never tried diving into one of the gates she didn't control, but Faldun's was the only one close. And she hoped she'd built enough goodwill with the queen that the soulwalk wouldn't anger her. Alena had no intention of harming the queen's connection.

It worked.

Alena dove into the gate, finding it to be identical to the one under Estern.

The obvious destination was the library of memories stored within the gates, but she hesitated. She'd spent so much time there. She'd found no strategies for dealing with Dezigeth within, and Sofra insisted none existed. Alena wanted to doubt the queen, but had little reason to.

Without a destination, Alena drifted within the gate, allowing her mind to float freely. The myriad connections of the world danced beside her, and in this state she could easily discern the vibrations in the web as lives were lost in droves on the distant continent.

In her fugue state, though, she noticed another presence, drifting among the gates almost like her. She turned her attention toward the stranger. With painstaking slowness it resolved itself into a familiar form.

Anders I.

Had she run into him months ago, she would have unleashed a tirade of insults at the very least. As it was, today she settled for glaring at him.

He smiled, and in that expression she saw a lifetime's worth of regrets. "Alena," he said, "will you believe me if I say that it is good to see you once again?"

The odd question gave her pause, uncertain of how to answer. She settled for the first question that came to mind. "What are you?"

Their surroundings shifted and Alena found herself sitting across from Anders in her mother's kitchen. She began to stand, her hand forming a fist and coming back to punch Anders right out of this memory. She hadn't created this. He had raided her private thoughts and uncovered those she held most closely.

The violation felt like a knife between the ribs, a

personal insult. This place was hers to share or use as she pleased.

It wasn't Anders' sudden retreat, or the way he threw his arms up to protect himself, that caused her to stop her fist before she struck. It was the horrified expression on his face. Not at the pain she was about to inflict, but at his own actions.

Alena released most of her anger in one slow breath. She returned to her seat and unclenched her fist. Deliberately, she pressed her hands flat against the table. The texture of the wood was just as she remembered it. Not only had he pulled up her memories, he'd dug deep.

"I'm sorry," Anders said. "But perhaps my mistake will prove illuminating. The short answer to your insightful question is that I don't know."

Alena allowed her silence to express her disbelief.

Anders gestured to the room around them. "You are angry because this place, this memory, is special for you. It is yours, and it upsets you that I would intrude in such a way, that I was even able to learn of this place."

Alena tilted her head in acknowledgment.

"I see as much now," Anders said, "but it didn't occur to me earlier. I thought only about creating a comfortable place in your memories we could speak, and in the soul-walk, it is easy for me to see a person's innermost thoughts." He paused. "When I formed the empire, I never would've displayed such a basic lapse of judgment. My rule wouldn't have lasted long if I did."

He opened his arms wide, as though inviting her to study him. "But the longer I remain here, the more I lose of the man I once was. Sometimes, I think that I am a ghost, a soul untethered from my physical body, long since rotted away. But a ghost is doomed to float through the world without touching it, an eternal observer. I am permitted a much greater freedom of action."

Alena thought of the village Sheren had lived in, the ghosts denied their rightful passage through the final gate. She agreed with Anders about that much, at least. He was no ghost.

"I do not know what I am," Anders continued, "but I know how I got to be this way. When I died, I appeared before the gates, the same as anyone else. I just decided not to walk through."

"I didn't realize that was an option," Alena remarked.

"For most, I don't think it is. You've been there. You've had some taste of the pull the gate exerts, but you don't really understand, not so long as your heart pushes blood through your veins and your lungs breathe the air of the physical world. When you die, all you want is to go through that arch to whatever waits on the other side. It's the greatest desire you'll ever experience. It's impossible to resist."

"And yet you did."

"Only with the strength of the gate below Estern aiding me. And the clues left to me by the gates themselves. I was lured in by Tisha's dream."

"Why? If the pull is so great, why fight it? And why haven't your successors done the same?"

"Because I've dissuaded them. This existence is nothing to desire, and I have more reason to stay than them. I have a vision not yet complete. My attachment to the world overwhelmed my soul's last desire. And now I fear I've doomed myself for eternity. As the years have passed, the pull of the gate has faded, and now I wonder if my soul will ever find a final release."

His voice sounded far away, as though it had traveled countless leagues to reach her ears. His tone was that of a weary traveler, worn by leagues of endless journeying, an explorer fondly remembering the long past days of his youth.

"And what was this vision that denied you even the final release of death?"

Once again, his smile made her want to cry. "I dreamed of a perfect world."

If not for the expression on his face, she would have scoffed. "A perfect world is nothing more than a dream for idyllic fools and tyrants."

The first emperor stood from the table. "Perhaps. Maybe the best that will ever be said of me is that I was an idyllic fool. But I believed. Through all the years of conquest and the backstabbing of friends and allies, I believed. The others heard my vision and mocked me, much the way I see you are tempted to do now, but I had a vision in my mind of a world that could be better, that could serve everyone." He paced the room. "But one of the curses of a life that stretches beyond its natural bounds is that I see the unintended results of choices that seemed the best so many years ago."

Alena leaned back in her chair. This was a side of the emperor she had never heard of, nor ever expected to see. "What do you mean?"

"Paid work for everyone becoming a tool of enslavement. A line of philosopher-emperors who bore the greatest burden of protecting the empire on their own shoulders, now little better than any other ruler history has ever seen. Secrets, kept to protect the continuation of the empire that now threaten to topple it. Have no fear, Alena," the emperor said, "my mistakes are legion, and are far worse than even you can imagine."

"So why keep fighting? Why visit me?"

"The same reason, Alena. Always the same reason. And today, I start with you." He reached out and laid his hand against her forehead. It was warm, and before she had any idea what was happening, her world faded to black and she fell into a deep rest.

61

Eight small spheres of water hung in the air between Brandt and Ana. The spheres danced, following no particular pattern. Their training, such as it was, more closely resembled a game than the disciplined sparring most would associate with martial skill. The rules of their contest were simple. The spheres had to remain intact and never come in contact with either of them or the environment. They each controlled four drops, pushing and pulling the water in equal measure.

The game went from stillness to chaos in a moment.

Ana sent one of her drops at one of his. Brandt let the target drop fall, only to find Ana had predicted the move. A second drop of hers raced in, hoping to strike his as it fell. Brandt shifted it to the side, then attacked with his own drops, hoping to elicit a mistake. Handling four spheres of his own in addition to keeping an eye on hers consumed his entire attention. While they played, he thought of nothing else.

Which, he suspected, had been a large part of why Ana had suggested it in the first place.

When the water did collide, either with another sphere, the floor, or one of them, the game would pause. They would each set up four new drops, drawing water from a nearby cup if needed, then resume. More than one good-natured argument over who had lost erupted, but they were short-lived.

Winning wasn't the point.

Playing was.

But eventually their clothes were wet enough Brandt figured he needed to change. Ana was little better. Water was her natural affinity, the one she had first discovered she could manipulate. His strength was greater, even with water, but he lacked the fine control and familiarity with the element she possessed, allowing for a relatively even game.

"Thank you," he said.

She looked down at her clothes, dripping wet. The fabric clung to her, revealing not just the swell of breasts, but of her stomach, too. Brandt imagined that soon he would be able to see the child kicking. "Thank you," she replied. "I was hoping to wear more changes of clothes today."

Brandt helped her to her feet.

She caught him staring. "What?"

"You're beautiful, you know."

"I know."

He smiled and opened his arms for an embrace, one she slipped through with ease. "I'm already wet enough, thank you. I don't need you drying off on me."

Although he knew the request wouldn't go over any better than his last several attempts, he couldn't help himself. "I still wish you would leave. You should find some corner of the empire and make a home for us for when this is all over."

"When you agree to come with us, I will. Where you go, I go. It's as simple as that."

"Eventually, my path is going to cross with Dezigeth's again."

"Even so."

"You know, when Alena asked Jace and Toren to leave her behind, they agreed, even if they didn't like it."

"And she's very fortunate to have such agreeable family."

Despite his frustration, Brandt laughed. "I only want you to be safe."

She took a quick break from her search for dry clothes. "I know, and although it may not seem like it, I appreciate the thought. I do. But if we lose against Dezigeth, it doesn't matter where I travel to. So we need to find a way to defeat it, and I think I'm more useful to you here than hiding in some cave."

She caught his look before he could hide it. "You disagree?"

His moment of hesitation was answer enough. But she didn't raise her voice at him. "Tell me," she demanded.

"You don't even have a gatestone," he answered.

"So the years I spent surviving our countless battles as a wolfblade were an accident? A stroke of luck?"

"No—"

"Then why do you so badly want me to leave?"

"Because I don't want to lose you like I did them!"

His outburst quieted the room. She didn't need to ask who he meant. She'd been a part of that fight, too, the night he'd lost his wolfblades, who were closer to him than family. Lola, Ryder, and Kyler. After all these years, memories of their faces came quickly to mind, accompanied by the familiar pang of regret.

Her response was quiet but firm. "Stop being so selfish."

She might as well have slapped him across the face. "What?"

"Do you somehow think it will be easier for me to live without you? That your death would devastate me any less than my loss would you?"

Brandt stammered, but had no clear answer.

"When you think of fighting Dezigeth and the Takaii, do you only think of how to overwhelm it? Do you only think of affinities and strength?"

He took a step back. Though her voice was calm, she battered at his defenses.

"We trained for years to fight the Etari, to find effective counters for their affinities. Even as wolfblades, we knew that martial skill was more important than the tricks we could do with the elements. You've tried to overwhelm Dezigeth, and you can't."

Her voice built, constructing her argument. "You need to find another way. Ever since you acquired that gatestone, all you think about is strength. But cunning has won just as many, if not more, battles."

"But when its strength is so much stronger—"

She put her hand up. "Stop thinking only of the gates. If the solution lies in that realm, we have little choice but to rely on the queen and Alena. You need to focus on what you can. Go back to your own training. You've studied plenty on how to defeat a superior force. Start with the basic questions. What do the supply lines of the invaders look like? What are their strengths and weaknesses? How much food do they need to eat? How much ground can they cover in a day? What do you know, and how can you take that and turn it to your advantage?"

For several long moments, Brandt just stared at his wife. She had been beautiful before, but now she was radiant.

She was right, of course. The gatestone and the powers at play blinded him to other factors. But the conflict with the invaders had been intense, and it was only now, for the first time, that he even had the time to consider the situation from a more detached perspective.

He felt the first stirrings of hope in the ashes of his resignation. Or if not hope, at least purpose. Ana had given him a way forward.

She stopped him by placing a hand under his chin before he could turn away. "One more thing."

He paused. Eager as he was to get to work on the problems facing him, he had learned that when she wanted to say something, he would be wise to listen. She leaned in and kissed him.

"This is why I worry when you think that you need to fight on your own," she said. "It isn't that you aren't capable, or strong, but when you follow these paths alone, you weaken yourself. Think back to the wolfblades. Strong as you were, we were always better together. The same is true today."

"You're right," Brandt said.

"I know," Ana said, a smile on her lips.

"And I will find a way to keep you and our child safe. Even if you won't leave."

Ana's smile grew.

"I know."

62

When Alena awoke it was in the physical world, and something had changed. She stretched, the muscles in her body tensing and then relaxing into a state of ease.

Then she realized.

She was rested for the first time in weeks. She felt like she had slept for a whole day and night. Turning so she could look out the window, she saw that it was dark outside. She frowned. *Had* she been asleep for an entire day? When she had dropped into the soulwalk, the sun had just risen.

That couldn't be right. There was no way she could have soulwalked for that long.

And yet—

Toren's movement caught her eye. He had been in the adjoining room and glanced through the door at the sound of her movement. When he saw her, an enormous smile spread across his face.

"What happened?" she asked.

"You dropped into the soulwalk this morning, then fell asleep, as near as we can tell."

She twisted her torso back and forth. It felt like she'd been sleeping for a long time, but how? Nightmares had been stealing her sleep consistently, fueled by the things she had done. Her memories remained, but not as they once had. As they came to mind they lacked the sharp edges and biting discomfort she had grown used to. They felt more as if they were events in the long past, memories that no longer troubled her.

Which made no sense, until she remembered the soulwalk.

Anders.

Alena's stomach rumbled loud enough for their neighbors to hear. "And I'm guess I'm hungry too."

One of the benefits to living in Faldun was that there were many places which served food. Unlike the empire, though, most dining halls weren't operated for coin. Most of the people living in Faldun at any given time were transient. The dining halls solved the problem of food both conveniently and efficiently.

Alena and Toren walked to the nearest dining hall and were pleasantly surprised to find Jace there. Alena almost laughed out loud when she saw him. She'd heard Jace's reputation as a storyteller had become something of a legend in the city. But this was the first time she'd seen the evidence with her own eyes.

He was a king holding court. While everyone else sat on benches, he sat above them on a table, ignoring the angry looks given him by the Falari serving food. He was surrounded by nearly a dozen Falari women and a few men. His voice rose and fell, his flair for the dramatic almost comical in its intensity. No doubt, whatever story he told featured tremendous heroics no one else would have remembered in quite the same way.

And the Falari were hooked.

Within these lands, imperial was only spoken by the warleaders, Senki, and a few others. While Alena wouldn't be surprised if she learned that most of Jace's audience had at least some basic imperial, she also had little doubt that most of them had no idea what he said.

But something about his storytelling transcended the boundaries of language. From his expressions and his gestures to the dynamic lowering and raising of his voice, Jace held his audience in thrall, even if the details were lost in translation.

In her mind's eye she saw Jace as a young boy, regaling them with tales of his trials, tribulations, and triumphs at academy. Given that the rest of the family tended toward taciturn, Jace's behavior had always made him the center of attention at home, a position that he alone in the family desired. For all that he had grown over the years, that much of him was still the same.

She hoped it never changed.

They collected their food and watched for a few moments unobserved, but when Jace spotted them he waved them into his circle of admirers. If it was possible, Jace's grin grew even wider when he saw his sister. "You're looking well."

"You don't need to say that as if it's such a surprise," Alena commented. They ate their meal quickly.

Well, Alena thought, perhaps it was more accurate to say that she finished all their meals quickly. She wasn't sure she had ever eaten more in one sitting. Toren and Jace shared incredulous looks, but wisely held their tongues, and it appeared the satisfaction they felt at seeing her eat a full meal overwhelmed any concerns.

They didn't remain long. Jace's crowd looked impatient,

and after the siblings assured one another they were both doing well, Toren and Alena returned to their chambers. They left Jace to tell one more story of mostly imaginary adventure.

Back in their chambers, she told Toren what she intended.

His look in response said more than enough.

But he deferred to her, and she returned to her bed and fell once again into the soulwalk, diving deep into Faldun's gate.

Once there, she waited. She possessed no certainty about what Anders intended, but she suspected that he had more to share. He wanted her to join him again.

So she waited, and eventually her patience was rewarded. The figure of the emperor once again formed in front of her, coalescing slowly. She couldn't say for sure, but it appeared as though he struggled to take shape. Perhaps there was truth to his claim. Perhaps his soul would never pass through the gates, and instead just fade into a gradual oblivion.

"It is an ending I fear, as well. For all that I have dreamed, I fear that I will not be able to take that journey which is a right of our kind."

As much as she detested his ability to see into her thoughts, she forced herself to accept it. "Do you regret any of it?"

"Some of it, and every day."

"Would you do it all over again? Would you fight to create the empire?"

"I'm not sure."

His responses didn't satisfy her, and there was little point in debating the past when so much of the future was at stake. "Was there something you wished to show me?"

"Everything," he replied.

He gestured and she followed him into the library, the memories of a world long lost.

Alena didn't bother to hide her disappointment at their destination. Here, where Anders could see into every thought, there was no point. "Sofra says the answers we seek are not here, and you already know how much searching I've done myself."

That ever-present sorrowful smile remained on the emperor's face. "The answers that Sofra seeks are not here," he confirmed. "But that does not mean there are no answers."

"A way to become stronger?"

"No. When it comes to sheer power, no one has gone further than Sofra. In that regard, she is correct."

"If not strength, what?"

"Life is not all about strength, no matter what both Sofra and Brandt believe."

Alena repressed her frustration. If Anders knew the answer, why wouldn't he just share? Why the obfuscation? "You don't actually have a way, do you?"

"Not yet." At this, Anders suddenly looked like an old man lost. The moment passed and his eyes were sharp once again. "But as I said before, I am not the man I once was. Let me show you what I know, and perhaps our minds working together can find what we seek."

Without waiting for further permission, he began a guided tour of the memories of those who had come before.

Their first stop was Tisha's memory and the completion of the first gate.

"I've seen this," Alena said.

"You have, but were you really watching? Tisha may have built the gate, but to her, not even the gate was sufficient achievement. She had her eyes on a more difficult problem."

Alena remembered. The woman had hoped to solve the riddles of death. The gates had been nothing more than a tool.

The woman's dream had infected others, though. Anders implied it was Tisha's vision that gave him the idea to reject his journey to the last gate. And Alena wouldn't be surprised to learn the queen's efforts at eternal youth were inspired by the same memory.

Alena shook her head. She wasn't sure either person was better for their pursuits.

Anders made her experience the memory two more times. "Watch Tisha, and watch how her vision changes as the generations pass."

Skeptical as she was, Alena did have to admit something about Tisha's memory tickled at the back of her mind. But she couldn't understand why. So she followed Anders as he continued the tour of the memories. Most were new, although some she had seen before. Anders would point out behaviors, commenting on each vision.

They watched those that came before evolve as more of them learned to connect to the gates.

For her part, Alena fought her growing disappointment as memory after memory revealed nothing to fight with. She had the sense that the emperor sought to construct some larger pattern that she didn't comprehend.

It wasn't to say the memories and the tour weren't interesting. Not only did she learn more about those who had come before, she learned more about Anders and what had pushed him to make his fateful choices.

Those who came before fascinated her. They were explorers and philosophers, and while they built some cities, most seemed to prefer a more nomadic existence. She wondered how much of both the Falari and the Etari traditions were echoes of these ancestors long forgotten.

She watched memory after memory of the shamans, as they styled themselves, traveling the land while working with the gates. She observed large gatherings that took place at the end of every harvest, when all those connected to the gates would discuss any issues related to the governance of the people.

Alena observed that even though the shamans were capable of great feats using the power of the gates, the power was rarely used. She asked the emperor why.

"They believed very strongly in the idea of balance. They feared that if they pulled too much from the gates they would forever destroy that balance. I believe their idea has merit. It is, after all, the problem that has been affecting the Etari gate."

"Is there an upper limit on what we can pull?"

The emperor shrugged. "Perhaps. But if so, we have not reached it, despite Sofra's best efforts."

As Anders led her through the memories and she watched his reactions to what he saw, a new understanding dawned on her. "You wanted to create a society inspired by those who had come before, didn't you?"

"I did. I knew that I couldn't copy them. The empire has always been responsible for many times the number of people they had. The tools that worked to govern them wouldn't work for me. But I wanted the same results. Although they had their fair share of conflicts, I was impressed by the longevity of the peace they had formed. It was the spirit of their society that I hoped to emulate, to create a society where everyone would have the opportunity to become philosophers in their own right."

"And yet, vast differences remain."

Anders took no offense at the comment. "Human greed and corruption are difficult beasts to tame," he admitted. "Still, I feel there is something here. I do not know what drives Dezigeth's kind, but I am convinced it has something to do with how we relate to the powers of the gates. Study those who came before. They lived without interference for many years, and I believe we can find out why. I must believe we can convince Dezigeth to leave."

"You think it can be persuaded?"

Anders shrugged. "I believe, like you, that it is our use of the power of the gates that has brought it here." He reminded her of some of the latest memories of the gates. "When Dezigeth's predecessor arrived, hundreds were connected to the gates, and were using them more frequently to solve their problems. Perhaps there is some threshold, or some particular action, that summons them."

His form wavered. "I'm sorry, but it is not as easy as it once was to maintain this form. I know that what I've given might not seem like much, but I'm certain something important changed between Tisha and the first visitation. If you can find it, perhaps we can better understand how to convince Dezigeth to leave."

Anders faded from view, leaving her alone in the library. She sighed. She wasn't sure how much she believed him, but she had no better ideas, so she continued her search.

63

Three droplets of water struck Brandt in the face, and he sputtered as he lost his focus. As punishment, Ana seized control of the remaining water and flung it all at him, laughing as he sputtered some more. "That was almost too easy," she said.

Brandt coughed and wiped the rest of the water from his face. "Sorry."

"That's three times in a row," Ana said, her eyes on his now-soaked tunic. "And I'm beginning to think that you are distracted."

She waited for him to explain his worry.

"I don't feel like we're doing enough," Brandt said. He stood up and stripped his tunic off while he searched for a dry one. "Everyone feels too at ease. It's easy to think that with Dezigeth on Palagia that we have nothing to fear, but it will be here before we know it. Every day we sit around is another day it gathers its forces."

"Alena is soulwalking from morning to night looking for answers. The queen is settling her people and healing them from the wounds they've suffered. I know it doesn't feel like much, but we are preparing. Don't you think you might be asking too much?"

Brandt grimaced. "If anything, I worry that I'm not asking enough. I think Alena has the right idea, but it feels to me almost as if everyone is going their own way and trying their own approach. There's not enough coordination."

"Then do something about it."

Brandt looked at his wife, wondering how he had been born such a fool. Again, she had given him the way forward, one he should have seen on his own. By that afternoon, Brandt found himself walking the streets of Faldun, searching for the elders. He didn't need them all, but at least a few who possessed enough authority to push a collaboration forward.

Finding elders proved more difficult than he imagined. Given the numbers he'd seen in the chamber, he figured Faldun must be full of them. But it was difficult to convince any of the Falari to hear him out. If Weylen and Ren had been here, he would have turned to them, but the last he had heard, they were still journeying with their people toward Faldun. They wouldn't be here for days, at least.

Eventually he found an elder willing to meet. It was a woman he didn't remember from the chamber, but he spoke to her about his fears.

The elder didn't look convinced by his pleas to work more closely with the Lolani, but she reluctantly agreed to send representatives from the council of elders to a gathering the next morning.

Buoyed by his initial success, he proceeded to the queen. She and her people had been given one of the lowest sections of the city, otherwise unoccupied.

Like the Falari elder, she wasn't enthused. Despite her

efforts, a cloud still hung over her, her failure to defend her people haunting her. After enough gentle persuasion, she capitulated. Brandt left feeling like his victory was only due to her saying what he wanted so that he would go away. But a win was a win.

Alena and Toren were last. Unlike the others, they agreed easily, and even seemed excited by the possibility.

And so the next day he had people from all corners of the world gathered together, all looking to him for guidance. They sat at a round table, and before Brandt cleared his throat and focused their attention, he took a moment to admire what had been accomplished. As far as he knew, never before had people from all the lands been gathered together.

But it would all be for nothing if they couldn't find ways to work together.

"Thank you for being here," he began. "We all know the problem we face, and Dezigeth will be here sooner than any of us would like. Do we all agree that our chances of survival are best if we work together?"

The challenge was plainly stated, and he looked to Alena and Toren first. Alena nodded, and Toren gave him an affirmative hand sign. Next he turned to the three Falari elders in attendance. They nodded as one. Last came the queen, and for a moment, he worried she might dissent. But even she inclined her head slightly.

"Good," he said. "Let us keep our shared goal in mind as we speak."

And so they began, each party updating the others on what steps they had taken in response to the threat. In most cases, the news wasn't surprising. The queen worked at settling her people and healing those she could. The Falari summoned all their people to Faldun to prepare for war, and although Toren represented the Etari in this meeting, he had no way of knowing how events stood in his homeland. For his part, Brandt had done little except gather them together. The mood around the table soured as they shared the growing realization that nobody had an easy answer.

Then Alena spoke, and changed the tenor of the discussion. "I've been in conversations with Anders I."

The queen scoffed. "That old man is a fool who should've taken his final journey to the gates long ago."

Alena raised an eyebrow at that, and for a moment Brandt feared Alena's backlash. The obvious retort was that the queen was far older than Anders and likely deserved the same fate. Fortunately, Alena chose a path of peace and held her tongue.

She continued her report. "Regardless, he doesn't believe that Dezigeth can be defeated in any contest of strength. He says that the queen has reached the pinnacle of achievement in that regard, and argues that no more can be done."

"So what does he want us to do? Grovel before its Takaii and beg for mercy?"

Alena remained unperturbed by the queen's bitterness. "He believes, as I do, that there is a link between the power of the gates and Dezigeth's arrival. I'm exploring the matter more deeply in the memories of the gates."

"That's what you've been connecting with my gate to do?" the queen asked. "How many times do I need to tell you that the answers don't exist there?"

Alena stood her ground. "Until you convince me. The ones who came before had far more people connected to the gates than we do, and they controlled the power for generations before Dezigeth's kind arrived."

Something tickled at the back of Brandt's mind, but the argument between the two women distracted him.

"Would you have us give up our only defense?" the queen scoffed.

"I don't know," Alena retorted, "but I also know I won't be satisfied until I've explored the possibility."

The queen stood from her chair, ready either to fight or leave the room. Protests erupted at the breach of decorum, and the council was moments away from spiraling out of control.

Brandt shouted, "Quiet!"

His outburst brought a moment of silence around the table.

The idea was right there, right on the tip of his tongue. Then he had it. "Alena, you said that those who came before had many people connected to the gates?"

She nodded and began to explain, but he cut her off. "What if we did that?"

She frowned. "What do you mean?"

"What if we give the gifts of the gates to everyone?" Brandt asked. "Then every soldier could wield such power." He looked up, his excitement building. "We could field a force the likes that this world has never seen."

"And for good reason," the queen objected. "To give so much power to so many, you would be creating pandemonium. And what happens after? What if we do win? Once so many have a taste of that power, they'll never give it up. We'll trade a quick death at the hands of Dezigeth for a slow death at the hands of one another."

"Perhaps that's the best we can ask for," Brandt argued.

The queen shook her head. "Look to your own peoples. The Etari allow no more than the smallest gatestones into their possession. The Falari shun affinities completely, and the empire pretends the gates don't exist. Don't you think there is a common wisdom here?"

Alena's voice butted in, quiet but still commanding attention. "There's a greater problem. It's not just as simple as connecting people to the gate. Without training, without some ability to soulwalk or manipulate affinities, I don't know how it would work. Perhaps some of the queen's acolytes might survive the connection, but with the level of compulsion the queen has them under, I'm not sure they would survive the process."

Her argument stopped Brandt. She was right. Even if they could share a gate, where would they find the army? The number of people in the empire who had trained with affinities with low, especially within the military. They would either have an army of untrained tradesmen with incredible power or they would kill most of their own soldiers.

And that was even if they could find a gate to use. Given the queen's attitude, and the certainty that Olen would refuse, they didn't have many options.

"The Etari could do it," Toren said quietly.

Everyone in the room turned to him.

"All of us are trained to use the gatestones. If anyone could connect to the gates in numbers, it would be us." He shook his head. "The tough part would be convincing them to do so."

There was a moment of silence as everyone considered the offer. It was Alena who spoke, and it was Alena, Brandt realized, that everyone in the room looked to as a leader. Though she made no claims to a throne, her actions had put her first among them all. "I believe Toren is right. I do not like the thought of attempting to battle Dezigeth again, but if it must be done, this is the best way I can think of."

There were slow nods around the table.

"Then let it be so," Brandt said.

64

A lena stood once again on the walls of the queen's city, her knuckles white as she gripped the stone for support. If not for the presence of Anders beside her, she was certain that she would have fled.

But the first emperor of her land possessed a quality she didn't fully understand. So long as he remained near, the nightmares that had destroyed her dreams and pursued her daily waking life lost some of their power.

It wasn't as if they were gone. The memories still troubled her, and although her sleep had improved, it still wasn't what it had once been. But the jagged edges of her terrors had been filed away, their threat reduced.

While Anders made her relive the experiences, she did so with a thick, comforting blanket wrapped tightly over her. She knew the nightmares still pounded on the doors, but she also knew they could not reach her.

Still, it didn't make reliving these scenes an easy task.

She had been skeptical at first. When Anders proposed that they revisit her memories and once again experience the nightmare of those days, she had turned him immediately down. But he gently insisted, telling her that the only way he knew to conquer a fear was to face it directly.

It wasn't wisdom that changed Alena's mind, but desperation. Despite her better nights of sleep, she still struggled to focus, her thoughts drifting in various directions during important moments in her day. The whole land was mobilizing for war, but all she could think about were random stories from her childhood.

She didn't believe, not for a moment, that her efforts alone would turn the tide of this war. But she did control two gates, which made her important to any effort. If she couldn't find the focus she needed, it could spell the end of their resistance.

And so she had finally turned to Anders, and he in turn had brought her here, back to the places where she took the lives of the Takaii in droves.

Finding the source of her troubles had been one of their first, and still most important, discoveries. Anders had guessed, his ability to see objectively into her thoughts a useful shortcut to uncovering her worst fears. For all the horrible scenes Alena had seen over the years, it wasn't what she had witnessed that haunted her. It was what she had done.

She had fought against coming here. Some memories, she believed, were better left alone, abandoned, to develop cobwebs as the years covered them in dust. But Anders was firm, arguing the memories couldn't fade until they were addressed.

In her soulwalk, in this memory, she saw herself as though she was viewing the event from a distance. The walls of fire rose up and took lives all over again. She trembled as she forced herself to watch, wishing, more than anything, that she could just take everything back.

Wishing she could try again.

Anders replied to her unspoken thoughts. "What is it, exactly, that you regret?" He swept his hand across the vista. "It was because of your actions that hundreds, if not thousands, of lives were saved. This is the essence of warfare, to meet an inferior advance with overwhelming force, to destroy your enemy before they can destroy you."

She knew he challenged her intentionally, and that he well knew her answer. But he insisted she speak.

Speaking a truth out loud gave it power a silent thought lacked.

"But I am no warrior. And this was not a battle."

The emperor's response was almost immediate. "I don't believe you."

Alena opened her mouth to protest, but the words died before they left her lips. In their time together, he had never lied to her, and his knowledge of her was uncanny. If he didn't believe her, it was because she lied.

But she hadn't. She was no warrior.

Anders interrupted her thoughts. "Think, Alena. I grant that you do not seek battle, but when have you ever run from a conflict?"

"When I ran away from Governor Kye in Landow," she said, the answer easy.

The emperor shook his head. "Even you know that's not true."

He fixed her with an unnerving stare. "You weren't running *from* anything. You ran because it was the only way to protect your family. It was not cowardice, but courage, that defined your actions that day."

"It doesn't feel like it."

He smiled at that. "After watching humanity for almost two hundred years, I can tell you this: The courageous warrior rarely feels brave in the times that matter. It is only the fool who feels confidence in such situations."

The battle before them continued. Alena forced herself to keep her eyes on it

Anders continued, "You have always fought in whatever way you thought best. You've stood up to Kye, to Sofra, and to every challenge put in your path. You are a warrior, but your real problem is that you do not feel like this was a battle."

Alena nodded. "It was murder."

The emperor again looked over the field. "Perhaps you've spent too much time around Sofra. Here, you acted as she would've acted, because you saw no other choice. Maybe it was right, maybe not. Only history will tell. But strength will not save us from Dezigeth. You see this battle as a stain on your soul. I think you must take how this made you feel and learn from it. Maybe, as you do, you will find a better way."

Alena felt a tug, a summoning from someplace else. The emperor, perceptive to all events in the soulwalk, smiled. "And speaking of Sofra, it sounds as though she desires your company."

"So it seems." The timing couldn't have been better. The battle was coming to an end. She didn't know if confronting the memory had changed her, but she swore to revisit this day to find her own way forward.

Anders began to fade, but Alena held him back for a moment. "Thank you," she said.

Anders nodded and was gone.

BEFORE LONG, Alena approached the queen's chambers.

She hadn't spent much time in these parts of Faldun.

She wouldn't exactly call them decrepit, but if they suffered a few more years without care, they certainly would be. It turned out that even in cities shaped by the power of those that came before, there were places one did not want to live.

Alena wondered at the queen's decision to live here. She'd been given a choice, offered lodgings much higher up the mountain, rooms that would be offered to any honored guest. But she had refused, electing instead to remain with her people.

Perhaps there was hope for her yet as a ruler.

She knocked on the door and the queen called for her to enter. Alena did, surprised that the queen didn't even have any servants attending her.

Inside, the room was warm and smelled of baking bread. For a moment, Alena was transported back to a different time, a different life. It smelled surprisingly like home.

The queen offered her a slice of warm bread topped with rich butter. Alena accepted the offering and bit into it greedily.

The queen wasn't as good a baker as her mother, but she was skilled. Alena shook her head, still surprised by the hidden talents of the queen. But, she supposed, when one has been alive long enough, one had time to pick up all sorts of skills.

The queen directed the conversation to the reason she had summoned Alena. "You intend to leave for Etar within the next day or two."

Alena nodded, predicting the direction of this conversation. It was little different than others they'd had recently. "I am. We're just waiting on the possible arrival of a trading delegation for the most recent news. They've been expected for the past few days, and we decided to give them a day or two more. The information could prove to be invaluable."

"Is there no chance that I could convince you of the foolishness of this endeavor?"

"Not unless you have an argument that I haven't heard."

"I still fear that your solution is worse than the problem we face."

"And I still contend that nothing quite holds up to the complete extinction of humanity."

With a visible effort, the queen suppressed her frustration. "It's too risky," she muttered, as much to herself as to anyone else. She turned back to Alena. "Will you still travel on foot?"

"Some," Alena said. "I do not wish to use more power than is useful, and to make a grand entrance into Etar would most certainly be a mistake."

"You are foolish to restrict your abilities."

"That may be true," Alena conceded. "But it stands to reason that if those who created the gate conserved their power, it behooves us, as their successors, to do the same."

"For all their understanding, they barely knew what they had created. Surely you've seen enough to recognize as much."

Alena rubbed at her chin, tired of the same arguments. "But there's no reason not to be cautious." She turned the challenges back on the queen. "Would you reconsider your own plans? Or at the very least, sharing your gate with Brandt? I understand your fears, but surely with him you have no need to worry."

The queen lifted her head a bit in acknowledgment. "I will consider it, but that is all I promise."

Alena raised her eyebrow in surprise. That was a larger concession than she'd ever gotten from the queen. Given her choice of lodging and her demeanor, she seemed to be changing before their eyes. They still couldn't push her to share her power, but every step brought them closer.

The queen stood from the chair she had taken, signaling the end of the brief meet. All she had wanted was to try one last time to dissuade Alena.

Alena supposed it was quite the change, that the queen was resorting to persuasion instead of violence. When they met again, how much more would have changed? "Whatever happens, I wish you the best, Sofra."

The queen didn't even bristle at the use of her birth name. "And you as well, Alena."

And surprisingly, Alena believed that the queen meant every word.

65

When Brandt looked out over the walls of Faldun to the valley below, he couldn't help but recall memories of the last time he had been here, when the city had been under siege. Now, as then, the Falari were lined up in the valley. And as before, they wanted in.

Brandt shuddered at the thought, mindful of the eerie parallels between now and then. Still, there was one crucial difference.

Today, no one would fight to gain admittance to the safety of Faldun. The streets wouldn't be patrolled by archers hunting for their kin.

The Falari had decided to recall everyone to Faldun. Apparently, the elders claimed, there was historical precedence, but Brandt was amazed that there was room within the city for every Falari. It confirmed a suspicion, long held but never proven, that the Falari lands were more empty than the empire believed.

In the valley, warleaders and Senki organized the people, and a constant stream of runners sprinted endlessly between Faldun and the encampments outside. Brandt only understood the barest outlines of the process, but even that impressed him.

Each warleader would have a section of the city to settle, a place to call their own. Each section held dining halls and armories. The permanent residents of Faldun were relocated to make space for the new arrivals.

It should have been chaos, and the city should have been up in arms.

But the whole process seemed calm and orderly. Everyone pitched in, and few complained. It was remarkable, Brandt decided, what cooperation imminent extinction could inspire.

His thoughts couldn't stay focused on the relocation long. They kept wandering to the friends he was about to meet.

He stood outside the tavern Ren had taken him to several months ago, a place run by a former Senki, designed to accommodate warriors as they passed through Faldun. It was a place he felt comfortable in, a place that he hoped brought out fond memories in his guests.

He supposed he would find out soon.

He didn't hear their approach, both of them far too practiced in the art of moving silently, but some vestigial sense informed him that he wasn't alone. He turned from the spectacular view of the valley to see both Weylen and Ren watching him.

The sight of them brought a smile to his face. Though it hadn't been that long since he'd seen them, it felt as though years had passed. His departure from them had been sudden, but he possessed nothing except fond memories of the two warriors. They'd fought side by side, and in Ren, particularly, he felt as though he'd discovered a kindred soul.

Judging from their expressions, though, he wasn't sure the feelings were mutual. Weylen's frown was deep, and neither man made any move to approach closer once they were noticed. They looked almost as if they considered Brandt some sort of dangerous animal, one they didn't dare approach too closely.

He was well aware of the reputation he'd developed in his absence, and he wished he could say that it was completely undeserved, but it still pained him to see these men treat him so.

Brandt swallowed the lump in his throat, knowing that this conversation would be as difficult as any duel.

He bowed deeply to them. "Weylen, Ren, I'm honored that you were willing to join me today."

They remained motionless, unimpressed by his greeting. Had his actions pushed him too far away from them? Brandt gestured to the tavern behind them. "Will you join me?"

There was a long moment of hesitation between the two men, but then some sort of unspoken signal was given. Ren nodded and led them in.

Brandt fought the powerful twisting in his stomach. He'd known, of course, this would be a difficult meeting. His first clue had come when the two warriors hadn't made any effort to visit him once their war party had resettled in Faldun.

Brandt supposed he could have let them alone, but he wished to mend the wounds he'd caused, and Weylen's influence had grown considerably in the months Brandt had been gone. Brandt hoped the war leader would be an ally, but truly hoped that at the least, they could still be friends.

Ren found them a table, and they were quickly served three mugs of ale.

Perhaps the drink would loosen them up a bit. He took a long pull of his.

When they didn't provide any easy openings, Brandt swallowed his pride and began. He bowed again, as well as he could at the table. "I am deeply sorry for whatever harm my actions have caused. What may I do to earn your forgiveness?"

Weylen shook his head. "Forgiveness is not something earned. It is granted."

His cold tone made it clear that forgiveness remained well out of Brandt's reach.

Ren continued where his warleader left off, his tone sharp. "What would you have of us?"

Brandt gripped his mug tighter. Truthfully, he'd expected a more charitable meeting. This already didn't bode well for him. "I had hoped for your aid in convincing the other warleaders that a stronger alliance with the queen is wise."

Ren's reply was vicious. "You hope to utilize our past friendship to aid you in your foolish plan?"

Brandt first grimaced, but he thought he caught a hint of something in Ren's response. A thread of hope, perhaps. He decided to gamble on the strength of their past relationship. "Yes." He let his pause hang between them for a few moments. "I still consider us friends, despite my actions. And I absolutely intend to drag you into even more foolish choices to come."

He waited for a moment, and then waited for several more. The faces across from him were as stony as the city of Faldun.

"I told you," Ren told Weylen, his face cracking first.

Weylen cursed and a coin was passed between warleader and Senki. Ren pocketed it with a smile on his face.

Brandt looked between the two men, unable to hide his confusion.

Weylen soon had a grin to match Ren's. "What you have done here, it would never be done among our people. A duel between Senki, perhaps, but nothing like this. Ren predicted not just your actions, but most of your words as well."

The wave of emotion that came over Brandt surprised him in its intensity. After the judgment he had suffered, however rightfully so, at the hands of so many others, to be understood by such men was more than he could ask for.

He didn't get the sense, though, that their scene had been entirely an act. There was an element of truth within. One that he needed to address.

Brandt supposed there was no better way than to tell the story from the beginning, which he did. Mugs of ale were refilled, and the conversation went long into the night. Doubtless he filled in more detail than was necessary, but he wanted these two men to understand why he had chosen as he had.

And when he was done, Weylen only had one question for him. "Do you trust her?"

Brandt grimaced. It was a question that had no short, easy answer. "I trust her to help us fight Dezigeth. As much as I would like to hope that the change to her character is something real and lasting, I'm not so foolish or naïve as to make that promise. I worry that even in the midst of battle, if she sees an opportunity to gain an advantage against us, she will take it. But not at the cost of defeating Dezigeth. That is her first concern, as it is mine."

Brandt glanced between the two men, but ultimately, the decision was Weylen's. He was warleader, and the voice that other warleaders would listen to.

When the older man nodded, Brandt felt as though he'd won his first major battle.

66

Alena looked over at Toren. "You sure you want to try this?"

Toren looked at the creation Alena had made, floating as high as his head off the ground. It wobbled, a problem that only seemed to get worse every time she tried to fix it. "No."

To her ear it sounded as though he wanted his refusal to carry even more vehemence, and for once she was grateful for his tendency to rely on understatement.

She hadn't told the queen the entire truth during their last meeting. She didn't want to fly into Etar. That had been true.

With a thought, she brought the platform back to the ground, its landing causing the ground to rumble.

The real reason why she didn't just fly everywhere was because she wasn't sure she had the control to do so.

Had they been in the soulwalk, Alena could have controlled her platform easily. She could imagine it without problem, but in the physical world the act required a level of focus and control with her affinities that she hadn't yet developed. She could fly the platform, but she couldn't ensure they reached their destination intact.

But they did have to make good time to Etar, and her fiddling with the platform wasn't helping.

Alena frowned, and then an idea occurred to her. She ripped two stones from the ground, each just a little bigger than her hand, and gave one to Toren while keeping the other for herself. "There. Hold onto this. If something happens to the platform, we can just jump out and I can hold these in the air."

Toren looked dubiously at the rock, as though it might be trying to take his life. But eventually he shrugged.

Without further comment, Toren stepped onto the platform. The shape that Alena had decided on was similar to a bowl, except the platform had a flat bottom. She figured that if they were going to be traveling long distances, the walls would help keep the wind off them. At least, that was what she told Toren.

Really, given her lack of control, the walls were more to keep them in than wind out. As extra aids, she had fashioned a few handholds for them to grab onto as well.

She ignored a strong temptation to send Toren up on his own. Entertaining as that might be, it was no way to repay the trust he had shown her. So, trying to keep the worry off her face, she joined him on the platform.

It felt sturdy enough under her feet, and she hoped she wasn't deceiving herself. She sat down and pressed her back against the wall, reaching out to grab one of the handholds. "Ready?"

Toren flashed her a sign of uncertainty.

She lifted them into the air.

Any dreams of a smooth flight were immediately dashed as they rose, tilting precariously one way and then the other.

Only their tight grips on the handholds and their feet braced firmly against the floor prevented them from careening into one another. Even so, Alena saw that Toren was clutching his safety rock as though it was the only thing that would save his life.

If they were going to suffer like this, Alena figured they might as well be moving, so she pushed the platform northwest.

She brought them higher so she had to do less maneuvering, and could spend more of her attention on keeping the platform steady. In time, she became confident enough that she released her death grip on the handholds. She couldn't master a smooth flight, but they were moving, and fast.

There was no denying how effective this idea was. She kept pushing them until they were travelling far faster than a galloping horse, and unlike a galloping horse, she needed no breaks. Using the power of the gates, she barely felt the effort at all.

And not only was their speed greater, but they could fly in a straight line while the trails below them twisted and turned, gaining steep elevation only to lose it again. The journey that would've taken them days passed underneath them in the course of a single morning.

From time to time, Alena would gather the courage to glance out over the edges of the platform. From up high, her feelings about Falar changed. The mountains were still imposing and majestic, but they no longer instilled in her the same fear as when she had traveled those paths on foot. From the air, she saw only the beauty of the land, not the effort it took to eke out a living here.

Wisely, Toren said little on the trip. He would've been a distraction, which she didn't need.

She improved with practice. By noon she had reduced the wobble to something that didn't constantly slam her teeth together, and in the evening, when she finally brought them to a stop, they were well within imperial lands.

She didn't want to stop, but her focus had been slipping, the wobble of the platform becoming almost unbearable. So she had landed them in the middle of empty land, hoping no strangers came by and found them. She was too tired for trouble.

While Toren set up camp and prepared their food, Alena debated whether or not she should enter the soulwalk. She had come to depend upon her sessions with Anders, but wasn't sure a visit was a wise idea after a full day of using her powers. Toren, attuned to her thoughts, asked, "Are you going to meet him tonight?"

"Not sure," she answered. "Going to bed sounds incredibly enticing."

"What you did today would be a legend in any other story," he said. "And even with my affinity for stone I would never have imagined such a mode of transport."

"Is that your polite way of telling me that I should rest?"

He signed the affirmative, and she laughed.

She wasn't sure what caused her to tell him, but she blurted out her idea regardless. "I'm thinking of asking Anders to erase my memories of Palagia."

The only indication of Toren's surprise was the brief hesitation of his knife as he prepared the food. "Why do you think that is wise?"

The question surprised her a little. Toren knew, better than anyone, what those memories cost her. But like the emperor, he seemed to share a belief that speaking was more beneficial than just thinking. "I still worry that when I face the Takaii again, I'll freeze."

Toren didn't respond for a long time. When he did, she was disappointed to find that it was with another question. "Are you certain?"

Her voice came out louder and more forceful than she intended. "You've seen what those memories do to me. Of course I'm certain."

Again, Toren was silent. She was used to him taking the time to think through his responses, but all the same she wished that he would just say what he thought.

Eventually, he spoke. "Back in Etar, when we were kids, did you know that we were encouraged to fail often?"

She nodded. Although it had never been stated so bluntly, she'd seen enough of the behavior from the Etari parents when she had been among them. She had always admired their insistence that children push themselves to the limits of their abilities and beyond.

"For some of us who were less gifted, fulfilling our parents' wishes was an easy task," he said. "It was those who were accomplished, who were used to success coming easily to them, that struggled most with the idea. Many parents had to push, harder and harder, until even the successful children failed. But most parents wouldn't give up until their children were pushed beyond their limits. Do you know why?"

"Because it makes the children stronger."

"It does. Failure is a far better teacher than success. The things that hurt us are the things we learn most from."

He paused, making one last addition to the dish he prepared.

"If you were to erase your memories, what is to say that you wouldn't just make the same choices again? Sofra's thinking would infect your own, just as it did in Palagia. Your strongest belief right now is that you want to make new choices, better choices. But if you aren't driven by the pain of Palagia, don't you think that you'll lose your motivation to do so?"

She absorbed his words and her anger died. She wasn't entirely convinced. But he made a good argument. And he was worth listening to.

She stood up and moved toward him. "You're wiser than you look, you know."

He smiled as he handed her a bowl of food. "I'm glad you think so. Now eat up. Tomorrow, we enter Etar."

67

Weylen was as good as his word and then some. That evening, he'd returned to his war party and waited for his hangover to fade. At least, that was what Ren reported. But the next morning he was up, visiting warleader after warleader, speaking to each individually.

In just one day, Weylen made more progress than Brandt had made since the Lolani arrived on the Falari doorstep. Before, the Falari had cooperated, but more as young people grumbling that they didn't want to work with others. With Weylen, they were almost enthusiastic. Today had been Weylen's idea, and it marked a giant leap forward in the cooperation between the people.

If they didn't accidentally kill each other first.

Brandt sat on a horse, well behind an assembled mass of both Falari and Lolani warriors. His station was on a low ridge across the valley from Faldun, giving him a view of everything happening below.

But for the moment, Brandt looked across the valley instead of down it. Though he couldn't make out any individual figures from this distance, he could well imagine many curious eyes waited with even more impatience.

The joint exercises were a symbol, a chance to show what was possible. But they could just as easily serve the opposite purpose. If they failed miserably, hostile warleaders and elders would argue for the end of their fragile alliance with the Lolani.

Too much rode on the shoulders of the unfortunate soldiers.

The commanders from both sides had more or less forced their warriors together. Though initially awkward, the troops soon found commonalities.

A warrior was a warrior, no matter where they were born. Brandt saw at least three archery competitions spring to life, as well as what he hoped were some friendly wrestling matches.

If their exercise had been examined and completed solely on paper, the cooperation between the forces seemed a natural fit. Although distance and language separated them, both cultures had a strong emphasis on martial skill. In Brandt's estimation, both the Falari and Lolani were enemies to fear. If they could make this alliance work, they would be even more terrifying together.

The logistics of managing separate armies was always challenging. The magnitude of the problem was one Brandt hadn't fully appreciated until they began preparing for the exercise. One of Anders I's innovations that didn't earn the respect it deserved was that of the shared system of signals used by all imperial forces. As Anders had rolled over the land and absorbed enemy soldiers into his army, every recruit went through a training that built them into a single army.

That same training continued, largely unchanged, today. It was one of the empire's greatest strengths.

The Falari and Lolani had developed their own systems of battle, their own methods of communication. Much preparation had gone into finding a system that worked for both armies, but it was anyone's guess what would actually transpire when the system was tested.

Based on the reports provided by the queen and Brandt, the Falari and Lolani commanders had developed a joint strategy to defend against the Takaii. As most good plans went, it was nothing complex, and Brandt hoped it would be effective.

The Lolani and their shield walls would form the front lines of any engagement, supported by Falari archers. The Falari bows were stronger than their Lolani counterparts, as the Falari's terrain had forced them into specializing in archery for generations. In contrast, the Lolani archers were just as comfortable with sword and shield as their ranged weapons.

Brandt's suggestion had been taken straight from Anders I's own strategies. Instead of forcing units to assume tasks they weren't comfortable with, they leaned into what they were good at. The Falari would use their bows, protecting the Lolani advance.

Eventually the commanders forced the groups into formations, and the exercise began.

Brandt watched the first attempt with a keen eye. It was the details, compounded one after another, that often doomed a maneuver. The initial formations held together easily, and for a moment, Brandt had hope.

But the start was about all that went well.

The Lolani marched faster than the Falari expected. The goal had been for the Falari to fire five organized volleys of arrows before the Lolani reached a marker in the valley. The Falari only managed three, and at least one archer commander ordered his warriors to fire far too late. The arrows came close to striking their allies.

Against a wave of Takaii, Brandt couldn't help but imagine their forces being run over, weaker together than they were apart.

He hadn't expected the first attempt to go well, but the failure pained him all the same.

The commanders formed their soldiers up. Arrows were retrieved, and they tried the exercise again.

The second attempt was better, but still not anything to be proud of.

As the units re-formed, Brandt was joined by Weylen, Ren, and a few of the other warleaders and Senki. He couldn't judge their mood from their expressions.

"What do you think?" Weylen asked.

Brandt noted the details he'd observed, adding suggestions for strengthening the attempts. All the warleaders nodded along as he spoke. "We've thought much the same," Weylen said. "You would make a fine warleader, with some more experience."

Brandt shook his head. "I'm honored that you think so, but I'm afraid I disagree. My skill is on the battlefield, not behind it."

"But you have a good eye," Weylen retorted.

"There's a vast difference between seeing what is going wrong and commanding an army."

"But knowing what is wrong is a valuable first step," Weylen continued. "Brandt, there are those among us who would offer you a command."

Brandt refused. "Again, I appreciate your generosity, but I am a soldier. Large-scale tactics and strategy are beyond me. I simply never had the gift. And besides, with the gate-stone I am far more useful if I'm in the heart of the battle. That is where I can make the biggest difference."

The warleaders looked to one another, and Brandt couldn't tell if they were disappointed or not. But in this, at least, he was certain. Command was not for him.

They didn't press further, and together, they watched as two armies struggled to become one.

68

The rest of Alena and Toren's journey to Cardon was uneventful. They flew to the border, then crossed the Alna River by ferry. At the border they were met by one of the trading clans. Both Alena and Toren were known to the clan, and were given some of the clan's best horses.

Long days in the saddle followed, the two frequently supplied with fresh horses by other clans. They reached Cardon within a week, far faster than any journey Alena could have imagined years ago.

Her legs protested, though. She hadn't ridden so far in years, and they'd pushed hard. More than once she dreamed of forming another platform, but she feared how the Etari would react to such a blatant use of a gate's power.

The last time she'd been to Cardon, the tent city had been almost deserted. Now, the opposite sight greeted her. More tents were gathered than she remembered being present even during the large annual gatherings.

The traders they'd passed had told them the Etari were

congregating, but none had indicated just how many. Both Toren and Alena paused for a moment at the sight.

"They prepare, too," Alena said.

Toren signed his affirmation.

She'd noticed a slight change in his demeanor since they'd returned to Etar. He was more relaxed, as though he'd let down a guard he'd been keeping up for months. This was his home, after all.

What surprised her was that she felt much the same. She'd spent more of her adult life traveling the plains of Etar than she had near her home in Landow. The quiet open spaces comforted her. She slipped into the patterns of the Etari as though putting on a comfortable coat. She spoke less and relied more on the hand signs that formed the backbone of Etari communication.

It made her think, however briefly, about her future. If they defeated Dezigeth, what would she do?

She could think of much worse ideas than spending her days traveling through Etar with Toren.

They rode into Cardon, seeking out their respective families. Toren found his first, and they parted while Alena searched for her own. Knowing Sooni, it was likely Alena's family wasn't here. But she maintained her hope.

Which was rewarded before long. Alena's whole clan was closer to the center of Cardon than she expected, a position of honor. And among the clan she found Sooni and her family.

Although it had only been months since they had last seen one another, the greetings she received made her feel as though she had been gone for years. Friends squeezed her until it was difficult to breathe, and more than one question was asked about Toren. All her family knew she had left with the mysterious Etari soulwalker.

She promised to explain what she could, but her first destination was Sooni's tent.

The leader of her family greeted her with a smile and a warm hug. She offered tea as Alena began recounting her adventures since she'd last departed for Falar.

Sooni listened attentively, asking a few questions when Alena skipped over details. When Alena finished, the tea was long gone.

"I'm afraid your story will have to be retold to the elders," Sooni said. "Although you will find little doubt as to its veracity. We've felt the groanings of the world since Dezigeth's arrival, and knew it was time to gather."

Sooni placed her hand over her stomach, where her gatestone was embedded. "But we all owe you a debt of incredible gratitude. Our gate no longer fails as it did when you were here last."

Alena's eyes shot up at that. She'd thought, occasionally, of the Etari gate since the Battle of Faldun, but not closely. Her attention had been focused on other matters, and the Etari gate had always seemed a lesser problem.

"It hasn't faded at all?"

"There were a couple of days when we worried the problem had returned," Sooni admitted. Alena inquired and found those days correlated with her battles with Dezigeth. Though not conclusive, she suspected that it was more proof of her belief that pulling massive amounts of power disrupted the balance between the gates.

All of which brought Alena to the question she'd been too afraid to ask. "We have an idea for fighting Dezigeth," she said. "But it requires the Etari, and I don't think the elders are going to like it." She explained their idea.

When she finished, Sooni took a long moment and looked into her empty tea cup. "You're right," she said. "But

I, for one, have come to trust you. Although she'll never admit it, Dunne does, too. The reason we're so close to the center of Cardon is because of you."

The rest of the day and night passed in a blur. She was given a tent, and the whole camp turned out to greet Toren when he rejoined her. Toren spent most of the evening engaged in various contests with the men of Sooni's family. Good-natured wrestling matches were interspersed with rounds of drinking. The atmosphere was celebratory.

The difference between this return and her last was striking. Toren, as an Etari soulwalker, had never been accepted by most of the warriors and traders. But now it didn't seem to matter. He was an outsider, but so was Alena, and Sooni's family had the capacity to welcome them both. When Toren and Alena finally got a chance to speak, he admitted that his own reunion hadn't gone nearly so well.

She felt for him, but after a lifetime of being excluded, his family's rejection seemed to roll right off him. And the welcome Alena's family offered seemed more than enough recompense.

That night was one of the happiest Alena could remember.

THE NEXT MORNING WAS COOL, and waves of light rain passed over Cardon. Most of the Etari remained inside their tents, and Alena found it difficult to convince her body to emerge from the blankets that covered both her and Toren. What she wanted was to remain snuggled next to him while the clouds passed them by.

But she was to meet with the elders today, so rest was out of the question.

She rose and stretched. One downside to their rapid

pace of travel was that she hadn't settled on an approach to win over the skeptical Etari. Her plan, such as it was, was to speak to them directly. What it lacked in subtlety she hoped it made up for in persuasiveness. Against the threat of their complete extermination, surely the Etari elders would bend against the force of their traditions.

Her summons came not long after she woke, during a break between rainfalls. The smell of wet grass filled the air, easing some of the tension she carried.

The elders summoned her to the center tent, the heart of Cardon, where the remains of the shattered gate stood.

Alena wasn't sure if the choice of location boded well for her or not.

The flaps of the tent were held open for her by the guards, and she stepped in.

As she did, she felt as though she was stepping into a new world, a sacred place set apart from the mundane activities of the outside world. It was quiet within, not even the elders speaking without reason.

She signed the most respectful greeting, then bowed. A reminder that she was a child of two worlds.

Dunne, the elder of Alena's clan, spoke first. "Welcome, Alena. My daughter Sooni tells me you have a tale we need to hear."

Alena signed a respectful affirmative gesture.

"Then proceed," Dunne said.

Alena took a moment to gather her thoughts. She'd come more prepared to make an argument for the use of the gate, but they would reach that point in time. She began her story, starting from when she had last met with this council, when they had sent her to Falar in an attempt to restore balance to the gates.

Within the tent, there were few external signs of time

passing. The air became warmer as the sun rose, but that was the only clue Alena had. When she finished her story, it felt as though she'd been speaking for days.

Water was offered, which she gratefully accepted.

The elders didn't confer after she finished. Instead, Dunne once again assumed the responsibility for asking questions. "You've clearly come before us for a reason. What is it?"

"We believe that our only chance to fight Dezigeth is to bind the Etari to a gate."

Looks of consternation passed between the council members, and Alena charged forward. "Only the Etari have such a large number of warriors gifted with affinities. The use of the gatestones prepares one well for the use of a gate."

Another elder spoke, one Alena didn't recognize. He practically spat the question. "You would have us all become soulwalkers?"

Alena made a negative sign. "There is no need. I can perform the bindings if your permission is granted. For the warriors, it will be much like connecting with their gatestones, only much more powerful."

Another elder, this one familiar from her previous appearances before the council, spoke next. "If this technique works, why hasn't it been used before? Why didn't Zolene and her followers attempt something similar?"

"I can only guess," Alena said. "The power of the gates deserves cautious respect, and I am unsure of how the pulling of so much power will affect the gates. I wouldn't attempt linking so many unless I absolutely believed it was necessary."

Dunne asked the next question. "You believe that if we don't do this, we stand no chance against the creature?"

"It is the only idea that seems to have a chance of

success," Alena said. "I continue to search for another way, but for now, this is all I know."

When no further questions seemed imminent, she added another thought. "At times, there seems an order to events that surpasses my understanding. Although the Etari are the only people capable of this task, they are also the only people I would trust," she said. "Should we succeed, I would intend to cut the bindings between the Etari and the gates once again."

"What you ask goes against generations of tradition, of the wisdom that has been handed down from elder to elder," Dunne said.

"And I am grateful you have even listened to me," Alena responded.

She almost said more but stopped. One of the earliest lessons the Etari had taught her was the value in saying only what needed to be said. They would either choose to trust her or not. That was up to them.

Alena grimaced. Her head had started to throb, a deep pain near the base of her skull. She reached back and rubbed her neck, but the pain didn't seem to be physical. It intensified.

"Alena, what's wrong?" Dunne's voice sounded distant.

Stars exploded in Alena's vision and the ground seemed to shake beneath her feet. For a heartbeat, she thought it was a figment of her own illness, but then she saw the elders swaying. A high-pitched whine filled the tent, and Alena saw the others turn to stare at the gate.

She followed the stares, and her eyes widened with all the rest of them when she saw the gate begin to glow. Not the blue she was now familiar with, but a bright white, so intense that it washed out the normal colors of the tent.

And that was just the beginning.

For the first few moments of the event, Brandt wasn't sure that what he felt was real. He was eating lunch with Ana when his stomach felt as though it had been filled with fire. He bent over and clutched at it, unable to respond to Ana's concerned cries.

His gatestone.

It hurt, as though it had grown claws and was trying to gouge its way through his torso.

The others in the dining hall gave him concerned looks, but he saw how they backed away.

Then the world began to rumble.

At first, he was convinced it was his imagination. But when the others started glancing around the room, looking afraid that the building would collapse, he knew it wasn't just him.

The whole mountain was shaking.

His agony increased in time with the mountain's distress. Ana reached under his armpits and pulled him out of the dining hall into the open air. Not that it would matter if the city began to collapse, he supposed, but she saved him from having to worry about the dining hall crashing down on him.

He tried to help, but every move he made only increased the agony in his stomach. This was no pain he could fight through. It commanded every iota of his attention.

Outside, the scene was one of chaos. Faldun stood, but any loose rock plummeted down, crashing into the levels below. Ana, seeing this, positioned them close to the wall of the dining hall. "Is there anything I can do?"

Brandt couldn't even find the words to respond. The pain in his stomach was causing stars to swim in his vision.

And then, as soon as it had hit, it was over. His suffering disappeared as though it had never existed, and the mountain stopped shaking.

"What was that?" Ana asked.

Brandt looked down at his torso, where he kept the gatestone wrapped tight around his stomach. "The gates. Something happened." He looked up at Ana. "I need to find the queen." He stood up. "Will you be fine?"

She nodded, and Brandt tested his gatestone. It still worked, the same as it always had.

Still, he didn't feel comfortable trusting it. If something happened while he was using it to fly down to the queen, he might not survive. Better to choose a path of safety. He made himself light and started dropping down to the city, leaping from one level to the next.

It didn't take long for him to reach the section of the city where the Lolani lived. Most were out in the streets, but there was a different feeling here. Up above, the uncertainty fed into the fears of the Falari. Down below, the Lolani appeared resigned, pursued by the troubles they couldn't outrun.

He made it to the queen's chambers without problem,

leaping from rooftop to rooftop to avoid the crowds. A contingent of guards stood outside the queen's door, and Brandt spotted an acolyte among them. They tensed at his sudden arrival, but he held his hands up, far away from his sword. He gestured toward the door.

The guards turned to the acolyte, who nodded. Brandt offered them a short bow, then went to the door and knocked. When he heard no answer, he turned to the acolyte. She gestured for him to enter, and he did.

Inside the rooms there was no light. Brandt took two steps in, closed the door behind him, and summoned a small flame. He found a lantern hanging by the door and lit it. The first room was empty, but he thought he heard something coming from the bedroom beyond. "Sofra?"

There was no reply.

Brandt walked toward the other room carefully, not sure what he might find.

When he came close enough for the lantern to light the room, he froze in place.

The queen was on the bed, curled tightly into a ball, weeping.

When she saw him, she snarled and yelled, "Get out!"

He almost did.

But something in her demeanor stopped him.

She had lived alone for too long.

He stepped toward the bed.

She swore. "Leave now, or I'll tear this whole mountain down!"

She almost did. He heard her gather the strength of her affinities. He took the last step forward and sat on the edge of the bed. Then he reached out and put his hand firmly on her shoulder.

At his touch, her anger broke. She released her hold on the affinities and she wept.

Brandt let her. Eventually he removed his hand, but he stayed by her. With only the lantern for light, he wasn't sure how much time had passed, but it had been considerable.

Eventually, her tears dried up. Her breath steadied. She lay still for some time, and Brandt glanced over to see if she was asleep.

She wasn't. Her eyes stared into the darkness, and he didn't know what she saw there.

He worked up his courage, then spoke. "What happened?"

Her voice was hollow. "It destroyed my gate."

Brandt shook his head. "That's not possible."

"It appears that it is."

"It can't be. Even the Etari gate can still be used."

The queen sat up in the bed. "This isn't like that. The weaving that built the Etari gate remains intact. It is only physical damage that gate suffered. Mine wasn't broken. It was undone."

Brandt couldn't picture it. "It's gone?"

She nodded.

Brandt felt as empty as the queen sounded. A part of him didn't believe, though he had no reason to doubt. The gates couldn't be destroyed. They were the hope of the whole world. And, Brandt realized with a start, they had become one of the foundations of his existence. He believed in the gates with the same passion he believed in Ana.

What did it mean?

New questions assaulted him from all sides.

Could the other gates still be used?

Were the other gates now weaker?

The temptation was to pose the questions to the queen.

If anyone knew the answers and understood the implications, it was her. But when he looked at her he saw how unwise such an action would be.

Whatever loss he might have felt at the news, it didn't compare to what she must be feeling.

"How are you?"

She growled at him, but Brandt didn't back away. "It's just me."

Her fist clenched, then fell. She shook her head and stared back into the darkness, unwilling to meet his gaze. "That gate has been my only companion for most of my life. I spent a lifetime learning how to connect with it, and then I spent even more lifetimes trying to understand it." Now she did meet his eyes. "No matter what happened, it has always been there."

From the tone of her voice, one would almost think she was speaking of a lover or friend.

But Brandt understood, at least in part. He'd felt something of the same when the queen had destroyed Highkeep. People could attach to places or objects just as easily as they could to others.

There was nothing he could say. Whatever he did, it wouldn't be enough.

So he sat while the queen continued to grieve.

70

When Alena finally woke from the rest Toren had forced her to take, she worried something more had happened. The rain had come again, and the soft drizzle against the outside of the tent made her want to roll over and return to sleep.

The silence of the camp concerned her, though. Cardon was rarely loud in the way that Estern, Tonno, or even Landow were. Unless the annual festival was occurring, there was little of the shouting that filled so many other streets. But even by Cardon's standards, it was too quiet.

Alena had been the first hurt, but she had been far from the last. She squeezed her eyes shut, trying to force out the memories of the elders, doubled over in agony, falling to the ground as they lost control of their limbs.

She'd shared their pain, her own gatestone raking across her stomach like an angry creature attempting to escape. But all of that hadn't mattered at all the moment Dezigeth undid the gate. A flash of white had seared her mind, erasing all thought with it. How long the moment had actually lasted she couldn't be sure. But it had been the opposite of the void the queen had once stranded her in.

Where that had been a perfect, never-ending emptiness, this had been everything. Every sensation and fear crammed into every fiber of her being. In those moments, nothing of her had remained.

And then it had been gone, and she was Alena again, doubled over in pain, clutching her stomach just like the elders. Except there was no more pain. Just a memory of what had once been.

There had been confusion and questions, and the council had disbanded. Toren had pushed into the tent, heedless of the guards outside. After a brief exchange with Dunne, he'd taken Alena back to their tent and they'd fallen asleep beside one another.

The covers beside her were empty. She looked across the tent and saw Toren meditating.

She rolled onto her back and stared at the ceiling of the tent. As he'd escorted her back, she'd seen the damage that the Etari had suffered. Men and women were everywhere, doubled over. Most were on the ground, but a few leaned against tents, sweat pouring from the exertion of simply standing. Children, not yet old enough to have the gate-stones, cried as their parents writhed in agony.

She hadn't even had time to ask how Toren had felt, or how he had managed to escort her to the tent. She knew that if she did, he would just wave her questions away and pretend they were nothing.

But he had stood when no one else could.

She smiled at the thought. Her friends, long ago, back at the academy, might have laughed to hear her speak of her love now. There were better warriors, and certainly more charismatic men. But Toren was always there. Through all her travels these last few months, he'd followed her without question, supporting her every step of the way.

And he never asked for anything in return.

Eventually, he came out of his mediation and smiled when he saw that she was awake. "I was worried about you for a bit," he said.

"How are the others?"

"Everyone will live," he said. "The attack was momentarily painful, but as near as anyone can tell, there was no lasting damage to the Etari gate."

Alena could barely start to consider the ramifications. What did the loss of a gate even mean? Did it affect the source of energy they drew from?

There would be no answers within the gates themselves. No memory of those that came before would cover this. If she wanted answers, she would have to find them herself.

Alena sat up, waving away Toren's attempt to help her. She felt a little tired yet, but otherwise fine. Tentatively, she reached out and connected with the gates. To her relief, they responded as they always had. Their power remained at her fingertips, and her abilities felt undiminished.

She thought of Sofra. It had been her gate that was undone. A gate she had been connected to for hundreds of years. Even if her power remained the same, Alena was certain the queen was anything but fine.

Alena stretched. She wasn't finding any answers sitting on top of her covers. She stood and stepped out of the tent and was surprised to find two warriors squatting in the rain, waiting for her. The one on the right spoke. "The elders wait for you."

Alena gestured that they should lead, though she well knew the way.

They didn't pass a single person. Everyone remained in

their tents. Even given the rain, Alena had never seen Cardon so quiet.

It concerned her. She'd never seen the Etari silenced so effectively. She needed them, and hoped that their spirits hadn't been broken.

Her escort ushered her into the tent without first announcing her. The elders were caught by surprise, many of them lying on the ground with their eyes closed. They slowly worked their way to their feet when she entered, the breach of decorum ignored. Alena politely turned her eyes down until they spoke.

Dunne asked the first question. "Has the loss of the gate changed your plans?"

"No. I remain connected to my gates, and I do not think the destruction of the gate has affected my abilities. If anything, it is more important than ever to prepare ourselves. We cannot let the same fate befall our gate."

The elders looked to one another. Alena could read them well enough. In her absence, the elders had made their choice, but they feared the consequences.

It fell to Dunne to make their pronouncement. "We have decided to allow you to connect with the gates, and to connect and train our warriors who volunteer. Tonight we will speak to all. You may begin tomorrow."

Alena signed her deepest gratitude. "I'm honored by the trust that you have in me, elders. I will do everything I can to ensure that trust isn't misplaced."

With that, the council dismissed her, and she returned to her tent. She walked quickly, her mood putting a spring in her step. For the first time since she'd first felt Dezigeth's approach, she felt the first glimmer of hope.

And hope was powerful.

. . .

ALENA ENTERED the tent at the center of Cardon the next morning with Toren at her side. What once had been the most secret place in all of Etar was now hers to visit as she pleased. At times, it still surprised her. What would her childhood self say, if she could see where she'd ended up?

She held his hand, and together they dropped into the soulwalk.

Their first task was to tie themselves more closely to one another. They already possessed a strong connection. But for this they wanted to be even closer.

In the soulwalk, Alena wrapped several strands of string around her wrist and his, tying each tightly. With each new connection she could feel his emotions more clearly. Remarkably, he was just as calm on the inside as he appeared on the outside. She basked in that quiet strength, preparing herself for what came next.

When he nodded, Alena dove toward the gate. Finding it in the soulwalk took time, but before long she stood before it, alone. She hesitated for a moment. The Etari had believed for many years that no one should do exactly what she was about to attempt. It was what needed to happen, and she had their permission, but it still seemed a bit of a desecration.

Then she pushed forward. She began weaving the connection between herself and the gate, using Zolene's connection as the model.

The weaving was completed without complication. Alena didn't feel any different than before. It was the final piece of evidence that suggested she'd been right about the gates. She could be connected to one or all four. They drew the same amount of power.

Next came the part she was less certain about. She began another weaving around the gate, then carried it back up the levels of the soulwalk. Toren could have joined her deeper, but he was a trained soulwalker. No one else among the Etari could. If this was going to work, Alena had to be able to connect them to the gates through no effort of their own.

She found Toren waiting for her, and she completed the weaving, connecting him to the gate. His eyes widened when she completed the last knot.

Together they returned to the physical world. She looked at him, hesitating. "Did it work?"

He signed the affirmative as he pulled dozens of stones from the pouch at his hip. His control defied her understanding. Then he smiled. "The next time we have to fly, how about you let me?"

"With pleasure. Now let me return to the gate to see if the connection has changed anything. If not, we can go to the elders and report our success."

So one last time, Alena returned to the gate again without problem. She came closer, studying the gate closely. As near as she could tell, it suffered from no ill effects of having multiple people connected to it. She would keep an eye on it, of course, but given what Anders had shown her, she suspected the gates didn't care much one way or the other how many people were connected.

She took a step back, examining her handiwork one last time. This could work, she decided.

When she thought of the ramifications of their plan, she shuddered. She hoped it would be enough to stop Dezigeth. But the queen's warnings back in Faldun had affected her, although not in the way the queen intended.

Alena didn't worry about so many having this power. She had no empire to rule over, no worries about being usurped. But she did worry about the balance of the gates.

She suddenly felt as though she wasn't alone. She didn't turn, knowing who it would be.

The voice of Anders spoke from beside her. "I thought you, at least, would think differently."

She took the insult in stride. She'd been expecting this visit for a while. "We're doing the best we can."

"You'll destroy the world."

"You don't know that. But we do know that Dezigeth will kill us all if given the chance."

"I can see the doubt within you," the first emperor said. "There's no point in trying to hide it from me."

She sighed. "Then what do you hope to accomplish? Were you in my shoes, would you gamble everything on the hope that we can find another way forward?"

To this, she received no answer. She turned so she could see him. He stared at the gate, his lips pressed together in a thin line. "I want it all," he admitted. "I always have. I want to defeat Dezigeth, but do it in a way that doesn't upset the order I understand."

"You know that's not likely. It might even be impossible."

"I know." He looked down at his hands. "But pride has always been my burden. Even though I sidestepped death, my ability to influence the world is little. I keep thinking that if only I was truly alive, I would find a way. That none of you possess the same gifts I do. But that's not true, is it? If our positions were reversed, I would be just as desperate."

Alena almost felt sympathy for the emperor.

Almost.

"Or perhaps," the emperor said, "I am just terrified of non-existence. If the gates are destroyed, I imagine I shall depart as well."

Alena considered comforting him by suggesting that perhaps such an end would allow him to make his final journey. But she didn't believe it. He was right. He'd missed his chance to die properly.

He sighed. "I find you remarkable, Alena. Had you been alive in my time, who knows what we might have accomplished. Just keep the needs of the world in mind."

She started. "I won't see you again?"

"I don't think so," Anders said. "Forming myself, even here, becomes more tiring. My soul is weary. I shall keep searching the gates for a way to defeat Dezigeth, but I no longer hope. There is not enough time, and I do not think I will suddenly discover what is needed. For the first time in my life, I will trust that someone else will find a way."

"Thank you, for what aid you've given."

"And thank you, for allowing me to hope that maybe there will be a way forward."

Then Anders disappeared, perhaps for the final time.

71

The problem with fear was that it wasn't an emotion that could last for long. Fear needed fuel to sustain it.

And with Dezigeth on another continent, fear faded.

Brandt didn't think it disappeared completely, at least not for the Lolani refugees. Every day they woke up in Faldun was another reminder that they had lost their home. That their future sprawled before them in an unknown land.

And somewhere, in the back of their minds, they were also reminded that Dezigeth would come again.

But as the days passed, the fear became less. It was replaced by routine. The lower levels of Faldun had become their home, or perhaps something more. In Palagia, they'd never had the freedoms they currently enjoyed. And disaster had brought them together. No longer was the queen the focus of their attention.

Sofra wandered often among her people. Brandt saw her more and more as the days went on, walking the streets, talking with other refugees. No longer did her subjects cower or sneer as she passed. She didn't have their respect, not yet, but was on the path toward it.

Both Brandt and Ana spent considerable time with her. Sofra still fell into fits of melancholy, and Brandt knew she was thinking of her gate and the people she had lost.

Once, Brandt had worried that her failure to protect the gate and her people would be the end of her. But Sofra proved resilient. If anything, her losses shaped her into a better ruler.

For the Falari, the routine was more problematic. The war parties had converged on Faldun because of a perceived threat. But that threat hadn't appeared, and the Falari missed their homes. Some of their frustration was taken out on their Lolani guests.

At times, Faldun felt like a pile of kindling, with a group of children striking sparks all around it.

Having the Lolani and the Falari separated helped, but Brandt wasn't sure how much longer the fragile peace would hold. The elders were already allowing some war parties to depart. Even the queen admitted that Dezigeth had been surprisingly still.

But Palagia was huge. It took time for the Takaii to sweep over it. Brandt knew the queen wished to return to fight for the remainder of her people, but she hadn't found a way.

One morning he emerged from his rooms to find the queen standing outside, on the balcony that overlooked the valley. He hadn't expected her, but he joined her.

They watched the valley in silence for a time. A war party was leaving the city, eager for an early start. Brandt didn't like to see them go, but at the same time, they traveled fast. When Dezigeth did reach this continent, the Falari would respond. It was more than they could say for the empire.

"Do you ever wonder what the purpose of life is?" the queen asked.

"Not since I was a much younger man," Brandt admitted.

"Why not anymore?"

"Life has no purpose other than the one we make for ourselves."

"And you've found yours?"

Brandt turned back to the door he'd just emerged from. Ana and his unborn child still slept. He nodded.

"For so long, I believed I would be the one to save this world," the queen said, her voice soft. "I believed it even when Dezigeth arrived. Some mornings, I still believe."

"But not every morning?"

The queen shook her head. "How could I? I would have to be blind. Dezigeth is far stronger, and I can't imagine how its might could be matched."

"So tell yourself a different story," Brandt said. At her inquisitive look, he continued. "When I see you, especially now, I don't think of you as the one who will save us all. I think of you as the protector of your people. You've brought them here. I've seen the actions you taken, both large and small, to ease their pains."

"But I can't protect them from Dezigeth."

Brandt shook his head, realizing he wasn't being clear. "Because you're only thinking of success and failure. The final result of your efforts is out of your hands. But that doesn't change what we do. When a farmer plants a seed, he can't guarantee a crop will be harvested. When a soldier charges into battle, she can't be sure she'll emerge victorious. But the results don't make them any less a farmer or a soldier." He took a deep breath. "It's the same for you. Ultimately, you can't control your fate. But you can *live* as their protector."

She didn't respond for some time, and when she did, it was with a command. "Come with me."

He followed her as they climbed up several levels. By now, Brandt's body had gotten used to the steep and narrow stairs and the higher altitude.

Sofra led him to the tunnel which led to the gate. The Falari had eight warriors guarding the entrance, but they let the queen pass. Brandt noted their disdain as they did, and wondered if the Falari would ever be able to forgive Sofra for the desecration of their sacred spaces.

"Do you believe that I have been a good queen?" Sofra asked.

"No."

Her step didn't even falter. "Once, I would have killed you for that."

"Not that long ago, I believe."

"I think, though, that perhaps you are right. One can so easily do the wrong things for good reasons."

Brandt rarely saw this side of the queen. He knew she thought deeply about many subjects, but she rarely shared such thoughts. It seemed the changes wrought in her by the loss of the gate were deeper than he expected.

"I would like to do better, if I can."

"From what I've seen, you're already doing more than you once did."

"And now I will do even more."

They came to what had once been the maze, destroyed in a single act of vandalism by the queen upon her first trip to Faldun. She stopped at the sight, and Brandt thought he caught the slightest hint of regret.

Then they were at the gate. Like the lost one in Palagia, it did not glow. The queen's control over it was such that no power leaked out. The awe, partially instilled in him by the sense of sheer power the gates usually exuded, faded as well.

"I'd like to connect you to the gate," she said.

Brandt's heart skipped a beat, and he didn't dare reply, for fear that he might say something that would cause her to change her mind. He bowed deeply to her.

"I know how you've longed for a gate, and Alena suggested I share mine with you before she left. I now believe she was right."

The words sounded like a confession of weakness. The moment felt fragile.

"I'm honored," he said.

Then the moment was gone and the queen was in motion. She gestured for him to join her near the gate and a bubble formed over them. He was about to ask, but she cut him off. "I might trust you, but to do this quickly will require my full attention. I don't want someone coming to take advantage of the situation."

Brandt nodded, and the sword on his hip had never felt heavier. Once again he had the opportunity to take the queen's life.

But it wasn't even a temptation. Not anymore. Humanity needed Sofra.

She closed her eyes and began forming the connection.

He could hear something of her efforts, but allowed himself to bask in ignorance, at least for a while.

There was no mistaking the moment when the connection was complete. It wasn't that Brandt felt a rush of energy, but more that he felt a sudden potential, like an athlete primed to run their fastest race. Waiting for the queen to return from the soulwalk was an exercise in patience.

When she opened her eyes and saw his face, she smiled. "Go on, then."

He did. He summoned fire, and it filled the air. As quickly as he'd summoned it, he released it. He bowed once again. "Thank you."

He had some idea what this gesture had cost Sofra. Possessing the gates had long been her dream, a dream she'd reserved for herself. His words couldn't accurately express his appreciation.

But they didn't have to. There would be a fight, and when it came, there was a part of Brandt that was eager to show Dezigeth what he was capable of.

72

Months passed, and despite the calamity hanging above her head, Alena believed they were some of the best of her life.

When she'd been younger, and first living among the Etari, she'd thought of herself as a woman who had two halves: equal parts imperial and Etari. In some way, she thought the halves would never meet and reconcile.

Azaleth had been the first to strike the barrier separating the two parts of her life. He'd shown her that it was possible to be part of two vastly different worlds without having to become another person. Surprisingly, it was Jace who destroyed most of the barrier that remained. He symbolized her imperial half, a warrior who would likely have someday been governor in Landow. But he'd followed her into Etar and found friends there.

And finally there was Toren, who didn't care if she was imperial or Etari. Toren, who walked by her side no matter where she traveled. He'd taught her that the division had always been an illusion. She was simply Alena.

Her time in Cardon was the longest she had spent

among the Etari since she'd lived with them. It was a home-coming, but in a different way. When Alena had first returned to her parents, after a decade away, she felt the warm embrace of pleasant memories. In time, though, she'd recognized that feeling as nostalgia. Landow would always be the place where she had grown up, a place she would think of fondly. But it wasn't home for her, not really.

The honor belonged to the Etari.

She quickly fell into the routines she remembered so well. The Etari worked from the rising of the sun until its last rays disappeared behind the world. Everyone had a task, and hers was connecting warriors to the gate.

Not everyone volunteered, and not everyone who did succeeded. If she ever had more time, Alena intended to find out why. But no harm came to those who failed, and there was a constant stream of new warriors lined up outside the tent. So she didn't explore the question. She suspected it had something to do with the curiosity and youthfulness of the warrior's mind, a quality that had nothing to do with physical age. Her impression of many who failed was that of a fixed, unquestioning mind. They were warriors that had stopped exploring their worlds, who stuck to trails and camps they were familiar with. But it was only her best guess.

So she sat in the tent by the gate, connecting people one after the other. It wasn't physically demanding work, but by the time the day was done, she felt exhausted all the same.

After the sun set, the campfires were lit and the meals were prepared. Most evenings, Alena found Toren by one of those fires, cooking the food for the evening. He had a remarkable ability to take whatever was available and create something delicious, and Sooni had put him to work around the fires as soon as she knew. His cooking won him even more friends among Alena's family.

The various families and clans would gather, sometimes apart, sometimes joined by other families or clans. But embraces were freely exchanged, as was food and drink. It was rare for her and Toren to climb under the covers until the night was late.

And she wouldn't have it any other way.

She might have been born in Landow, but Etar was her home.

She wished she had realized that earlier.

Because all good things had to come to an end.

Alena didn't actually feel Dezigeth stirring first. The queen did, who then reached out to Alena in the soulwalk. The two women spoke briefly, in hushed tones, and Sofra told Alena the time was coming.

Though she'd enjoyed months of reprieve, it seemed all too short to Alena. Just as she grew comfortable with her new life, Dezigeth took it away.

"It's not enough time," Alena told Sofra.

"It never is," the queen agreed. "For all my years, this is too sudden, even for me."

The two women soulwalked in the queen's caves. Sofra had chosen, and Alena hadn't asked.

"We need the empire," the queen said.

Alena grimaced. "I don't think Olen will listen."

"We must try."

Alena supposed. At the least, she couldn't imagine Olen overpowering her in the soulwalk, so she would be safe. They had nothing to lose. The empire couldn't be less helpful than it already was.

When Sofra disappeared, to gather those close to her for

the meet, Alena searched out Olen. Thanks to his connection to the gate, he remained easy to find.

She didn't choose her mother's kitchen, not this time.

Instead she pulled Olen into a soulwalk in the Etari plains. He greeted her with a glare.

"We need to speak," Alena said.

"There's nothing you can say or do to convince me to listen to anything you say," Olen replied. He looked out over the endless grasslands. "Since your departure, I've been speaking more with Niles Arrowood. He knows you killed his father, and he's told me all about your childhood. How smart you thought you were, and how he suspected that dozens of unsolved thefts were your doing."

Olen looked up, a satisfied look on his face. "So you see, Alena, I understand you in a way that none of your new friends and allies do. You might have blinded them to the truth, but my eyes remain clear. No matter what tricks you pull to convince me your case is real."

"Tricks?"

"I thought the appearance of Anders I was a particularly nice touch. He was just as my father described him, too. But when he tried to convince me to trust you, well, I recognized your game."

"But surely you felt the queen's gate being destroyed."

"Is that what you're claiming?" Anders scoffed. "I don't know how you've managed all these different techniques, but I tell you again, I won't be tricked out of my birthright."

Alena imagined, for one glorious moment, all the harm she wished on him. She'd never met a man so intelligent and yet so obtuse. He refused to see the world as it was. But she caught herself quickly. In this realm it was dangerous to imagine too vividly. Here, such thoughts soon became reality.

She took a deep breath. "Is there any evidence you would accept to prove my claim? Dezigeth is coming, and both the Etari and Falari are preparing for war."

Olen's eyes were sharp. "You've given away too much, Alena. You plan to invade the empire, don't you? To take by force what you couldn't take by guile."

"What?"

But there was no time to speak further. Olen ripped himself away from her soulwalk, leaving her alone on the empty prairie.

73

Of all the queen's accomplishments, Brandt figured that getting the Falari elders to join her in the soulwalk might be her greatest. The Falari had a long history of distrusting affinities, and soulwalking was considered the worst of all. The fact they allowed anyone with affinities to live in Faldun was surprising enough. But meeting in the soulwalk? Brandt never thought he'd see the day.

They gathered in a small room. Jace, Ana, and he represented the empire, for what that was worth. Sofra joined on behalf of the Lolani, and a handful of Falari elders rounded out the group. Several of them looked like they weren't sure if they should relax or run out the door.

The queen looked around the room. "Ready?" she asked, in Falari. She'd been picking up some of the language of her hosts over the past few months.

At their nods, she instructed them to close their eyes. Brandt fell into the soulwalk, and the queen gathered them all together. Even that was an impressive feat. Brandt soon found himself back in Palagia, in a room in the queen's palace that he'd walked by several times but had never seen used. It featured a long table, now filled with imperials, Falari, and Etari. Alena had brought a group into the soul-walk on her end, too.

The queen sat at the head of the table. Brandt wondered if the decision had been intentional, or if that had just been her instinctive placement. Alena sat at her right hand, and Brandt her left. She greeted them all and gave them a few moments to be at ease.

"As you know, we've summoned you here because Dezigeth begins to stir once again," the queen began. "I would guess that it will arrive on this continent within the next few days, and then our final fight will begin. Today we coordinate that fight."

"Is there no one who can speak for the empire?" one of the Falari elders asked.

Brandt glanced over at Alena, who was about to speak, a guilty look on her face. But the queen spoke before Alena could. "I am afraid not. As you know, my relationship with many of the peoples on this continent is antagonistic."

The queen continued to surprise him. She'd assumed the blame for Olen's behavior, saving Alena from her own guilt. It was the sort of small gesture that won over hearts, and one he wouldn't have expected the queen to be capable of.

Sofra continued, "Emperor Anders VII has been unable to look beyond the events of the past, despite our repeated efforts to persuade him of the threat."

Brandt studied the reactions of the others. There was little love between the empire and its neighbors, but both the Falari and the Etari watched the empire closely. Doubt flickered across their expressions, and Brandt knew at least a few were wondering if perhaps they weren't the ones who were fools.

It was the Etari elders who eased the minds of everyone present. "Then the emperor is a fool. We have felt the loss of your gate, and we fear this creature that comes."

"Thank you," the queen said. "I, too, wish the empire would join us, but for now, we shall have to do without."

She paused, looking around the room one more time. "The unanswered question is where Dezigeth will land. It stands to reason that it will wish to attack the gates, but that leaves four possibilities on the continent."

Brandt raised his hand, not sure what rules were followed during this meeting. All heads turned to him. "Does it even matter?" he asked.

The queen gestured, inviting him to expand on his question.

"Of the four gates, two are in the empire, and might as well be forbidden to us. As much as I hate to admit it, if Dezigeth lands there, we must wait to move our forces until the emperor allows us in."

"We could just overpower them," one of the Etari elders pointed out.

"They are no less human than we are," Brandt replied. "There's no point in helping Dezigeth with its task of wiping us out." When he was satisfied the challenge was settled, he continued. "The other two possible destinations are Cardon and Faldun, and both of them are guarded to the fullest extent possible. We could concentrate our forces in one city or the other, but I don't see that the benefit outweighs the risk. We'd be just as well to wait to see what Dezigeth does, then respond."

"If it arrives near Cardon, we'll attack," an Etari elder said.

"If you can, you should hold off on your attack until I can arrive," the queen said.

"Why?" challenged the elder. "Alena has bonded over a hundred of our warriors to the gate. No living creature can withstand such an assault."

"We don't know its limits," the queen replied. "And I'm offering to help. If there is nothing to be lost by waiting a day, why not?"

The Etari elders looked unconvinced, but Alena nodded, which the queen seemed to take as promise enough.

Brandt didn't have the same experience with the Etari that Alena did, but their confidence made him fear the future. They were untested, reminding him of a talented but inexperienced recruit. They always thought they were invincible until battle taught them otherwise.

He'd been no different, long ago.

Still, over a hundred warriors bonded to the gate? If, as Alena and Sofra told him, each was as powerful as the next, such a force was beyond imagining. And terrifying. They could, once they defeated Dezigeth, turn to their old enemies in the empire. With a hundred gifted with gates, they could roll over the empire as fast as their horses could carry them. Nothing would stand in their way.

Sofra had made her arguments against the Etari months ago, but after their flight from Palagia, he could only think about how they defeated Dezigeth. Now, for the first time, he truly understood what the distant consequences of their action might be.

One of the Falari elders spoke, interrupting Brandt's thoughts. "And what if the creature chooses Faldun?

Though we have summoned our war parties once again, we do not have the power the Etari possess."

The elder didn't look at the queen, but the subtle insult was aimed her way all the same.

It was a foolish problem they'd been dealing with for weeks now. Very few Falari were in touch with their affinities, and attempting to connect them with their gate would be a death sentence. But the Falari elders saw the Etari growing in strength and hated to be left behind.

"If Dezigeth chooses Faldun," Alena said, "the Etari will bring our gate-connected forces to you."

"We can't hold out that long!" came the retort.

"One day is all we need," Alena said, refusing to raise her voice to match the elder's.

Brandt's stomach sank. He hadn't even considered the advantage of mobility. With the cost no longer a factor, they could fly wherever they chose. They could conquer the whole continent within a week.

The Falari elder seemed to realize the same. Tension built within the room as everyone realized there was one dominant force at the table.

Remarkably, it was the Etari who put the room at ease. An older woman spoke. "You fear what Alena has given us, and there is wisdom in such fear. These powers, I do not think they belong to us. You may view these as empty words, but they are backed by my promise. If we defeat Dezigeth, the Etari will not invade Falar or the empire. Not until there is a new chance to negotiate a treaty."

Throughout the empire the Etari had a reputation of being determined traders, and perhaps some part of that reputation was deserved. Perhaps they wouldn't start a war, but they wouldn't hesitate to use their power to their own benefit.

In the end, it was agreed. The Etari and Falari would provide mutual aid, no matter where Dezigeth landed.

Which was good, because two days later, Dezigeth arrived.

74

I n so many ways, the scene was an exact replica of what had come before. Replace the desert with the grasslands of Etar and the thick walls of the queen's city with the tents of Cardon, and it was all the same.

Dezigeth had landed the day before. Its arrival didn't shake the world the way its first one had. According to witnesses, it had extended its wings, slowing its descent, and it had landed softly in the grass. It arrived alone and without fanfare, and as soon as it landed, it began building another gate.

From her tent in Cardon, Alena could feel it. The presence was the same she'd gotten used to in Valan, the same feeling she had tried to forget once they fled.

What came next was easy enough to guess.

Their goal was to stop it before that could come to pass.

She'd spoken briefly with Sofra in the soulwalk. The queen had promised to come, and she implied she'd be bringing guests with her.

Now they waited. Toren sat behind her, massaging her shoulders and kissing her neck and back. Despite the fact they were likely going to battle tomorrow, there had been little said between them. Alena found that it didn't feel necessary. She understood Toren, and he understood her.

Someone came to the entrance to their tent and informed them that the queen was near. She'd been spotted in the sky. They thanked the messenger, put on their clothes, and went to wait with the rest.

The queen flew a platform similar to the one Alena had created. The craftsmanship was far superior, and she landed it softly, but Alena didn't begrudge her stronger abilities.

Brandt stepped out first, signing a greeting to the elders who stood in front of all the rest. The greeting was returned, and Jace, Ana, and the queen all stepped off the platform. There was one moment of silent awkwardness, and then Alena broke through the lines and nearly tackled Jace with her embrace.

With that, less formal greetings were exchanged, and the visitors were welcomed among the Etari.

A brief planning session was held, but there was little to discuss. Their strategy, such as it was, was to surround Dezigeth on three sides and attack it with as many of the Etari as they could. The training every Etari youth went through proved invaluable here. The riders were already used to maintaining open lines of sight between themselves and enemies. The queen and Brandt would reinforce the center.

Alena barely paid attention. The plan hadn't changed in any meaningful way since she'd gone over it last, and her thoughts were with her brother, standing near the back of the command tent.

When the planning session ended, the Etari invited everyone to that evening's feast, already being prepared. Jace joined Toren and Alena as they went toward their family's cookfire. He looked like there was much on his mind, but he wasn't quite sure where to begin.

"I wasn't sure you would come," Alena said.

Her brother looked hurt.

"Not like that," she chided him. "I just thought you might want to return home to Landow, to protect our family."

He shook his head. "Depending on how tomorrow goes, I might. I can't contribute to the battle, but I will witness it, all the same."

"With Ana?"

He nodded.

She wanted to tell him to watch over Ana, should they lose tomorrow, but held her tongue. The Etari were confident in their chances, and why shouldn't they be? Not even Dezigeth could stand against such a force.

Alena couldn't dispel her doubt, though.

She didn't want to voice her fears to Jace. Doing so might prompt him to do something foolish.

And anyway, her brother would do the right thing. Of that, she had no doubt. He didn't need to be reminded.

The mood around the fire than night was boisterous, and it didn't take long for Jace to get in the mood of the celebration. As the sun set, Jace's stories became louder, and he'd traveled with Toren long enough to have some basic fluency in Etari.

Out of the corner of her eye, Alena saw Brandt and Ana retire to a tent that had been set up for them. They walked hand in hand, and from the looks they gave one another, it seemed to Alena that the wounds between them had finally started to heal. She was glad of that.

The night wore on, but Alena felt no tiredness. She wanted to stay awake, to listen to the crackling fire as her brother's voice held his audience spellbound. With her hand in Toren's, it was as good a life as she could imagine.

At some point in the night, when another speaker took the focus away from Jace, her brother came to sit next to her. "Alena—"

She held up her hand. "There's no need to say anything, Jace. I know."

Their eyes met, and she saw that his were watering. "I'm worried," he confessed.

"Me too," she admitted. "But for tonight, all I want is to listen to your stories. For a little while, at least," she said, as she flashed Toren a mischievous look.

"I love you," Jace said. "I don't want to lose you tomorrow."

"I love you, too. And I'll try to stay safe. I promise."

Partly in the soulwalk, Alena felt the bond between them glowing brighter than it ever had before.

Jace stood back up, gave her a smile, and returned to his storytelling. A handful of the Etari women sat closer to him than was strictly necessary. Alena smiled, hoping that Jace found his own happiness.

Later, Toren stood, gently pulling Alena to her feet. They returned to their tent, also walking hand in hand.

ALENA AWOKE to the sound of the camp coming alive. Toren, of course, was already up, the space beside her empty.

She rolled out of bed, pulling her clothes on and stretching out stiff joints. They ate breakfast with the rest of the family, and from the looks of it, Jace had enjoyed a long night himself. When their eyes met, he grinned from ear to ear.

It was, she decided, a good day to finish this fight against Dezigeth.

They'd elected not to ride horses into battle. Dezigeth's landing had only been about a league from Cardon, so walking was no problem. And against the energies that would be unleashed, no one was certain how horses would react.

After breakfast there was one final round of goodbyes. Few of Sooni's family had been connected to the gates. Their primary function within the clan was to serve as traders, and others had been prioritized. When Alena hugged Sooni, the woman said, "I'm proud of you, daughter."

Alena had to turn away before she teared up.

She told Jace she would see him soon, and then she and Toren met with the rest of the Etari.

And they marched to war.

75

A s Brandt and his allies positioned themselves against Dezigeth, he thought one last time of Ana. Despite the import of this battle, his greatest desire was to return to her, to spend more time in her company.

The greatest danger in loving someone for years was taking them for granted. The endless routine of days together made it easy to assume they would always continue.

Until life reminded you that nothing in this world lasted forever.

Brandt felt as though he'd just won Ana back, only to risk losing her again. Once this battle was over, he planned on taking off his sword forever.

The final Etari reached their position, and the sudden stillness around Brandt focused his attention. He looked up and down the line, if it could even be called as much. They formed almost half a circle, stretching for hundreds of paces. When they attacked, Dezigeth would be assaulted from all sides.

A commander couldn't ask for a better group of warriors, though. The lines of the Etari were spread out well. As they used their affinities, there was little chance they would strike one another.

Dezigeth paid them no mind, which unsettled Brandt. The queen accused the creature of too much confidence, but Brandt feared they underestimated their enemy. He couldn't imagine Dezigeth withstanding their assault, but a few years ago, he wouldn't have imagined a single part of today.

But Dezigeth continued building its gate.

They had decided the queen would have the honor of landing the first blow. It was as good a signal as any, and the elders agreed she deserved the right after Dezigeth's cleansing of her land.

The queen strode forward and her steps were matched by the Etari. A portion of a circle began to close in. Dezigeth remained uninterested. It let them approach within three hundred paces without so much as stirring.

This close, Brandt could see the ghostly outline of the gate Dezigeth built. It was a glowing arch, almost shapeless but not quite. For now, it was only a potential, a possible future. For as much as Brandt hated what that gate would bring, he couldn't help but admire the beauty of its construction.

The queen seemed less impressed. She formed a glowing ball of flame before her, focused heat that threatened to sear Brandt's skin. The Etari responded by setting their own stones to spinning at incredible speed. Brandt was curious to see what their famous technique would look like when powered by the gate.

Not to be left out, Brandt summoned his own fire, focusing it the way Sofra did. Though his wasn't quite as powerful as hers, it was orders of magnitude more than he'd ever created before. Thanks to the gate, it wasn't even hard.

Sofra released her attack, flinging it toward Dezigeth. Her aim was true, and although Brandt couldn't see if it hit Dezigeth or a shield, the devastation from the eruption of power was incredible.

Brandt threw his own attack, and the Lolani launched their stones. They cracked the air with their speed, a sound unlike any Brandt had ever heard.

Dust and smoke obscured their view of Dezigeth, but Brandt felt its presence. It had lived through their first strike, which no doubt disappointed most of the Etari warriors. The queen attacked again, but Brandt noticed the Etari left their stones spinning ahead of them.

Brandt joined with the queen, and off to the side, Alena supported them. Their attacks made the ground rumble, and the cloud of fire and smoke ahead of them grew.

But as near as he could tell, Dezigeth remained unharmed. And the Etari had stopped helping, unable to see well enough to aim.

A powerful gust of wind rose, clearing the smoke from around Dezigeth. The creature unfolded its wings and launched itself into the air.

As soon as it did, the Etari responded. Cracks filled the air as stones zipped toward the creature. They hit with uncanny accuracy, and for the first time, Brandt saw the creature injured. It shuddered as some of the rocks struck it.

Its vengeance caught them all by surprise. Dozens of points of light appeared, and they all struck out at the defenders.

Most of the Etari were able to create shields, but not all. The technique wasn't second nature to them, and in the heat of battle, some failed to protect themselves.

They were the first casualties.

Wherever the points of light touched the ground, devastation followed. Brandt was thrown from his feet as one landed just a few paces ahead of him. His own shield kept him safe from harm, but it couldn't protect his balance as the ground lifted in response to the assault.

The battle began in earnest then. The Etari lines shifted to accommodate their losses, and the crack of rocks being accelerated to unimaginable speeds became common.

The Etari didn't often miss. And Dezigeth's protection couldn't stop them all. Brandt saw more hits, but it didn't see blood. Shadow seeped from its wounds.

Its rage was palpable, filling the air. The Etari and their stones battled the dark creature and its weapons of light. He, Alena, and the queen fought as well, most often utilizing fire to keep Dezigeth at bay.

Dezigeth howled, the deep sound paining Brandt's ears. It folded its wings into a dive, crashing into one of the Etari. The poor warrior's protection couldn't withstand Dezigeth's focus, and Dezigeth tore the man limb from limb, revealing its physical strength.

Even the Etari closest to the victim didn't break, though. They stood firm, and more stones than ever assaulted Dezigeth. It was among the greatest acts of courage Brandt had ever seen.

For all the progress they had made, though, Brandt couldn't say for sure which side would win. Dezigeth, of course, had inflicted more casualties, and Brandt didn't know how much damage they had done to the creature in return. Could they kill it before attrition decided the battle for them?

Dezigeth took to the air again, but there was no corner

for it to hide. Stones tracked it across the sky, and Brandt saw holes in its wings.

Their progress wasn't without cost. Dezigeth crashed into another Etari, killing the young woman with one devastating punch. It released more of the balls of light. Explosions knocked Brandt back again to his knees. In ones and twos the Etari fell, and with every passing moment, victory became just that much more elusive.

The hope that had once bloomed in his chest began to die.

They needed something that changed the course of the battle. He watched Dezigeth release another assault, then braced himself as the light hammered against his shield.

Beside him, the queen stood in defiance of all the forces Dezigeth brought against her. Energy cascaded from her in an unending torrent, wrapping Dezigeth in flame. The invader retaliated, focusing for a moment on the queen. As their blows collided, the air trembled and warped.

Through it all, the queen stood tall.

From the first time they'd met, he had been in awe of her indomitable will.

Memories of their first meeting made him think of Dezigeth's gate. Back then, he'd destroyed the queen's connection in the soulwalk and prevented her from invading the empire.

He could destroy the gate today, too.

There would never be a better time. Attacks struck Dezigeth from every side. Brandt wasn't sure how much attention the creature could spare to defending the gate.

He broke from the protection of the formation, covering the remaining distance between him and the gate in little time. He glanced toward Dezigeth, but it was busy enduring the queen's assault.

The ground constantly shifted under him, but Brandt made himself light, skimming across the ground like a bug across water.

When he reached the gate, he put his hand against it. Though the surface didn't look solid, his hand stopped as he reached out. Brandt grinned and attacked the gate with all the power he could summon. A wave of energy blasted into the structure, and from above, the air shook with the rage of Dezigeth's scream.

In that moment, Brandt became the sole focus of Dezigeth's attention. The creature dove at him, two globes of light leading the way. Brandt pushed one more surge of energy into the gate, then defended himself.

The gate cracked, but it didn't break.

The light struck his barrier, and his world erupted in fire. Brandt grimaced as his barrier cracked, then shattered as Dezigeth slammed into it.

Brandt half-scrambled, half-rolled away from the creature's swipe. By instinct, he drew his sword, which he got up just in time to block Dezigeth's next swipe with his inhumanly powerful arms.

Brandt's sword shattered and he was thrown back, into Dezigeth's gate.

The creature advanced on him.

He could defend, or he could attack the gate.

Only one option had the possibility of ending this war.

Brandt closed his eyes and focused, pulling all the power from his connection to the Falari gate as he could. He blasted Dezigeth's construction once more.

He heard the shattering, a sound so loud it deafened him. He fell back as his support vanished, and Dezigeth's hand passed barely in front of his face.

And then Sofra was there, attacking Dezigeth for all she was worth. She forced him back a step, and then another.

The Etari redoubled their efforts, and stones cut into Dezigeth from all directions.

Never in the history of this world had so much force been focused to a single end.

And even Dezigeth wasn't enough.

It stumbled to its knees, and Brandt saw disorientation in its eyes.

The queen took a step toward it, hand outstretched, a small sphere of incredible force held before her. She placed it against Dezigeth's head and released it.

Once more the world filled with light as her attack struck true.

But this time, when it faded, all was quiet.

Where Dezigeth had knelt, now there was nothing but empty space.

76

Cheers went up from the assembled Etari. Even Alena fell to her knees. She wanted to weep.

But it was Toren, prone to neither extreme sadness nor joy, who noticed first. "It's not dead."

As he mentioned it, she felt it, too. Though its body was gone, its presence was not.

Not only was the presence not gone, it was active. Alena spun in a circle, looking for the creature, but unable to find it.

No one else seemed to realize. Perhaps the queen, who remained rooted where she had last attacked Dezigeth. From here it was too hard to tell. But the Etari were whooping, throwing their fists in the air in celebration. Toren signed frantically, warning them an enemy was nearby, but his motions were ignored.

Given that she couldn't see Dezigeth, Alena dropped into the soulwalk. Its presence was like a blight, a twisting and ripping of the web of life wherever it went. She followed its trail.

Alena had never developed a reliable sense of direction

in this realm. She wasn't sure if one even existed. But Dezigeth's trail never faltered once. It had a destination.

Her stomach twisting, Alena pursued faster, ignoring the risk of ambush.

The trail dove deeper into the realm of souls, into a place where there could only be one destination.

The gates.

Alena followed.

She found herself floating in the ethereal space the gates occupied. Two figures stood before her. One was Dezigeth, its shape now a familiar outline against the light of the gate. It clutched another figure in its hands.

Anders.

Alena rushed forward, but she wasn't in time. Anders saw her coming and smiled a bloody grin. There was a flash of power, and he was gone.

Gone for good.

But his sacrifice had delayed Dezigeth long enough for Alena to join the fight. Her knife, given to her by her father, appeared in her hand, and she struck at it.

Dezigeth snarled and backhanded her away.

Alena was up and after it a heartbeat later.

Dezigeth reached out and touched the gate.

She thought she had more time. She reached out and grabbed his other arm. But it was the work of a moment. Lifetimes worth of study and memories, and Dezigeth destroyed it. There was no cut, no eruption of energy. It just expanded for a moment, and then it unraveled, filaments of the incredibly complex weaving drifting away on invisible currents.

Alena's world went white, and she went senseless.

Motion brought her back to her senses. Dezigeth was

rising back up through the soulwalk, on its way to the physical plane.

Alena was groggy. Was the gate gone? She channeled affinities through her gatestone, embedded near her navel.

Nothing happened.

The gatestone had become simple stone, without a connection to the world's energy. The Etari, and the culture they had built since the death of those who had come before, were now a dying people.

Too late, she understood Dezigeth's intent.

All the Etari had been connected to the one gate. Their army, possessing a power the world had never seen, was now nothing. The Etari couldn't even rely on their gatestones for support. With one decisive move, Dezigeth had won the war.

Alena cried out and pulled on Dezigeth's arm, bringing it to a stop. She needed an answer.

"Why?"

Dezigeth looked down at her, and she could not read its expression. On a human, she might have termed it pity, but that didn't seem to fit the creature. "You have stretched too far," it said. "And this is the order of the universe."

With that, it continued its ascent.

Alena pulled and tugged, but it would not stop. Reluctantly admitting she had no hope of stopping it, she let go and returned to the physical world first.

The Etari warriors were in various states of distress. Some, like Toren, had already found their feet again, but not all. Alena formed a platform, the largest by far she'd ever made, pulling stone from deep beneath the grasses. "We need to go," she said.

Toren didn't argue. He started gesturing and yelling, pointing to the platform as their means of escape. Slowly, the Etari stumbled to their feet and staggered toward the platform. The queen and Brandt met Alena.

"It destroyed the Etari gate?" the queen asked.

Alena nodded. "We need to retreat, before it re-forms."

The queen stepped away from them. "This will be my final battle. You two run."

Alena grabbed Sofra's arm and met her answering stare. "Your people will need you, and you still know more about the gates than anyone alive. You need to keep fighting. Don't give up. Not today. Not after everything."

Brandt joined in. "We can move the Etari to Faldun, and join them to that gate. We're not done yet. Today we came closer than we ever have."

For several long moments the queen hesitated. Alena looked over the plain, expecting at any moment to see Dezigeth once again forming. So far, she saw no sign of it. The queen agreed and turned toward the platform. She eyed its size and the number of people on it skeptically. "I imagine you want me to fly?"

"Seems wise," Brandt chipped in.

About half the Etari had reached the platform, and the other half were closing in, supported by friends who had found their feet.

That was when Alena saw the dark shadows begin to congeal in the distance. She swore. "Hurry!" she cried, gesturing the same.

The Etari moved as quickly as they could, but every moment stretched into an eternity. Dezigeth regained more of its physical body with every wasted breath.

The final few Etari reached the platform, and the queen grimaced as she focused her energies. The platform lifted, ponderous and slow. As it lifted it began to move toward Cardon. It moved at a crawl, but slowly gained speed. Within a few moments, it was moving at a walking pace.

Excepting the queen, all eyes were on the figure behind them. A chilly wind sprang up, as cold as any that Alena had ever felt. It was no wind from this world.

Dezigeth had returned, and it turned its cold regard on the fleeing Etari.

Alena closed her eyes.

They weren't going to make it.

Even if the queen did manage to move them more quickly, they couldn't outrun Dezigeth. And if they somehow could, where would they go? It would reach Cardon in no time at all, and the Etari there were now defenseless.

She felt a strong hand on her shoulder. It was Brandt. He looked forlorn but determined. "I will slow it down." He took a deep breath. "Tell Ana—" He stopped himself. "No, there's nothing more. Just kill that creature, will you?"

Brandt stood tall and began working his way toward the rear of the platform.

He looked a noble figure.

She thought of Ana, and the child growing within her. "Brandt!" she called out.

Off in the distance, Dezigeth spread its wings and launched itself straight into the air. It moved with a speed Alena hadn't seen from it yet.

Brandt turned to her call. She thanked Olen for forcing her to learn the technique. "Sleep," she said.

And Brandt collapsed, limp and unconscious, to the platform.

The queen had her people. Brandt had a child who would need a father.

Toren reached out to her, but she'd predicted his move,

and deflected it easily enough. She met his eyes. "You're tired," she said, putting the force of her will into the soulwalk.

Toren resisted, but his body relaxed.

She knew that even if she asked, Toren wouldn't leave her. Not this time. But she wanted him to survive. That knowledge would help her take the journey to the gate with confidence. He would hate her, but hopefully, in time, he would forgive her.

She bent down and kissed him. "I love you," she said. "And I know you love me. Our days together have been some of my happiest. Thank you."

Tears trickled down his cheek, but his eyes were drooping.

"Now sleep," she said.

And he did.

Alena stood tall and met the queen's gaze. Sofra gave her a small nod.

Alena tore off a bit of the platform, stood on it, and launched herself into the sky after Dezigeth.

Bright lights came to meet her, and she extended a wide shield, catching them all.

She flew through the fire and into the clear skies above. She flew until she was close to Dezigeth.

Its attitude had changed. Before, it had fought with something resembling passion and emotion.

All that was now gone. It was again the creature she remembered from her first visions, cold beyond anything humans were capable of. It manifested as a physical sensation, sending a chill down Alena's spine.

They stood, separated by only a few paces, but as far away from one another as two beings could be.

"We want to survive," Alena said.

"Your wants are irrelevant," it replied. "Your predilections are clear. Your future only leads one direction. And that cannot be permitted."

Alena wondered if there was any way to win this fight.

They'd tried everything she could think of.

So probably not.

But the longer they remained up here, the longer the queen and the others had to escape.

She waited, as did Dezigeth.

Eventually, though, it tired of her. It closed the remaining distance between them, and Alena moved the platform under her feet, allowing her to drop beneath its swing. She responded by launching a small stone at it, which struck it in the chest.

She saw the flicker of disgust.

Good. So long as she had its attention.

It came after her again, and she launched another stone at its head as she directed her small platform to escape. She led Dezigeth on a chase through the sky, constantly attacking with stones, keeping it off balance.

But she could only dodge for so long.

Her luck ran out, and Dezigeth struck her with its full power. For a moment her world went black, and when she came to, the wind whistled in her hair as she plummeted down.

She reached down to the pouch at her hip. Her clothing snapped at her as she grabbed a stone and held it tightly in her hand.

The ground rushed toward her, growing ever larger.

She focused on the stone, slowing its descent, and with it, her own. By the time she hit the ground, she was falling slowly enough that she could collapse and roll safely.

A shadow crossed above her and she looked up to see

Dezigeth aiming straight at her. Her eyes went wide and she just had enough time to form a sphere of protection around her as it struck.

The force of the impact drove her into the earth.

For all the viciousness in his attack, there was no emotion on his face.

Surrounded by earth, she had no place to run.

Like a cornered animal, she lashed out with everything. She struck with fire and pulled stone from the ground, throwing it at Dezigeth with reckless abandon. In a way, knowing that she didn't need to win freed her actions. She now understood there was a world of difference between killing Dezigeth and surviving its attacks.

Alena lost sight of the creature, but she felt its presence directly in front of her. There was no missing it.

As she attacked, it did the same. They exchanged blows and reinforced their shields, waging a slow war of attrition.

It could only end one way.

Alena left nothing in reserve.

But it wasn't nearly enough.

Her shield cracked and Dezigeth landed on top of her, driving her onto her back with its feet. It crouched on top of her, driving its powerful fists into her chest. She heard her ribs shatter, and all she knew was that she couldn't breathe.

She yelled, spending the last of her precious breath to draw Dezigeth's attention for a few more moments. Fire engulfed both her hands, and she launched it at Dezigeth's face. Fire swirled around it, but it remained unscarred.

She found the strength to attack again, more fire to blast at it.

And then her focus started to fade.

Dezigeth extended its arm, one of the balls of light held in its palm.

She thought of Toren and her body was filled with warmth, the memory of his embrace when he'd held her for the last time.

Of her parents, whom she missed desperately. Perhaps she would see them again, but hopefully not for a long time.

And of Jace. The child who had become a man in the blink of an eye, but who always had a story ready.

The memories faded, and she offered Dezigeth a bloody smile. Let it remember that. It had defeated her, but it hadn't broken her.

The gate hovered before her. The true gate, the one that summoned them all at the end of their days.

She stepped toward it without regret.

She had done all she could.

And Dezigeth released its attack, destroying Alena's body, never knowing that she was already dead.

INTERLUDE

Interlude

It found itself troubled.

When it fought against them, it abandoned the cold yet comforting rationality that defined its existence. But it could not help itself.

These creatures angered it.

Of course they fought to remain alive. Such was the course of all life. Very few humans had the wisdom to proceed quietly into oblivion.

But these humans went to extremes. Their abuse of this world was a crime they didn't seem to comprehend. It defied all reason. To so crudely use the gifts offered to them sickened Dezigeth.

And yet, a part of it lamented their destruction. Not that it would consider for a moment sparing them. But for all their crimes, they displayed startling nobility. The girl—

The girl had been special. One who might have understood. One who might have ascended, if given proper instruction.

Dezigeth knew that fate was a myth of lesser creatures. And the girl had abused the powers, just the same as the rest. But it regretted that their paths had been pushed towards inevitable conflict.

It looked to the south, where the structure had once stood. The humans fled, most likely to defend another one of their gates.

Two ideas warred within it. One was to pursue. By the time the sun set on this world, its threats could be eliminated.

Or it could finish its own portal.

Rationality reasserted itself.

The others, it knew, posed no danger. Efficiency was prized among all else. The Takaii, as these humans called them, would begin their work sooner if it built the gate for them to come through.

So Dezigeth turned from the site of the girl's last stand, and once again began to build.

77

The world continued to turn. The sun rose and set. Rarely did Brandt set his head down in the same place two nights in a row.

There were councils, and what seemed to be a never-ending retreat.

They ran, and they grieved.

They lived, only because she had died.

None of it seemed real.

Brandt felt as though he was watching a play of his life, like he was a puppet being pulled by invisible strings. He didn't think he was alone in that. Jace, too, walked around from morning to night with his eyes sunk in his skull, staring at nothing in particular. His once-ready smile hadn't appeared since that day.

Brandt had lost friends before. But never someone so close, and not like this. He'd lost his wolfblades, so many years ago, but Kye had stolen those memories from him. He'd regained some thanks to Alena, but they weren't his. They were Ana's, and they lacked the same impact his would have had.

Alena had taken his sacrifice away from him.

At times, he felt violent anger toward her. He had been ready, and she had still been so young. She had more years ahead of her than he did.

He'd known, in that last moment, what she intended. But he couldn't stop her. For all the strength given to him, he seemed cursed to be surrounded by those with greater abilities. Sometimes, that thought angered him, too.

Dezigeth hadn't followed them. The queen reported that it was uninjured, and once again they couldn't begin to guess at its motives. It had them all at its mercy, and it simply let them run. It began to build the gate again, erasing the progress they'd made.

In his darker moments, Brandt figured it had all been for nothing.

After a brief meet in Cardon, they decided to flee to Faldun. It was the only defensible place left to them. The only place that might welcome them.

Brandt barely remembered the journey. An enormous caravan had departed Cardon. The queen flew her platform to Faldun and back several times, preparing the way for the new set of refugees and carrying those who couldn't make the trek.

If they survived Dezigeth, the whole world would owe the Falari generations of hospitality. The mountain warriors didn't exactly welcome the refugees with open arms, but they made space, and with nowhere else to go, even that felt like an act of extreme generosity.

Brandt led the refugees over the land. They couldn't be sure that Dezigeth wouldn't attack, and he volunteered. He wasn't sure he'd have the focus to fly one of the platforms, even if he wanted to.

They passed into Falari territory without a problem.

Their borders were now undefended, as they'd recalled everyone back to Faldun. The refugees climbed into the mountains, and the days passed, doing nothing to deaden the loss Brandt felt.

Ana tried to help him grieve, and he appreciated her efforts, but this was something of his own to deal with. And although he wouldn't ever say this to Ana, he felt a pang of guilt whenever they spent time together. He didn't deserve happiness. Not at this cost.

None of it was fair.

On the day before they reached Faldun, Toren found him. He hadn't seen much of the young man. From what he'd heard, the warrior had been killing himself every day serving the refugees. He cooked enormous meals and shouldered the burdens of the weary. His old family tried to welcome him back, but he gently refused all offers. It was as though he wanted to be alone, not just now, but for all the days that followed.

Brandt couldn't judge. He'd seen warriors deal with grief in as many ways as there were ways to die.

Toren asked Brandt to follow him. They found a ridge, hidden from sight. Jace was there waiting for them.

Toren gestured for Brandt to sit and he did. The Etari pulled out a flask and joined them. "I thought it was time that we grieve for Alena properly."

His pronouncement was greeted with silence, but it didn't seem to bother him at all. He took a sip from the flask, coughed once, and passed it over to Jace. Jace looked at it for a long moment, then shrugged and took a swig. He coughed harder as he cursed. "What's that?"

"Don't know." A hint of a smile played upon Toren's face. "But it was the only drink I could find."

Jace took another swig and passed it over to Brandt, who

sipped. It burned from the moment it hit his tongue, all the way down his throat. Despite his best effort, he also coughed. "That's not good."

"We all loved Alena," Toren said, "and we haven't had the time to properly mourn. Nor will we. I imagine once we reach Faldun we'll be busy with deciding what to do next. Without a body, there can be no proper ceremony, but I hoped we could honor her tonight."

"When we were little," Jace said, "we didn't fight the way most brothers and sisters did. We never came to blows like some kids, and truthfully, we didn't even yell at each other that much."

Jace extended his hand and Brandt passed the flask back. Jace took a more gentle sip. "After she left, sometimes I felt cheated, like I'd missed a rite of passage. Most of my friends fought viciously with their siblings. Sure, Alena and I disagreed all the time, and I'm sure I got on her nerves every day. But her patience with me, I now think, was part of the reason I eventually found the success I did. I just wish I had given her something more in return."

"You did," Toren said quietly. "You taught her how to forgive. For the longest time, she didn't understand you. She couldn't believe you could move past the harm she had caused you. She spoke often of it."

Jace nodded and took another sip.

Toren gestured for the flask. "She taught me what courage really meant. Growing up among the Etari, I came to believe that courage was charging an enemy, or fighting against overwhelming odds. And maybe that's a type of courage, too. But I saw something else from her."

Toren took another sip from the flask, searching for his words. "Alena possessed a courage I had never seen before. It wasn't brash, nor boastful. But she challenged the elders and traditions long held, not with violence, but with her persistence and her character. If we live through this, I am convinced she will have done more to change the Etari than anyone since Zolene, long ago. She taught me to stand up for my own beliefs."

Toren fell silent, and Brandt looked between the other two men. They were both lost in places long behind them. Brandt thought of his own experiences with Alena, and one came immediately to mind. "When I first met Alena, it was when she was a thief. When I last met her, she was one of the strongest people on the continent, and a bridge between people. When I think of Alena, I think of how much she grew." His voice grew hoarse. "I think that made her the best of us."

The flask made another round, and this time, Brandt drank more deeply.

Toren spoke. "We need to mourn, but we also need to move on. I don't think any of us believe she would want grief to control our lives, and there is much to be done. I, for one, want to make her proud."

Ana had said much the same to him. But coming from Toren, whose love for Alena was unquestioned, it had a different weight. And by the young man's own actions, he put the other two of them to shame. Since Alena's death, he'd done more than any of them to keep her spirit alive.

Grief hardened into resolution.

"You're right," Brandt said.

They looked at Jace, who was slower to reach the same conclusion, but he did. When Alena's brother met their gazes, he said, "After we reach Faldun, I'm going to head back north, into the empire. It's time for me to return home."

Brandt understood. Of them, he was the only one with a home to return to. "What will you do?"

Jace shrugged. "At first, hide so the empire can't find me. But more than anything, I want to be with my parents. I need to tell them about Alena, and try to make them understand what she did for us all. But I want to be with them as the Takaii come."

There was a hint of finality in his voice. But then he brightened, if only for a moment. "Who knows, perhaps I'll be able to organize the defenses of Landow? We've got thick walls, and I've got people who know me there. I don't know how hard the emperor will be pressing for my arrest, now that Alena has passed."

"I think that's wise," Brandt said, and he saw Jace relax, as though he'd been nervous Brandt might disapprove.

And then Jace told another story, of an Alena the other two had never met, one much younger.

They sat and drank long into the night, sharing their memories of the life that had touched them all.

78

Brandt walked among the refugees. He lacked a specific task, but aided them however he could. From moving furniture to providing directions, no favor was too small. In another part of Faldun, he knew Toren was doing the same.

The simple act of offering aid did wonders for his grief and his worry. He appreciated the gratitude shown him, but the acts themselves were reward enough. They kept him busy and allowed his mind a break from constantly worrying about Dezigeth and the Takaii.

The Falari hadn't been pleased about the arrival of the Etari, but they hadn't turned the nomads away, either. Faldun was now filled from top to bottom with people. The streets were more crowded than Brandt had ever seen, and children played at his feet.

The spaces between Dezigeth's attacks filled Brandt with wonder. Everyone here knew a final fight was coming, but it was amazing how quickly the mundane needs and desires of humanity asserted themselves. Here a child was crying because she had kicked the ball over the side of a wall, sending it plummeting down three levels before landing. There, an older Etari man complained of feeling cramped up in the city.

They didn't infuriate him the way he expected. Instead, he smiled and helped as he could. He wanted to live in a world where these concerns mattered, because it meant so much else was going right.

When he saw Sofra descending a stair, he knew his brief idyll wouldn't last much longer. He joined her, and together they walked the streets of Faldun. They'd been here several days now, but he hadn't seen much of her. Part of this was by choice. Brandt had elected not to take part in the councils between the leaders of the people. He didn't speak for the empire and felt his presence was unnecessary. He much preferred to spend his days assisting the recently resettled refugees.

"You appear content," the queen remarked.

"Thank you," Brandt said. "But I fear it will be short-lived. What news is there?"

"Little you don't know. Dezigeth completed its gate on the continent. I have little doubt Takaii are pouring through, but we don't know what they're doing. Which is why I wanted to speak to you."

"You want me to scout for you?"

She nodded.

"Even flying, I won't be able to cover enough territory fast enough to be useful," Brandt pointed out.

"Which is the second reason I'm here. The Etari, and now the Falari, are both pressuring me to share my gate. If I connected the Etari again, they could also fly the platforms, and we could know more of the advance of the Takaii."

"It's a reasonable request," Brandt said. "But you're not sure."

"It is a problem I have difficulty articulating. I no longer fear sharing the gate, not as I once did. But I do not like the pattern we are establishing. Even though those who came before shared freely of the gates, their power was rarely used. Now we speak of using the gates for a task as mundane as scouting. Though the situation demands no less, it still feels like a desecration."

"Does it matter, if we lose?"

The queen bit her lower lip. "It feels like it does."

"I think you should. Even if the scouting feels mundane, the Etari remain our best hope for defending against Dezigeth. We didn't kill it outside Cardon, but we got closer than we ever have before."

She paused and looked out over the valley. "Very well," she said.

THE QUEEN WAS as good as her word. That very afternoon she began the process.

Brandt watched a few times, amazed at the ways that Dezigeth had brought them together. The Lolani queen connected the Etari to the Falari gate. Such coordination would have been laughably unthinkable even a year ago.

A shame they had to be so close to the end for them to come to this point.

Brandt began the first scouting missions. Twice, he actually landed himself and his escort close to groups of Takaii, instigating small battles. He wanted the warriors to have some experience against these mindless warriors.

With his assistance, they were never threatened, and with each battle they learned. They ravaged several small groups of Takaii.

Their efforts mattered little, though. Day by day, the

creatures expanded throughout Etar, eventually reaching the wide banks of the Alna River. Brandt and the other Etari scouts watched them closely, curious if they would expand south or choose to cross the river into the empire.

They did both, dividing roughly in half. One part continued south, but the creatures also proved capable of swimming, much to Brandt's consternation. Had they not, they might have been contained. But they waded into the Alna, and eventually they emerged on the other side.

When they strode into the empire they were scattered and disorganized, but that didn't last long. They had an uncanny ability to find one another regardless of distance or terrain.

At first, the advance was slow. The Etari, not satisfied with being scouts, often used the power of the gates to destroy enormous numbers of Takaii while scouting. Eventually, though, Dezigeth chose to intervene. Three Etari scouting parties were lost before they realized what was happening.

Then, for a couple of weeks, the battle for control of the continent went back and forth. The Etari would strike when they had the opportunity. The Takaii never retreated, but their losses were horrendous.

But Dezigeth remained active, and the Etari took losses, too.

For a while, Brandt thought they might contain the advance long enough to develop a new strategy. But the Takaii were tireless and eventually covered more territory than the Etari could protect. Once they broke free, they flooded the land, including the empire.

Thanks to the Etari fleeing their land, initial losses were low. Even in the empire, it was mostly farmsteads and small villages attacked. Brandt suspected Olen didn't even know the danger his land was under yet. At least, he didn't see any response from the imperial armies.

The advance of the Takaii was slow but relentless. But to this point, major catastrophe had been averted.

Until they hit Tonno.

79

Brandt heard about the assault from the queen. When the scouting missions first began, Brandt had imagined that scouts would fly to and from Faldun, but the queen had far better ideas. Every scouting group was responsible for their own territory, and at night, the queen connected with the leader of each group through the soulwalk.

Brandt had never imagined information could flow back and forth so easily. It changed the landscape of warfare completely, and was the only reason their pitiful forces had any success against the invasion.

His scouting party had been in the middle of their daily patrol when he felt that familiar tug near the base of his skull. At first, he thought it was Alena, but then he had to remind himself that Alena would never summon him to the soulwalk again.

He and the queen met and she wasted no time. "Another group of scouts has just reported that Tonno is being overrun."

Tonno was a large city, situated on the Alna River, close

to the Etari border. It was an important trading post, and given its vulnerable location, there was always at least a regiment of army there. If it fell, it would take no small number of Takaii. Brandt hadn't realized so many of the creatures were in the empire.

"I want to help."

"That's why I'm letting you know," the queen said, as though she was surprised Brandt hadn't already figured it out on his own.

The soulwalk ended abruptly, and Brandt gathered his scouts on their platform and sent them flying.

The plains of Etar passed below them, and soon they found the Alna River. Brandt followed it north, soon spotting the smoke from the burning city.

He looked at each of his warriors, all prepared for a fight. Although they numbered only five, Brandt believed they could turn the course of any battle, if they weren't too late. Brandt would make sure of it. Only Dezigeth would have anything else to say on the matter.

Dezigeth.

Brandt hadn't used his gate for much more than flying them around the past few weeks, wary of Dezigeth attacking them. Should he use it in Tonno?

The question was easy enough to answer. He would do all he could to save Tonno, including using his gate if needed, and hope it didn't bring Dezigeth. He had to try.

But as they neared, Brandt realized it didn't matter.

They were too late.

The walls had been breached and Takaii flooded the streets. Brandt snarled and summoned fire. Kane, one of the Falari scouts who often served as a reasonable voice on their expeditions, rested his hand on Brandt's arm. "Are you sure?" he asked.

Brandt looked down at the streets. No matter what he did, the city was lost.

But as they flew overhead, he could still hear screams.

"There are survivors, still," Brandt said. "I can't save the city, but I can save them."

Kane nodded, satisfied.

Brandt sent waves of fire down the street. The Takaii, as they always did, died silently.

Their work was slow. As hurried as Brandt felt, it was more important to be thorough, and he cleared every street and alley. The docks, where buildings crowded upon one another, were the worst, and Brandt had little choice but to leave sections of the dock untouched. The spaces were too crowded and he didn't want to injure someone innocent.

The other scouts mostly watched. Helping at this stage would be little more than a waste of arrows. They did fire if they saw someone in immediate danger.

When the streets in the area were mostly cleared, Brandt set them down in the docks, where the fighting was close in and brutal. Against the organized tactics of his scouts, though, the Takaii didn't have a chance.

By the time the sun was down, Brandt thought the city had been pretty well cleared. Tired as they were, Brandt ordered them to begin the search for survivors.

After a few blocks, Brandt felt his soul separate from his body. He observed his actions over his own shoulder, unable to experience the sights directly. The citizens who had fallen to the Takaii had died violently, and their corpses hadn't been treated with respect. Even burned by Brandt's cleansing fires, he could see the bite marks, the flesh torn from the bones of men, women, and children.

It was too much. Sickness roiled his stomach, and the

only way he found to continue on was to keep calling for survivors.

In ones and twos they began to emerge. Covered in grime and mud, jumping at every unexpected sound. Slowly, they became a crowd, and Brandt had his scouts direct them to an open town square where they could begin to gather what they would need to survive the next few days.

Eventually, they were met by a commander, his insignia half ripped off. He'd been cut by the sharp forearms of the Takaii, but he looked as though he would live. He approached Brandt nervously. "You're the one who brought the fire?"

Brandt nodded.

"I've never seen anything like that before."

Brandt wanted to tell the man there would be more terrors soon, but didn't have the heart. He just nodded. "We've beaten them back today, but I wouldn't count on them giving up so easily. You'll have to decide what you want to do."

"What were they?"

"You wouldn't believe me if I told you," Brandt said. He'd seen plenty of wonders in the past few months, and it was a struggle to remind himself that not everyone had seen the same. For the average citizen, and even the average soldier, in the empire, life had proceeded largely without interruption. Their awakening would be rough.

"Sir, today I've seen creatures that don't look like anything I've ever seen in a lifetime of service tear through our defenses with no regard for their lives. I've seen a man on a flying platform destroy those same creatures with an affinity that defies everything I know about the cost. I'm open to new beliefs."

Brandt laughed despite the tragedy surrounding him.

The empire would be in for a rough time, yes, but it would still be a mistake to count them out, especially if it was in the hands of men like this. "They are creatures from another world, brought here to kill us."

"The Etari did this, didn't they?"

Brandt laughed again, but this time at the absurdity of the statement. Then he turned somber. "Hardly. The Etari lands have already been overrun by these creatures. Most of them have fled to Falar."

The commander digested that. Brandt imagined that for the last several years, the threat of the Etari was all he'd been concerned about. To learn your enemy had been wiped out by a force that now threatened you was a lot to take in.

But the man did so. "You won't be staying long, will you?"

Brandt shook his head. "This war is happening on many fronts, and I'm needed in many places. Besides, the emperor isn't exactly in the mood to welcome me right now."

"He will once I tell him what happened here."

Brandt nodded. "Look to your people, and spread the word about the danger coming. The empire needs to be prepared."

"I'll do that, sir."

It pained Brandt, but he ordered his scouts back to the platform and out of the city. He wanted to provide aid, but there was little he could do to help the victims that others couldn't.

What he could do was clear the area surrounding the city of Takaii and give the commander and the survivors room to breathe.

And that was exactly what he did.

80

When Brandt saw Ana again, he could hardly believe the change in her. He'd only been gone a few weeks, but there was now absolutely no doubt that she was ready to give birth. She still moved well enough, but she grumbled about the baby overstaying its welcome.

Once Brandt returned to Faldun, he rarely left his chambers, except to go on walks with Ana and to the meals prepared in the dining halls. Otherwise, they sat and talked, or sometimes played games. In the world beyond, the Takaii continued their relentless advance, but he and his scouts were exhausted. They'd been out for weeks, fighting however they could, but always retreating.

The queen had set up a system that allowed the scouting parties to return and rest, an effort to keep their fighting forces as fresh as possible. Brandt and the others had another two days before they were scheduled to leave again, but he wasn't certain he wanted to.

Seeing Ana this pregnant changed his priorities. It was a selfish decision, to be sure, but he wanted to be present for the birth of his first child. And anyway, it wasn't like his presence on the front lines was turning the tide of the war. There were now dozens of Etari equally capable.

For the first time in his life, he truly just wanted to rest and be with Ana, ignoring his other commitments.

By unspoken agreement, they didn't talk of the events in the world beyond. They built a shield of their own and hid behind it, safe from the sharpened arrows the world thrust at them. They did some training, although Ana's focus was worse than Brandt's had been the last time they had sheltered in Faldun together. It was no fault of her own, though. Their child was incredibly active.

They rested throughout the day, Brandt letting his hand slide across Ana's stomach, enjoying the feeling of his child kicking.

In those moments, he wanted to leave it all behind and run away with Ana and his child. Then guilt would set in, and he knew he would have to leave to ensure that his child had a safe world to grow up in.

It all felt tremendously unfair.

Brandt and Ana were playing a Falari board game when there was a knock on their door. Brandt answered it, surprised to find the queen there, all alone. His stomach sank. If she was here, it didn't mean anything good.

"Come in," he said, suddenly self-conscious of their small space.

Sofra came in, but gestured for Ana to remain seated.

In so many small ways, Brandt couldn't believe how she had changed. He offered tea, but the queen refused. "I'm afraid I come bearing bad news," she said.

Brandt gestured for her to continue.

"The Takaii are making their way toward Landow."

Brandt absorbed the information, understanding quickly enough. "It's going for the next gate."

The queen nodded. "It seems to be, yes. Given its behavior so far, it doesn't want either us or the gates to be here when it leaves."

Brandt thought of Jace, and of Alena's parents. Landow had been where this all began for him. "What would you have of me?"

"Landow isn't their only destination," the queen said. "Another prong of their advance is marching toward Falar."

"So we have to defend two locations at once."

The queen shook her head. "Thanks to the terrain here, the Takaii will likely funnel into one of three different valleys, depending on where exactly they cross the border. A handful of Etari should be enough to prevent their advance."

"Until Dezigeth arrives," Brandt said.

"Exactly." The queen paused. "I would like to remain here, both as a strategic decision, and to remain close to my gate. But I believe we should defend Landow as well."

"As much as I'd like to," Brandt said, "I don't know how wise that is. We're still criminals in the eyes of the empire."

"Olen is in Landow," the queen said. "I felt him connect with the second imperial gate two days ago. I expect he'll know what happened in Tonno. It's possible he might listen to you now."

Brandt looked to Ana for advice. She shrugged. "At the least, you can ask Olen."

"Can you connect us?" Brandt asked Sofra.

She nodded, and a moment later they were in the soul-walk. Sofra placed them within the desert of her homeland. Brandt glanced to her. "I wasn't expecting you to join us. Your presence might not be welcome."

"He knows I am on the continent, and even were I not a part of this conversation, he would know I'm nearby. There's little point in hiding anymore."

Brandt nodded, not entirely convinced.

Not long later, Olen appeared. Brandt had expected him to appear ready to fight, but Olen just eyed the two of them suspiciously.

Brandt began. "The Takaii are approaching Landow with the intent of capturing the gate for Dezigeth. We'd like to offer our help."

"You were the one who came to Tonno?" Olen asked. "The man that the survivors there remember matches your description."

"It was," Brandt said.

Olen looked from Brandt to the queen. "And you're here because your land was overrun?"

"I am."

Olen turned his back on them. "This is your land?"

"It was. And perhaps one day, it might be again."

He nodded, but whatever thoughts ran through his mind, he kept them to himself. "I'm afraid I've been a fool," he said. "The wise men say there is no one easier to fool than oneself, and I'm living proof of that. I was so convinced, both by my own paranoia surrounding the gates and my closest advisers, that you all were lying. But then I saw Tonno and heard the stories, and I knew the truth of it. It was one piece of evidence too much to deny. If I had just acted earlier—"

"Sir," Brandt interrupted, "you cannot afford to get bogged down in past decisions. We've all made mistakes. You know the truth now, and we'd like to help."

"Can you?" Olen asked. "If what you say is true, you've

had little success doing anything but get driven back. And Alena is dead. Her connection to the gates is gone."

"We want to fight," Brandt said. "Give us permission to join you in Landow. I do not know how likely we are to succeed, but I do know that our only hope is to try, together."

Olen nodded. "Very well. How long will it take you to arrive?"

"A couple of days at most," Brandt said.

"We'll try to hold out until you arrive," Olen said as he disappeared.

Back in the physical world, Brandt escorted the queen out of their chambers.

"When are we going to Landow?" Ana asked, her intuition as sharp as ever.

"By tomorrow," Brandt said. He looked at his very pregnant wife. "Is there any way to convince you to stay?"

She shook her head. "It sounds as though either Landow or Faldun will be the next focus for the war. Either way, I would like to be with you at the end."

Brandt laughed. "You know, some days I wish I'd married a coward."

81

The queen and Brandt walked side by side as they inspected the last of the preparations. Half of the gate-connected Etari would join Brandt. The other half would remain behind with the queen, preparing a very warm welcome for the Takaii once they were funneled into a valley.

"Are you certain you don't want more?" the queen asked again.

"I am. It's not wise to short yourself protection, even if you believe Dezigeth will attack Landow first."

"It's not just that. They won't be needed here. The mountains will act as funnels. I could probably stop the Takaii myself."

"And if Dezigeth decides to attack here next, you'll be alone. We'll only be separated by two days. Wherever it strikes, we can respond."

"We've never lasted two days once Dezigeth is involved," the queen pointed out.

"In which case the extra Etari wouldn't matter."

The queen went silent. She didn't agree, but they'd also

had this argument several times between last night and this morning. Brandt refused to take a bet on which target Dezigeth would attack first. Their attempts to predict its movements thus far had failed. An even split gave them the best odds, slim as they were.

The queen was certain Dezigeth would attack Landow first, based, as near as Brandt could tell, on little more than the fact that Landow was closer. But she wasn't so certain she would abandon her people, which only confirmed Brandt's argument.

The preparations for their departure were nearly complete. The warriors packed weapons, arrows, and what food Faldun could spare.

Their eventual leaving was a quiet affair. A somber mood hung over Faldun. The whole city knew the state of affairs. Brandt wondered how many watching secretly wished the departing warriors would remain and leave Landow to its fate.

The platforms took off and began their flight through Falar. Brandt led the way, setting the pace for the rest to follow. They passed over majestic peaks and thundering waterfalls. The land was devoid of people, though.

Just the way Dezigeth wanted the whole world.

Perhaps there was some comfort in knowing the world would continue on, even if they failed. Humans liked to believe they were somehow necessary, but as he passed over Falar, Brandt understood how much of an illusion that was. If Dezigeth succeeded, most of the world would hardly notice.

Their passage was quiet. Brandt's warriors spoke a little to one another, and to Ana, but the language barriers prevented a free-flowing conversation. And flying the platform wasn't the easiest of tasks. It required most of Brandt's attention.

They paused briefly for lunch, and to allow those flying the platforms to rest their minds. Then they resumed their journey, the mountainous regions of Falar transforming into rolling hills and then the plains of the southern edges of the empire.

As evening began to fall, Brandt watched the progress of the other platforms. They were all starting to wobble, evidence of their mental exhaustion. He pushed on, hoping to put as much distance behind them on the first day as he could. Every league they flew today was one they didn't have tomorrow, and he wanted to arrive in Landow as early and as fresh as possible.

Eventually, though, they had to stop. Brandt landed them in an empty field and they made camp.

The next morning, they began as soon as the sun shone the first rays of light over the horizon.

Brandt made no effort to hide their flying platforms. They passed over villages and farms, eliciting both screams of terror and wide-eyed looks of awe.

One way or another, change was coming to the empire.

In more ways than one, Brandt soon found.

The queen believed that the Takaii were focused on Landow. Perhaps it was true, but Brandt discovered it wasn't the whole truth. They spread throughout the empire, and had already reached far beyond Landow. They passed burned villages, abandoned towns, and parties of Takaii.

The first time, they'd stopped and killed the creatures. But as they passed more, Brandt ordered his warriors to fly over them. Guilt almost doubled him over, but they needed to reach Landow.

Some of the other platforms had more than one gate-connected warrior, and they obeyed the letter of Brandt's orders while ignoring the spirit. One warrior would fly the platform while another launched stones back and forth, destroying groups of Takaii without even having to slow.

The sight of it nearly brought Brandt to tears. This wasn't their land, but the Etari protected it all the same.

Soon mountains rose off in the distance, and Brandt knew they were nearing Landow. The forest grew beneath them, and Brandt saw the Takaii moving in large groups underneath the protective canopy of the trees. The ground seemed to be covered with them, and Brandt knew no other reinforcements would reach Landow.

Brandt almost lost his focus when he saw the walls. The Takaii might have reached other parts of the empire, but nowhere like this. The walls hadn't fallen yet, but it wasn't due to any lack of effort on the Takaii's part. Bodies were piled high against the wall, and Takaii used the corpses of their comrades to scale ever closer to the top.

Flame erupted off in the distance, and Brandt marked it as the emperor's location. Using the hand signals so useful among the Etari, he ordered the other platforms to find places to land near the wall. They were to spread out and burn the piles of corpses to cinders.

He was glad they had pushed hard yesterday to arrive when they did today. Had they been much later the walls would have been breached. As soon as there was a way in, the city would be lost. Brandt thought of Tonno and shuddered.

Never again.

Brandt directed his own platform to where he had seen the ball of fire. He found a place to land and became light, scampering up to the top of the wall as his warriors followed.

Brandt hadn't seen the emperor physically for many years and never so close. Olen probably hadn't been much more than a boy.

Any trace of the boy was gone now. Olen was leaner than he projected himself in the soulwalk, and sweat poured off him. He looked like he hadn't slept in days. Given the number of Takaii piled against the wall, it was possible he hadn't.

Brandt summoned a wall of fire that cleared a large swath of swarming Takaii. Olen turned, seeing Brandt for the first time. He nodded a silent thanks and looked up and down the wall as the Etari went to work.

The import of the moment wasn't lost on Brandt. Landow wasn't far from the Etari border, and although traders frequently came through, the relationship between imperials, particularly in these parts of the empire, and the Etari were contentious at best.

Now the city was being saved by those it had once loved to hate.

The siege, at least for the moment, continued. Fire devoured the bodies of the Takaii, erasing the progress they'd made.

Brandt turned to Olen. "Rest now, sir. We'll hold the walls."

He was as good as his word. The Takaii were already re-forming, and Brandt formed a wall of fire to meet their relentless advance.

82

The siege of Landow bore little resemblance to the siege of Valan. The Etari made the difference. With so many assuming the defense of the city, it was almost a casual affair. Despite the Takaii's persistent attempts at breaching the wall, they had no chance against the defenders. More important, Dezigeth was nowhere to be found.

Brandt and Olen created a schedule for the gate-connected warriors, and Toren communicated it to the Etari. They fought on the wall for a third of each day and rested for the other two thirds.

After two days, the Takaii finally relented. They could still be seen swarming in the woods. If anything, their numbers swelled once again.

Brandt watched the shadows flitting through the trees and wondered how many Takaii even existed. Tens of thousands of the creatures had died on this planet, and that was only in the battles Brandt knew of.

He couldn't summon any sympathy, though. Perhaps they were willing servants. Or maybe they were stuck between two far stronger forces. Either way, their mindless behavior prevented him from seeing them as sentient.

Brandt turned from the wall. The city's forces had taken charge again in absence of an assault, providing Brandt and the Etari a well-deserved rest. The main gates remained closed, but with the flying platforms, there were few immediate worries about food or supplies.

Brandt passed one of the platforms as he finished descending the wall. Such a simple creation, once the cost was surpassed. But they changed everything. Warfare, commerce, and travel would be revolutionized. If they survived this, the world would never be the same.

And he was eager to see what it might look like.

He let his imagination wander until someone bumped into him. He shook himself out of his reverie and saw Ana walking beside him, an innocent look on her face. "You seem like you're thinking deep thoughts," she said, her tone light.

"Just imagining what a world without the cost might look like."

"And?"

"It's wonderful. And terrifying. I'm not sure we're ready."

"I think we'd figure it out. We usually do."

Brandt laughed. "An optimistic belief."

She shrugged. "When I see what's happening in this city, it does give me hope."

She gestured toward a teahouse. A group of imperial warriors and Etari were sitting together, smiles on their faces. A year ago, they would have been one wrong move away from drawing swords on one another.

"There's been trouble, too," Brandt reminded her.

"Sure, but they've been minor incidents, and it's too much to ask everyone to change all at once."

They strolled through the streets, no particular destination in mind. Again, this was like no siege Brandt would have imagined. They were still surrounded by thousands of Takaii, but within the walls, life seemed almost normal. The Takaii only knew one method of attack, and it couldn't break the walls. Not with the Etari here. There was no reason not to be out.

The unceasing ability of people to adapt always surprised Brandt. They found a new normal, no matter what occurred.

Their pleasurable stroll didn't last nearly long enough. Jace found them, looking every bit a leader in his new imperial uniform. As soon as Olen learned Jace and Alena had been speaking the truth, he'd reinstated Jace and then some. The young man slipped into the role as if he'd been born for it. His look didn't indicate good news, though. "The emperor wishes to see you. He's gotten new birds in today."

"And?"

Jace shook his head. "He wouldn't say. But from the way he paled when he read them, it isn't good."

Jace led them to the governor's mansion. Not nearly as large or ostentatious as some, Brandt found that he liked the design. The governor now shared the residence with the emperor. They were admitted quickly.

Jace stopped outside an otherwise unremarkable door and knocked. When invited, they entered.

Olen was hunched over maps of the empire, paper surrounding him. He was alone, and didn't even look up at his guests. He gestured for them to consider the maps with him. Brandt saw the problem immediately, and even he was taken aback. "They've already reached Estern?"

Olen nodded. "I've just received word today. They've

been marching for days without pause, and as we speak, they're tearing up the estates outside the walls."

To that, Brandt felt little sympathy. They were the estates of the wealthy, built beyond the walls so that they could retreat to the thick defenses of Estern if needed, but didn't have to deal with the crowded conditions otherwise. They were a defensive nightmare, and a bitter part of him was glad to see the Takaii finally illustrating the error of their ways.

Still, if Dezigeth's pattern continued, it meant they were now fighting a war on three fronts. Was the queen wrong? Did Dezigeth plan to just skip over Landow and destroy the gate in Estern?

That wasn't the only difficult news, Brandt saw as he looked at the map. The Takaii were everywhere. If Olen's map reflected reality, they had already advanced across half the empire. No doubt there were places like Landow that held out, but the empire was crumbling even faster than Brandt had feared.

Olen met their gazes. "I believe we need to abandon Landow. With your platforms and the Etari, we can fly up and down the line, killing the Takaii and halting their advance."

Brandt shook his head. "We don't have that many people. We couldn't cover enough ground fast enough."

"Then call the remainder from Faldun." Desperation tinged Olen's voice.

"Even then," Brandt said.

When he looked at the map, he saw a timer, grains of sands slipping away too fast to catch. They couldn't stop the Takaii. Weak as they were individually, there were too many spread out over too far. Their chance for containment had been lost at the Battle of Cardon.

Their only option left was an assault on Dezigeth. And based on the map, it couldn't wait long. "Sir, do you mind if I contact the queen?"

He didn't know how much she knew, but when she saw this map, he expected that she would feel much the same as him. It was time to roll the dice and attack. Before they were spread too thin to do even that.

He reached out in the soulwalk, finding the queen before long. They connected and appeared in Highgate.

The queen looked surprised. "You know?"

"Know what?" Brandt asked.

"Why did you reach out?"

Brandt recalled the map and materialized it in the soulwalk. "Estern is under attack and the Takaii are making rapid progress through the empire. I think we need to attack Dezigeth, and soon."

A grim smile appeared on her face. "Convenient, then. I was just about to connect with you."

"Why?"

"Because I'm coming to Landow."

Brandt didn't understand. "Why?" he asked again.

"Because Dezigeth is stirring, and its heading toward you."

83

Even without the queen's warning, Brandt would have suspected Dezigeth's arrival the next morning. The Takaii didn't attack, but they gathered in the trees, massing for their advance. They only waited for their herald.

Dezigeth arrived around noon, first seen as a black speck far off in the distance. The speck grew rapidly, evidence of the creature's incredible agility. Brandt watched it come and wondered how long it would take to cross the entire continent at such speed.

For all their advances, they were still children compared to Dezigeth.

But even children could fight.

Dezigeth streaked overhead, and the Takaii advanced.

They were greeted, as they always were, with walls of flame. The grounds just beyond the walls of Landow were little more than scorched earth. Today, the only thing that burned were the Takaii.

Dezigeth had little patience for the slaughter of its

minions today. It swooped down to strike at the wall's defenders. Brandt allowed himself the barest hint of a smile.

They were starting to understand it.

Dozens of stones split the air, too fast to see.

With so much recent practice, the Etari's aim had only improved. The attacks did little damage, but Dezigeth veered from its course.

It wasn't tied to its physical form the way Brandt was to his, but it still didn't like being hurt. Not at all.

Predicting it did little good, though, if they couldn't hurt it. Each of those stones would have blasted holes through any city wall, and Dezigeth bore their impacts without complaint.

Brandt formed several flames, each focused into a small ball. He didn't delude himself into believing they were as strong as Dezigeth's creations, but they would hurt. He threw them.

Flame engulfed the dark form, and at least a half dozen Etari launched stones into the maelstrom. Here in Landow, stone was plentiful, and the Etari were free with their attacks.

Dezigeth burst from the cloud of flame, aimed straight at Brandt.

As expected.

More balls of flame struck Dezigeth from the side. As it dealt with the surprise attacks from Olen, Brandt threw more fire, the heat almost unbearable.

Dezigeth broke through it all.

Brandt caught a glimpse of its face. Eyes glittered with cold fury. It swiped at Brandt, but Brandt had seen the same attack at least a dozen times now. He sidestepped the blow and wrapped his arms around Dezigeth's legs as it passed.

That he was successful seemed to catch them both by surprise.

Dezigeth's momentum carried them both off the wall, tumbling to the burned and blackened ground beyond. Brandt made himself light a moment before impact, but the landing still drove the breath from his lungs.

He was on his feet with sword in hand a moment later. Dezigeth didn't stand, exactly. It re-formed itself from the form of a person lying down to one that was vertical.

The action froze Brandt before he struck. Dezigeth took the form of a winged human, but that was just a mask.

Did Dezigeth even have vital points to strike? It couldn't, not if it survived the attack the queen had unleashed on it outside Cardon.

Brandt struck at Dezigeth anyway, who stepped back and avoided the cut. It flexed its wings and flew straight into the air.

Brandt switched to a one-handed grip and pulled a stone from his pocket with his left hand. He smashed it into a flat disc, then made himself light, stepped onto the platform, and launched himself after Dezigeth.

Points of light formed around the creature as it resorted to yet another predictable attack. Brandt heard the cracks as Etari stones tracked Dezigeth. And then Brandt was close, swinging his sword as he passed by.

The points of light faded as Dezigeth dodged backward.

Brandt pursued.

He wasn't as agile, but he could always reach it before it released one of its devastating attacks.

Below them, most of the Etari maintained their defense of the wall. The flames surrounding Landow remained unbroken, and the Takaii spent themselves to no avail. The defenders' strategy was succeeding, at least as much as anyone ever expected it to.

But Dezigeth, as always, was the deciding factor. The number of Takaii dead didn't matter if Dezigeth attacked Landow with its full strength.

Brandt chased Dezigeth across the sky. He relied on the edge of his sword, knowing that in a battle of affinities he had no chance.

And it worked. Dezigeth, it seemed, didn't want to be cut. It kept dodging, abandoning its attacks before they could fall on the city below.

But it couldn't last forever.

Dezigeth stopped trying to remain close to the city. When Brandt came close, it launched itself higher at a speed Brandt couldn't hope to match. Brandt followed anyway. He couldn't catch it, but there were also no other choices. If it had a moment, Landow would be destroyed.

Brandt flew higher, higher than he'd ever been. Tears streamed from his eyes as the wind whipped across his face. Brandt heard the song of fire above him. He knew that Dezigeth prepared.

Still he rushed forward, hoping against hope he would reach the creature in time.

He didn't.

Dezigeth let him close, but only to ensure Brandt had no time to dodge. It unleashed a stream of fire that engulfed Brandt. Brandt fought against the current, absorbing the heat and pushing it back at Dezigeth.

He slowed to a stop, their strength at a temporary equilibrium. Brandt started to sweat, the first sign he wasn't absorbing the surrounding heat fast enough. He groaned and pushed, but there was nothing left to give.

With a last, desperate gasp he thrust his sword toward Dezigeth. He felt it strike something.

And then the fury of the flames became far too much for him to bear. A wave of energy threw him off the platform, a wall of air and fire that sent him tumbling.

Another blast hit him, and then another. Earth and sky twisted wildly as he fell, spinning upon every axis. For a few heartbeats there was nothing but the wind in his ears and a complete sense of disorientation.

He returned to his senses slowly, then fumbled with his free left hand for one of the remaining stones in his pocket. His clothes flapped in the wind, and he still felt slow. One of Dezigeth's blows had struck him in the head, he thought.

Finally, he found a stone and held it tightly in his hand. He tried to make himself light and gradually slow his descent.

He saw ground, then sky, then ground again, and the concept of up was harder to grasp than he'd ever expected it could be. But by using small efforts, he slowed his spin to the point where he knew what to do. He fought against his fall using the stone, and he slowed himself down so that when he finally landed on a roof, it did little more than knock the wind out of him again.

Brandt struggled back to his feet.

He heard the songs of the affinities first. When he looked up, two dozen lights were descending upon the city of Landow. Brandt focused and managed to move just one out into the forests beyond.

Then the lights hit.

Brandt had never seen such destruction. Not even when Dezigeth had thrown the boulders at the queen and her city. Buildings exploded where the lights touched, destroying their neighbors along with the inhabitants inside.

The people had known to find shelter today, but their shelter couldn't protect them from this.

Brandt stood on the rooftop, far enough away from any of the lights that he didn't need to fear. For long moments, all he could do was watch.

So many lives, lost in an instant.

Worse, it appeared that Dezigeth had targeted the edges of the city, near the walls. Brandt saw enormous breaches in at least two places. The Etari who had been defending those sections had to be either dazed or dead, as the walls of fire had dropped.

Before Brandt could spring into action, though, others stepped in. Members of the city guard filled the breach, resorting to spears and shield to defend the gap. They met the Takaii, and they didn't give up a single pace of ground.

Brandt tested his abilities and found he could still become light. He did so, skipping across rooftops to reach the breaches. He found Jace at the first one, commanding the city guard with a sure hand. Brandt unleashed a few waves of fire, clearing the grounds beyond the wall of the endless Takaii. The city guard made short work of those who had made it close to the wall.

Jace nodded his appreciation.

After they were cleared away, the Takaii didn't return. Brandt didn't question why, but turned to the other breach.

He stopped before he even took a step. The breach was being closed by a handful of Etari, led by Toren. They lifted enormous boulders and placed them in the gap. Another warrior kept the besiegers away with fire.

For the first time since the battle had started, Brandt had a moment to look around. Up and down the wall, the Takaii were retreating back into the forests. He looked to the clear sky above, but could see nothing there, either.

He wasn't sure why the attack had stopped, but they'd survived the first day.

He looked at the portions of the shattered city behind him.

It hadn't been without its losses, though.

And he had the sinking feeling that tomorrow would be worse.

84

Brandt almost didn't leave Ana's side the next morning. It felt as though he was always leaving, and now, he wasn't sure his leaving would have any noticeable effect on the battle to come. They had tried everything. Even with the queen arriving today, what difference did it make?

There were times to fight a hopeless battle.

But they gained nothing here. At best, they prolonged what was quickly becoming an inevitable conclusion. Why not spend his last days with the woman he loved? He didn't believe they could run forever, but they could buy themselves more time together, and wasn't that worth it?

Ana was the reason he wanted to run, but she was also the reason he stayed.

While he fought, she had helped Landow however she could, from tending to the wounded to being a shoulder to cry on. Given how late in her pregnancy she was, Brandt thought the most she should be doing was resting in bed, but any suggestion of that nature was rewarded only with a harsh glare. She had decided to stay and fight in her own way, which meant he would, too.

As he walked to the wall, he watched citizens moving closer to the center of the city. Barricades were being constructed in the streets.

Jace had been responsible for the decisions. He feared the walls would be breached again today. He wanted the citizens closer to the center of the city to protect them both from Dezigeth's attacks on the walls and the flood of Takaii that would threaten each breach.

The young man had the hallmarks of a great commander. Brandt remained unsure of his tactical or strategic genius, but he wasn't sure how much that mattered, especially now. Jace knew enough not to make mistakes, which was enough for this defense. And his soldiers loved him. Quick with a joke or story when needed, but uncompromising in his orders.

He hoped Alena would be proud of her brother.

Brandt was.

Olen was almost the opposite. His warriors followed him, but more out of tradition than any particular desire. He'd largely handed off the defense of the city to others. Although it was the right decision, it also sent a clear message to his soldiers he wasn't experienced enough to command them.

Emperor Anders VII stood alone on the wall until Brandt joined him. He stared out at the trees, where the Takaii gathered once again. "If we fail," he said, "I'll be known as the last emperor. The one who let the empire collapse."

Brandt shook his head. "That's nonsense, sir. You have nothing to worry about on that account."

Olen's hope at the comment almost made Brandt feel

sorry. "Really?"

"Of course, sir. If we fail here, there won't be anyone left to write a history."

Olen's hope died and he glared at Brandt, who acted as though he didn't notice.

Brandt remained by Olen's side, waiting for the Takaii to attack.

They didn't.

Dezigeth struck first.

They didn't see the creature this time, not until it was too late. It flew just over the tops of the trees. Then it dove into and through the wall, sending a section about three hundred paces north of Brandt into the sky.

Then the Takaii advanced.

Put on the back foot from that first strike, the morning didn't go well for the defenders. Immediately some Etari broke from their positions to repair the wall. Others grew the wall of flames to keep the Takaii away.

But Dezigeth wasn't finished.

It repeated its act, destroying another section of wall and the Etari guarding it.

With each strike, their attention was divided. Few Etari remained to watch for Dezigeth and attack it with stones.

A third attack by Dezigeth brought them to their breaking point. It focused its attacks on the Etari on the wall, and the protective fire surrounding the city began to falter. Some Takaii poured through, climbing on the backs of one another to reach the top of the walls, while others aimed for the breaches.

Jace and the city guard filled the collapsed sections long enough for some of the Etari to come and repair the wall. But then Dezigeth killed more of the guard by another section.

The creature moved too fast and didn't remain in one place long enough for them to attack.

Brandt formed a platform and floated above the city, looking for Dezigeth before it struck. Sometimes he could spot it but not always. And it moved too fast. Brandt was just as likely to strike an ally as Dezigeth.

Brandt swore. The fire around the city was collapsing now, and the Takaii were against the walls, spreading all over.

He dropped to the wall. He couldn't figure out how to fight Dezigeth, but he could help against the Takaii. He cleared large sections of the wall, giving the Etari time to reposition. Still, it wouldn't be long before their defense folded.

He kept looking around, worried that at any moment, Dezigeth would strike at him.

For now he avoided that fate.

He spent so much time looking at the trees he didn't remember to look up. High above, Dezigeth formed its deadly lights. Brandt didn't notice until they were already falling, and by then, it was too late.

Brandt threw up a shield as the lights landed. Several hit the wall in different places. Some were contained by the Etari, but when the dust cleared, another half dozen breaches existed.

The Takaii didn't hesitate.

Brandt formed a platform. As dangerous as Dezigeth's earlier tactics had been, they didn't match the widespread destruction it could unleash from above.

But he didn't need to respond. Flame engulfed Dezigeth, even as Brandt prepared to fly. He followed the line of the attack to the floating platforms that approached the city.

The queen and the rest of the Etari had arrived, and not a moment too soon, either.

Dezigeth didn't stay to fight. It dropped to the level of the trees and returned to picking off the defenders as it could.

Brandt didn't understand why Dezigeth fled. It wasn't as though they'd done any true damage to it.

Or had they?

It said something about their lack of knowledge when Brandt couldn't even be sure if they were winning or not.

Regardless, the arrival of reinforcements changed the momentum of the battle. Fire was reinforced along the walls, and there were now plenty of Etari to repair the walls and keep watch for Dezigeth as it approached.

The creature tried a few more attempts, but only once did it get to the wall without being spotted.

By noon, the Takaii were retreating, and the fighting seemed over for the day.

That night, the queen found Brandt and Ana. She entered the room they'd been given in a building near the center of the city. They offered tea and she sat down beside them. Something in the queen's demeanor had changed, and it took Brandt some time to figure out what it was. She still moved with the easy grace she always did, but her footsteps seemed lighter, as though she was just brushing the ground.

Brandt knew then what the queen intended.

After sitting in silence for a while, she spoke. "If you survive this," she began, "I would like you to look after my people. They wait for you in Faldun."

Which was confirmation enough. The queen planned to fight, giving herself no option of retreat. Perhaps it was the best chance they had left. He wouldn't dissuade her, but he did have questions. "Why me?"

"There's none else that I trust in this," she replied. "I would have chosen Alena, were she still alive. But you are the only person who has any understanding of both the Lolani and this continent. I do not ask that you lead them for the rest of your life, unless you choose to. I only wish for them to become a part of this new world. If I die, let the Lolani die with me. Then they can choose their tomorrows without me."

Their gazes locked, but Brandt didn't flinch away.

Sofra was all steel within. Anything soft in her had started to burn away back when her childhood had been stolen from her. She was capable of horrible deeds. Was guilty of terrible deeds.

If she won tomorrow, would it matter? Would they say it had all been justified by the result? There were few enough Lolani left to remind them all of the price paid for such strength.

Brandt didn't know.

He couldn't forgive her, and although he had some measure of respect for her, he couldn't bow before her. He'd seen her choices firsthand.

But he didn't hate her anymore, either.

It was hard to hate somebody that he understood so well.

He nodded, and it was finalized. She stood up to leave.

"Would you like me to fight by your side tomorrow?" he asked as she was about to step out the door.

She paused for a moment, then shook her head. "Thank you for the offer, but no. And let the others know, too. They can use their stones, if they like, but they should stay away. For their own safety."

And then she was gone.

85

The Takaii attacked before the arrival of the sun the next morning. Brandt woke to the alarm bells, bleary-eyed, the days of mental focus and existential fear slowing his transition to awareness. Ana was even slower to rise.

Brandt threw on clothes, then bent down to kiss his wife. In the predawn darkness, his courage almost failed him.

The queen had decided that Landow would be decisive. Brandt wasn't ready to make that commitment.

He lingered. The Etari would be reaching the walls by now. They didn't need him right away. He held Ana's hand as she grumbled her way into a sitting position.

She was the one who pushed him out. After another kiss and a long look, he left. It was her courage that sustained him, her courage that he felt as he made his way to the wall.

When he arrived, the defense was as routine as this new type of siege could be. The newly arrived Etari had integrated into the ranks of the more seasoned defenders, and the walls of fire kept the Takaii well away. Watchers scanned the sky for Dezigeth, but in the darkness, they had little hope of spotting it in time.

No doubt, that was its plan.

No one saw it before it struck the wall. The old stonework collapsed, and the flickering wall of fire meant at least one of the Etari had lost their lives.

Then Dezigeth disappeared again, lost to the darkness of night.

Brandt wasn't alone in watching the sky with worried anxiety. Again, the urge to run almost seized him. But now he remained so as not to let down the warriors beside him. Any of them could run. They all had the strength to fly a platform as far as their focus would take them.

None did.

They stood, defending a city that wasn't even theirs as Dezigeth picked them off one by one. No one ever saw it coming.

When Brandt saw Dezigeth flying for a section of wall not far from him, he barely had time to brace for the impact.

It never came.

Brandt only caught a glimpse of a figure, speeding down from the sky like a dark shooting star. It struck Dezigeth on the back, driving both to the ground. The impact threw up dirt higher than the wall, and there was now a crater where two figures stood facing one another.

Brandt ran along the wall to get a closer look.

The queen stood against Dezigeth.

The Etari on the walls, finally given a stationary target, launched their stones. Dezigeth stopped most of the projectiles, but the Etari didn't relent.

Dezigeth spread its wings, but before it could take flight, dozens of lights appeared, forming a small dome around the two combatants. They were more a deterrence than a cage, but Dezigeth hesitated for a moment, and that was all the queen needed.

She closed, her footsteps impossibly quick, a short sword leaping to her hand.

Brandt had only seen her physical abilities once, back when she'd taken on several attackers while connecting to the gate at Faldun. But he'd forgotten that her skill with a blade surpassed even his own. Though she'd lost the one hand, it had been her weak one. From the grace of her first two cuts, it appeared she'd been refining her one-handed technique.

Dezigeth retreated, but when it put space between itself and the queen, the Etari were there, their deadly stones another threat.

It lashed out with its arms, and the queen's sword blocked.

They had it retreating, circling around the edges of the queen's trap. Brandt had seen them corner it before, knew that it would find some way to give itself just a moment. As soon as it did, the fight would be over.

He prepared, three focused balls of flame held ready.

The moment lasted the blink of an eye. A wave of uncontrolled power blasted from Dezigeth. The walls underneath Brandt's feet cracked, and though he was expecting something, the attack still knocked him off his feet.

He attempted to stand, but more explosions erupted, one after the other, a chain of concussions that shook the foundations of the wall. Brandt shielded himself, unable to do anything more. A section of wall, about the size of his head, smashed into his shield a few moments later.

It was all too easy to imagine his skull crushed by the debris.

Brandt fought to his feet, expecting to see the queen dead before the wall. The explosions had to be her points of light detonating. He stumbled forward, still unbalanced, and caught himself on the edge.

He blinked, not sure he believed what he saw.

The queen's clothing was in tatters, which told Brandt she hadn't shielded herself from the blasts. The reason revealed itself in the sight of her sword struck through Dezigeth.

She'd sacrificed her defense for the opportunity to attack.

Everything for one last strike.

And she'd hurt it.

Whatever Dezigeth's body was, it felt pain. Agony was written on every line of its face.

The sword began to glow, the queen channeling fire into the blade. She twisted and cut more.

Against a human, Brandt was certain the blade would pass through a body without resistance. But Dezigeth was formed of something stronger, and as the queen strained, the blade only moved the width of a finger at a time.

Still, the pain of such a stab had to be excruciating, even for Dezigeth. Light grew in the pit of its stomach.

The queen drew the sword out, so bright it almost hurt Brandt's eyes. Before Dezigeth could recover, she stabbed again, twisting into its body.

Then again.

Dezigeth howled.

And Brandt dared to hope.

Until he saw the lights.

They appeared, one by one, around the two fighters. At first, Brandt thought they were the queen's, but they weren't. Although the attacks looked similar, Dezigeth's were more focused, more powerful than anything the queen could create.

The queen didn't notice. Her focus was entirely on Dezigeth as she continued to cut at it. He shouted for her, but she didn't hear. She was in her own world, taking revenge for her mother from so long ago.

He didn't dare soulwalk. His message might get through, but if he consumed her attention, even for just a few heartbeats, Dezigeth would kill her.

It now looked like a cloud of fireflies surrounded them. He turned to the others on the wall as more lights appeared. Brandt had never seen so many in one place. Dezigeth planned on ending this. "Run!"

The Etari obeyed, but for the first time that day, Brandt had no desire to run. The queen was hurting Dezigeth. She was maybe even killing it.

Could she succeed before this final blow?

Either way, Brandt felt her act had to be witnessed. He formed a shield around himself, and then another over that. He reinforced them with as much power as he could pull.

The queen stabbed again, but Brandt could see her strength begin to fail her.

The sword, now embedded in Dezigeth where a man's heart would be, started to glow even brighter as the queen channeled everything into it.

Dezigeth's agony was matched only by the queen's satisfaction.

And then the lights fell.

86

Brandt's world became chaos. He closed his eyes against the blinding white, but it did no good. The glare burned his eyes even as he covered them.

He was lifted from the wall, as though a giant hand had picked him up. Then he was flying, though in what direction, or how far, he had not a clue. Forces thundered against his shields, and even using the power of the gate, they strained under the assault.

He hit something, and then something else. His outer shield cracked, then shattered, and Brandt's only thought was to keep his inner shield intact.

Brandt struck something solid, and his movement was finally arrested. A distant thunder rumbled in both his ears and his bones, and then the light faded, leaving nothing but blissful darkness.

He didn't know how long he lay there. It felt like a long time, but it probably wasn't more than a couple dozen beats of his heart.

His shield held, but barely.

He breathed deep, then opened his eyes.

It was dark, but thin beams of light shone through. He heard the low hum of stone surrounding him.

A building had collapsed over him.

He moved the stone easily enough. Tempting as it was to throw it everywhere, he moved it gently, well aware there might be others nearby. In time, he was able to climb out of the building. He was sore, but his shields had protected him.

The Landow he emerged into was not the one he remembered from before. Where the queen and Dezigeth had fought, there was now only an enormous crater. The wall for hundreds of paces was gone.

Takaii poured into the city, clogging the streets and alleys with their numbers.

Brandt fell to his knees.

The queen had to have been close.

Again, it was all for naught.

Brandt remained on his knees as he watched even more Takaii flood into Landow. He knew he should fight. Bursts of flame in his peripheral vision let him know that some of the Etari still lived.

But he couldn't bring himself to stand.

Determination could only last so long.

Eventually, truth won.

They had no hope.

They never had.

Shakily, he got to his feet.

Not to fight, but to run. He needed to find Ana. He would get them out of here, and he would steal every precious moment he could.

Perhaps they would even survive.

He turned toward the center of the city. She would be there, helping however she could. She was always helping.

Time lost its grip on him. His journey to the center of

the city became a jumble of moments, barely connected. He was ambushed by Takaii in an alley, but with a gesture, destroyed them with fire.

On another street he saw a young family running in the same direction he was heading. The father held a crying boy in his arms, no more than three. Brandt killed a group of Takaii who followed them.

He passed horrors, too. Places where the devastation of Dezigeth's attack had leveled buildings on top of those hiding within. Places where the Takaii had already visited, leaving mutilated and half-eaten corpses behind. But the sights couldn't quite reach him. He'd built a shell around what remained of his heart, and only Ana existed within it.

Closer to the center of the city, he found Jace and Toren, fighting side by side. Both were bloody, and Jace had a long but shallow cut running from his shoulder nearly to his stomach. They looked a mess, but they protected dozens as citizens fled to the very center of the city.

Brandt wanted to tell them there was no point, but they already knew. And they fought anyway.

As he watched, Jace killed two Takaii with beautiful swings of his blade, demonstrating his admirable martial prowess. Toren killed a half dozen more with his spinning stones. Then they searched for the next battle, the next group to protect. Brandt knew they didn't see him, or if they did, it was as no more than another survivor fleeing for shelter.

He turned away, ashamed.

But he continued onward, to where he knew Ana would be.

He found her outside a city square, where many of the wounded were being cared for. She moved from person to person, cleaning and wrapping wounds.

She was the most beautiful thing he could imagine.

Then everyone around him began to look up. He continued on, not realizing the import of it for a long moment.

A shadow passed overhead, and he realized his mistake.

He turned to see Dezigeth flapping its wings slowly, floating overhead.

The people in the square screamed and ran for the cover of buildings, but there weren't many places for them to go. The Takaii closed in from all sides.

From a distance, Dezigeth appeared unharmed. The damage it had suffered at the queen's hands had vanished. And yet, Brandt thought, it wasn't entirely healed. There was something in its bearing that gave it away. It might look whole, but it was hurting.

Not that it would matter, though.

Even hurt, Brandt knew he was no match for the creature.

But Dezigeth's eyes were focused on him. It hunted him.

And in that moment, Brandt knew that he wouldn't be fleeing Landow.

Dezigeth pointed a finger, straight at Brandt's heart. "You!"

Brandt stood, alone in the square, and drew his sword.

Dezigeth snarled. "You are the last, the last of those that showed true promise on this world. The others have spent their lives against me. Once you are gone, it is over."

Brandt looked at the sword in his hand. For most of his life, he'd trusted the blade to keep him safe, to be both a weapon and a shield against harm. Now it seemed almost laughable that he'd put so much trust in something so meaningless.

But perhaps it had one more kill within it. Brandt

thought of the queen and how close she had come to killing Dezigeth. "Then come down, and we'll see who deserves to live."

Dezigeth shook its head. One glowing orb formed in its hand. "No," it said.

And then the line of fire reached down for Brandt.

87

Concepts formed slowly.

First was *here*. Place.

Then *wrong*, like a wrinkle on an otherwise perfect sheet.

The ideas linked and grew into a seed, a seed that grew into something more.

Something was wrong here.

Or here was wrong.

There was suffering in a place where there should be no suffering. Cries for help, where there should be only peace.

Then came separation.

It wasn't separation, not really. Everything was connected, in ways much deeper than they understood. Causality was only the surface, a ripple on top of a bottomless ocean. But it was the illusion of separation, of uniqueness.

With uniqueness came identity. Another illusion, but a powerful one.

The suffering was unbearable.

And it should not belong. Not here.

It reverberated like a plucked string.

A weaving existed here, something else that shouldn't exist.

It had been brought here, where nothing should be brought.

The weaving was strong, a thread that had been tested countless times. But it possessed a unique property. Stretching it made it stronger.

It pulled now, demanding attention.

And she pulled, too.

She answered the call.

88

Brandt met the fire with a shield. The heat swirled, and he pushed away what he could.

He stood against the onslaught as long as he could. Sweat dripped from his brow. He thought of Ana and the fate that awaited her if he fell, and he found the strength to stand longer.

Against Dezigeth, though, it was futile.

Brandt had never been a match for the creature. And he wasn't today, no matter how he wished otherwise. He collapsed to his knees, the last of his strength pushed toward the shield. His shield cracked. Heat seeped through, more than he could absorb.

Only a handful of heartbeats remained to him.

And then the pressure suddenly lessened. The flames died, and Brandt squinted as he looked up to see Dezigeth flying high into the sky.

Strong arms pulled him to his feet, then supported him as he found his balance. Brandt found himself looking into Jace's grinning face. Jace's mouth moved, but Brandt could hear nothing over the ringing in his ears. Brandt shook his head. Jace spoke again, this time louder. "I figured I would find you here."

"How?"

"Dezigeth, big pillar of fire. Seemed like something you would be a part of."

Brandt stared at Jace. In the midst of all this, where did he find the courage to jest?

Shame flushed his cheeks. He had the strength, the affinities, and the training, and yet here he was, leaning on a man with none of those gifts.

"Chin up," Jace said. "Toren and the others drove it off, but it won't last long."

"It's after me," Brandt said.

Jace looked unconvinced. "I know you think you need to save us by yourself, but I doubt Dezigeth is that interested in you."

"Normally, I'd like to agree with you," another voice chimed in, "but in this case, Dezigeth said as much." Brandt turned to see Ana behind them.

Jace grimaced. "Then don't you think you have better places to be than the center of my city?'

"You want me to run?"

"If it gets the flying monster out of my city, then yes."

It made sense. Perhaps if he ran and Dezigeth followed, he could buy the city some time. Brandt looked at Ana, but Jace cut him off before he could speak. "I don't think being near you is the safest place right now, do you?"

Jace turned and flashed a hand sign to Toren, up on a nearby rooftop. The Etari scrambled down to join them.

While they waited, Ana and Brandt enjoyed one last moment together. "Come back to me," she said.

"I will if I can," Brandt said. He hated the conditional,

but anything else was a lie. "Try not to give birth while I'm gone."

She laughed and shook her head, but then Toren was there, and Jace was giving him orders.

When Jace finished, he turned to Brandt and Ana. He smiled. "Don't worry," Jace said. "We'll take good care of her until you return."

"How do you do it?" Brandt asked. He swept his hands across the ruins of Landow. "How can you smile when this is what you see?"

Jace gave him a hug, then let him go. "You can't take life too seriously, Brandt. None of us can control what happens, and none of us get out alive."

Smiling at his own wit, Jace turned and left Brandt alone with Toren. Toren gestured, and the two of them took off for a platform.

In moments, they were soaring up and over the destruction. Toren flew them quickly, and Brandt sat, huddled up against a wall.

Dezigeth would return soon, and if it spoke the truth, it would come for him. Below, forests were filled with Takaii. He had left his wife again.

There was nothing to smile about, but memories of Jace filled Brandt's thoughts.

In another person, Brandt would have called the attitude callous. But that didn't apply to Jace. Jace had traveled across multiple continents for his sister and had always been there to help when needed. He cared deeply, but somehow managed to keep the tragedy from dampening his spirits.

It was a strength Brandt wasn't sure he could match.

Brandt squeezed his eyes shut. He should be focusing and resting, preparing for his next battle with Dezigeth.

But all he could think of was Jace.

He gave a short, bitter laugh, low enough that not even Toren heard it. Jace was right that they couldn't control their lives. He couldn't even control his thoughts.

He glanced over again at the forest that passed beneath them. There were fewer Takaii the farther they got from Landow, and Brandt hoped that meant there would be an end to the creatures soon. There were still a number of Etari to guard the walls. So long as Dezigeth wasn't there, they could hold out.

Something nagged at him, a thought he couldn't quite form completely.

He considered Jace's words, and an idea occurred to him... or more, the beginning of an idea. He checked the surroundings, but Dezigeth was nowhere to be found. So he dropped into the soulwalk.

This realm didn't come as easy to him as it had to Sofra or Alena, but he could feel the power of the gates nearby. He dove deeper, fighting against the currents of power until Alena's words from so long ago came back to him. He relaxed, and the current disappeared. Then he was before the gate. He felt his connection, could visualize it here. This was what he pulled power from.

He walked around the gate, studying it from all sides. He could see the connections to the source, a pool of power he couldn't even begin to comprehend.

But the gate wasn't well. The power came in irregular bursts.

Brandt put his hand against the gate. It burned, and he pulled away, staring at his hand.

Alena believed that the queen had been pulling too much power, and it had upset the balance of the gates. But that didn't make sense to Brandt. The source still had more than enough to give, but there was a resistance between the gates and the source.

He frowned.

There was something here. He knew it. Like a word at the tip of his tongue.

Toren suddenly materialized in the space next to him. Brandt jumped, having forgotten the young man was a skilled soulwalker. "We need to leave," Toren said. "Dezigeth is coming."

Brandt stared at the Etari. "You can fly the platform and be here?"

Toren signed the negative. "I put the platform down to reach you. I can't outfly it, regardless."

Brandt looked at the gate. The answer was here!

It had to be.

"I think I have an idea. I need time, though."

Toren only hesitated for a moment. Considering the price of the favor was most likely his life, Brandt was grateful when he signed his affirmation. Toren disappeared.

Brandt studied the gates again. The Falari gate was the one with the most connections, and Brandt sensed the most resistance.

Maybe?

It was nothing but a guess, inspired by Jace's distaste for seeking control over life. But he had nothing left to lose. He couldn't beat Dezigeth as he was now.

He materialized a sword in his hand. He stared at his connection to the gate, then, with a loud yell, sliced the connection.

The loss of strength brought him to his knees. But he stood, bracing himself against the gate. It no longer burned. Brandt pressed his forehead against the gate. Though he was alone, he still felt embarrassed. "I need your help," he said.

Nothing happened.

Then a nasally voice spoke. "There you are."

Brandt turned to see Dezigeth standing beside him. The creature grabbed Brandt by the throat and threw him forcibly out of the soulwalk.

89

Alena had been born in Landow nearly three decades ago. When she emerged from the gate into the physical world, she returned to the same place. This was where the call had come from.

She opened her eyes and her senses were assaulted. Sight, taste, smell, and the rest were familiar, if more vivid than ever before. If she focused, she could hear a whisper a block away, a battle from nearly a league.

But there was so much more. The soulwalk, too, was present, an infinite spiderweb of connections between all living things. She saw it vividly, and she straddled both planes at once without effort.

She remembered dying.

Remembered walking to the gate.

And nothing else.

Nothing before the call, the weaving that had pulled her back.

She stared at her hands, uncertain of everything. Did she dream?

No.

She couldn't say why, but at the same time, was certain. As certain as the fact that both her parents still lived, and were in fact that moment just two blocks away, waiting for the Takaii to breach the remaining defenses.

She loved them, but no longer longed to return to them.

They had grieved her passing once already.

She opened herself up and knew everything. The suffering of past neighbors struck a chord in her heart. She saw how they'd come to be here, both the heroic sacrifices and the poor decisions that had led to this time and this place.

"Alena?"

She smiled, recognizing that voice anywhere. She turned. "Brother."

Jace stood less than ten paces away, looking like a man on the edge of a cliff, not sure whether he should jump or not.

But he was Jace, and he would always jump. He ran to her and wrapped his arms around her. She returned the embrace, the feeling and the smell of him more intense than anything she remembered.

After a moment, he broke away. "Are you—?"

She looked down at herself. "I don't know."

"What—?"

She smiled and shook her head. "I don't know."

"How—?"

She shook her head again.

"Right. You don't know." Jace took another step back. "You're her, though, right? My sister?"

"I am."

"Then we'll figure out the rest later."

Alena felt Dezigeth, blighting the web of life wherever it

went. It had found Brandt. "I'm sorry, Jace, but I need to go now."

He stepped forward and grabbed her shoulders. "But you'll be back?"

"I will."

His grin could have lit a room. "Then go. We'll clear the city of the Takaii."

Alena took a step away from her brother, then vanished from sight.

90

Brandt opened his eyes and found himself in a mountain valley. One that seemed vaguely familiar. It led up to the gate.

Had Toren known?

Brandt had more pressing problems on his mind, though. Dezigeth stood a ways from them, ignoring Toren's attacks as though they were pebbles thrown by children, rather than sharpened stones launched fast enough to cut through trees.

It looked tired, though Brandt couldn't say how closely the creature's appearance reflected reality. But it had its gaze focused upon Brandt.

A single point of light burst into existence between them. And Brandt had given up his one defense.

If he was going to meet his end, though, he would meet it on his feet, head held high.

The light flew toward him.

It struck him square.

His world went white.

But then the light faded, and he still stood.

He looked down at his hands, as though they might have the answer. But they were the same hands he'd always had. Only now, an incredible energy ran through him. It felt as though he was connected to the gate.

But he wasn't.

He searched for his connection, and it was not there.

Dezigeth stepped closer, squinting at Brandt. A wave of energy rolled toward Brandt, struck, and then passed on.

Brandt still stood, protected by a shield he didn't understand.

And wondered if he could reply. Fire and air responded to his will, and he attacked with his own light, nearly as focused as Dezigeth's own.

The blast staggered Dezigeth.

Encouraged by the result, Brandt turned to stone, attempting to pull some from the nearby mountains.

Nothing happened.

Brandt didn't understand.

Dezigeth's next attack was more powerful, more focused. It hit Brandt and sent him skipping back dozens of paces. Even with the shield, it hurt.

Brandt sat up as Dezigeth approached. He tried the first attack again, and it worked. But Dezigeth was prepared and shrugged it off.

Brandt scrambled backward, cursing his fortune. If he'd had just a bit more time, he was certain he could find a way to beat Dezigeth now. This was the breakthrough they'd been waiting for! But he had no more time.

A stone split the air, but Dezigeth stopped it before it connected.

It glanced at Toren, who had tried one last time to save Brandt's life. Dezigeth spread its wings and launched itself at the Etari, moving far faster than the young man could evade. Brandt reached out, a desperate act from a helpless man.

Less than half a heartbeat before Dezigeth struck, another figure appeared from nowhere. It held up a hand, and Dezigeth stopped as suddenly as if it had hit the side of a mountain.

"Not him," a voice commanded, familiar yet not. "Nor anyone else."

Dezigeth stumbled back, and Brandt saw the mysterious figure for the first time. His eyes widened and his jaw dropped. He saw, but he didn't believe. "Alena?"

She turned to him, but her gaze made him profoundly uncomfortable. Her eyes were familiar, but not quite human. Not anymore. They saw too much. But then she smiled, as though Dezigeth was nothing more than a nuisance, and Brandt knew that whatever had happened to her, she was still the woman he remembered.

She walked to him and offered a hand. He reached out and took it. Her hand was warm and soft, exactly as he remembered. When she pulled him to his feet, though, he sensed her strength.

It terrified him.

"How?" he asked.

She shook her head, dismissing the question. She looked him up and down. "You figured it out, didn't you?"

"Figured what out?"

"The final secret of the gates. I was close, before I died. But you, you did it."

"I did?"

She laughed, and warmth flooded Brandt's heart at the sound. "You did."

"Did you?"

Her smile faded. "No." She tilted her head toward

Dezigeth. "I'm more like it, unfortunately. You've found a different way. You've become a steward."

"What?"

"Later," Alena said. Brandt noticed that Dezigeth had stepped forward. She gestured to Toren, who joined them. Brandt almost laughed at the Etari. He looked as implacable as ever, as though he'd always expected his partner to return from the dead.

Together, the three of them faced Dezigeth as lights began to appear all around it.

With a thought, Alena snuffed out Dezigeth's lights. She understood how they were created, and undoing them was a simple task, like untying a loose knot.

Her act focused Dezigeth's attention on her.

Two dozen more lights appeared. And she saw them as they were intended: a test with fatal consequences. Not for her, but for those she loved. She unmade them as well.

Another test passed.

It wasn't that she was as strong as Dezigeth. That measure, Alena now saw, had always been wrong. Better to say she now had all the same abilities as Dezigeth.

That wasn't to say she could beat Dezigeth in a fight. Two trained fighters both knew how to throw a punch, but it wasn't the knowledge of the technique that led to victory. It was experience and how many ways one could use their skills against their opponents.

Dezigeth had far more experience than she could ever dream of. Because of that, when they fought, it would win.

If they were dueling.

But she wasn't alone, and it wasn't as focused as it could be. It commanded the Takaii, and although its physical form was healthy, its battles against the queen, the Etari, and all the rest had taken their toll. It wasn't limitless, much as it had once seemed to her.

And it feared. It feared destruction and shied away from pain. For too long it had ruled uncontested. Long ago it had stopped growing, stopped adapting.

In her rebirth, she understood it.

It spoke to her mind. "You see now. You should not exist. Your ascendancy is a blight."

She did not think it intended access to its memories, but she saw them nevertheless. Long years of idleness. Brief flashes of activity. As it aged, it stagnated, focused only on maintaining the order to which it was accustomed.

This was not the first planet it had visited.

They were not the first humans it had hunted.

But they would be its last.

"You cannot stop us," she said.

"I must. It is for the good of all."

She didn't agree. Dezigeth believed in its actions. Of that, there was no doubt. But she was tired of those who justified their horrible deeds by claiming they were needed to create a better world. If it really wanted a better world, it needed to find a better way.

Dezigeth prepared to attack, a complex weaving Alena wasn't sure she could unravel.

But she wasn't alone. "Brandt, attack it, as fast and as often as you can. Toren, do the same, but in the soulwalk. Don't stop until it's gone."

They listened.

Brandt struck first as Toren slipped into the soulwalk. She admired him for a moment. Controlling the gates had never been the point. They had only been a stairway to something greater.

Brandt no longer controlled a gate, but he could direct them, to a degree.

And now he did.

Flame had always been his natural element. And now he unleashed an inferno at Dezigeth.

The creature had no choice but to defend, lest it lose its physical form and the strength that came with it.

Moments later, Toren dragged Dezigeth into the soul-walk, where he repeatedly pierced the creature with spears, too many to count, and almost too fast to track.

As with its physical body, Dezigeth had to react. It had to defend its soul, too.

Alone, Dezigeth had the strength and experience to deal with both attacks at once. It fought in two realms simultaneously, and advanced in both.

Then, Alena launched the real attack. It lacked the violence of Brandt and Toren's approaches. But she saw now the weavings that held Dezigeth together. She attacked its essence, unraveling its very core.

Dezigeth responded in kind. Her own essence frayed as it attempted to separate her. She felt her limbs break, then knit themselves back together as her sense of self fought to remain intact. Memories vanished, only to reappear a moment later.

Both attacked and defended in equal measure.

But Dezigeth fought two other battles as well.

Their wills clashed, invisible to all but them.

She gained the upper hand. Her advantage grew. It spent more time repairing itself than attacking, but she could unravel faster than it could heal.

She sensed its fear when it realized that its immortality was at an end. That it had been beaten.

By humans.

It raged and redoubled its efforts, mad with terror.

But it was too late.

And then she completed the unraveling, and Dezigeth was gone.

For all the destruction it had caused, its own end was remarkably peaceful. It faded until Alena picked apart the last of its essence. It vanished immediately from the soul-walk, and in the physical world, the darkness of the creature lost its form, becoming a cloud that blew away in the mountain breeze.

Alena looked down at her hands again.

Amazed at what she could do.

Both men looked at her, near the edge of collapse themselves. "Is it over?" Brandt asked.

She searched for Dezigeth, not quite believing it herself. But she couldn't find it. Its end was final.

She smiled. "It is."

EPILOGUE

Two years later

Alena grabbed the pan from the fire. Her mother turned, suddenly nervous. "Careful!"

Alena gave her mother a look. She felt the heat from the handle, perhaps even more vividly than her mother realized, but it didn't hurt, at least not the way she remembered pain feeling.

Her mother gestured to a spot on the counter she'd prepared for the pan. "You should still protect yourself, you know."

Alena just smiled and put the pan where her mother had indicated. "Sorry, I just didn't want it to burn."

But her mother was already onto the next task, her every move the very image of efficiency. She glanced over Toren's shoulder and took an exaggerated sniff. "It smells delicious. Will it be ready soon?"

Toren signed the affirmative, and her mother nodded. As she passed by Alena she whispered loudly, "If only I could get your father to cook for me someday."

"I heard that!" came their father's cry from the next room, followed by a happy squeal, not from her father.

"You're good?" Alena asked Toren.

"Go," he said. "I'll be done soon."

She stepped into their living room, currently filled with people. Her father was in his usual chair, an enormous mug of ale in hand. Brandt and Ana sat on the floor, playing with their child, a precocious girl named Clare.

Alena sat down next to Clare, who was rolling a wooden ball across the floor to Brandt.

Before she could get settled, though, there was a knock on the door, followed by the sound of it opening before anyone could answer it.

"You're late!" their mother called from the kitchen.

"I was busy running the city!" Jace shouted in response.

Clare's eyes went wide at the sound of Jace's voice. She got to her feet and walked smoothly toward the front door. She'd been walking for well over a year already.

Brandt shook his head as he pushed himself off the floor to grab his own mug of ale. "Sometimes, I think she loves Jace more than me."

"We all do, dear," Ana said, as Brandt offered her his hand.

Jace swept into the room, looking resplendent in his formal governor's uniform. He picked up Clare with one arm and tossed her high into the air, earning a squeal of absolute delight. "The truth can be difficult to bear, right, Brandt?"

Their mother's call interrupted the banter. "Enough, you all. Supper's on the table and it isn't getting any warmer. Come eat."

They all lined up and made their way one by one into

the dining room, where the long table had every place set. Bowls and platters of food dominated the center.

Brandt pulled Alena aside as the crowd shuffled into the room. "Sorry to ask, but the elders wanted to know. How is the transition coming?"

Alena had expected the question, and was grateful Brandt had asked now, avoiding serious subjects at the table. "It's already done."

"Already?"

"We felt it wise to sever the connections before the ceremony. You're the only one who had done it before, and we both wanted to ensure there were no ill effects, and that no one would fight the process."

"No one did?"

"Not one."

"Thank you."

She nodded, and Brandt left her to go into the dining room.

As of three days ago, not a single human remained connected to any gate. Tomorrow, they would make it public. The planet could begin to heal, guided by the hands of the stewards.

Jace kissed their mother on her forehead as he sat at the table. "Everything smells delicious," he said.

"I was starting to get worried you wouldn't make it," she replied.

"There's no crisis in the world that would keep me from a meal like this."

Their mother didn't miss a beat. "Unless your crisis had long hair and a pretty face, then I'd never see you again."

After no small amount of confusion, they all found their seats. They passed food around, and all took hearty portions. Even Alena, who no longer needed food, helped herself. The necessity of the act was gone, but the flavors carried more power than ever.

They ate and they spoke. Brandt and Ana lived in Faldun most of the year, where the Lolani and the Falari continued to become one people. Though not without conflict, Brandt reported that there were less challenges than he'd expected. Fortunately, Falar was a large land sparsely populated. There was room to grow. And both cultures had a long martial history to share with one another.

Ana divided her time between motherhood and commanding part of the city guard. She enjoyed both responsibilities.

Alena and Toren spoke little about their own adventures. They had both been part of the armies sent to clean the land of Takaii. It had been difficult enough across this continent. But Palagia had been a nightmare. They'd endured nearly half a year of living among the ruins of the Lolani. The Takaii were no more, but the devastation they'd brought would be evident for generations. No one knew if anyone would ever attempt to settle Palagia again.

This meal, in part, celebrated their return. Tomorrow, on the anniversary of the end of the Battle of Landow, peace would be declared. A new truce would be signed, allowing easier passage between the people of these lands. Olen had pressed for a unification, all under the empire's leadership.

The Etari, Falari, and Lolani had flatly refused.

To Olen's credit, he took their refusal with grace.

The Massacre of Tonno and the Battle of Landow had changed the young emperor. His intelligence remained, but he consistently sought a greater diversity of opinions, including, not infrequently, Alena's. The empire was far from perfect. But they were safe for now, and Alena believed they were in good hands with Anders VII. Even he had given up his connection to the gates on Alena's request.

Brandt turned to Alena. "Now that the fighting is over, what will you do?"

She glanced at Toren and shrugged. "Travel. There's more of this world to see, and I would like to do so. Also, the source, whatever that is, remains a mystery. I'd like to find out more, wherever that knowledge might take me."

As Alena looked around the room, she wondered if this would be the last time they would all be together. She hoped not. But for all her knowledge, she couldn't see if all their lives would intersect again.

It left her with a bittersweet feeling in her chest, something she'd felt more often as of late.

This world was beautiful, but everything within it constantly changed.

Jace, as usual, had no problem jumping into the silence. He began a tale of a thief who stole the keys to the jail, apparently to break in.

As with any story Jace told, she couldn't quite tell where the truth ended and his exaggeration began.

Nor did she care. It was her brother, and she loved his tales.

She looked around the room, basking in the companionship of her friends and family.

This was her world.

And it was good.

THANK YOU

Before you take off, I really wanted to say thank you for taking the time to read my work. Being able to write stories for a living is one of the greatest gifts I've been given, and it wouldn't be possible without readers.

So thank you.

Also, it's almost impossible to overstate how important reviews are for authors in this age of internet bookstores. If you enjoyed this book, it would mean the world to me if you could take the time to leave a review wherever you purchased this book.

And finally, if you really enjoyed this book and want to hear more from me, I'd encourage you to sign up for my emails. I don't send them too often - usually only once or twice a month at most, but they are the best place to learn about free giveaways, contests, sales, and more.

I sometimes also send out surprise short stories, absolutely free, that expand the fantasy worlds I've built. If you're interested, please go to https://www. waterstonemedia.net/newsletter/.

With gratitude,

Ryan

ALSO BY RYAN KIRK

The Nightblade Series

Nightblade

World's Edge

The Wind and the Void

Blades of the Fallen

Nightblade's Vengeance

Nightblade's Honor

Nightblade's End

Relentless

Relentless Souls

Heart of Defiance

Their Spirit Unbroken

Oblivion's Gate

The Gate Beyond Oblivion

The Gates of Memory

The Gate to Redemption

The Primal Series

Primal Dawn

Primal Darkness

Primal Destiny

Primal Trilogy

ABOUT THE AUTHOR

Ryan Kirk is the bestselling author of the *Nightblade* series of books. When he isn't writing, you can probably find him playing disc golf or hiking through the woods.

www.ryankirkauthor.com
www.waterstonemedia.net
contact@waterstonemedia.net

 facebook.com/waterstonemedia

 twitter.com/waterstonebooks

 instagram.com/waterstonebooks

CPSIA information can be obtained
at www.ICGtesting.com
Printed in the USA
BVHW072344120822
644459BV00008B/683

9 781953 692009